H A S D A I

IN THE GOLDEN AGE OF AL-ANDALUS

H A S D A I

IN THE GOLDEN AGE OF AL-ANDALUS

A HISTORICAL NOVEL

R I C H A R D   M A L M E D

Kravitz & Sons
INNOVATORS IN PUBLISHING, MARKETING AND ADVERTISING

Kravitz and Sons LLC
1301 Farmville Blvd, Suite 104
Greenville, NC 27834

Published by Kravitz and Sons LLC.
ISBN: (sc)   979-8-89639-127-2
        (hc)   979-8-89639-128-9
        (e)   979-8-89639-126-5

Library of Congress Control Number: 2025904115

Table of Contents

I AM HASDAI

Permit me to introduce myself: I am Hasdai ibn Shaprut, a Jew living at the pleasure of Caliph ar-Rahman III in Cordoba, al-Andalus in the year 956 CE. I am hurrying to the livery stables near the Alcazar where my horse is being readied. I have been summoned by the Caliph as one of his advisers on what I am told is a matter of great importance. When ar-Rahman calls, your humble servant is quick to respond.

I am dressed in a caftan which conceals a short sword. I carry it because the streets can be mean even in the center of Cordoba. The Moors, or Umayyads, are Muslims who, after controlling North Africa, crossed over the Strait of Gibraltar and, in 712 CE conquered the southern half of Iberia, or al-Andalus as the Moors call it. Under Muslim rule, Andalusia, the southern section, began a period of prosperity, learning and tolerance. Muslims, Jews and Christians lived in harmony and exchanged learning in the fields of medicine, mathematics, astronomy, botany and poetry. Algebra and the concept of zero were introduced to the west. Although not given equal citizenship rights with the Muslims, Jews and Christians are permitted to pursue their businesses, learning and religion. We Jews are not permitted to carry weapons, but we usually carry knives under our loose fitting garments in case trouble should arise.

The Caliph Abd-ar-Rahman III is the son of a member of the royal line and a Christian concubine. His paternal grandmother was also a Christian. He has white skin and blue eyes and is thought to be quite handsome. Although sturdy and stout, he has short legs, but when seated on a horse he gives the impression of being quite tall.

His grandfather Abdallah had chosen ar-Rahman as his successor instead of any of his four sons. Since then, our Caliph ruled for many years and succeeded in subduing the many factions which surrounded him in Cordoba until a calm seemed to pass over southern al-Andalus, the former Roman Hispania, and the arts and sciences began to flourish.

He built the immense palace complex he called the Medina Azahara and modeled after the palace in Damascus. Just west of the city of Cordoba, it had ceremonial reception halls, government offices, gardens, a mint, workshops, barracks and baths. It had an exquisite landscape of gardens, pools and mosques. It was dedicated to the Caliph's favorite concubine Zahra.

I have been summoned for a meeting with ar-Rahman III, the Caliph of al-Andalus, the ruler of southern Spain. Since his grandfather ar-Rahman II had started the magnificent complex of government and palacial buildings at Madinat-al-Zahra, several leagues to the west of our city of Cordoba, most meetings have occurred there. Of course, the Caliph lives there with his entire family and servants, and nearly all activities necessary to govern the realm occur there too. As I said, it is several leagues to the west, so I must ride my horse.

And my horse is a different story. For some of my missions on behalf of the Caliph a few years ago, he gave me this magnificent arabian stallion. For centuries, the Arabs have bred and trained some of the most extraordinary horses in the world. Long before Mohammed, before Alexander the Great, as far back in time as we know, the desert people have bred these horses, Thoroughbreds. Compact muscular bodies, mounted on slender legs with shiny coats and long manes. To watch them trot or gallop was to watch a tribute to God for having created such beautiful creatures. And the Caliph has given me one.

I walk out to the livery where my horse is stabled and cared for just outside the Juderia near the Alcazar. The Alcazar had guarded the bridge crossing the Quadalivir since early Roman times and houses many soldiers, but also is the center for local city government and the residence of the mayor. It is also the local prison. It is a pleasant walk through the gardens and pools shaded by orange and palm trees. A few vendors in the early morning sit by their wagons bearing sliced fruit, tea and pastries. I collect a small meal for myself for the ride out to the Madinat. At the livery, the servants who care for the horses greet me as if I am a notable. First, the Caliph has granted me permission to stable my horse with those of the senior officers in the Alcazar, but also my horse is the finest of the lot.

Although they have no idea why a Jew is so honored and even needs a horse, they count me as one in power. In the Caliphate, power and rank is very important. They must think I am powerful, although I am in reality a humble Jewish doctor. Of course, the Caliph sends me on diplomatic missions, but only he and sometimes his generals and chief advisors know what I am doing. In the meantime, I busy myself as a doctor amid other things.

But today, there is a matter of some import I must meet with the Caliph about – as yet I do not know what. So they ready my horse. The young groom, Aziz, gives me a big grin as he leads my horse out. He, of course, is happy because he is the one to exercise my horse every day and brush him down. He loves this beautiful creature, as a true Arab would and considers his duty a divine blessing. He has named him Rashiq. This is a presumption on his part because, after all, it is my horse, but he takes such wonderful care of him that I ignore this. Rashiq means swift and this thoroughbred is. Way too swift for such as me, and often eager to gallop off like the wind over the dry flat stretches of our arid countryside. That is a job for Aziz, not me. Today, I will travel in a small group from the gate of the city along the well-worn road to the Madinat and Rashiq will want to canter gracefully kicking his feet down the road. I wonder what people think as they see this Jewish scholar bouncing on this magnificent steed. I can only thank the Caliph for this illusion. But when Arabs see my horse, they see a person of importance in his saddle and clear to the side of the way as I go past. Some even bow or salute. Not me, but my horse. I have no illusions.

So, I fall in with some of the soldiers going out to the Madinat who now canter spritely in formation past the few forts and checkpoints along the way.

The ride through our countryside is somewhat dull. For leagues around, dry flat stretches of parched earth, occasionally covered with dried grass, and even less occasionally a few cattle lying in the shade of the rare acacia tree that has found root in this soil. A few hardy souls have ministered to some groves of olive trees along the river to our south. Otherwise, the countryside is arid and barren and the day is hot. I munch on my orange and chew a few almonds as we go.

In the distance, the Madinat rises from the plain and is set against a hill rising in tiers. Much of it is completed and much is still in the process of being constructed. We pass a guardhouse where they check our documents for the Caliph's seal. The guards know me from my previous trips out, but are thorough in looking at the seal. They greet me by name as I rode up. The guardhouse has two passages in each direction and a three story tower. From the top of the tower, it is possible to see the plain up to the Quadalivir River and beyond, so any enemies advancing from the south could easily be observed.

From there, the road splits four ways with the lower road leading to the kitchen and service area where food is prepared for the entire complex, and the second level is for the military barracks and command center. There, a large open expanse is where the soldiers mustered and trained, and where the horses are ridden or put through jumps. The next highest level is for official state business such as meetings with the chamberlain, or other officials, and for other bureaucratic functions. On this level, there is a long garden with pools. The higher level officials could take their meals along the walkways or hold conferences in the comfort of the gardens. At the highest level is the residence of the Caliph and his family. The Caliph's residence faces a large pool surrounded by trees, exotic plants and birds. In the ponds, large koi float languidly by. On the outside of the ponds there are cloisters where one can walk shaded from the heat of the day. As was common among the Moors, these gardens were open to heaven and served a religious function for prayer and meditation. They look upward unimpeded to heaven.

I was again welcomed at the fourth gate and escorted into the room where I and the Caliph's advisers would meet. The fourth level was a heavenly oasis overlooking the plain south to the Quadalivir River. Pools surrounded by trees, flowers and stone benches. The floor itself is a walkway of polished stone, surrounded by mosaics of smooth river stones. Cisterns above the fourth level collect rain water which enters an intricate series of pipes and sluices to flow through all four levels. The water flow was connected to the toilets, the ponds and the baths at all levels.

On each level is a mosque – four ornate walls surrounding a marble courtyard open to the sky. At each, a tower arose where the muezzin call the faithful to prayer five times a day. On each occasion, the men perform the ritual washing outside and then enter, to get to their appointed prayer rug to pray and remember their subservience to Allah.

I had to marvel at the devotion of the Caliph's people to their rituals. In this arid obscure location, the Caliph had gathered together his government, his military and his family and servants. All responded to the calls to prayer wailed from the prayer towers every few hours to bow their heads on their knees facing Mecca and reconsecrate themselves to a life of submission to the will of Allah. And yet, Jews and Christians have lived in peace alongside them. It was a gift from God. I said a few prayers in thanks to God for this hallowed time in the world. Surely, he had given wisdom to our Muslim ruler.

I have always been the doctor to the Caliph and his family, but now I am one of his chief advisers. I am to appear at court for regular hearings of legal matters and, then, to discuss matters of importance to the Caliph along with the rest of his small circle of advisers. While I entertain the idea that I am here because of my superior intellect, in reality, I am here as a Jew. I have no political aspirations, no ties to any faction, and can be expected to be neutral and rational in the opinions I give the Caliph rather than pursue some personal agenda. Others on the council are fearsome of what I might do or say, but I enjoy the Caliph's protection and my independence. The one person who is most unhappy with my selection by Rahman is my wife, Rachel.

She must run our household and her business with the help of our 14-year-old daughter, Yael. My father, of course, went on a search to find me the appropriate wife and picked out the very attractive daughter from one of his friend's friends from Seville. I was 30 years old and she was 15.

I was most apprehensive before I met Rachel. I mean some wives can be terrible and destroy a man. From our first conversation, I knew I would be pleased with her. She had long wavy black hair in shiny locks flowing down her back and over her shoulders, bright shiny dark eyes and striking white teeth. Her olive face was complimented by a long aquiline nose. And she could read! I had hoped that my wife could converse intelligently with me and she could. She knew the Torah and could recite Arabic poetry and she was not a dunderhead. Her reasoning and observations were clear and sound. She would be a fine companion. As in Proverbs 31, she would be an eshektal – a splendid helpmate. But enough of Proverbs. After waiting 30 years, I was eager to explore the Song of Songs. Would she be worthy?

Praise be to the Eternal One. She was. Her mother had given her a few instructions in love making and she applied them with alacrity. She was a blessing. As I would walk through the door of our house and she would look at me with a sideways glance, I knew the Holy One had found favor in me.

And that is not all. I have been trained as a physician and ministered to many in the city. All came to me – Jews of course, but Muslims and Christians as well. I had trained with my mentor Solomon Shalom Rodeph, a kindly and peaceful man who sought the well-being of all God's creatures. He was rigorous in insisting I learn both the Hebrew form of treatment as well as that of the Muslims. I worked hard as his assistant tending to patients he was too infirm to see. When his time came, may he rest in peace, he left me with a great body of knowledge and a desire to help my fellow man.

Rachel insisted on learning from me elements of my profession. She became my apothecary. She too became fascinated with the properties of herbs and minerals. She quested not only after our knowledge, but that of the Muslims as well as the healers of strange pagan faiths throughout the countryside. I was required to rent and refurbish our neighbor's storage shed so she could collect and sort out remedies of all sorts. She would make frequent trips to the country fairs and villages to learn about and collect samples of cures, herbs, and elixers. I soon had to rent a small shop for her to meet her customers to prevent them from crowding our tiny street. She has served them all with grace and concern during our fifteen years of marriage.

And now, our eldest, our daughter Yael, had been insistent on helping her mother. She also now went on her mother's trips to the country fairs and into the forests and fields to collect specimens. I think she did this in part to escape from her little brother, who would pester her every waking minute.

David is our son, and what Jewish parents aren't tempted to name their son after God's beloved, the flawed hero-king. Our David was not much different. He was strong and active – too active. He would run in the streets with his friends and indulge in all physical activities. For a brief time, I considered asking the Caliph to let him train as a soldier with the Caliph's and the other nobles' sons, just to pour off some of that energy.

But it was a bad idea. Jews could never become officers and were never permitted to bear arms. Rather, the Jews paid a special tax, the vizya, to be exempt from military service. And it was not cheap. It was really a way of taxing us more than the Muslims. The arrangement suited both the Jews and the Caliph. But we were permitted to worship in our own way. As Rahman says and his father before him, "the Quran says there is no compulsion in religion." (2:256) So we are free to pray, to hold our own courts for legal matters, and to earn a living in peace, perhaps more so than at any time for the past 1000 years.

Soon, I am at the gates of the Palace and it is a splendor to behold. The Caliph has designed a huge complex west of Cordoba and named it Madinat al-Zahra, a tribute to his favorite concubine. The Moorish builders have crafted a masterpiece. The entrance was, of course, guarded by soldiers at attention in colorful uniforms each with a long spear with a curved tip knife blade, both sharp and polished to a high gleam. Today the guards wore bloused pants in red and shirts of orange with a green vest. In view of the rising temperatures of the spring season, they did not wear the heavy leather armor and instead had waist coats of a light green. To amaze the onlookers, but I assume also to stretch their legs, the guards marched through an intricate pattern changing their respective locations along the wall, all to shouted commands and drum beats. It was a marvelous spectacle. I have to wait until the march is finished before presenting my credentials at the gate. Although I was well known to the gate keeper, he went through the complete process of inspecting my leather wallet case of documents signed and sealed by the Caliph's Chamberlain himself. After he was done, he came to full attention and saluted me. "You are most welcome, Hasdai ibn Shaprut." I was admitted through a door in the gate to a splendid courtyard.

In the center was a pond running the length of the courtyard. Plantings of small bushes clipped into spherical shapes and a variety of yellow and blue flowers surrounded the pond for a distance of eighty cubits. To reach the ceremonial hall, one could walk along the outside of the pond in the open air or under the colonnade which skirted the walls. The colonnade had wondrously carved columns, footers and headings as one passed along the side of the pond. At the far end of the courtyard, two more colorful guards stood and a large double door of heavy oak with windows of intricate, almost lacy, wrought iron. As I approached, the doors swung wide for me to enter into the interior of the palace. Here, a large throne commanded the floor of polished granite of about 60 by 80 cubits. Along the walls were hung either shields of burnished steel with cloisonné emblems or intricately woven tapestries in designs of maroon, navy blue or ivory. Now no one is in the throne room but a few slaves mopping the floor. I am motioned to a room off to the side and through a small door giving onto a meeting room. There, a large table of polished mahogany is surrounded by heavy chairs upholstered in maroon leather.

As I was the first to arrive, a servant inquired if I wanted something to drink, pastries or fruit. The Caliph's pastries are highly esteemed everywhere and I could not resist selecting a few from the tray proffered. (Although I could hear my wife Rachel clucking in my head at my excess.) The tea is also most welcome on the cool spring morning. The entire wall of the east side of the room was covered with a tapestry showing a map of al-Andalus. Rather than tempt fate, the boundaries of the Moorish area controlled by the Caliphate of Cordoba and the Christian area controlled by the Kingdoms of Leon, Aragon and Castille were not depicted. These boundaries were constantly changing as large and small confrontations shifted the territories from Christian to Moorish and back again. The rivers, the mountains, the deserts and the valleys were woven into the pattern in bright colors. From time to time, pins or brooches were affixed to the wall hanging as the fortunes of war waxed and waned between the two sides. That was to be the subject of our discussion today, the fortunes of war and the preparations for the future.

As I sat in the room at one end of the table, two large Christian knights were ushered in the door. They grumbled that their large broadswords had been taken from them. I could understand their chagrin. These swords, made in Toledo, were magnificent. With hammered gold and silver pommels, and cloisonné inlays, they were indeed works of art. But the steel in the blade was balanced, polished and honed to the finest degree in the known world. The swords were made for display and not battle. But a man without his sword? They might as well have taken his manhood. Both were large men with pale faces; each wore a heavy leather tunic and some kind of legging and heavy riding boots. Although it was only early spring, I was sure that the men were uncomfortably warm today. Apparently, this is what they always wore. And judging from the rank smell of body odor and unwashed hair they gave off, it was apparent that they rarely changed these very clothes. Of course, they can be forgiven somewhat because they had ridden in from the northern area of Cordoba in the mountainous area near Merida. But I must say that I thought it very strange that they wore these legging things. At the front was something they call a codpiece, a flap which had buttons on either side which they could undo to expose their members and urinate. It seemed that there was no rear flap which they could undo in order to defecate. In many cases, there were colorations at the rear of these leggings which had curious stains that made one question their hygiene. In a similar manner, their beards were unkempt with stray items of food or straw in them. Nevertheless, these men were the Christian nobles, liege lords now to the Caliph and part of our meeting called to discuss the security of the realm. Some history had alienated them from the kings of Leon, the Christian kingdom to our north.

There was good reason for the Jews' status in the inclusive realm of the Caliphs. They had helped the Moors overcome the cruel Visigoths over 200 years before and were now rewarded for their service. The new Moorish rulers had been magnanimous to the Christians as well. They permitted them to keep their imposing cathedral as well as their religious rites and practice. Only lately, as the Christian leaders began to look to Rome for its guidance and abandon their Arian beliefs, that the Caliph began to suspect their loyalty. Before now, the Visigoths practiced a dissident form of Christianity called Arianism which questioned the divinity of Jesus, but held him not to be the equal of God the father, nor part of a trinity. It also began to create some hostility between the Christians and the Jews as the new doctrine included strong pressure to convert the Jews, voluntarily or involuntarily. Thus, a tradition was born of Jewish observance in secret, and Christian practice in the open. During the Caliph's reign, this tension had disappeared and the three religions profited greatly from their exchange of cultures. The Jews were exposed to the Greek and Arabic advances in medicine, poetry, philosophy, mathematics and biology. The few educated Christians, primarily the monks, readily absorbed the Greek influences in religion and developed practices in medicine, astronomy and engineering. It was a profitable exchange and an enrichment to all.

I knew the Christian knights from previous meetings. One had married the King of Castile's niece and had been given a number of towns in Toledo, just to our north. The politics of the changing fortunes in our Christian kingdoms to the north had encouraged him to throw in his lot with the Caliph. He was Rodrigo of Merida. His compadre was a very accomplished knight owning no particular land, but who was well compensated by the Caliph as a soldier and a commander of armies. Both men were important allies of Rahman III against the expanding Kingdom of Leon, which had been pressing ever further south and had taken a vast area including Toledo. It was now important for us to consider not only the incursions from the north, but also the continuing threat of the vicious Berbers from the south. These puritanical, uneducated Moors, the Almoravides, resented the wealth and sophistication of the earlier Moors, the Umayyads, but most of all, they resented the close ties the dhimmis held to the ruling Moors. The dhimmis, as we were referred to, were the Jews and Christians not only tolerated but welcomed into the Moorish world, and given various degrees of freedom. The Jews paid an additional tax called the vizya, and so were exempted from military service. So, Rahman III faced threats from the north and the south and needed to prevail against both. Could he rely on his Christian allies to ward off the Leon armies? Could he defend against the fanatical Muslims from the south. Certainly, he was beset by both. Hence a meeting.

I could only marvel at the convenience and comfort of my dress. These simple cotton shirts which fell directly from the shoulder to the knee were cool and comfortable and an ease to arrange when nature called. Today was a bit cool, so I had added an embroidered vest emblazoned with the symbols of Cordoba in honor of my meeting today.

I greeted the knights warmly since I had known them for some time now. Sir Rodrigo and Sir Alphonso were from families which stretched far back to before the Moorish conquest of the area. They had strong infusions of Visigoth blood, but the past 300 years had mingled with the remainder of the Romans. The Moors had been quite generous to those Christians and allowed them to keep their magnificent churches and pursue their religion without interference. Consistent with medieval practice, they owed duties of loyalty to the Caliph – to pay taxes and supply men and arms in the event of a conflict. Their ways were different, however. A nobleman's life consisted of drinking, hunting, dealing harshly with his serfs and romancing women in his castle. They were versed in the arts of the battlefield from the time they were very young - even five years old. Most of them were not literate and few could appreciate the Moorish world of poetry, arts, music, philosophy, science, and mathematics. Of course, we Jews were in paradise with these Arabic niceties. But occasionally, the monks, Irish and a few French, would join us in our discussions. We also had many scrolls and codexes to exchange. The Moors had kept and copied many of the Greek volumes and added vast stores of their own poetry, mathematics and medicine. The Jews were anxious to share their codexes of poetry, medicine and the sciences. But the Christian knights were not so inclined. Although they enjoyed their safety and tolerated existence here in Moorish Iberia, as they called it, they were wary. They viewed the Jews with some indifference. While in their churches they were told that we had killed Jesus. Fortunately, St. Augustine long ago had come to our defense. He had said that Jews should be preserved as witnesses to Jesus, but not permitted to thrive. If I am quoting him incorrectly, I apologize, but that is what I have heard. So it was with some consternation that the Christian knights observed us thriving under the protective arm of the Moors. They accept us begrudgingly and viewed us as strange beings: we did not bear arms in battle, but paid a tax instead; we did not usually own land or tend the fields or the livestock, but we were literate and kept to ourselves. So I asked after their wives and children and they asked me to convey their greetings to my family. And we took voraciously to the immense fruit platters servants had brought in as well as tea poured from brass pitchers with elongated spouts.

Soon, the Caliph and his two advisers came to join us. The Caliph was a short, elegant man, and exceedingly accomplished in diplomacy. He greeted each of us, not only by name, but told a simple but complimentary tale of each man to enhance his standing at our meeting. But he was worried. The wonderful Caliphate under his rule was being threatened. The advances in learning, the beauty of the new Moorish architecture, the wonderful cross-breeding in the arts and sciences were threatened. From the north, the Kingdom of Leon – driven at least nominally by a desire to spread the Christian faith, but primarily inspired by greed for land and booty, was making mischief at the borders. From the south, the fanatical Berbers sought to advance their extremist Muslim faith which they believed required far stricter devotion and a suppression of the more sophisticated ways of the Umayyads, known for their learning and liberality. Yes, he was worried. He wanted advice to fend off the two barbaric forces which were trying to impose their brutish will on the forces which might bring civility and grace to the world not seen since the fall of Rome a half millennium ago.

The Caliph, Abd ar-Rahman III, was dressed in an elegant djellaba of blue and gold. Like my simple white shirt edged in embroidered thread, his also hung like a shirt from his shoulders with a slight collar. But there were alternating panels of gold flecked thread in a silk weave, and blue cotton dyed with pigment derived from the Mediterranean clams imported since ancient times by the Phoenicians and Carthaginians. He wore gold slippers turned up at the ends. His retainers pulled out a chair for him at the head of the table and stepped back to a position several feet to the rear and came to attention.

The two Moorish nobles who joined the meeting were also elegant in their dress. Much to the chagrin of the Christian nobles, they wore the ornate swords from Toledo, with highly polished steel blades and hammered brass designs along the shaft and exquisite jewel encrusted pommels and guards. They also wore brightly colored djellabas and gilded sandals. Their beards were neatly clipped and trimmed.

It was a pleasure to feel the change in atmosphere as the Moors took their places around the table. I guess it was the light scent of almond and roses the Moors gave off which defeated the odors of the Christians. But it was also their manner – sophisticated and bright – that overcame the hulking intimidation.

"Gentlemen," our Caliph said, fixing each of us with a warm smile. "You know, in part, why I have called you here today. As has unfortunately been our lot, we have been under occasional attack from unknown Christians from Leon to our north, and unknown Berbers to our south. No formal war has been declared, but there is a continual series of incursions where men steal our cattle, raid our villages, and then retreat. It is a factor of intimidation which may precede actual warfare. I seek your guidance.

"In years past, the Kingdom of Leon paid my predecessors tribute and now, we pay tribute to them in some areas. This was supposed to buy us peace along our borders rather than sacrificing men and engaging in the costly logistics of war. Also, in the past, the Berbers were a motley band of crude, unwashed beggars more interested in war. Now, both impinge on us. What do you suggest?"

The room was quiet for a while. Sir Alphonso spoke first. "Your excellency, we know little of the Berbers. We do not know what they want, how they fight or what language they speak. What good are we?"

"Good advice. My Moorish lords Tariq and Kadim will give you a brief description of their battle formations, their tactics, their weapons. I want fresh ideas. Speak without fear of being wrong. It may suggest a new approach."

The Moorish noblemen, looking at each other, described the exquisite Arabian horses, the curved bladed scimitars, and the graceful horsemanship the years of desert warfare had created. Lighter and faster, but not adaptable to swamps or heavily forested areas. If they could be lured into hand-to-hand combat on the ground, the ponderous Christians would hammer the Berbers into submission. Areas were staked out on the tapestry hanging on the wall where there were open flat plains, and where heavy forestation or bogs covered the land. Unfortunately, southern al-Andalus, or Iberia, as the Christians called it, had precious few forests and many bare desert areas. The Caliph clapped his hands and sent one of his retainers with the tapestry to be drawn out on parchment and colored to identify the areas in question. Now it was the Moors' turn. How do we defeat the Christians from Leon? Of course, the opposite was true. Those large, broad-chested heavy-limbed knights were mounted on warm blooded horses. They had heavy broadswords made of crude steel, maces, spiked balls on chains, hammers, and clubs – heavy weapons which crushed and maimed the enemy but required great strength to wield.

The Christians held an advantage. Between Cordoba and Leon there was the plateau of Estremadura – an almost desert-like formation that for years now had been a neutral zone between the Christian kingdom and the Moorish Caliphate. On either side were dense mountainous regions which were difficult to climb and traverse, especially with large warring parties. The land itself had protected each side from the other. A column of men could only march at best two or three abreast and often single file through thick forest. Not only did it make for an easy ambush, but the supply wagons and baggage lagged far behind. The pace of the march was slow and difficult even in the best of times. Bogged down by rain, it was impossible.

It would be ideal if the Christians could hammer the Berbers on the south, and the Moors could move swiftly to harass the Christians in the north. Again the Caliph clapped and sent the other retainer out for a map of the south with appropriate colors and drawings to depict the natural features of the terrain.

Now came the time to identify the Caliph's vassals or allies to number who would form points of the army's array for battle. It would be time to send envoys in all directions to see who would support us, among our neighbors. It was always a bit delicate to send the Christian knights who were loyal to the Caliph to talk to the King of Leon, since they were often viewed there as traitors. By the same token, the Caliph's emissaries sent to talk to the new Berber invaders to the south were often viewed as lapsed Muslims who had fallen into the easy life and were unable to follow the strict puritanical demands of Islam. These new Berbers believed in conversion by the sword. The Caliph was an intelligent man, well read in the Greek philosophers and he would have to make a difficult decision. But he had other things on his mind as well. He gave Hasdai a furtive but telling glance and Hasdai, long a confident of the Caliph knew exactly what he was troubled by. Not merely the thought of war, but of betrayal.

The discussions on tactics, the dispositions of the enemies at the borders, and the names of allies and foes went on at length. More fruit trays, more tea, and eventually a sumptuous lunch was brought in. Game fowl cooked in a sauce of oranges and figs was laid before everyone by multiple minions of the Caliph's servants. I, alas, was strictly bound by kosher dietary law and was even warned against eating in the house of a non-Jew. But the Caliph was well aware of my compunctions and, diplomatically, had special dishes brought for me, unbeknownst to the rest of the guests. The Christian knights were served an excellent red wine, while the Moors had a blend of fruit juice. The Caliph was quite discreet in not pointing up the differences in his advisers. Eventually, the talks ground to a halt with little concrete resolution, but many interesting ideas. The knights would sleep in the palace before taking the long trip home. The Moors resided nearby and would return home before the afternoon prayers. As everyone got up to leave, the Caliph, with a minimal gesture of his head, asked me to stay behind. Now, the real strategy would be discussed.

As the other men trundled out, they were handed small silver and brass jewelry boxes for their wives. The Caliph well knew how the marital politics were played. While the women in both the Christian and Moorish households were treated as chattel and had few rights, they nonetheless, were forces to be reckoned with in their husbands' political decisions. A small gift would endear these women and give him a somewhat small but incessant voice in the household as the men chose their loyalties. Woe betide the man who ignored the demands, while not binding, but nonetheless persuasive, of their wives (or whomever their favorite bedmates happened to be). A cross bedfellow is not conducive to the joys of the bed chamber.

I waited until the men had passed under the long cloisters and were out of sight. He returned to the table and the Caliph motioned everyone else out. We would now get down to the real affairs of state.

While the Caliph regarded me as a Jew, but I was perhaps the most trustworthy man in the entire Caliphate. While accepted and even treated cordially by the Christians and Moors alike, I would never have any real power and was worthless as an ally so long as no one knew my relationship with the Caliph. I was no fool when it came to evaluating my secret but close tie to the Caliph. The rest was all show. Why? You need ask why? The head of the Caliph was always a target to someone. In the blink of an eye, the Christians could reunite with the King of Leon, or even their co-religionists in Cordoba. The change of regime in such a land, and for that matter, everywhere else was accomplished by murder. One poison cup, a few well-armed soldiers could empty the seat of power with few regrets. The Caliph had to keep a delicate political balance and reward his allies handsomely and punish his enemies brutally and publicly. Except me and the Jews. They and the Caliph were well aware of the peace and prosperity they enjoyed in Cordoba at this time. The Jews had a long history of living under rulers who were not so kind to them and they well knew what a regime change might bring. In case they had forgotten, however, the Caliph was persistent in reminding them. It was perhaps the best time the Jews had enjoyed in a thousand years, and they were not about to invite trouble.

The Caliph waited until the door was closed behind the last of the servants before he turned to me. "Now, what do you really think?" The Caliph reached for a sugared pastry, poured himself a glass of tea and settled back for what might be a long presentation.

"In all honesty, your excellency, I fear more trouble from within than without. There is no doubt that your realm is the most productive, most peaceful, most learned of any for 1000 years. Since the Moors came to Andalus, they have ruled with patience, tolerance and wisdom. But there are those who are jealous, greedy or simply stupid. We should watch everyone to see with whom they communicate. I suspect that neither the Christians in the north nor the Almohades in the south would move against you without some help from the inside. By the same token, we should have our own sources among them – men who could keep us abreast of developments in these areas. I have thought about this for some time now and believe we should have merchants who visit these areas regularly and do business with the capital cities where the rulers and their courts reside. We should develop contacts who will tell us which way the wind blows. We should know their armaments, who has become a regular ally, and what military strengths these allies possess."

"Ah so. A spy network. Very good, very interesting. Of course, I already have in place many informal contacts, but nothing on a regular basis. Who could set up such a network?"

"That is something we must discuss. Should they be Christian or Moorish?"

"An important issue. But loyalty must be a prime concern. Perhaps the Jews could be the traveling merchants. We would be honored with such a task. We owe much to you for the peace you bring to us. But we know little of military affairs. We have only been permitted to carry arms in defense of the realm in the past several generations."

The Caliph said, "Ah, but we are well aware of the efforts the Jews made in our behalf at Cadiz. They practically delivered the city to us. In my case, I will have you speak to my generals and be given a list of information we might need."

"It would be my pleasure to serve your excellency."

"In that case, I have something for you." With that, he clapped and a servant appeared at the door.

"Your excellency called?"

"Yes, Sirhan. Please bring me the box by the door in the next room." The servant disappeared and returned with what looked like a crate for oranges.

"Leave it on the table." When the servant had disappeared, the Caliph opened the box and drew out a magnificent djellaba for a woman. It was mostly white with insets in colors of royal blue, stitched in silver thread. A magnificent piece covered in an intricate design of grape vines and small antelopes in various postures of leaping or running.

"I would like to have your wife wear this."

"Oh excellency, it is magnificent. You are most kind."

"And this." At the bottom of the crate was a small pouch of leather with a draw string. The Caliph opened it and poured out several gems on the table. As they bounced on the table, the gems were throwing off colors of blue, yellow and opaline. There were emeralds, topazes and sapphires. It was a treasure. "I want you to have this to use in your travels to compensate those loyal to us. You may keep half for yourself. I know I can trust you to do this fairly. Bring me what I want and I will consider it a cheap price to pay."

"Most gracious your excellency."

"And now, I would like you to go on a diplomatic mission to the north with our Christian friends to speak to the King of Leon. Visit his court. Make contacts. Bring along a few who might like to be our merchant-messengers. They will be supplied with goods for trade, but they will also keep their eyes and ears open. You will need merchants you can trust."

"I am most grateful for this charge you have entrusted to me. I will not disappoint."

"I have every faith in you, Hasdai." The Caliph rose and that was a sign the meeting was over. He reassembled the contents of the orange crate and handed it to Hasdai. "My blessings go with you."

"Thank you, your excellency."

As I was walking home with the Caliph's orange crate securely under my arm, I chose the wide streets and those with many pedestrians. It was beginning to dawn on me how clever the Caliph had been. He knew all along what the comments would be from our Christian vassals and allies and our Moorish compatriots. I was not surprised that their thoughts would be the usual advice we had learned over the past two hundred years. He was simply honoring them with a call to counsel him on the threats we faced. I also guessed that he was shrewdly observing them during the discussion to see if anything was unusual or suggested some hint of betrayal or self- dealing. I had to leave those judgments to him. As for me, I realized he had played me like a fine stringed instrument. I flatter myself that I am not a drum. He knew well my propensities for rooting out betrayal and he also knew that he could trust me as one of his neutral Jewish citizens who could be depended on to support his regime. I was sure that the speed with which he adopted my plan for a diplomatic visit, and to develop a cluster of informants suggested that he had already considered this himself but wanted a neutral Jew to carry it out. What better person to carry out the scheme than one who believed he had suggested it to him. The old fox. He let me design my own mission and had the gems ready to support it. Gems were easy to carry and did not betray their origins as coins might. But more importantly, they could easily be exchanged through Jewish merchants who trafficked in such currency, if you will. The old fox was ahead of me, but I was not far behind. We were singing a duet in fine harmony.

DJELLABA COMES HOME

I plodded through the narrow streets in the Juderia and went into my house. I placed the orange crate on the dining room table and sank onto the large silk pillows in the front room. As I traced the intricate patterns in the silk woven rug hanging on the opposite wall, I drifted into a pleasant nap, stuffed with the rich meals I had consumed heartily at the palace.

"Hasdai, what is this?" She was pointing at the dirty-looking orange crate on her shiny dining room table.

"Oh, I don't know. Some disreputable fellow put it there. Probably from a secret admirer of yours. Open it. Let's see." Gingerly, she opened it and open-mouthed pulled out the exquisite djellaba with the intricate silver and blue embroidery.

"Who? . . . What? . . ."

"Aha. You must have a secret lover." I beamed. I knew my wife was not a material person. Always modest in her dress and manner, she preferred to spend her time with her apothecary herbs and helping her patients. Although quite beautiful with her olive skin and her long finely etched nose and full lips, she rarely considered her looks. Most of the time, she puttered about in a plain white linen caftan and a head scarf. "Hasdai, this is too much!"

"Ah, the Caliph didn't think so. He must have made an effort to determine your size. You can wear this at the high holy days, Rosh Hashana and Yom Kippur." While these days were the time for reverential prayers, the women appeared at the synagogue in their best finery to show their standing in the community and gossip about their peers. Rachel was never one to compete with the wives of the merchants who, every day, sported the fanciest dress and jewels. Often, I had to get my sisters-in-law to take Rachel to the bazaar to select some appropriate fashionable wear. This year, Rachel would astound those shallow, fussy wives and make me proud. She still stared at the djellaba open mouthed.

"Is that all?" I asked.

"Oh, there's a pouch." She shook the contents on the dining room table. Out fell two large gemstones, a sapphire of a misty blue-gray color with a star in the center and a large yellow clear citrine. "Oh Hasdai, look at this."

"Yes, dear. I know. Take them to the jeweler and have a nice brooch made up."

"But . . ."

"You will be able to dazzle sometimes."

"But . . ."

"Don't I get a thank you?"

With a few tears glistening in her eyes, she managed to get out an "Oh, you." And came over to kiss me.

"Tell your father and mother. I think they don't think I feed you enough."

"Oh, Hasdai." It is nice to be appreciated once in a while in your spouse's eyes.

I lay awake after a light supper. My mind was racing over the plans for this diplomatic mission to the King of Leon. It dawned on me that I would have to recruit two knowledgeable merchants from Cordoba to accompany me; they had to be able to conduct trade in something Cordoba had that Leon did not. Of greater importance was the ability to evaluate the information they would get from their sources. I scanned through lists of subjects in my mind, tossing and turning. It slowly began to dawn on me that I would have to have some long discussion with Alphonso and Rodrigo, his supposedly friendly Christian knights. I would need a layout of the city and a list of possible targets for the merchants to approach. Yes, that was a priority. The Christian knights. They were leaving for the north tomorrow traveling to Merida and I had to reach them before they left. Yes. First thing. Up at dawn. Slowly I faded off to sleep. . . . First thing tomorrow. . . .

HASDAI SEEKS KNIGHTS

I was restless about my talk with the knights the next morning and tossed and turned as I went over my talking points. I awoke before dawn after a few hours sleep and got up to urinate and make tea. I knew the knights would have been carousing the night before as guests of the Caliph and would be sleeping late. So I got down from my shelf a few scrolls to read by candlelight. Thoughts came crashing into my conscious state so I could not completely concentrate. A few pieces of orange and some pastry and milk still did not calm him down. So I went to the stables to talk to my horse at the military stable at the al-Kazar, a short walk from the Juderia. The livery people were already awake feeding the horses and shoveling the horse droppings. (They were a valuable commodity and were treated with great care.) I nodded to the stable boy who was by now used to the odd-hour conferences I had with my horse as I thought through some notions. Eventually, I fell into a light sleep on the straw at the side of the horse pen and awoke into broad daylight and smelled of horse. Should I change? Maybe this smell would endear him to the knights. No. I was a man of letters. I should conduct himself as such. I went home first, splashed some water on my face, and changed my clothes, and sprinkled water smelling of almond and rose on my torso and left for the castle. By now, the city streets were full and business was brisk. At the castle gate, I was greeted by the familiar guards and admitted. I went to the guest wing of the castle and inquired after the knights. I was directed to two adjoining doors. Knocking on one, I was greeted after a few knocks with an unintelligible snarl. A pretty young girl answered the door with a blanket wrapped around her shoulders and clutched at her breast.

"Yes, sire. Oh! It's you, Dr. Shaprut." She was one of the Caliph's harem. "Sir Rodrigo will be with you shortly." She was a bit tousled, but had a pleasant smile as she closed the door. She obviously had been an accommodation to the knight by the Caliph. She seemed not to be unhappy with her royal duties. In fact, it would have been an honor to be selected by the Caliph for a visiting nobleman, although she probably was a bit put off by his body odor and heavy breath. But she appeared to be from a Christian land herself and was probably immune to the smell of such men. Only these Moors (and I am pleased to add, the Jews) indulged in habits of personal hygiene. Besides, if she was sufficiently pleasing to the visiting knight, he might purchase her from the Caliph and elevate her to a position in his own court. On the other hand, if they pleased the Caliph with dutiful service in their youth, the Caliph might marry them off to one of his soldiers or servants, a life vastly superior than one in which they toiled in the palace kitchen or cleaned the castle and also superior to the wife of a poor peasant.

Sir Rodrigo eventually lurched to the door and greeted Hasdai with a hearty growl. "What can I do for you, Doctor?" Sir Rodrigo was the older and more intelligent of the two. His hair and beard were graying and he was becoming quite stout, but still had the heavy muscular build of a man trained from childhood in the art of war. His hair was quite dark otherwise and his face quite pale. This appearance suggested he came from a line which had mixed Roman blood with that of the earlier inhabitants of Iberia– before the Visigoth invasion centuries ago. He owned several castles and tracts of land outside Merida to the north. Generally, he was a jovial fellow and appeared to be happy in his role as vassal to the Caliph.

"Sir Rodrigo, I have been asked by the Caliph to go on a diplomatic mission to the Kingdom of Leon and would like to ask you and Sir Alphonso a number of questions to prepare. Could I have breakfast with both of you before I go?"

"Of course, of course, anything for the Caliph and certainly for you, whatever we can do to help." He banged on the next door to his and bellowed for Sir Alphonso to wake up and pull his member out of the harem girl assigned to him. By this time, Sir Rodrigo's companion of the night had brushed past us, fully clothed by now. She greeted us as she left and, showing a nice pendant hanging from her neck, thanked him for her present.

Sir Alphonso came to the door, peering around, for it was apparent he was in the altogether. A young girl was still in the bed, rubbing her eyes, as she, quite tousled and a bit bruised with a swollen lip, was only partially awake.

"The good doctor is going on a mission to Leon and wants to ask us some questions."

"Sure, sure. I'll be ready."

Servants were already carrying trays of fruits and pastries to the rooms for breakfast. Sir Rodrigo and I sat at a table in his room as a large brass ewer of tea was brought in with several porcelain cups.

"So, what would you like to know?" Of course, I wanted to know the best route to Leon and all the usual travel arrangements, but I wanted to do several things as we talked. Prime was judging the loyalty of these two men. Of course, they were Christians and must have had a natural propensity to side with the Christian king, but for some reason they had chosen to side with the Caliph. Of course, their land was on the border, so they could be expected to switch allegiance with the tides of war. Many loyalties became blurred along the boundaries of the two realms and it was not unusual for Christians to side with the Moors on occasion. I already knew that Ordono of Leon was a descendant of the Visigoths and Sir Rodrigo looked to be of Roman or Astinian origin. He was a rough fellow which suggested his family had earned their nobility and lands by military service to someone in the past. Who and how were good questions, so I asked.

"My great-grandfather had fought for the King of Leon and held a command years ago. He was given several towns then. But, when Ordono usurped the title from Sancho, it was time to side with the Moors. My father and I had sided with Sancho and lost." Simple enough. "The Caliph has been good to us and we keep his northern boundary safe. It has been peaceful up there since Ramiro II declared Estremadura a no-man's land to separate the north from the south. It was a no-man's land anyway. It is mostly desert and worthless. This ended the trouble Ordono II started when he set out on a military campaign to conquer Seville, Cordoba and Guadalajara. As with most wars the king ran out of money, could not pay or provision the soldiers, so he retreated back up north. Besides Ferdinand, the Christian king of Castile, sided with the Caliph. Now, apparently, he sides again with the north and Sancho I of Leon. We don't know what Sancho I intends now."

"I thought I had heard all that, but it is good to hear it from someone much closer."

"Well, I married one of Sancho's cousins when I was fourteen and she was a widow at 25, so I am in Sancho's good graces for now, but I am still a vassal to the Caliph."

By now, Sir Alphonso came into the room alternately rubbing his eyes and scratching his member and sat down for some tea. He was taller and thinner than Sir Rodrigo and had dark blond hair and an unkempt ginger beard. It suggested his heritage was from the Visigoths who were often tall and blond. My knowledge of Sir Alphonso was that he was a surly, spoiled dolt and he had not disappointed me in the past.

"Good morning all," he mumbled with a mouth full of boiled egg, fruit and pastry all at once. "I understand you have some questions about your mission." His Arabic was mumbled and not completely clear, so I responded in the language of the north – a corrupt Latin and part Frankish.

"Yes, I will be going through Merida on my way north in a few weeks and wanted a lay of the land." My use of their language pleased them both.

"I live a good bit to the east and have not gone north much. I don't know if I can help you." My senses perked up because we knew he had also married a cousin of Queen Toda, Sancho I's wife, in Leon and had only recently split from Leon to seek our union. He was spotted at two weddings since then in Leon. Suspicion started to grow in my mind. The Caliph was not without his sources already.

"Tell me about the city. What is where?"

Rodrigo drew a circle on the table top out of the tea on his finger. "Here are the walls, here's the palace, the main streets and the gates. That's about it. It's not a big town, just an old Roman fortress. It sits on the Douro River and has a drawbridge to let travelers into the main gate. Aside from the main street through the gates into the castle keep, it's mostly small narrow streets. It is popular with pilgrims on their way to the shrine of St. James at Santiago de Compostela."

"So what is the shrine?"

"Well, in the 800's, the local bishop put out this story that St. James, that's "Santiago" in the local dialect, came here to preach after Jesus' death and for some reason returned to Jerusalem where he was unfortunately beheaded. Legend has it that his followers brought him back to this area where he was buried in some unknown location 800 years ago. As the story goes, a shepherd followed a star to a field of rocks about 150 years ago and determined that this was the burial spot of St. James. The local bishop backed him up and named the town "Santiago de Campostela", St. James' field of stars. Pilgrims have been flooding through Leon to the shrine for the past 150 years. So there is a section of town devoted to inns which cater to the pilgrims and vendors who hawk religious items. The church has become wealthy as well as the town.

"You mean people come to worship the suspected bones of an apostle."

"Yes. Quite right." I had to suppress my reaction. People were worshipping the supposed physical remains of a deceased human as if he were a god. I resisted the urge to go further. Our commandments forbid the worshipping of idols or other gods. Of course, my own religion had its peculiarities, but some local bishop had endorsed the myth that some 800 years ago a follower of Jesus was buried nearby on the strength of a shepherd who had a vision from a star. Better left any comment unsaid.

"So, is there a season for the pilgrims."

"Oh yes. Summer. Definitely summer."

"So I might masquerade as a pilgrim."

"Very easily. The town is overwhelmed with them."

"Now, who might I contact for information helpful to the Caliph in the town."

The two knights looked at teach other. This question might ask them to betray friends still loyal to Leon. They had to depend on my confidentiality.

Rather than answer the question, Alphonso asked, "So why did the Caliph pick a Jew for this mission?"

"Good question and worth a straight answer. He did not wish to compromise either of you by going to Leon to spy on your fellow Christians. Not only would it be more dangerous, but it would expose you and your lands along the border to attacks. Me, I am just a man on a mission from the Caliph. My loyalty is only to him. No one might suspect that I would report my contacts to the King of Leon."

"I see."

"We have many good friends and family in Leon. It is always difficult for us."

"Oh, I understand. I have no such problems. So I will be going through Merida, near you, on my way to Leon in the next few weeks with some others. Let us meet again then and discuss this further."

"Fine. But who will you bring with you?"

"A few soldiers to protect me on the road."

"Well, we could provide you with some of my men." This gratuitous offer implied danger. These same men could easily waylay me and foil the mission. I needed protection loyal to me and the Caliph, but I could not refuse. It would be a sign I did not trust them.

"That would be most kind."

The discussion rehashed a number of issues, but reached no important points as I thanked them and left with more than a few suspicions. Rodrigo offered to let us stay in one of his houses in Merida as we came through. While this was most generous, it also drew immediate suspicion. First, he would have advance notice of our travel plans and could kidnap or kill us, but also it might identify him closely with our mission for the Caliph. We did not wish to compromise our northern vassals any more than necessary. It would be much better if we traveled totally incognito.

I thanked the men for their help and agreed to meet with them in Merida when I came north. This was a polite diplomatic evasion.

CONVERSATION WITH DAVID

It was time to pick up my son, David, from the Inn where the caravans from Seville discharged passengers. He had been visiting my sister, his aunt, and her family in Seville for the Passover holiday. David attended both the local school open to all students and the Jewish yeshiva in our neighborhood. Fortunately, Easter and Passover occurred at the same time this year, so he had a week off to visit his cousins. It was a long walk to the Inn at the center of town, but it was a nice cool spring evening on Saturday.

I found David sitting on a bench with a group of other passengers waiting for their bags to be unloaded. After I collected his, I noticed a calm and pensive expression on his young face. He was just ten this past fall, and beginning to get a picture of the world which confused him.

"David, you look distracted. Didn't you have a nice visit with Aunt Esther and your cousins?"

"No, Papa. That was great. But some boys in the wagon up here were saying things I didn't understand."

"Like what?"

"They were Christian boys, older than me, and were saying something about the Jews. They were mad because we killed Christ. Did we?"

"Did they do anything to you?"

"No, I just kept quiet and listened. Did we kill Christ? I mean, they say we killed God."

"Well, let me say first that we did not kill 'Christ.'" By the way, we don't say Christ, we call him Yeshua, which is his given name. The Romans killed a man named Jesus a thousand years ago. The Romans were the rulers of Jerusalem and Jesus was making trouble so they killed him."

"In Jerusalem? Where the Jews lived?"

"Yes."

"And the Romans conquered Jerusalem?"

"And the rest of the country and made the Jews pay high taxes."

"So the Jews lived in Jerusalem like we live in Spain, like the Moors rule over us now?"

"Exactly. Except that the Moors treat us like everyone else and we are free to do many things, like run our businesses, go to synagogue and go to school."

"So the Moors are not like the Romans. They don't kill Jews?"

"No. In fact, they seem to like us very much. I am an advisor to the Caliph and I run my business. Any other Jews can pray, run their businesses and go to school."

"But why do the Christians say we killed their God?"

"Because they were afraid of the Romans and had to blame it on someone."

"But Jesus wasn't Jewish."

"Yes, he was."

"So their God is Jewish, and yet that hate Jews? How is that?"

"That is difficult to answer. I don't know." It was beginning to look like this was going to be a long question and answer session, so I took David over to the lemonade seller and got us both lemonades so we could sit on the park bench at the square.

"Why isn't Jesus our God?"

"Because we believe he was human, and we do not make humans into Gods, only the pagans and the Christians do."

"What do the Moors think?"

"They agree with us. They think he was human and think he was a prophet."

"What's a prophet?"

"Like a wise rabbi."

"These boys say that this land was Christian and would be conquered by the Christians again and that they would expel the Jews along with the Moors."

"They said that?"

"Yes. They went to church on Easter and their priest said so."

"Ah. That's sad."

"Why?

"Well, this land did used to be Christian, but then the Moors came in 200 years ago. We have had mostly peace and prosperity since that time. The Moors let everyone live in peace, but the Christians do not."

"Why do the Christians want to conquer the Moors if everything is going so well?"

"First, they think everyone should believe as they do, and second, they want us to pay taxes to them and not the Moors."

"But if we don't want to believe as they do, how can they make us?"

"Good question. Some people they kill. Some people they exile and some people fake being Christian and secretly stay Jewish."

"How come the Jews always live in somebody else's land? How come we have to pay taxes to someone else?"

"Good question. Only God knows."

"Is God mad at us?"

"No. I don't think so. I mean we have survived for 2000 years. The last 1000 we have always lived in someone else's land. Sometimes we were happy, most of the time we weren't. It is all part of God's plan. At least we are still here. The Romans were the most mighty empire in the history of the world, now they are gone, and we are still here. Go figure. Maybe we are God's lesson to the world."

The lemonades were finished, so we started back home.

"Papa, the Christian boys wanted to be soldiers and were practicing with swords. The priests said their time would come to fight. Can I have a sword?"

"No. The Moors won't let Jews have swords."

"Will the Christians serve in the army with the Moors?"

"Yes. But only certain ones."

"Will they fight soon?"

"Oh no. I don't think so. The Moors have lived here for 200 years now and are very powerful."

"So what can I be when I grow up?"

"The best thing you can be is a scholar. That leads to everything else. You can be a doctor like me. You can run a business. You can be a rabbi."

"So instead of sword fighting, I learn to read and talk to the learned men."

"Yes, exactly."

SELECTING MEN FOR MISSION

The travel to Leon through Merida would not be particularly difficult. Some old Roman roads were on the way and elsewhere well-trod trade routes filled the gaps. Only the way from Cordoba to Merida would be through forests or hilly terrain, but that was expected to be friendly territory. One had to be on guard, however, because the threat of ambush or raid by bandits was always a possibility. Once past Merida into no-man's land, we might meet enemy soldiers, but the high plateau was flat and rather barren. It was possible to see other travelers a long way off.

The proposition was more appropriately who would I bring. Of course, the Caliph would send two of his best warriors with me, not only to protect me but to keep an eye on me and the others. I would need two Jewish merchants who would set up trade connections between Cordoba and Leon, but also the Caliph would rely on these men to bring continual information from Leon from informants they would develop. The Caliph would provide them with an opening supply of Cordoban goods and it would be their responsibility to develop trade for goods from Leon. Jews were the obvious choice. It was rare that we could own agricultural land or bear arms in the military, so we were known as traders and could make contacts through Jews and Arabs easily in Leon without raising suspicion. And then, two Christian soldiers would accompany us, purely for protection. So two Arabs, two Jews, two Christians and me – empowered by a letter from the Caliph for a diplomatic mission. The merchants would ride in a cart carrying our supplies and their trade goods, but also my medical instruments and a selection of Rachel's herbs and cures.

Like all good travelers, I needed to hide my money and a list of the men I would contact written in code. Hopefully, we could go to Merida and then on to Leon, make our contacts, sell the goods and come home. Mission accomplished.

The more important part of the mission was to keep an eye on my traveling companions to seek out any hints of betrayal. While our world in Moorish Iberia, al-Andalus, was prosperous and successful, there was always a plot, some spies, some evil which threatened. The Caliph and I must protect his realm at all costs.

I, of course, explained this to Rachel. While she was proud of me, she said that while I was on my mission, it would be an excellent time for her and Yael to visit the town fairs and buy more herbs and cures. I had to explain to her how important her personal security was. If she was captured and ransomed, it would jeopardize my whole mission and the Caliph's security as well. She would be a target. She understood, of course, the plots and counter-plots were daily conversation pieces. She would have some of the Caliph's best soldiers as her guards on her trip. I noticed that she had had the sapphire and citrine mounted in a lovely pendant which she carefully allowed to hang under her djellaba. She was too modest to display such expensive things in public.

AFTER SERVICES – ELI AND SAMUEL

The men began to file out of the Sabbath services and chat in the street outside. I sought out the two younger men laughing among a group apart from the elders. As I approached, the group quieted down. I was an acknowledged wise man in the Juderia and my presence meant something significant. I motioned to two of the men.

"Eli, Samuel, can you come over here? I want to discuss something." Eli and Samuel were not the prominent members of the younger generation. They were somewhat smaller and unobtrusive, but had cheerful engaging personalities. Eli was about medium height among the Jews, had a pale complexion and straight black hair. Samuel was a bit smaller with an olive complexion. Both came from modest families among the tradesmen in town. Both were working as apprentices in a business which could only support one family. Neither had the wherewithal to pay a decent bride price and neither had prospects. I had shuffled through the members of the congregation carefully to select two young men who I could enlist for my mission. Both had the combination of factors to be itinerant merchant/spies. Both men followed me to a quiet area and eagerly awaited what I had to say. It was already an honor that I had called them over.

"Eli, Samuel, I have an interesting proposition for you both. It involves an excellent opportunity, but involves some risk and danger." Hearing no objection, I went on. "The Caliph and I have conceived an idea to, shall I say, maintain contact with our neighbors to the north, Leon. He has asked me to select two young men to become merchants traveling between Cordoba and Leon, and parts in between on a regular basis. Taking some goods from Cordoba and selling them en route, while buying commodities along the way in exchange."

"But we have no such resources."

"I agree, but the Caliph has agreed to stake you to an initial inventory at his expense from goods here: copperware, knives, swords, textiles, spices, all from his personal stock of high quality. We will discuss very favorable terms for the repayment of such an advance. He will supply a wagon and horses for the trip. You will also be given a permit to carry personal weapons. As you may guess, the trip north and return will have some risk of bandits, so we expect you may have to defend yourselves. We will also supply two soldiers to serve as your bodyguards until you can afford your own. This will be considered your military service, so you will be exempt from the tax. Above all, you will acquire a good friend in the Caliph."

"Good Dr. Shaprut, this is indeed an excellent prospect. But now I must ask what we must do in return."

"Several things. Some relatively simple. First, you must accept those who would travel with you in a caravan and add more guards as necessary. You may charge others for the privilege of joining your traveling body."

"Simple enough. But I believe something else is coming."

"Quite right, Eli. Your name betokens the wise one from the Torah."

"You will also carry mail and messages back and forth for a small fee."

"Ah, a minor task. Dr. Shaprut, what else is involved?"

"Another good question, Samuel. You must listen."

"So, listen. Listen for what?"

"When you travel through the Kingdom of Leon, you must listen for what the king intends against Cordoba and the south: what knights he has assembled, what alliances he has formed, who among the Christians in Cordoba might become his allies and betray the Caliph."

"Ah, so we will be spies."

"No less. You will develop sources, friends who may seek to ally with the Caliph and be rewarded for their trouble. Those who like to drink and babble. Those with secrets they must hide. All in the Kingdom of Leon. And on your return, you will relate what you have learned to the Caliph and his generals. You must be discrete, use your wits to meet and befriend. Have I made myself clear?"

"How are we to do this?" Samuel said with a smirk, as if he did not know this already. He and Eli often lead some of the antics of his generation.

They often bought rounds at the tavern or romanced women with gifts. They were now having a bit of fun at the expense of their learned and a bit stiff elder.

"You know, I was your age once. Do not think I did not enjoy myself."

"Yes, Doctor. Have you asked our parents?"

"No. This is for you to do. But your first test is discretion. You must limit the amount of information and know who you can trust to be told and keep silent. Your parents must understand the word of your true mission may put your lives in danger."

"Yes. We do not need to be told that. When can we start?"

"Let's say in two weeks. If you accept, I will tell the Caliph. He will want to meet with you and select your inventory and your guards."

"About how long is this trip?"

"A sensible question. About a week to two weeks depending on the weather and the bandits along the way. Now, tell your parents and then come for dinner at my house."

RACHEL WITH MOORISH WIVES

Now that I was the Caliph's doctor and adviser, Rachel was invited by the Caliph's wives to join them in an entertainment. She nervously consulted some of the other Moorish women to find out what this meant. Was she expected to bring a dish? What should she wear? Were they kosher? What if they served something that wasn't kosher? Should she wear a veil? Would the Caliph's wives be wearing a veil? I got a great deal of enjoyment out of my wife going into such a tizzy.

Of course, she also asked the other Jewish women the same questions. They did not know, of course, but it was a less than subtle way of letting everyone know that she, Rachel, Hasdai's wife, was to be a guest of the Caliph's wives. She wanted to lord it over her friends, but didn't want to look too obvious.

But answers came back. Yes, the Moors kept something like kosher. They called it "Bilal". They didn't eat most of the things forbidden in Deuteronomy and butchered their animals the same way because, after all, the Moors looked to the Hebrew Bible as their own, and Abraham as the founder of their race. They also looked to Moses and the other Jewish wise men as their prophets including Jesus. So, yes, they kept the equivalent of kosher.

No, they didn't wear veils in their own houses. Like most women, in their houses, they slipped off the uncomfortable but fashionable clothing — shoes, girdles, hairpieces and relaxed and wiped off their eye makeup.

Yes. It would be nice if she brought a particularly Jewish dish. She settled on a nice desert, haroset, a spread of oranges, raisins, dried apricot, cinnamon and dates rolled into balls and covered with sweet dough.

She decided to dress up a bit. She put on her good jewelry, put kohl on her eyes in the Egyptian fashion and put her best mother-of-pearl comb in her thick, black, shiny hair. As she fidgeted around the house, Hasdai chuckled.

"How come you don't get dressed up for me like that?"

"Oh, Hasdai, be nice. I am so nervous."

"Relax, they are women like you. Just be yourself."

"But what if I mess up. What will happen to you? Will they tell the Caliph I did something wrong?"

"Relax! Relax! Be yourself. I put up with you. So will they." He gave her the money for a cart because he knew she would be worried about her hair, and whether she would sweat on the long walk. Finally, she was out the door and the house was quiet again.

As she alighted from the cart, she was ushered into the palace and directed to the wives' quarters. The Caliph's bedroom and quarters were to the right side of the throne room, while each of the wives had their own separate apartments for themselves and their children to the left. In the middle of the wives' complex was a small open atrium with a long pool of water running down the middle with a small fountain at one end. The fountain was a bronze peacock spewing water out of his mouth. His fine tail arrayed behind him with the eyes of his tail burnished in white, blue and green. Along the sides of the pool were small palm trees and low plants. In the pond were small fish darting back and forth. As she entered, a servant was feeding the fish. A few parrots cackled from large perches under the eaves of the cloister that surrounded the edge of the park. Chairs and couches were arranged in small groups under the cloisters.

As Rachel walked in, she was greeted by an older, but striking woman in her forties. "Hello, Mrs. Shaprut, I am Yasmine, the senior wife. Please come sit with me." While Rachel stood gaping at this woman, three other ladies walked out of the gateway to the building and came up behind Yasmine.

Rachel had never seen such an exquisite interior and couldn't take her eyes off the peacock fountain. She turned as the other women approached. They ranged in age from 15 to 30. Each was dressed in long silk pantaloons and a bra top with a shawl over their shoulders. As they walked, they tinkled. Anklets with bells were on everyone's feet. Yasmine introduced them all. A servant came up to take Rachel's haroset in the covered dish.

The women all sat in a semi-circle facing the pool with Rachel next to Yasmine. Rachel babbled nervously, "You women are all so beautiful. I never would have guessed what was under your veils."

They giggled. "Ah, that is the mystery. Everyone guesses, no one knows. I am Malala. Nice to meet you. I am from Yemen." She was much darker than the rest and had several pearls imbedded in her forehead. She was somewhat plump and had gold bracelets on her arms.

"How did you come to Cordoba?"

"The Caliph is distantly related to my family and came on a visit years ago. I am from the Almorads, a different branch of the Moors and the Caliph thought it was a good idea to cement relations with our families."

"Ah. We too have arranged marriages. My father picked me out for Hasdai, but he has only me."

The youngest one, a very petite young girl of fifteen, shyly spoke up. "Does he sleep with you every night?" The other women stared fiercely at her. This was a bold breach of privacy. It did not seem to upset Rachel.

"Yes, of course. We sleep in the same bed." The other women looked at the floor. They were only with the Caliph when he sent for one of them and to keep jealousy from arising, the others were never supposed to know when one of them had been summoned. Sometimes he selected none and sent for a concubine. But they knew. Anyway, this was a very touchy subject. Yasmine, a wise diplomat steered the conversation away. Concubines were never mentioned in this group. In truth, they all knew the Caliph had a harem as well and a favorite concubine, Zahra. But this was never mentioned in their quarters.

"You must be very proud having your Hasdai as the only Jew on the Caliph's council of advisers."

"Yes, we very much appreciate the honor. But it does take him away for many days. Then, I have to run the business by myself. Of course, my daughter helps."

"You work in a business?"

"Oh, yes."

"You are very lucky to have such responsibility. We do not have such important things to do. Only the peasant women work. All the other wives stay home."

The servants had been coming in bearing delicacies and placing them on the low table in front of the women. Rachel noticed that her own plate of haroset had been brought in, but two of the balls had been eaten. Perhaps someone had tested them to be sure they were not poison. They obviously passed. But then, these were the Caliph's women. They were always at risk.

"I can tell you it's no fun. Our Bible instructs women to be the helpmate of their husbands. We are to be an eshektal from Proverbs 31. We are to help him in his business matters. It has always been so."

"Aren't you proud to do so?"

"Proud, but tired, I also have to take care of the children, and tend the house and do the cooking."

"Don't you have servants?"

"Sometimes, but it is difficult. Many do not know how to keep kosher and they are not used to Jews."

"Well, I wasn't used to Jews or Moors before I got married. Now I am." Speaking was a tall blond woman in her thirties. She was much larger and heftier than the others, and spoke with a Spanish accent. "Please call me Astrid. I was raised Christian, but I am some kind of peace treaty. The Caliph married me so he could be friends with Aragon." She laughed. "But I am happy here."

The wives chatted pleasantly as the afternoon wore on. It was interesting for each of the households to learn about the other. As Rachel rose to leave, she was embraced warmly by the Caliph's wives. She walked home slowly with much to think about. She was now thankful for the life she led. She said a short prayer.

ELI AFTER THE SABBATH

Eli went to the Saturday morning service with his family as usual. The prayers were familiar, the people from the community sat together, they sang together and the Torah portion was read. It felt comfortable to look around and feel the whole community together. And then they filed out.

At first, Eli stood with his parents and his sisters. He was the eldest of the siblings. His family was not wealthy and stood to the side and chatted with the other families from his row of houses. But Eli's thoughts drifted to the circle of young women gathered in a group. They were laughing together and speaking loudly. Eli was now of marriageable age, but his family could not afford a bride price and Eli was working only as an apprentice with his distant cousin, the silversmith. He was a decent craftsman and turned out nice work in copper and silver, but he was an employee. He had no funds to buy the metal necessary to work, nor could he afford a shop. He might remain an employee forever. Yet he had been fortunate to get this apprentice opportunity years before when he was 14.

His mother had been friendly with the wife of the silversmith and had interceded. The smith was happy now to have him. He was good with customers, his work was fine and he was beginning to learn how to buy silver and cooper and then judge a proper price for the finished product.

When Samuel, his friend since they were toddlers, had told him about Hasdai's interest in working with the Caliph as merchants to Leon and the opportunity to develop their own business, Eli could not imagine his good luck. He could get along easily with people and knew he could get information for the Caliph. Plus the intrigue. To be of service to the Caliph, to enjoy his gratitude, to be partners with his good friend Samuel in their own business. It was like God had plucked him out of the multitudes and given him a purpose in life.

Now, his mind was drifting over to the young girls laughing together. He had known one of them briefly from the neighborhood and was attracted. He would saunter by as casually as possible to greet her. He had a bit more confidence now that he might have a future.

"Hello, Iliana." He tried as he came near their group.

"Oh, hello." She did not repeat his name. Iliana was somewhat pretty with a full face and a pale complexion with mounds of curly black hair, dark eyes and full red lips. Under the layers of clothing, she looked a bit plump, but a bit plump was not necessarily a bad thing. It was far better than to be thin. But Iliana had a whiney voice. She came from the family of a well-to-do merchant and was used to having her way. Among the girls she was standing with, she had the most expensive clothes because they were in the rare colors of blue and purple from expensive imported dyes. After the brief response to Eli, she turned to her other girl friends. Eli was a born salesman and not one to object to an initial slight.

"So Iliana, what are you doing this summer?"

"Nothing much, I have school and then I go to the mountains."

This answer was well rehearsed and told Eli and the rest of them several things. Only wealthy girls went to school because, usually, few women were educated past a certain point, and most could not read. So school was an expensive proposition for a family and a marked distinction. A summer trip to the mountains was also. It meant the entire family would escape the heat, the dust and the smells of summer and live in a nice villa in the foothills to the north where little work was done. While her wealthy father plied his trade in town, she and her mother and a few servants would pass the days idly and pleasantly in the cool of the mountains in their villa. There were a few small communities where the wealthy gathered during the hot months. Eli and his family certainly could not afford any such thing. But Iliana sounded bored, as if it was something so expected and to which she was so entitled, that it held no suspense or even interest for her. To say this in front of her girl friends and Eli, she was laying on thick her social standing. It was an intimidation.

Undaunted, Eli persisted. "Perhaps we could meet at the cafe." In those days and forever, marriages were arranged and shrewdly bargained for. Love was not a consideration. But, somehow, in all communities, the boys and girls could meet and express a preference. This was dangerous because it might be out of all proportion to what the father, or often the mother could foresee for their children. Such notions could become tragic if the children persisted in defying the choice or designs of the parents. They were not to be encouraged. What Eli was attempting was dangerous. To seek to rise several social ranks above himself might be foolhardy, but his new secret self-confidence from his mission for the Caliph had stiffened his backbone.

But it was unknown to Iliana. In her shrill whiney voice, she rebuffed him. "It would be too much to fit in these days." This was a pale excuse. All the singles showed up at the café at one time or another. It served tea, fruit juices and pastries and seemed to have become a magnet for the young singles.

For Iliana, not to say when she would be there so they could meet in a safe social setting among many others was clearly a rejection. To imply that she was too busy or bored to attend was a pretense. The Jewish community was not large and its young singles population was minimal. To imply that she was not interested in going to the café was a boast. Everyone went there. But mainly, she didn't want to meet Eli at the café and she wanted to let her girl friends know how indifferent she was to the necessary life at the café. Eli was getting the message. He gracefully chatted with some of the other girls in the group and left at his earliest and best face- saving opportunity.

A VISIT TO THE CALIPH

I and my two would-be merchants walked from my home up to the Caliph's palace. We were to be given the Caliph's blessing for their respective missions. Once again, I was saluted by the guards and we were escorted down the cloistered walkway to a small room. They were instructed to sit as platters of fruits and a tea service was brought out. Suddenly, the Caliph and two aides came through the door and we sprang to our feet.

"Please be seated" said the Caliph as he and the two aides, now apparently generals of the army dressed in mufti. "Gentlemen, you are about to embark on an important mission. Several things are important. First is discretion and secrecy. Only you three will hear what you know or have learned and you will report only to me, or the two men seated across from you, General al- Hakin and al-Mansur. No girl friends, wives, drinking buddies, no one. Is that clear? Otherwise you endanger yourselves, your compatriots, your sources and most of all, me. Is that clear?" Nods all around.

"Next, you must get your information to me promptly so it can be used." Nods.

"I have authorized you to draw an extensive inventory from our warehouse. This is an excellent opportunity. You will pay no interest on this loan. You will repay me upon each return from Leon until the loan is repaid. If you are successful, I may forgive the loan. You may become very prosperous and rise far above your present station. You will have beautiful wives and fine houses. The reward is great, but so is the risk. Are you ready to undertake this mission?" Nods.

"Hasdai Shaprut is your leader. He speaks for me. He has selected you as worthy for this work. Everything you do reflects on him. You must protect him. Do you understand?" Nods.

"Very well, General al-Mansur will take you to the warehouse where you may draw your goods. I have also given you these documents which say you are my agents and under my protection. Do not show these to anyone except in emergencies. Hide them about your persons. These documents could mean your death if they fall into the wrong hands. Do you understand?" Nods. With that the Caliph stood and abruptly turned to leave with General al-Hakin. General al-Mansur saluted and turned to us.

"Gentlemen, if you earn the Caliph's trust and regard, things will go well for you. Now, please follow me." There was no hesitation as we followed him to the warehouse.

CARAVAN TO LEON

On the appointed day, I and the rest of the men assembled at the Caliph's warehouse at dawn. The carts had been loaded. The two Christian soldiers sat upon large brown horses who nibbled at oat bags. The two Moorish soldiers sat on small sleek Arabian stallions who twitched nervously in the cool morning air. I had hired a large brown horse while Samuel and Eli sat in the front of the cart. I did not take my fine Arabian, because I felt I needed a more serviceable sturdier stallion for the long trek. I had taken my medical equipment and a stock of herbs and spices needed for various cures. Also concealed in the carts were various weapons, a supply of Leonese coins, some gold and gems, and documents executed by the Caliph. The lead Moorish soldier signaled to form up and depart. With that, the small caravan wended its way north to the road to Merida. Leading from the city, the old Roman road going north was well maintained and we kept a brisk pace for several hours. As they reached the foothills with a few scattered farms, we went into the woods and climbed the steeper roads. Under the foliage, the air was cool and there was little talk among us except Eli and Samuel who chattered nervously about the inventory and the prices they could charge in Leon and what they should buy for the return home. Around noon, we stopped in what was apparently a rest area along the route. A small brook came past a flat grassy clearing in the trees. The men pulled out a satchel or two and distributed bits of nuts, fruit and water. After a half hour, they started once again. We had neither seen nor heard other travelers on the route thus far. The afternoon passed in the cool roadway under different trees. A few people had passed going south, but little, if any traffic passed going north or south otherwise. After a few more rest stops, we came to a large open area by the road where numerous old campfire sites remained and a few lean-tos had been erected. It was decided to make the first nightly stop here.

After laying down their gear, the two Christian soldiers went off into the forest as the rest of us built a fire and began to brew a concoction of lentils and some dried grains. It hadn't taken long before the Christian soldiers returned with a rabbit and two squirrels they had hunted. They busily assembled a spit on one of the arrows and placed it over the fire. They were eager to offer some of their kill to the Jews and the Moors. Politely, both groups declined. Looking somewhat hurt, one of the soldiers eventually asked why.

"You see, the animals cannot be eaten under the rules of our religion."

"What, what do you mean?"

"We do not consider these animals to be 'clean'" explained Hasdai. "The Muslims and Jews can only eat certain animals, and only if they are properly butchered."

"It is hard to believe someone would turn down a nicely turned rabbit." He pointed to his soon to be dinner. "What game animals can you eat?"

The Jews and the Moors looked at each other. One of the Moorish soldiers decided, "Deer would be acceptable if he could drain all of its blood before cooking it. As Jews we looked doubtful. After some hesitation, I decide."

"If the animal is dead, it would not be kosher. That is inedible. But if it is still alive so I could kill it and drain all of its blood, a deer would become kosher then." The Arabs nodded.

"Yes, it must not be completely dead when you bring it back to us." The Christians seemed delighted to be able to contribute something to the trip.

"OK. So a wounded deer is acceptable." They enjoyed hunting and were happy to comply. "So, tomorrow we eat venison. Can we dry it and salt it? Is it acceptable then?"

I nodded. "Yes, if it is without blood, it can be eaten." With that the Christians nibbled on the skewered rabbit and squirrel while the Moors and Jews dipped helpings of the lentil stew. There was also flat bread and a hummus dip.

"You know, not to be impolite, but may I ask why you Jews are so different. You don't eat our food, you don't go in our taverns and you have such strange rules."

Everyone turned to me. "You know from your Bible that Moses received the Ten Commandments which we all believe in, as well as the Moors." The Moors nodded in agreement. "But over the centuries after that, our wise men added more rules, some from God, some for health reasons, so that is now part of our religion. I am advised that Mohammed and the Arab wise men also adopted many of these rules." The Arabs nodded again.

"But why are you people so smart and why do you get rich?"

"Good question. I think some comes from the fact that every boy of 13 must read from our holy scroll the first five books of the Bible to be accepted as a man in our community. So every man can read. We also worship the act of reading and practice it regularly."

"We do not read. At least almost all of us do not read. Except the priests and they can even read Latin."

"I understand. So I think reading helps us to understand things better." The Christians pondered on that for a while. The one asked, "Why are you always making money?"

"Another good question. First, we are often forbidden to own land, we are not accepted into the armies of the Christians, and we are not permitted to train as soldiers."

"So that makes you rich?"

"No, but it forces us into being merchants or doctors or coppersmiths or something like that."

"Is there money in that?"

"Yes. If you know your trade. If we were to work as serfs in the fields, we would always be poor as the serfs are. If we fought in the wars, we would lose all our men. So, we keep our men and we learn a trade and we live where we are told."

"Uh huh. But you all can read. So you all read the Bible."

"Yes."

"Only our priests can read the Bible."

"So we hear."

"But yet, our people rule."

"Yes, that is true. Your people."

"Why is that?"

"I don't know. Of course, there are more of you."

"But your God permits you to suffer and be ruled by others."

"That is true."

"Don't you distrust your God then."

"Well, our God is your God. So his ways must have some meaning. It is something we do not know."

"Yes. That is so. Well, we all serve the Caliph now, and we all are doing well. Is that not so?"

"Yes, I imagine that is true. So we must protect his rule"

"I must agree."

"But you are Christian. The king up north in Leon is Christian. Why do you not join him?"

"The Caliph has been good to us. We have our cathedral and we are doing well with his rule. It would be stupid to change now. I am a soldier, my family is happy and I live well here."

"So you see no reason not to serve the Caliph well on this trip?"

"My family has been under the Caliph's rule for many generations. My grandfather was a farmer, but my father was sent to the military school at Cordoba and learned to be a soldier. I did the same. We have been loyal to the Caliph and it has been good for us. I may be a decion soon and lead a squad of men. The kings of the Christian kingdoms are always killing each other and life is not good up there. No. If the Caliph calls, I will answer."

I nodded.

"Dr. Shaprut, next time we bring deer."

"Now remember, the deer must be wounded, not dead. I must kill it with a knife and drain its blood." He turned to the Moors. The Moors nodded, each with a piece of flat bread in their hand dipping in the stew.

"Dr. Shaprut, we must post guard. Pietro and I will take two hours each. The Moors must take the next two each."

"Very well." He turned to the Moors. "Is that acceptable."

"It will be our duty to serve. And yes to the deer, we will dry what is left over for later."

"Ah. We have an agreement. It will be God's will." All nodded and Eli and Samuel smiled. So far, so good.

ON TO MERIDA

The troop of seven made its way steadily but slowly through the forested foothills on the way to Merida. The cool air under the trees was pleasant and the forests were alive with game – kosher for the Jews, bilal for the Moors, but trapped or wounded by the Christian soldiers who were enjoying the sport. The animals were brought back to the camp and slaughtered ritually before being placed in the stew or roasted on a spit. Breaks in the expedition were taken at the regular prayer hours of the Muslims, who unrolled their prayer rugs and kneeled facing east while the Jews and Christians lounged on the side of the trail and sipped water. After a few days, the town of Merida came into view. It was an old Roman capital and still had many Roman temples to the Roman gods as well as aqueducts and paved streets. With the defeat of the Romans several hundred years earlier, most of their improvements had fallen into disuse. Goats and cattle nibbled at grass on the floor of the temple of Diana, now covered amply with trash and manure. The streets survived nicely but were worn into tracks for the wagons. Around the center of town were ramshackle huts spreading in all directions, with a few neighborhoods of row houses built of mud bricks and mortar.

I announced that I was funding a stay at an inn and a healthy dinner for all as we passed the row of taverns lining the street on the way into town. Merida was more or less in the area of no-man's-land these days, between the Christian and Moorish kingdoms. Both Christians and Arabs were among the townsfolk who did not seem to object to each other, although they lived in different parts of town. But the population was small enough that most people knew each other. During the day the men, and occasionally a few women, went out into the fields to cultivate the crops and tend the livestock. A few were hunters. The town was owned by a Moorish vassal of the Caliph who collected taxes and maintained a standing small army of soldiers and knights.

It was one of the soldiers who stopped the troop as we entered the town proper and demanded to see our right to enter. Although the men could not read, they were awed by the well-known seal of the Caliph that I showed them and with great ceremony ushered us into the town while pointing out and describing the better taverns along the main road. They offered to escort us to a few in particular. (For which he undoubtedly would be paid by the proprietor.) His disappointment was evident as we said we wanted to present ourselves to the Caliph's vassal. We proceeded along the road over the old Roman bridge crossing the river. It was a magnificent piece of work with many spans all of carved stone. On the right as we entered the main gate through the town's wall was the Al Cazaba, the Moorish castle and fortress guarding the western and main gate into town. Our escort departed as we entered the western gate guarded by soldiers in capes of yellow and red. I again showed the Caliph's letter to the guard who did not appear to read it, but made a humming sound as he saw the Caliph's seal and passed us through. One of his soldiers peeled off and escorted us on foot to the main palace door, another wrought iron affair with birds and vines in silver adorning the cross pieces. We had drawn a large crowd as we rode into the main courtyard. We were after all, an odd contingent – two Christian soldiers on large horses, two Moorish soldiers on delicate Arabians, and three men in a small wagon with a fine horse trotting tied to the rear. This town was an outpost and drew few travelers except on market days.

We dismounted and entered the castle door to be greeted by a vassal and his entourage. "Gentlemen, I am Al-Tariq, mayor of Merida. You are welcome and my regards to the Caliph." He went on for several minutes reciting the praise of the Caliph and praying that his and his family's reign would be prosperous, but that he was his loyal liege and was always on call to serve. The late afternoon sun was beating down, we were tired, our horses were tired and sweaty and we wanted a cold drink and a place to sit, but first we must hear out this flowery welcoming speech, which mercifully came to an end.

"Gentlemen, you must stay in my castle, the magnificent Al Cazaba and dine with me tonight." Ah, music to our ears. Of course, we were not nobility and would be relegated to the lower level in the dining hall, but we indeed welcomed the hospitality. We walked our horses to the livery stables and had our gear carried by several servants to the wing of the castle where we would spend the night. The Moors used the occasion for one of the daily prayers, but the rest of us fell on our cots for a nap in the coolness of the stone walls. As we started to stir, a few older women rapped timidly at our door and asked if we wanted to bathe. A most welcome suggestion after several days in the same cloths, day and night on horseback and sleeping on the ground. The bath, alas was a large pool of cold water, but welcome nonetheless. We were not in civilized Moorish territory where we would be scrubbed clean in a Turkish bath with warm water. But a cool dip was heaven nonetheless.

We dressed in fresh linen djellabas and went to the dining room, lined with rough wooden tables and benches. While our Christian brothers may have had a thirst for wine, we were offered cool pitchers of a mixture of tea and fruit juice. Lamb stew was ladled into our plates along with hunks of fresh bread. We were again treated to a lengthy speech by the mayor praising the Caliph and praying for many more years of his and his family's reign. Fortunately, we were not standing, were no longer tired and were permitted to eat as he spoke. Out of respect, we dared not glance at each other with bemused scowls.

We went to bed early that night. I say we. The Christian soldiers both went out to sample the inns. We heard them stumble into their rooms just about as the church bell struck either two or three. At least it was still dark outside.

The next morning, the Moors and the Jews came down to a breakfast of milk, fruit and some type of bread. One of the Caliph's retainers greeted us and told us we would have a tour of the town. Since he was determined to show hospitality to those who might report back to the Caliph, we could not refuse. Surprisingly, the Christians came down shortly thereafter looking not a bit out of sorts, although they did smell of sour wine and loose women.

This town of Merida was very important to the Caliph. It might be a focal point of the next incursion by the Kingdom of Leon into the moorish holdings in Iberia. A series of skirmishes had been going on for at least a century with the Moors slowly losing ground. This, of course, emboldened the Christian kings to push further. My mission was to try to secure the peace for a least a generation, and particularly so because a different, cruder, more barbaric group of Moors were invading our Caliphate from the southern end.

I would have to prepare a report on the strength of the soldiers and fortifications of Merida for the Caliph. While I could depend on the Moors to be loyal to the Caliph, it struck me that the Christians might not and could well be examining the walls and other strategic places for a rich reward informing the King of Leon from a trip at our expense. Since the Christians although decently recovered from an evening of carousing, were not what you would call brilliant military tacticians or passionate aficionados of Roman architecture, I told them they could rest for the day. Without a second thought, they accepted and were invited on a hunt into the nearby hills.

During our tour, I was amazed at the many Roman structures which must have been at least 600 years old by this time. There was a large ampitheatre, large for provincial standards, and down the middle of town was a large forum. Most of the buildings had fallen into disrepair and served as shops for the several merchants in town. My two Jewish boys were quick to snap up a site for themselves which was vacant along the row. The Temple of Diana, but probably to Augustus, dominated the forum area but was now mostly a cattle and sheep pen. Pigs, of course, were not permitted to Muslims so they were raised and sold well outside of town in the Christian area. It seems Merida was a town built by the Romans for housing retired Roman soldiers to protect its interest in this outpost of the Empire, so it was heavily invested with Roman amenities.

I had already noticed that on our trip from Cordoba we had been in a fairly heavily forested area with very few inhabitants and only a few scattered farms here and there. This area could be easily defended as a long invading column of troops and an even longer trail of supply wagons took up the rear. Of course, invading troops would readily avail themselves of the crops of the farmers in the area, but there were precious few of those.

The town of Merida itself had been strategically placed to guard the Guadiana River which ran north and south past the walls and the Al Cazaba fortress in the walls. The old Roman bridge was still quite sturdy and could be used as a rampart to deter raiders on the trip south. The town also guarded the popular land route through a pass in the hills to the north. I made mental notes to be reduced to a letter to the Caliph. I would discuss it with the town's mayor as well.

In my humble opinion, as a non-military man, the invading army would have to skirt this town far to the east over what I was told was mostly a desert highland, similar to what we would see to the north on our trip to Leon. We were back late for lunch, only to be greeted by a large number of people. Apparently, one of the mayor's retainers had been bragging that Hasdai Shaprut, the famous doctor had come to visit. Of course, I wanted to keep my presence very quiet, but it seems a number of people with different maladies had assembled to ask for treatment by a famous visiting doctor. My two young entrepreneurs, Eli and Samuel, saw a major money-making opportunity and began to form the people in a line to see me while they collected my fees. Reluctantly, I sat in a cool area on the old forum and began to diagnose and prescribe. The boys hustled to get a tent for me so some of the people could undress or explain their illness in private. While I nibbled furtively at the midday meal they brought me, I examined eyes, ears, rectums, skin rashes and heard of indigestion, headaches and venereal disease. The list was exhaustive for such a small town on such short notice. I had the boys write down my remedies for the local apothecary and in some cases dipped into my collection for herbs and ointments. As the sun sank and I was staggering to dinner, I still left a number of people unsatisfied.

I sat down for dinner and had a large flagon of wine brought over to ease the headache I had acquired. The boys handed me a fat purse jingling with coins. I gave them some for their ingenuity. Meanwhile, they had laid out their wares in the adjacent stall and had also attracted a following. They were able to hire a nice middle-aged Arab woman to agree to tend a stall for them when they came through next time. They did not need to teach this woman how to negotiate the prices. It was part of their tradition to haggle. So far, the trip had been a nice adventure, but tomorrow we would head into the high desert plains of Estremadura – no-man's- land between the Christians and the Moors.

ON TO LEON

Many of our group were reluctant to move on to Leon. The Christians liked the inns and had made a few friends. My young Jewish entrepreneurs had done well in their very limited time in their stall at the forum. And the Moors were meeting friends and relatives their families knew. But the purpose of the trip was to go to Leon. So I had to whip everyone into line and get them ready to depart at dawn the next day.

Everyone showed, prepared to travel. The Jewish boys had repacked their wares and had their cash in the wagon. The Moors were mounted and packed. They were a bit apprehensive about going into enemy territory, but had faith that my letter from the Caliph would protect us. One of the Christians said goodbye with a long embrace to his female companion of the previous night. Yes, it was just two nights, but the heart has its reasons. And so we were off.

The area to the north of Merida was a continuation of what we had seen in the south. Not dense, but certainly full forestation with very few inhabitants. We were coming up the foothills onto the high plain of Estremadura. About noon, we stopped for a prayer session for the Moors and some lunch. The Christians struck off into the trees to hunt some game. The rest of us lounged around a small clearing.

Suddenly, out of the thickets sprang five disreputable looking characters brandishing broadswords and daggers. The men were extremely ragged and wore head scarves. Our Moorish escort rose to the attack immediately and bore the full brunt of the first wave. They had extremely sharp short spears with curved blades, similar to scimitars. The length of the spears kept the attackers at bay as the Moors slashed at them. One of the Moors was the first to draw blood as he swiped at the midsection of one of the men and sliced deeply into his abdomen. This angered the remaining four who now began to circle the Moors. In doing so, two of them had to circle past us and expose their backs. While not heavily armed, nonetheless, I and my two Jewish protégés had concealed short swords under the wagon. We each grabbed one as the attackers circled the Moors. With a cry, Eli sprang forward onto the back of one of our assailants and plunged the blade into the area near his collarbone by his neck. His companion to the left turned from the Moors and started a ponderous swing with the broad sword at Eli, but Samuel came to aid his friend and struck his short sword just under the ribs of the assailant and ripped the blade in an upward motion.

By this time, the Christians had heard the commotion and came running full tilt out of the woods. While they had a bow and quiver of arrows, the space was too small for them to load and fire. So they each took a mace, a heavy hammer-like weapon with a rounded metal head with spikes. In the confusion swirling around the loss of three companions, the remaining two were distracted watching their fellows fall and not prepared for the onslaught of the Christians. The first struck one of the attackers with a heavy blow to the right side which made a cracking sound as it crushed several ribs and began to draw blood. The other Christian feinted with a low blow and swung directly overhead, striking his foe at the top of his forehead. In short order, all five men lay silent with bloody mortal wounds and never moved again. We stood there, hands on our knees breathing heavily for several minutes. As we walked up to examine the men, it appeared that they were Moors, but extremely thin, dirty and in rags. Someone might have tipped them off about the direction of our journey and they followed us from Merida. We picked up their weapons and threw them in the wagon. But how did they follow us? We were moving slowly, at the speed of the wagon, but no one could have kept pace for six hours on foot. There must be horses. So we spread out to search.

I heard a cry from one of our Moorish guards after about ten minutes. He had found horses tied up and tethered about 150 yards away. These beasts were thin and haggard with large gaps of hair missing and a few disease spots. They were Arabians but not quite pure bred. We brought them into our clearing, fed and watered them. They would take some tending and care, but they were not that old, just ill treated. We fashioned a line to tie them onto the back of the wagon, and proceeded north again.

SALAMANCA

Before Leon lay the city of Salamanca. As we came into the edge of the huts surrounding the city walls, we could see for the first time the effect of the ravages of war. The walls at certain places were reduced to piles of rubble. There were still bits and pieces of what were once human beings lying about as birds picked at what was left. Only rags covered the bones now and the head, arms and legs were skewed at odd angles. A few horse carcasses lay on the side and there again, birds picked. A few shabby feminine figures were walking about as if in a daze, followed by children of various sizes, also in tatters. A mangy dog or two trotted among the ruins. Occasional pieces of broken armaments lay scattered about. These were the remnants of past battles. There were no men. As we came closer to the town center, a number of buildings had been heavily damaged, some with marks of fires, some merely crumbling as they stood. All was silent. There were no inns. There were few standing residences and the castle, such as it was, and the keep had been destroyed.

There was no need to ask to purchase food. There was none. Only a few wells for water. We were in the no-man's-land between the Christians and the Moors, and this must be what parts of hell looked like. Only women and children of indeterminate age, of poor health, with blackened or diseased skin wandered about the rubble on some uncertain mission. Some begged, some offered themselves. It all begged the question as to why there was war. Surely neither side had gained in the town of Salamanca. Yet, it was well situated on the bank of the Tormes River and a two-day journey from Madrid to the east, and on the old Roman road running north to Leon and south through Merida and Cordoba. The town lay as if dead – a monument to man's undefined quest to expand his territory at the expense of those in the way. We could not stay the night in Salamanca and must press on to safer and less gloomy camp sites.

VILLAGE FAIR

In the rural town of Andujar, just outside of Jaen, the center square was teeming with people. Vendors had set up their stalls, booths and tents in neat rows designated for them. In some places, vendors simply sat on a cloth with their wares arrayed in front of them. Most of the sites were run by women while their husbands worked in the fields of their plots. Children of all ages ran wild through the square, screeching as they chased one another. The older children were very pleased with their status as official helpers at the stall. The market had been assembled beginning in the hours before dawn and was in full readiness by early daylight. The more permanent stalls were the butchers who hung a variety of animal carcasses—rabbits, chickens, beef and pork in various states of dismemberment on hooks. Flies descended on the exposed meat and were whisked away by the children. Buyers would haggle with the proprietor until a suitable compromise could be reached and their purchase wrapped in a large leaf and bound in twine. Other stalls displayed produce including cabbages, lettuce, apples, lemons, and honey, eggs and cheese. At others, clothing, hats, sandals, boots, and copperware were stacked neatly, as the women of the family engaged the passersby surveying their merchandise.

Off to one corner two women sat on a cloth under a makeshift tent to shield them from the sun. I say women, but one was a girl of 14 and the other her mother of 30. Before them in neat piles were arranged an assortment of dried plants, jars of ground seeds or powders. Many of the fair's attendants knew of these women as healers since their many ingredients had been dispensed to cure various ailments in the past with some degree of success. Arsinoe, the mother, and Zastra, the daughter, were versed in the diseases their wares cured and could examine and prescribe these herbs to combat the ailments. In secret, these women were part of a scattered group formerly known as the Burgomils who had been chased from southern France because of the greed of the Pope, the King of France and his complicit noblemen who coveted their lands. The women wore colorful head scarves and looked like many of the Moorish women, but with pale complexions, long aquiline noses and intense dark eyes. These women could hold a man's gaze with their intelligent and piercing demeanor. Some men it frightened. But their customers could feel their nurturing and wise advice as a comfort and drew near their site at the fair to discuss family illnesses. Customers would advance, quietly disclose the ailment of some family member and leave with a wrapped herb with symbols for its use hastily scribbled on the outside. Some were to be boiled, some sniffed. The former had a bubbling pot, the latter a large nose.

Other symbols for other topical uses were inscribed on the outside as well. The Burgomil healers were busy, shuttling back and forth to the large chest and saddle bags behind them as they fulfilled the orders. It was a busy day in late spring and business was brisk.

A large woman customer motioned Arsinoe to the back of the stall. "Oh, madam, can I speak to you of my problems?"

"Of course, what can I do?"

"I have times when I am very warm and sweat, even on cold nights. My monthly flow is painful and my stomach hurts. Can you give me something?"

"Of course. What you have is not uncommon. I will mix a batch of herbs which you must make into a tea, three times a day." She shook a few sprinkles of ground herbs into a small piece of paper including alfalfa, wild yaur root, fennel and a special herb from Africa, hong quai. "I will be back in a month. Let me know if this has helped."

Another customer came up. She had been a beauty once with full lips and round high cheeks and wide eyes with heavy lashes. "Alas, madam, I am getting older. My skin is wrinkling and yet my love for my husband is stronger than ever."

"Ah, I see. I will prepare a lotion of aloe, apricot and eucalyptus. Put this on in the morning and at night and your skin will look younger. I will also give you something to make your husband pay you more attention. Sprinkle this saw palmetto on his food. I can't say he will be a raging bull again, but he will not stay in the pasture and eat grass!" The two women tittered knowingly.

Two large men pulled their master on a rolling wagon. The master had removed his right shoe and exposed a large red big toe. As the servant started to address her, Arsinoe said, "Stop, I know the problem. I will make a large drink. This may make your master vomit, but the pain will subside and he will be able to walk again. Tell him to drink fruit juice instead of wine." Arsinoe prepared a mixture of cherry juice and stinging nettle. "Tell him to make a strong tea of this three times a day. I will be back next month. Come and tell me what happened. And remember, no red wine until then."

Soon a crowd two and three deep were clustered before the small booth as the two healers ran back and forth to their herbs dispensing what were hoped would be cures. A commotion began to stir at the far end of the town square. Some had dismounted from their horses and were now walking down the center aisle of the market. As they began to emerge, it became clear that it was Sir Osric and several attendants. Yes. It was Sir Osric, a teenage boy. He wore a doublet of bright scarlet and hunter green with his family crest embroidered on the left about the heart. It consisted of a falcon's head and a castle. The attendants were large rough men dressed in heavy leather jerkins and at their side they wore broadswords. Sir Osric had a smaller, thinner epee hanging from his hip. Only the lords or their attendants were permitted to carry weapons openly. Many outlaws carried concealed daggers. As they walked through the market, the crowd parted and much murmuring was heard as Osric examined idly the goods at each stall. The town was not under Osric's control, but belonged to Duke Felipe, an ally of Osric's father, Alonzo.

Nevertheless, the presence of nobility was remarkable to the townspeople and the merchants. Some approached Osric, making pleas of different sorts, often begging some indulgence or money. They were swiftly brushed aside by Osric's attendants. Osric surveyed the proffered wares at his leisure, undisturbed by the riff-raff around him. He did step carefully in his high red soft leather boots among the puddles of unidentified moisture and animal blood. As he approached the booths at the edge of the square, he came to an abrupt halt some 30 feet from the area where Arsinoe and Zastra worked. He was taken with Zastra as she flitted from customer to the herb chest and back. She was dressed in a simple brown tunic belted at the waist. Osric's bodyguards looked at him and at each other. What was this? Did he need some potion?

In Osric's head, he was debating furiously an approach to this strange girl. Woman? She was petite, but had a worldly air about her. Unlike the blond, full-bodied women of his court, she was slim and had a serious look on her face as she dealt with the customers. Her dark eyes and jet black hair were set off by her pale skin. And her eyes and lips and nose were all delicate. She was an exotic creature. But he could hear her speaking the local dialects – a kind of Spanish mixed with Goth and Latin, and then over to the Arabic and on to Frankish. One after the other. Osric only spoke the local Spanish/Goth mix, but could hear the other accents and inflections. How to approach this woman? No, this girl! No, this low-born street huckster! No, this exotic bird! Should he assume a lordly bearing and speak to her as a feudal subject. No, try the new courtly love poetry he had heard sung at court. No, he would seem a besotted fool. Ah, bravado! That's what I can do. The bravado of a knight talking to a bar wench. Yes, that must work.

"So, my little sparrow, what shall I take for heart ailments?"

"Ah, sir. What does your heart feel like?" She had noticed his use of the familiar second person form in which one addressed children and servants. But he was a lord and this was a sale.

"I notice when I am near you it beats strongly and I begin to shake."

Oh no, a crude attempt. Does he take me for some stable girl. "I see, perhaps you need a dose of purgative. You need a dose of manners."

Osric's two attendants looked at each other at first with a bit of fear, and then a bit of merriment as Osric shook off the retort with a smile. They chuckled softly at the young master's discomfort. With a glance from him, they looked blank again.

"A dose of manners. I see. What do you have for a lord and a knight?"

"Fortunately, the cure for this disease is the same for everyone. One would need some hot pepper to burn out the pride and let the humility grow. Perhaps then you will feel more human."

Osric shot a glance at his attendants before they could react with more amusement. This girl was not to be trifled with. He advanced more closely to the booth, out of earshot from his companions. "Tell me, where are you from? You are neither Arabic nor Goth."

"I am from the Frankish lands, across the mountains."

"Do you always have a sharp tongue?"

"When I am not treated with respect."

"Oh, I see. I meant no harm. I like your spirit."

"Thank you, my lord." She said stiffly, as if he were not worthy to judge. "When do you come back here again?"

"We are here often on market day."

"When do you leave here?"

"Sir, we travel in a caravan with the other merchants."

"Do you need any help or protection?"

"Thank you, no. We fend for ourselves quite well."

"Perhaps we can meet again?"

"Sir, you are a noble. I am not. You must find a suitable mate among your father's choices."

"Ah. Quite so! Quite so!"

"Do you ever come to my father's domain? It is . . .?"

"I know where it is. You wear its crest. Yes, sometimes we come there, but your tariffs are high."

"Maybe I could get you exempt."

"That is up to my mother. She and my father consider such things, not I."

"Where could I reach you?"

"We travel, sir. We are in many places."

"But where is your home?" With that, Arsinoe, who had been listening at a careful distance caught Zastra's eye and made a short, negative twitch of her head. Zastra also knew well not to disclose such vulnerability.

"I'm sorry, sir. I do not reveal that."

"Oh, I understand."

"May I see you again?"

"We are at many weekly markets."

"Do you go to the church tomorrow?" Again a glance and a negative twitch from her mother.

"No, sir."

"Are you not confessed or in a state of grace?" "We are not of this parish."

"Which is your parish?"

"Please, sir, that is private." Although the mother was signaling, Zastra did not need to see her to be able to reply.

"You are Christian, are you not?" This question was more than intrusive, it was a threat. This market town was on the border of several domains. The roman priests had begun to seek out their version of true believers and take punitive measures against the rest. Either Osric did not understand the danger this question posed, or he was simply too naïve to see the risk it might create.

"Yes, I am a Christian." She had to answer. Not to do so would imply the contrary and that would lead to grave consequences. She could not reveal her true beliefs. She was now beginning to feel threatened. Did this young lord mean her harm for her rejection of his advances? Could this conversation now have lead to a situation which put her and her mother in great peril? What was his intent?

"At least, you are not a Moor then." At the time, Moors were travelers in Christian territory, but not welcome and could be robbed or attacked with little protection from the Christian feudal lords.

"No, sir. I am not a Moor. Now, with respect, I have several customers who await my attention. May I serve them?"

"Oh yes, yes." She turned and addressed some of the people at the edge of the booth, but she smiled inwardly. The young lord's attentions were very flattering and those around her booth had seen this exchange. As the crown thinned out in the afternoon, Zastra noticed her mother glaring at her. It was not a time to discuss things, but she could feel the heat from her mother the rest of the day. As the sun began to disappear over the hills to the west and the temperature began to drop, Zastra and Arsinoe started to pack up the herbs, powders and lotions in the trunk and saddle bags to the rear of the booth. As the last stragglers began to leave the town square, the man Arsinoe had hired arrived to put the trunk on the donkey cart and load the saddle bags on the horses. After paying him, Arsinoe deftly had the cash bags stuffed with coins under a floor board in the cart. The women led the horse and donkey to the caravan forming at the east end of town.

As the women stood off to the side, Zastra spoke first: "What mother? What? What was I to do?"

Arsinoe, who had been boiling since the young lord left the market said, "Zastra, we are not ordinary people and you cannot speak that way to lords." Then under her breath, "Zastra, we are Burgomils, we must hide our faith. The agents of the church are everywhere."

"But, I never said anything to betray us."

"But you acted like you had a right to address a man in that manner. Christian women do not do that. Only Burgomils give women equal status and let them speak. When we do this, we are defying St. Paul, who tells Christian women they must be quiet and are a source of sin."

"Yes, yes, mother. I understand that. I am almost ready for the consolamentum. When I am ready then, I will become one of the perfects."

Arsinoe and Zastra were Burgomils – a divergent Christian sect on the brink of extinction. Those who had not been massacred over 20 years ago had scattered, taking with them what they could. After living peacefully for several centuries and prospering in southern France, they fell afoul of Orthodox church doctrine which permitted only strict adherence to the

Nicean Creed – the strict belief in the Trinity with God the Father and Jesus being considered in mystic fashion to be one and the same, along with the Holy Ghost. Burgomils followed their own theology now considered heretical which considered the body and the material to be corrupt and the soulto be eternal. A distinction without a difference in everyday life, but of great importance to the Pope and the priests because the Burgomils also claimed that the Roman Catholic Church was corrupt and intervened improperly between man and God. Both concepts were indeed detrimental to the monolithic structure of the Catholic church. This bothered the papacy, who then sent the priests to convert the Burgomis to orthodoxy. When this move met with resistance, the Pope ordered certain priests to be the leading edge of the Inquisition, which was to "inquire" forcibly and violently among practitioners who were not strict Trinitarian Catholics. It certainly did not help the Burgomils that they had been prosperous, so much so that they attracted the greedy eyes of the French king who, with the equally acquisitory Pope wished to avail themselves of the Burgomils' land and treasure.

The Burgomils were not a warlike people. They believed the material world was corrupt and they sought to free their souls of material influence, so they could become "perfect." They looked to Mary Magdalene as a source of wisdom and, as a result, women were considered equal to men and often held the role of preacher in their community which recognized no hierarchy within their church, and sought a direct relationship between man and God.

So it was with great trepidation that Arsinoe, who had been careful her whole life to avoid being identified as a Burgomil, watched the contact between her still naïve daughter and the young Christian noble. One slip would bring the Inquisition down on them and maybe their entire small community. The caravan was following a path from the small market town to Jaen where they would be met by some of the Burgomil men who would shepherd them the rest of the way home. Meanwhile, they were safe in the caravan as it slowly wound down the trails southward back toward Moorish territory.

Suddenly, a thrashing was heard in the bushes behind them. The caravan guards wheeled on their horses and grabbed for their swords. "Halt, who goes there?"

"It is I, Lord Osric, son of Alfonso, a vassal of Castile." If true, this was a dangerous moment. The caravan was in Castilean lands, and not in the fiefdom of Alfonso. What were these men doing here in the twilight, coming up on a caravan? As the men trotted up, Osric held up his hands without a sword and gestured he meant peace.

"I would like to talk to one in your caravan, no more."

"Then sheath your swords and approach with your hands aloft." Osric and his retainers complied and nudged their horses forward. Osric stopped at the donkey cart where Arsinoe and Zastra sat. In front of the caravan, Zastra's pale complexion turned crimson. Arsinoe's eyes flashed anger, but looked only forward. Osric had now been schooled on the new poetry of courtly love and become besotted. Normally, his father would arrange a proper family alliance with a nearby lord's daughter of a similar station. The marriage might be pleasant or not, but since peace in the countryside depended on it, the couple would try to be agreeable. There was little sin in a young lord's dalliances with ladies of the court, or serving maids, or stable maids, or bar wenches, or . . . whatever. The wife would hopefully bear male children and she and the lord would marry off the daughters in a politically sage manner. For sons were very much needed.

What was the person doing? "Miss, may I speak to you?"

To say no would be dangerous. "What is it, my lord?" "I am Osric, son of Alfonso, a vassal of the Caliph, and I would ask you more questions."

"Please, sir. I am tired, I am on my way home and I have few answers."

"Are you married or betrothed?"

Little did he know that this was a question with a dangerous answer. Burgomils did not see reproduction as the primary function in life, they sought "perfection" meaning freedom from material or sensory pursuits. A love affair was out of the question. Disclosure of her community could mean disaster. "No, sir, but I am pursuing religious orders." A good answer. The safe denial was little different and, in a way, a true answer.

"Have you had religious training?"

"Yes, sir."

"Why are you not in an Order yet?"

"I must help my parents for a while."

"Would they consider a dowry?"

She did not need to look at her mother. "No, sir. It will not do."

"Well, you have not heard the last of me. I am persistent. What is your name?"

"I am called Zastra."

"Ah, an unusual name." With that he and his attendants pulled off and rode back up the trail. The entire caravan breathed a sigh of relief. Castilin lords could do what they wished.

Robbery, rape and murder could always be options. That would not happen today. The caravan rode on.

Of the many things that arouse, let us say, interest in the male of the species, rejection seems to be the strongest aphrodisiac. Not extraordinary beauty, not vulnerability, not the allure of sexual activity. The blow to the ego, especially in a social context created an outsized pull. Osric was no exception. The refusal of Zastra to countenance his interest sparked a demand in him in one who was not accustomed to being denied anything.

Yet Zastra could not do anything but fend off his approaches. As a Burgomil, her very existence was always in danger, especially from the orthodox Catholic Church whose religious Orders relentlessly sought to purify the faith. But it was more than that. One of the strongest considerations for women is safety and security, let alone survival. Especially in this lawless society, women were especially vulnerable. Beauty might not always be a virtue, but might draw unwanted attention, and often violent attention which they could not resist, even with help from their menfolk. Love was out of the question too. Mere love could never ensure security in the years past their few years of beauty and allure. They needed a provider and a protector as they fulfilled their roles as mothers to the next generation. Roles which changed their bodies, softened their skin and increased their need for material comfort.

But with Zastra it was stronger. She had been taught, and her people had believed for centuries, that the material and the physical were trappings of the devil. As they rid themselves of the physical trappings and desires of the world, they could become "perfect." They thought of themselves as spirits trapped within their physical bodies. Through each reincarnation, they sought greater and greater purity until they achieved complete salvation in a ritual called the "consolamentum." They pursued lives of what they considered to be bold pursuits, healing, nurturing and providing comfort to their neighbor as they believed Jesus had preached. They looked to Mary Magdalene as their guiding spirit if not their actual founder – a question lost in the mists of time. But women were held in equal esteem as men, as they believed Jesus held Mary Magdalene. Women were often preachers. The Gospel of Mary (Magdalene) was an important text, although often destroyed by their orthodox Catholic tormentors.

And yet, Zastra, despite her mother, despite her Burgomil concerns, could not help her attraction to the boyish, crude knight. Burgomil men were gentle, soft spoken and often literate. Osric was brash, probably unlettered, spoiled and had an unwashed smell about him. It was a vast compliment that he even recognized something in her. She was slight and dressed in a common shapeless shift. What could he see in her? And why would he bother? He and his father might have the pick of the young ladies in all of Castile. He could never marry her. He could never provide for or protect her. And yet, some stirring had occurred. But as he rode off, she knew it was nothing but an exotic adventure. As she looked across to her mother in the donkey cart, her mother slumped in relief and shook the reins of the donkey to hasten the pace and increase the distance from this Castilian pest.

Yet, Zastra thought. It wasn't the smell – an admixture of horse, body odor, leather, unwashed hair and maybe stale ale. No. That was repulsive. He was different, just different, and masculine.

Neither mother nor daughter noticed another rider quietly join the caravan.

IN LEON

The rest of the way to Leon was dull for Hasdai and his company. Few people were sighted and what had become no-mans-land between the Arabs and the Christians was barren and unbroken. After the attack, the soldiers had taken turns doing sentry duty during the night in shifts of three hours. As the group approached the outskirts of Leon, a few settlements and farms began to appear. A few carts drawn by mules or oxen were on the roadway. As the city itself came into view in the distance a large contingent of riders appeared in the distance. I got out a white flag and mounted it on a pike and sat in the front seat of the cart.

When the riders approached, they were dressed in a military uniform with a tunic bearing the seal of Leon over their mail. They wore crude metal helmets and carried lances at their right side. A commander barked orders and the riders surrounded our group. Although I could speak the Leonese dialect, a mix of corrupt Latin and some Visigothic words, I directed one of the Christian knights to translate so I could maintain the illusion that I did not speak the language. The Christian explained that we were on a diplomatic mission from the caliph to speak to the king and that I was the chief envoy. He further explained that the two young men in the cart had brought goods from Cordoba to trade in Leon.

The commander dismounted and inspected the letter I handed him explaining their mission to Leon with the seal of the caliph. Although it was written in Latin and Arabic, the commander had no idea what he was looking at. He handed it to a soldier in his troop to read and the soldier, after perusing it, seemed to acknowledge what it was. The commander then walked to Eli and Samuel's cart and lifted the tarpaulin covering it. He asked what was inside and was told what goods they had brought to sell. He seemed intrigued when the steel daggers hand wrought in Cordoba were mentioned and asked Eli to show him one. Eli unwrapped one of the sacks and slid a box out, opening it and showing the commander an inlaid knife with a blade running his from thumb to the other end of his hand. It was inlaid with geometric designs and the hilt was wrapped in a silk twine. The commander thanked Eli, put the knife under his tunic and waved Hasdai through. We all started back up with the Leonese horsemen riding ahead and behind my cart and the Arab and Christian soldiers. We crossed the old Roman bridge over the river and were directed to the castle near the front gate. Except for the castle, the city, if you could call it that, consisted of one-story wooden shacks built haphazardly along the old Roman road. Closer to the castle and along the main road where the agora lay in evenly laid out parcels, the houses were much nicer and the streets clean and paved. The rest was squalor. Muddy, rutted streets with gutters filled with things too awful to look at. Once inside the castle walls, we were directed to a low building along the row of castle buildings built up against the wall. The Arabs unsaddled, unloaded and released the horses and the mules and led them off to a livery area where the animals could graze, be fed and watered. They had had a long journey and could use the rest. They let it be known to the stable people that the bandits' horses were for sale. They were to be given extra feed to fatten them up and be stroked down with coconut oil to allow their lesions to heal.

The rest of us were led into a large stone building. The floor was earthen and covered with a thick layer of straw. The cart was brought inside. We were told that this was our place to stay. My God! It was a stable. A faint smell of horse manure and urine still remained. In the corner was a trough which collected rain water from the roof. Now it was only half full. The water though was clean.

We spread out tarps on the straw and arranged our belongings. Strangely, the soldiers had not taken the soldiers' weapons. After the long journey, we stripped and splashed ourselves with water from the trough and filled our skins. It might be a stable, but it was going to be comfortable. The soldiers and the rest lay down on the straw while Eli and Samuel rushed off to the main road and the agora to seek out a stall for their goods. Ah, youth! They could not contain themselves and were driven by the desire to get their business started.

I, of course, took the wiser course and dozed off. My guess is the soldiers did too. At the tolling of the evening bells, a servant of the king came to tell us that dinner would be in half an hour. By this time, Eli and Samuel had returned with a story about their new site. They also had told people that the great Jewish doctor, Hasdai Shaprut would be there to heal people. They, of course, wanted to attract people to their new store and believed a celebrity appearance would help. I was not very happy about this. I wished that my mission would not attract too much attention and rile up the politics of a possible truce. Many Christians in Leon wanted to evict the Arabs from what they felt was their peninsula. They believed that the Arabs with their heretical religion needed purging or conversion, if not by persuasion, then by sword or death. The king would be ill advised to stir up these violent emotions. Nonetheless, I agreed to appear. I had done very well with my healing in Merida and had a fat wallet from it. We all washed again for dinner and followed the servant to a large wooden hall with heavy wooden tables and benches. We were not able to see the king or any of his entourage and believed we were being fed with the working men. First, the stables and now the common eating hall. My mission was not being given its prestige. It looked like the king was trying to gain the upper hand in negotiations by belittling the caliph's representatives.

The food was brought out by serving girls. I say girls. These were sturdy middle–aged women with prodigious bosoms and sturdy bottoms. They carried large wooden bowls with large ladles which they used to slosh the contents into the diners' bowls. Only a wooden spoon sat by each bowl. I was sure that this food would never come close to being kosher, but inspected it closely. One of the sturdy women had a bowl of tripe mixed with pigs feet. I shuddered. One had a bowl with parts of hare mixed with rice. Not too bad. The mutton stew looked passable. Of course, none was kosher, but necessity could be invoked in these circumstances. The drink poured from large pitchers was a fermented honey mead diluted slightly with water. Even though only mildly alcoholic, the men drank huge quantities and began to get a bit rowdy. The fellows we shared a table with were a pleasant bunch. After a few quaffs of mead, we could ply them for a little gossip.

To their surprise, Sancho I, whom I was supposed to meet had fled. Sancho I had been replaced on the throne by Ordono the Wicked over a year ago and he was fanning the flames of anti-Arab sentiment. He was training and raising troops as of a few months ago, and he had raised taxes.

The Christians in the north had enjoyed a resurgence against the Moors under Ramiro II who 50 years before had retaken much of the land from the Moors and turned Estremadura and the Douro Valley into a no-mans-land, bereft of people, farms and vassals and, unfortunately for both the Moors and the Christians, no tax revenues. However, the extremely brutal tactics of Ramiro II earned him the Moorish title "the devil." He left behind him a vast wasteland.

Sancho I succeeded Ramiro II and tried to repopulate Estremadura and bring peace to the region. It was he who sent out feelers of peace to the caliph and encouraged the journey for Hasdai. But Sancho I had left under fear of assassination and had been succeeded by Ordono who tried to be as wicked as his name sake. It now turned out that this was whom I must meet on the morrow: thus, the stable quarters and the working man's menu. I faced little chance for success.

Meanwhile, Eli and Samuel, owing no duty of ambassadorial work, had sought out quarters in the Jewish community while they were prospecting the agora. There were ten Jewish families who lived near each other on the edge of town. So far, they were not in any danger, but paid hefty taxes and were not permitted to carry weapons or serve in the army. Many were merchants at the agora, but some kept small farms in the north. They welcomed Eli and Samuel and invited them to the synagogue – a small row house in their community for the Sabbath. Of course, more than a few local matrons checked them out for their daughters. They wanted to know who their parents were, what they did for a living and what would they be doing in Leon. Somewhat satisfied by the barrage of questions and the boys' answers, the younger women began to inspect them as well. The town matchmakers promised to meet the boys during the market day and do the due diligence necessary to verify the marriageability of the boys. Samuel and Eli returned later to the stable exhausted. Theirs had been the first foray.

Now the kingdom was in a state of paralysis, frozen in fear as to what revenge the new king might take on the old king's supporters. Were purges coming? Who would lose their homes to Ordono's loyal knights? So the men spoke in whispers but their tongues were loosened by mead. As I picked at the meal to piece out the morsels which might be kosher, I tried to formulate how to open my talks to Ordono in hopes of persuading him to abandon the new war- like course he was on.

And why did men choose to go to war? Spoils certainly. Rape yes. Adventure away from the humdrum existence of feudal living, scraping a living out of the soil. But what did they say to each other? Foster Christianity – the faith. Rid the country of these foul heretics, worshippers of a false religion. What was the religion? Who knew? But what of Jesus, preacher of love, turn the other cheek, gain the kingdom of heaven? No! Forget that! Make al-Andalus go away, bring back Hispania. But what was Christianity? Only recently had they been persuaded to abandon Arianism, a form of Christianity which doubted the concept of the trinity. But the locals were confused. They were further confused by the pilgrims. Every day pilgrims passed to the west through Leon on their way to Compostela de Santiago as penance for their sins.

As the pilgrims passed through Leon and stayed at the inns along the way, they preached the many variations of Christianity – Jesus was divine, not divine, the son of God, and the same entity as God, or not the same entity as God but subordinate. The locals could not fathom the niceties of these legalistic arguments but knew one thing – they had to kill Moors and take their land. Of course, raping and robbing along the way was a side benefit to their Christian mission.

But what was this shrine of Campostela de Santiago? Long ago, pagans followed a trade route along the north of Spain to see the interminable sea, throw their old clothes in it and wash away their old sinful ways in its waters. The place they sought was Fistere, a shortened version of Finisterre, the end of the earth. A local bishop saw this frequent traffic. He seized on a story that a local shepherd saw a shining in the woods and believed it was the spirit of St. James. This arose from an old local myth that St. James, the disciple, was buried where he saw the light. James was killed in 44 C.E., but was buried in northwest Iberia because it was said he preached there. Thus, the word Campostela means "field of star," the star seen by the hermit in 813 C.E. Santiago is a corruption of the name of St. James – the Great. So the town of Leon's primary industry became housing and feeding the pilgrims seeking either the "end of the world" or to have their sins expiated by the star of St. James burial location. Thus, a religious ferver was perpetually passing through Leon. Such was the environment I faced for my meeting with Ordono who had not asked for or agreed to this meeting. And on that note, I lay on the straw in the stable and steeled myself for my mission tomorrow as I drifted off to sleep.

RACHEL TO JAEN

After Hasdai had left, his wife Rachel, began to miss him and became listless, depressed and quite worried about his journey into dangerous territory. It was not lost on her that his guardians, two Christians and two Arabs, might not be loyal to him, the politics of Al-Andalus being what they were. Would they be loyal to the caliph, some usurper, or the Christians of the north. Her daily duties as a dispenser of medicinal herbs gave her some comfort as she chatted with the customers. But her silence and moping at dinner was obvious to her daughter, Yael, who was restless. It was she who suggested a trip of their own to purchase and gather herbs and tonics. After some resistance, Rachel conceded. A trip would be a pleasant departure. They could leave David, her son, with his best friend's family and take the next caravan out to the east. Yes, that might do it. David certainly had no objection.

As it happened, the next caravan out was going to Jaen and Andujar to the east. Rachel and Yael began collecting vials and bunches of their local herbs, and prepared a list of items to seek out. They also began to purchase kosher dried meats for the journey. Few women traveled alone or even in caravans, but the Jewish women were an exception. As the caravan began to assemble east of Cordoba, Rachel paid her fee to the leader who had assembled a polyglot of armed and dangerous men to protect the travelers en route.

It was early in the morning just after dawn when the leader bellowed out his orders and his men echoed them down the line. Most of the men were Arabs and wore head scarves and wrapped their faces in cloth. There were a few large Christians dressed in leather tunics, carrying massive pikes and maces. They ogled the women and made many suggestive offers, but did little to disrupt the journey. Rachel and Yael had covered their heads and faces in the Arab fashion. Few would bother them. It was well known that Moors sought savage revenge on any affront to their women. Better to be an Arab woman in this caravan. As the leader and the first carts began to pull away, a long line began to follow to the rear with the guards riding on horseback up and down the line. Rachel and Yael unwrapped their breakfast, a jug of milk and some fruit and fell into the pace. The caravan stopped every few hours so the Arabs could pray. Only the men got down on their prayer rugs and bowed to the ground chanting their prayers. On the short break about midday, a group of women from the local farms were squatting by the roadside to purvey produce and cheese. The caravan days were well known along the route and the women used the occasion to gather some coins for the family savings. As they walked up and down the line, they mumbled or intoned their merchandise and stopped when hands arose to buy their goods.

The journey recommenced and ambled along the slowly increasing foothills through what was becoming heavier forestation. Rachel and Yael huddled together and clucked to the mule pulling the cart. Sometimes they hummed songs. While they recognized some merchants from Cordoba, they made little eye contact with anyone, especially the large Christian soldiers who frequently hooted and made obscene suggestions as they rode past.

Eventually, the long train began the steep ascent to the City of Jaen. From below, they could see the Moorish Castle which surveyed the entire countryside around. As the caravan came inside the city wall, various members of the train pulled off among the narrow streets. Rachel headed for the small synagogue and asked the shamus where the best lodging might be. Of course, it was a market day so many of the homes with extra rooms to let were taken, but they were directed to an ancient widow's house on one of the narrow streets. As the cart pulled up to the widow's door, she came out and was delighted to see two females who wanted to take her spare room. Although Rachel and Yael were tired, the woman, Miriam, insisted on knowing the welfare of everyone she knew in Cordoba – some unfortunately long dead. She prepared a delicious meal of chicken in apricots. Rachel had taken down their bundles and put them in their bedroom, while Yael pulled the mule and the cart along to the local corral. They greeted the darkness of night which alone appeared to have their host draw to a close her many stories of the people she knew from Cordoba.

It had been a long day and they would have to be up early to claim a good stall at the market. They hired a porter with a hand cart to take their goods to the market and find a nice stall. After spreading out their wares, they each sat on a stool and waited for the customers. It did not take long. People with a variety of ailments came up. Some knew what they wanted, some did not. Rachel and Yael examined each carefully and prepared a remedy – a tea to be brewed, some leaves to be sprinkled into a stew or a soup, ointments for the eye or the skin and poultices. Parsley for bad breath, garlic and echinacea for boils, aloe for burns, goldenseal for cankers, eucalyptus for a cough, bilberry for diarrhea, fennel and dill for gas, red clover for menopause, yohimbe for impotence, ginger for indigestion, valerian for insomnia, white willow bark for pain, capsicum for shingles and many others. Many of the people seemed to be enjoying hanging around and discussing their maladies at great length.

As it would happen, two other women with Frankish accents had the stall next to Rachel. As the day wore on and the crowds began to dwindle, it became apparent that the two pairs were in the same business – purveying medicinal herbs. It was the two younger women, actually almost women, who began to chat. Yael learned the girl was Zastra, her mother Arsinoe. They had come into Al-Andalus, which they called Iberia, from France, over the Pyrenees. Arsinoe's husband had died and the women lived with others from the same area in France. There was some secret about this and Arsinoe was casting fierce glances at Zastra as she prattled on. As the women eventually began to pack up, they hired the same porter to take their things. But on Rachel's invitation, they agreed to stop at an open counter for some herbal tea and a bit of pastry.

As they sat, a group of soldiers swaggered down the street. The leader, a young nobleman by his dress, stopped at Zastra's side.

"I am blessed. You again." Only last month, this young noble had made crude attempts to talk to Zastra.

"Yes, sir." Oh no, she should not have conceded she remembered. "Please, miss. I meant no harm."

"As I recall you needed something for a heartache. Did you take the purgative I suggested?" She was referring to her prescription for him to learn some manners and purge his crude behavior.

"Oh yes. And you were quite right." The nobleman's two retainers glanced knowingly at each other and smothered a chortle at their charge's discomfort. "Let me do this properly. I am Osric, son of Alonso, a vassal of the caliph, but a Christian. As I recall, I asked you before if you are Christian." "And I told you to mind your business. And I do this once again." She could only say this in Moorish country. In the north, she might be arrested and interrogated.

Osric turned to Rachel and Yael. "Do you know these ladies?" he asked of Zastra. Zastra replied, "Yes, we both purvey medicines."

"Ah so." He said turning to Rachel. "Are you Christians? What is your parish?"

Rachel had to reply quickly. They were in Moorish territory. "No sir. We are Moors." To speak openly to a Christian lord might be trouble. At least here they were safe and they had their headscarves with them always.

"I detect a Frankish accent."

"Quite so. My people are from beyond the Pyrenees." Arsinoe shot her a withering glance.

"May I call on your daughter?" said Osric turning to Arsinoe.

"I think not, My Lord. You are a noble and she is not. Your family will find you a suitable match. Not such as we."

"Quite so. But I enjoy your daughter's wit. You may call on me. I am at your service."

"Thank you, sir." And Osric and his men sauntered along the roadway.

Well after they passed, Arsinoe turned to Rachel and said, "That was extremely dangerous. Those men live at the north of the Caliphate. Who knows which side they are on."

"But surely, as good Christian women, you are safe even so."

"Good madam, I heard you and your daughter speaking the Jewish tongue. I know these things. I know you are Jewish and would not betray you. We too are in difficult straits and must conceal our natures. We are Burgomils. The King of France and the Pope conspired to steal our lands and chase us from the face of the earth. They felt the path we practiced was not to their liking, but more importantly they coveted our lands. So they began a crusade to steal our lands and hunt us down. Many of us escaped into Spain. Where else could we go? Only the Moors let us live in peace and now the Christians threaten them. It is not an easy life."

Arsinoe had spoken in hushed tones as Rachel and Yael listened intently. "Call me Arsinoe."

"Arsinoe, you can always come to Cordoba. My husband is a physician there and is an ambassador for the caliph as we speak."

"Oh, madam. We would be most grateful."

"Call me Rachel."

"Ah, Rachel of the book"

"Yes, so I am named."

The conversation turned to the many difficulties in the politics and wars of the times. It was terrifying certainly for women who had little control over the events around them. The wheel of fortune could turn you to the top or cast you to the bottom without warning. The delicate balance on the Andalus peninsula could change overnight. The Moors had held sway for over 200 years, but even now the Christians in the north were gaining ground every year. Unlike the Moors, the Christians would doom both of the womens' communities to total disaster. The church, and especially the monks, would see to that. The mutual feeling of perpetual fear made a strong bond between the women.

Arsinoe invited Rachel and Yael to dinner among the Burgomils in the area. Rachel explained the kosher laws, but Arsinoe already had heard of them.

"Look, come eat what you can. It is probably a chicken."

"Well, there is a rule that says when you are away from home, and necessity requires it, do the best you can." So the women left the center of town to the small Cathar neighborhood. Zastra took Yael under wing and guided her successfully past all the eligible young men who needed no explanation about why she was here and who she was. After the dinner, which was the ubiquitous roast chicken, although maybe not ritually slaughtered, Rachel and Yael went home in the cart of one of the men and went to bed early so they could join the caravan by dawn. They counted it a great success. They had many coins and had been able to acquire a few of the rare herbs from the area.

When they got to the widow's house, she bustled around and clucked that she had been worried about them. They assured her that she had been an excellent host and they would come back soon for the market day.

BEFORE KING ORDONO THE WICKED

Arising early, I couldn't go back to sleep and went out to get some breakfast for everyone. I was lucky to get some milk, fruit, and a few eggs. When I got back, everyone was starting to #stir. Eli and Samuel had spent the night in the Jewish quarter and had rented a room for a week. My soldiers and I sat down to a decent breakfast while I prepared them for our meeting with the king. They did not need to be told how to stand at attention or be respectful, but I wanted them to understand they were in enemy territory and not to respond to jeers or insults, but to maintain discipline. They dressed in their best uniforms, rubbed their teeth and actually ran a comb through their hair, bringing straw, dirt and some unidentifiable items to the surface. When the king's servant knocked to let us know the king would be ready to receive us, we were ready. We did not march, but walked in an orderly fashion. I was surrounded by my guards the short distance to the castle. Quite a few people lined the street as we entered the main room of the castle which was already filled with a number of nobles and their ladies. My guards were asked to surrender their weapons at the door and did so. We then strode to the center of the hall where we were told to stop and wait. Murmurs ran through the hall as the assemblage inspected us.

The king took his time coming up to his elevated throne as did his entourage of knights in full battle attire. When he was seated, he nodded to a man standing and facing him. He turned and demanded in a loud voice:

"Be it known, that this is the court of Ordono, King of Leon, on this 104th day in the year of our lord 963. All those having matters to bring before the king, come forward." Then motioning to us, he said:

"Who are you sir and what is your business with the king?"

I stepped forward. "I am Doctor Hasdai ibn Shaprut, a citizen of Cordoba, and an envoy of the Caliph of Cordoba, his excellency, ar-Rahman III. I have come on a mission of peace to confer with his majesty, King Ordono, on matters between the two of our realms."

The King irritably interjected, "Why are you here? I never sent for you or permitted you to come?" He was putting on a show for the nobles. He did not wish to appear weak in public by suggesting he had sought negotiation, a position of weakness.

"It was my understanding that messengers between his excellency Sancho I and our caliph wished to discuss matters."

"Why has the caliph sent me a Jew, two Arabs and two renegade Christians? Does he insult us?"

"No, your majesty. I am a doctor of medicine and of letters and the caliph felt I could best deal with the fine points of a future truce and negotiate a lasting peace which might be of benefit to all. These men were my guards on the trip north. They are representative citizens of our realm where Christians, Jews and Moors live together in peace." A murmur arose through the court. I had implied that this Christian kingdom was intolerant as well as not peaceful or prosperous. It was true, these things that I now made clear. I was obliquely appealing to the nobles and townspeople who may have favored Sancho I or peace and negotiations. Would I succeed? For the king to reject me out of hand before hearing my offer would not only be rude, but stupid. Maybe I was offering a good deal.

"What could you offer that would interest me?" At least I had his attention.

"Well, your majesty, I had been thinking how to open our discussions until I came to the town of Salamanca. There I saw devastation and the results of war. The menfolk were mostly dead and bodies lay strewn about, rotting in place. The dead, Moor and Christian, were joined in a common fate. Their women and children now wandered about, dirty, starving and scared as we came through. The buildings in the town were destroyed, some leveled, some burned, while mangy dogs and feral cats crept through the rubble. This town now pays no taxes to anyone. It will be a generation before people will populate the area and make it productive again. Surely, a negotiated peace is better than a war which harms both sides."

"Enough of that." This king was not subtle or capable of public debate. He was used to trampling those weaker than he with brutal force.

"Do you have the caliph's authority?"

"Of course, your excellency." I produced the letter written in Arabic and Latin. One of his aides handed it up to him. He seemed to read it, though I suspected he could not read. He flung it back to the aide who returned it to me.

"What terms do you suggest?" I had none written down, but decided to try a ploy. I handed him the list of herbs my wife had asked me to bring back. I purported to fumble and look for it and then gave it to the aide.

He again seemed to read the list of herbs, all in their Latin names, and roared, "You expect me to agree to this?" He again flung it at the aide who returned it to me. No. He couldn't read.

"Perhaps we could sit and see if we can reach common ground?"

"Do we haggle as the Jewish tradesman in the market place?"

"Well, your excellency, that is how we reach bargains."

"Very well, back into my chambers. Leave your guard here!"

I followed the aide who directed me to a room just off the throne room. I sat alone. He sat with two knights on either side. He bellowed even though the room was small.

"I can wipe out your caliph and his Moors and march through to Gibraltar. Why should I listen?"

"War is a perilous adventure, always pursued at great risk. The Romans, great as they were, succumbed to the Visigoths." I knew this would appeal to him. He probably had lots of Visigoth blood in his veins.

"I have 8000 Christian knights, all battle trained and ready for war."

"They must cross Estremadura, a march of several weeks, over an area with no supplies and little water. I have just come from there."

He knew this to be true. He did not expect military strategy from a Jew. "What do you know of war? You are a Jew. Your people never bear arms."

"Quite so. Not by choice I might add. But we do listen and learn. I have been well taught."

"By whom, by Arabs?"

"They are an intelligent people and have conquered much by their military skill."

"Oh, they are a scared bunch of rabble. They are no match for my men."

"That remains to be seen. Besides weather, terrain, supplies and strategy, all play a part. Arabs are excellent horsemen and archers."

"Yes, but we are bigger and stronger in man-to-man combat. We have seen this in our past battles."

"Will they be so strong after two weeks without food in Estremadura?"

"Ach, you are talking nonsense. Go now! And come back with a decent offer, or go home and prepare for battle."

By now, the room we were in, all stone walls and small, had begun to smell. The body odor of the Christians who do not bathe had been augmented by the nervous sweat of our negotiations. The smell was now strong of body odor and garlic. Their breath was heavy and foul smelling. They had few teeth and did not take care of their mouth and teeth. I was happy to leave even though I had accomplished nothing with this ignorant blowhard. But I certainly could report on his character, which would affect his plans of battle. Straight ahead. With no nuance, no stratagem. He was a fool. Yes. I left and went to the agora to see how Eli and Samuel were doing.

HASDAI AT THE AGORA

I left the castle feeling a bit shaken. I could feel ripples of nerves tingle down my arms and in my stomach. I had a risky, high-level confrontation and was now outdoors. The warm spring sun shone down and there was a bit of gaiety in the air as the feeling of spring took hold. I went to Eli and Samuel's booth. They had somehow commandeered a nice table and a canopy tent and sat back as the people surveyed their goods as they walked by, occasionally stopping to ask prices. Some of the people from earlier in the day stopped by and were told, yes, Dr. Shaprut was here, over my protestations. I wanted to let this mornings meeting run through my brain so I could absorb the nuances and influences. I would allow the thoughts to mingle, coalesce, reform and recombine.

As the people showed up for various cures, I examined, prodded, questioned until I could diagnose and prescribe. Eli was most helpful fishing through my stock of remedies as I called for them and I applied these as and where needed. Indigestion, hives, scabs, fainting spells, gas, menstrual cramps, sore muscles, head lice, My patients came and went leaving a nice pile of coins as Eli fixed the prices – far higher than mine. But soon I begged off for lunch and a nap. I bought a few delicacies, a loaf of bread and a jug of sweet wine and headed back to the stable.

The welcoming cool stable and a bed of straw. My soldiers had also gone to the agora, but were still wandering around. The Arabs were not feeling comfortable in this crowd, so they stuck by the Christians who translated for them. They needed gifts for their wives and children and mothers. But I welcomed the calm and cool in the stable. I drifted off replaying the exchanges with Ordono, the proud and stupid. I awoke from dreams which again replayed grotesque versions of my exchange. Not much to tell the caliph except to prepare for war, which he was already doing. He knew the chances of my success would be slim if Ordono was king.

Ordono, some now referred to him as "the Wicked," would not listen to reason. I could not alter my arguments to persuade him to the contrary. His mind was bent on war, devastating, destructive, unproductive war. But did he have the support of Leon? Would they follow him into battle? And then it came. An idea. Who and where was Sancho I? He was the one who had written the caliph proposing negotiations. I had to ask about this man. I would have Eli and Samuel probe the Jewish community, my Christian guards and I would ask around subtly, sotto voce. Could I bring another element to these discussions? I ran back to the agora and outlined my plan to Eli and Samuel.

When the guards came back, I explained what I wanted from them and gave them a bit of drink money to help loosen the tongues of those at the taverns. I even hinted they should get pillow talk from the houses of ill repute which were numerous despite the pilgrim presence. I, of course, warned everyone how dangerous such talk might be. Ordono, the Wicked, would certainly brook no dissent.

Later that night, we had a quiet conference with all my travel companions at our stable. And I was surprised. The most common remark about Sancho was that he was fat. Too fat to be a soldier. He was raised as a pampered son of nobility. His father was Ramiro II, King of Leon and his mother was Urraca Sanchez of Pamplona. He was an educated and intelligent man in direct line to the throne. He shared the throne with a cousin for a few years until the cousin died and he became sole King of Leon. It was said he ate 14 meals a day and weighed 35 stone. A group of nobles deposed him after a few years and he fled with his court and many sympathizers. His whereabouts were unknown, but it was understood that he was alive. He had only left the throne a bare six months ago. It was generally agreed that Ordono's faction were crude and greedy men who showed little respect for the town's people or anyone not of their ilk. But they had terrified the residents into a grudging submission. Ordono was not well liked. A return of Sancho I offered some promise, but he too was untested and his attitude unknown.

Yes, I thought, yes, a possible option. Only recently fled into exile. A recalcitrant local population. A possible source of peace, but who knew? No one for sure. He was a fat, self- indulgent noble. But he was educated by the local monks. He knew Latin and Greek. Maybe some sense was residing in that regal skull. It was a chance that had to be pursued. How to make contact? Who were his people? A bit more investigation was needed. That night as I pondered who might lead me to Sancho I, I sent my people out to ask who might favor Sancho I enough to maintain contact with him. As I slept, I dreamed of my images – my meeting with Ordono, the day in the agora, were all conflated. I was already in a period of high agitation. It would be nice to return to my medical practice in Cordoba and have a dinner with my family. The dream faded into a scene with the family and I drifted back into deep sleep.

The next day, I guessed the offensive Ordono no longer wished to confer with me, so I wandered up to the agora to help the boys and buy some presents for the people back in Cordoba. I wandered about the market and found little of interest. Leon was just a provincial town and offered little at the market outside of produce, animal parts, but little if any ingenious invention that might serve as a gift. There were many religious items as well as some snake skins and a few fossilized rocks. I was sure Rachel and Leah would never forgive me for such gifts, but David would delight in things such as these. What ten year old boy wouldn't?

I got a bag of almonds, an assortment of berries and a cup of tea for lunch and wandered back to the stable. I took the back way down the narrow streets behind the castle, when suddenly everything went dark. A canvas bag of some sort had been pulled down over my head to my waist and I was being wrapped with ropes around my neck, shoulders and waist pinning my arms to my side. I was lifted by several hands to a horizontal position and thrown roughly onto a cart bed where my feet were being bound at the ankles. I heard a gruff voice say, "Don't cry out. It will be your life." I lay on my back trussed like a sheep bound for sheering and rolled and bounced as the cart made its way over some rough paving until I could feel the cart rolling on an earthen path. Someone was holding me in place as we jostled along.

It would be several hours as I lay like this. I puzzled who had done this and why. Maybe Ordono wanted to have me disappear. To what end? To embarrass my guards, to reject my negotiations, to send a defiant message to the caliph? At least, he hadn't lopped off my head and sent it in a basket to Cordoba to show how brutal he could be. Or maybe Sancho I's partisans.

Maybe I had struck a note with them. Did they wish to embarrass Ordono by snatching someone from under his very nose? Maybe to embarrass him by harming a diplomat who had come under a flag of truce. Maybe the caliph had sent men to snatch me out of a position of danger. No. The voice I heard spoke in the rough Leonese tongue. Whatever this was, I was now bouncing miles out of town on a cart bound for God knows where. After a few hours like this, the cart stopped and I was lifted out and put astraddle a horse. My legs were untied, but the canvas bag was still over my head. The ropes binding my arms to my body were loosened so I could hold the reins. This was much more comfortable and we moved at a faster pace. We went like this for the rest of the day with rest stops every few hours. I could see from the bottom of my hood that daylight was fading. I had now been gone over six hours. What were people thinking back in Leon?

I felt myself roughly pulled off my horse and forced into a seated position against a tree. The bag was pulled from over my head. In front of me a small fire had been set and a small animal was turning on a spit. A few large unkempt men were moving around the campfire. One of them came up and kneeled before me. In the Leonese tongue, he asked, "Are you Hasdai Shaprut?"

"Yes." Maybe I was being held for ransom. No sense denying. "Did you address Ordono yesterday?"

"Yes." The man got up and motioned to another man. He was not dressed in the rough leather clothes of his companions and appeared to be well groomed – neat beard, combed hair and a clean blue and white doublet and blue tights. He now asked: "Are you an envoy of the caliph?"

"Yes. My letter . . ."

"Yes, your letter is back in Leon. It was directed to Sancho I, not Ordono."

"Quite so."

"Do you seek a mission with Sancho I to secure peace in the lands between Cordoba and Leon?"

"Yes."

"An end of hostilities?"

"Yes." No sense dissembling. I had already said all this.

"Would you like to meet with Sancho I?" Ah, more was becoming clear. Sancho sensed an ally and I was his spokesman.

"I think that would be a good idea."

"Fine." He said, loosening the ropes and motioning for a man to bring me a plate. It was not a good time to quibble about being kosher. The plate had a roast squirrel and a handful of rice. I was poured a cup of wine. It was decent and had a fruity flavor, maybe seasoned with orange. I did not complain that a squirrel was not kosher. I was hungry. No time for ritual niceties. God would understand.

I ate in silence. I could hear one of the men mention I was a doctor, a Jewish doctor. His companion came up to me and asked me to look at a rash on his neck. I looked. I asked a few questions.

"Does your girlfriend kiss you on the neck?" He looked warily at his companions and mumbled.

"Of course."

"Do you wear her kerchief into battle?" Again the wary look. "Yes."

"The cure may be difficult. We must remove your head from your shoulders." He looked at me, disbelieving, speechless. Finally, his companions could detect a slight smirk on my face and began to guffaw, slapping their companion on his back. He began to give a slight, but hollow chuckle nervously.

"No, my good man. You have acne, yes even at your age. Refrain from drinking milk, wash your neck regularly and I might add all over more regularly. Find some calendula and rub it on the affected area and then rub on some marigold. Tell your girlfriend to stop kissing you on the neck and kiss you on the balls." A brief silence, then uproarious laughter from the companions and a weak smile from the patient. A little doctor's humor. Always worked on the peasants.

Now, the trip went a bit smoother. From time to time, the riders would trot up next to me and ask mumbling out of the side of their mouths a few hypothetical ailments someone might have. Boils, especially on the butt, redness on the penis, on the vagina, indigestion, insomnia, pulled muscles, coughing – quite a collection. I explained that it would be better if I examined them, but reeled off a litany of herbs. Some I wrote on a leaf they would hand me. Since they couldn't read, they tucked it away carefully to take to the apothecary at the town market. The ride was easy over low foothills and soft moist earth or sand in and out of overhanging trees.

After my unofficial clinical hours, I began to wonder what would be said about my disappearance. Undoubtedly, it would be blamed on Ordono. It looked to be the act of a coward to harm an envoy seeking peace, especially an unarmed one who was a guest in your own town. But had I been harmed, imprisoned or merely silenced? To silence me after my little speech would also seem cowardly to one who might be harmed by an opinion contrary to war.

But I also wondered about my companions, the caliph's soldiers. They would be ashamed that they had permitted harm to come to me. It was not their fault. I had chosen to walk alone. But back in Cordoba, when the tale was told they would face the wrath of the caliph. For their sake, I wished I could return home in one piece and relieve them of their guilt.

Now we were drawing up to an encampment of lightly colored tents surrounding a much larger tent. We drew up to the large tent and dismounted.

"Please, Doctor, come inside."

As I entered the tent, I could see in dim candlelight an extremely obese man sitting on a large upholstered chair in the middle of an immense kilim, an ornate woven rug from Turkey. Before him on a brass table were several dishes filled with a number of delicacies and pastries. I assumed that this was Sancho I, so I bowed deeply.

"Ah, Dr. Shaprut. How nice of you to stop by."

"Yes, your majesty, may I be of service?"

"Yes, you may. But first, wash up, have some dinner, rest after your long trip and we will meet in the morning for a long discussion."

"I am at your call, your excellency." No need to complain about the rude kidnapping, or embarrassment to my guards, or soon to come, the worry of my family. I bowed my way out and followed my captors, now apparently my friends, to a tent. A pleasant young woman told me she was to be my servant and would assist me in the bath. I was getting a much better reception here than in Leon. Sancho must need something he thought I could deliver. The tent I was to call my own was a nicely striped affair, in which I could stand upright, and there was a large sleeping couch, a small table with a basin and a water jug and a desk. All the comforts of home. The young woman began to pull my cloak from my shoulders.

"Sir, doctor, you may call me Chloe."

"Where are you from Chloe?"

"I come from across the big sea." I was sure she meant the Mediterranean. She looked Arabic, but had a strange accent and the mark of a slave on her arm. She brought me a fresh robe, bade me strip and said the bath was on the other side of the camp circle. I stripped and put on the robe, feeling modest for the first time in front of this young woman. I should say girl. She was about fifteen. She showed me the way to the bath tent and pulled the flap aside to reveal a large metal tub and several kettles sitting on a grate over a fire. She began to pour the water into the tub and test it with her finger. She motioned for me to get in. Apparently this was the custom, so I dropped my robe and strode naked over to the tub. Yes. The water was quite warm and soothing. But the girl was still there. She walked out, reached for an object that looked like a smooth stone and poured some oil-like substance on it. She then began to scrub me down. Thoroughly, quite thoroughly. Especially the nether regions. She smiled shyly at me as she looked at my erection as if she had accomplished a minor miracle. I was next dried thoroughly and directed back to my tent where I took a pleasant nap. Chloe now came into awaken me for dinner in Sancho's tent.

Dinner was a sumptuous affair for some. There was an entire roasted wild boar, heaps of vegetables and stewed fruits, mountains of greens and scantily attired women flitted back and forth bearing ewers of different wines. Sancho sent over a retainer to my table as I sat with a half dozen nobles. In perfect Arabic, the servant said, "Dr. Shaprut, we are well aware of your desires for kosher food. While we do not have the butchers in this encampment to perform the ritual slaughter, we have nonetheless drained all blood from the kid we will be serving you." I must say, the kid was very tasty, and surrounded by small potatoes and onions with a hint of garlic. I tried both the red and white wine and found them fresh and light. The entire room had a festive air. I was assured that Sancho's dinner tent was always like this and the food exquisite. Soon I was stuffed and groggy from the wine. Then a series of toasts were posed. The general theme was a desire to reimpose Sancho on the Leonese throne, always greeted with much table pounding and hoots.

I felt I had enough rapport with my immediate table companion now to ask about the general attitude toward the caliph and the Moors to the south. He was assured that I was not an Arab. He felt that as a Jew, I was basically neutral. So he launched into a long diatribe of his hatred for Ordono and the populist element who were notably the old Visigoths whom he considered degenerate barbarians. He admired the intelligent interchange of ideas in Cordoba which he felt were engendered by the caliph who encouraged such. Of course, he was a devout Christian who felt the entire peninsula should be reconquered for Christ, as he put it. He didn't begrudge the caliph and his Arabs a place in the realm, but insisted it must be a subordinate one. He could be tolerant and was grateful the Moors had permitted the Christians to retain their cathedral and their houses of worship and expected to do the same for them in a Christian Hispania. An interesting view. Would he accept a treaty specifying a no-mans-land in Estremadura and a cessation of all hostilities between Christians and Arab? After some thought, he felt he could live with such a truce. I must say I felt I could live with such a position. Was it similar to Sancho's? It probably was. He was an educated and worldly man. Why had he been deposed? To tell the truth, it was because he was so fat and overindulgent that elements of the nobles who controlled the military could not accept his leadership. He couldn't even ride a horse he was so obese. They were used to years of military training and took pride in their physical condition, although there was rampant abuse of alcohol. My companion, Sir Eldred, had been most helpful in educating me in the Sancho I would meet tomorrow. For now, I needed a clearer head and waved off more wine, much to think about.

As I walked to the edge of the dining tent, I discovered Chloe sitting among a group of other girls who apparently had eaten together.

"Sir Doctor, may I direct you back to your quarters?" I was a bit disoriented and could use a little help. She took my arm and lead me to the tent and patted at the bedding. As I took off my shoes, she asked if I required anything further. She had a sly smirk as she said this and her meaning was clear. I know I will regret this for many years, but I explained that I did not believe in slavery and could not in good conscience avail myself of her services. I did compliment her beauty. She seemed disappointed and went over to a bed roll in the corner and undressed slowly. I resisted temptation and rolled into bed and a deep sleep. It had been a curious day.

KING SANCHO I

I stirred early as I heard Chloe preparing tea at a beaker near the desk, where she had already arranged some milk, fruit and a few pastries. It was my meeting with Sancho this morning. I arose and washed my face in the basin near me, stretched and groomed. I could feel some fuzziness in my head from last night's wine, especially the sweet wine. I knew I needed some fluid in my body, but also knew it would reactivate the wine and make me tipsy again. I decided to dilute the wine as much as possible and gulped the milk and tea. I turned to Chloe.

"Where are you from Chloe?"

"I am not sure. People tell me they found me wandering the battlefield after a skirmish when I was five. They took me in and fed me."

"Do you know where your parents are?"

"I don't remember them now, only a few bits and pieces. I have served Sancho since then."

"Are you happy here?"

"Oh, yes. I have much to do and they tell me I am a bright girl. That is why they picked me for you. All the girls are jealous. I was given fine new clothes and told to make you happy."

"So you don't mind taking care of me?"

"No, Sir Doctor, it is an honor."

"But, the sex business. Does it upset you?"

"Oh, no. I am proud to give pleasure."

"Did you learn it?"

"Oh yes. We were taught by one of the King's senior wives and practiced on a few lucky soldiers."

"So, you don't mind?"

"Oh no, it is something I am good at."

"Interesting. What will become of you in the future."

"The king will arrange a marriage with one of his soldiers. Already there are many that ask the king about me. I am almost of age. I will have my own dowry and have some say in whom I want."

"So you are almost like a daughter."

"Yes."

"Interesting."

"In the meantime, I have nice clothes, nice food, and a warm place to sleep. I also help in the kitchen sometimes when I am not busy."

"Are you an Arab?"

"I don't know. I remember some words of Arabic, but I am a Christian from Leon now."

"Well, thank you Chloe."

"You will meet with Sancho soon. Do you know what he wants?"

"I will soon find out." I finished my breakfast, had a second cup of tea as the cobwebs were leaving my head. To increase circulation, I did some bouncing and stretching and took a nibble at some willow bark. As the sun rose, I went out and took a brief walk around the camp until one of the soldiers came and asked me to follow him to the king's quarters. It was a large tent, not where the King slept, but where he met with people. It was far less formal than the throne-type setting from the day before. Sancho turned from a large table and sat on a large couch covered with drapings of many colors. He was an extremely large, obese man and moved slowly and with some difficulty. From his face, he was not very old. I would guess late 20's or early 30's now that I saw him up close.

"Ah, good Doctor Shaprut, please sit. We have much to discuss." He waved all the servants and retainers out. I sat. Another tray of fruit and pastry, as well as a small beaker of tea was placed at my side.

"How may I be of service, King Sancho?"

"Alas, you have said it. King Sancho. I am no longer the king."

"I am guessing, with little doubt that you wish to return as king."

"You understand me well. But I must win the people back. The biggest complaint about me was that I was, I fear to say these words, too fat. The people saw me only as an overweight, self-indulgent man who might not be strong enough to lead. So Ordono, a hard and brutal military man, convinced some of the nobles to usurp my throne. Now, you are a renowned doctor, you must help me."

"I see. Your excellency, I have not seen my family for some time and I fear word has gotten back to them that I was kidnapped and I have disappeared."

"Yes. I apologize for that. I must keep your presence and my presence a secret for now. Can you understand that?"

"Most certainly. But my wife is a good woman and knows I am on a very sensitive mission. Can she be told?"

"Very well. I will see who could be trusted to communicate with her. I have no Jews in my entourage, but I will get a trusted man for that job."

"Alas, now as to your weight. I can do this, but I need your full cooperation. In short, the key is diet and exercise and time. This will not be easy. You must do as I say and tell others to listen to me as well."

"How long could this take?"

"Several months, maybe a year."

About this time, Toda, his grandmother came into the tent.

"It is difficult to rule when your subjects call you El Gordo or el Groso behind your back." Toda said. She also was born of the royal bloodline. "My grandson is a good man. He must get his kingdom back."

"But, your highness" (I presumed she had no right to enter the tent and dare talk so frankly if she was not some royal family member.) "Our countries are at war. Of course, I see that Ordono the Wicked will cause the Caliph great harm. But why" I said turning to Sancho I "Should I expect better from you?"

"I am certainly no worse. And a fight between Ordono and me for control of the Leonese throne cannot be bad for your country. But, sir, I am an educated man. I admire and envy the culture of the Moors. Toleration, fostering the sciences and the arts; I would like to see this in my kingdom.

I am well aware of your envoy to the Byzantine empire, and your treatises of plants and medicine."

"Sir, I am flattered, but I only translated the text you speak of."

"But you are surrounded in al-Andalus with Jewish scholars of many disciplines, all of whom answer to you and are even supported by you."

"The Caliph helps me in this to a great extent."

"Sir Doctor, you may be assured that I would encourage Jewish scholarship alongside our intellectuals."

"Do you really mean that? I mean that would be my fondest dream." I could not take this man at his word. Christian monarchs had almost never been kind to the Jews. In some ways, it was political. The church was a strong political influence and often had an iron grip on the Christian kings. A slight turn of the wheel could activate the Christian faithful and send the monarch and his family plummeting. I had good relations with the Turks, with Byzantines, and all along north Africa. But Christian Europe was never kind and often harsh to the Jews. Frequently, they were told to leave, to give up their businesses and be confined to very small parts of the towns, or often they were simply killed and pillaged. It did not take much encouragement to rile up a crowd of peasants, give them a religious motive and point them at the Jews. Sancho I was offering to be the first of his kind to offer support for the Jews. Could he be believed? As far as I was concerned, it was worth the risk. Could the Jews rely on a Spanish ruler to allow them freedom?

"Your Excellency, I respect your good intentions. I am prepared to have you start my regimen to lose weight even now. Will you hear me?"

"Most anxiously, good Doctor."

"Very well then. I will prepare a list of dishes for your meals. We must ban forever pastries, sweets, beer, heavy drink and I shall include pasta, rice and most starches."

"Oh, I am aching already."

"Your Majesty, it is the only way."

"I know. I know. I hear and obey."

"You will have chicken, fish, beef, game animals, pork and salads, some fruits and everything may be cooked in olive oil. You may use garlic. You may cook with white or red wine. I'm giving you a partial list. I will have a better one tomorrow. I will also give you a purgative to take regularly."

"A purgative. Is that what I think it is."

"Yes. You must cleanse the system."

After a few minutes of thought, I managed to bring to memory a number of herbal remedies. Of course, there was apple cider vinegar, a nearly universal product that seemed to be good for everything from indigestion and heart problems, but it also was a good weight loss remedy. Unfortunately it had a very strong taste by itself, so it had to be mixed with water and sometimes honey. It can also be used with oil and a salad dressing. Cabbage is a great vegetable for weight loss. But, my favorite was bottle gourd. I explained all these to Sancho and he immediately summoned his chef. The chef was not pleased, he delighted in making fancy sauces rich with butter and cream. He hated being denied starches and noodles. He was denied breads and pastries. He seemed to have been demoted to a scullery maid with all these mundane demands on his skills. But at bottle gourd, he drew the line. He knew of nowhere he could get this. He had never heard of it. Nonetheless, he slumped off resigned to his new menu. Sancho could only smile meekly at me and shrug his soldiers.

"Where can we get bottle gourd?"

"Your highness, the best I can suggest might be at the local market. Where might that be from here?"

Sancho summoned his head housekeeper. "Madam, can we send someone to the market at Jaen?"

"Of course, your highness. We go there every week."

"Can we get some bottle gourd there?"

"I will certainly ask around. What does it look like?" she said turning to me.

"Like its name, it is a gourd shaped like a bottle. It is long and thin like a cucumber, but does not curve. Some people call it a calabash."

"Very well, your highness, we will do our best?"

"Thank you madam."

"And now exercise. I want you to select one or more soldiers to aid you in a daily exercise course for six days of the week and on the seventh you may rest."

"What sort of exercise?"

"To start, I want you to walk as far as you can, accompanied by your soldiers, until you can no longer. Then, after I am satisfied for you to run at a slow pace, you will do this. Then, I will review your soldiers' military training and prescribe that you join in some of their events at least three times a week."

"When can I stop this?"

"Never, for your health, this must go on for a lifetime." He sat wagging his head. "Do you want your kingdom?"

"Yes, yes I do. But the pain."

"Nothing comes easily, it must be earned. Now I will accompany you from time to time, because I do many of these regularly myself."

"That will help."

"We will start this afternoon, after lunch. Eat something light – greens, maybe fish or chicken and water. Otherwise, you may vomit in front of everyone. That would not do."

"Can some of my court join me?"

"The more the better."

"What shall I have for dinner?"

"The same."

Toda had been listening. "Oh, good Doctor, God has sent you. Don't let him off easily. He was a very spoiled boy."

"Abuela, silence!"

"No, Sancho, it is true."

I left for a walk around the camp and said I would return after lunch.

AT JAEN MARKET

The King's housekeeper had reached the Jaen market by mid-morning accompanied by two young helpers to carry baskets to her carts. As she walked through the main street of the market, the permanent stands and stalls lined the streets. These were mostly butchers of beef, poultry, sheep and pork. Further along were the produce stands with tomatoes, lettuce, potatoes and fruits. It was easy to pick up the King's cabbage and apple cider vinegar as they were ordinary staples. Everywhere she went, the purveyors, most of them women from nearby farms shrugged when asked about the bottle gourd. As the day wore on, the housekeeper had filled her cart with the items, but the bottle gourd still eluded her. As she reached the periphery of the market, there were mostly irregular items, sold with the sellers sitting on tarpaulins spread on the ground with piles or stacks of items in front of them. Soon she came upon Zastra's collection of herbs and spices. Business had been slow this day and Zastra was chatting with Rachel who had come from Cordoba with her daughter Yael and taken the place next to Zastra who had now become a close friend.

The housekeeper asked if either of the ladies had ever heard of bottle gourd since their wares seemed to be the most exotic of collections she had seen that day. Both women brightened up at this request. They well knew its properties, but rarely fielded such a request. They looked at each other.

"Of course, madam, we are familiar with it."

"I have been instructed to get some. Could you tell me where I could find it?"

"Of course," said Zastra. "I am aware of an herb garden where this grows on vines. May I ask why you want it?"

"I have a master who has been prescribed a weight loss regimen by his doctor and this is on his list." Rachel stirred at this suggestion.

"A doctor prescribed this?"

"Yes, madam, for my master." Rachel recognized immediately her husband's predilection for this remedy. It was in a catalog of medicinal remedies he had helped translate from Greek. He was particularly fond of it because it was mentioned in the Bible as a plant the Lord grew for Joshua to shade him from the sun as he slept. It was known for its fast growing properties as well as the very beneficial, but only slightly known, effects on digestion and weight loss. It must be a coincidence, some doctor prescribing this in such a manner. She was intrigued.

"Madam, you say a doctor prescribed this for your master's weight loss?"

"Yes, madam."

"Who is this master?"

"I am not at liberty to say."

"Who is this doctor?"

"I am sorry, madam, I cannot disclose that either, with all due respect."

Zastra, at this point said, "My good woman, if you can come back this day next week, I will endeavor to supply you with the bottle gourd. How many would you like?"

"There are three or four men who will use it, so let us say a dozen."

"I could deliver it directly if you wish."

"No, thank you. I will see you next week on this day. I greatly appreciate your efforts." The housekeeper seemed quick to scurry away with her two helpers in tow. Such questions must have been an irritant. She had something to hide.

Zastra and Rachel looked at each other, questioningly. Yael said, "But mother, my father . . ."

"Hush, dear. We will talk about this later."

Fortunately, or unfortunately, young Lord Osric came swaggering into the side path where Zastra's and Rachel's areas were laid out.

"Ah, my pretty pigeon. It makes my heart sing to see you on market day."

Zastra averted her eyes. "Sir, your effrontery has no effect on me. Please do not bother me while I am working."

"But I am a customer. Do you have something to keep my heart from racing when I see you?" Yael could not help chuckling at this. Zastra fixed her with a glare and turning to Osric. "Please, sir, I am not some peasant girl who wishes to be trifled with."

"My little one. My father is a very powerful man now. Not only is he a vassal to the Caliph, but he houses a king."

"How can that be so?"

"Ah, that is a mystery. But both will be beholden to him."

"How so?" Such gossip was always of interest. Often it meant a cataclysmic change of fortunes when the affairs of kings and caliphs were in flux in this area so close to the border between Arab and Christian. What could this impudent little brat be talking about? Something he should probably keep to himself. After a few more gibes at Zastra, Osric and his companions swaggered off to show themselves and collect abeyances from the rest of the merchants who owed their safety to his father.

Rachel's mind was now spinning with possibilities. She well knew her husband was familiar with the properties of the bottle gourd, or calabash, as he called it. He had found it referred to in both the Bible and in Greek treatises and had included it in his translations into Arabic. Could he be the doctor prescribing it? It was not a remote coincidence. But then this posing pipsqueek noble bragging of his father – the Caliph's Christian vassal and a king. Who could the king be? Residing as the guest of the Caliph's vassal Lord Alonzo? There were quite a few kings throughout Hispania. Which king could it be? Much to think about.

As the market day ended, Zastra and Rachel began to pack up their wares and count their money. They embraced and said they would meet again next market day. Each promised to look for bottle gourds. And the sun was low in the sky.

MESSAGE TO CALIPH

That night, two riders left Sancho's camp which was situated just eight miles from Jaen in the fiefdom of Alonso, actually a vassal of the Caliph. The two riders, one a Christian loyal to Sancho, the other a Moor in Sancho's entourage. They had been waiting for the safe arrival of Hasdai. When he arrived in good condition, Sancho's chief aide dispatched the riders. One carried a letter of passage with the seal of Sancho, the other a letter with the seal of the Caliph. Nonetheless, they were heavily armed and rode swift horses. The journey to Cordoba at their speed would take six hours. They rode through the night along the old trail, with brief stops to water the horses, both magnificent Arabian thoroughbreds.

Just after dawn, the Moor presented his letter to the guard at the gate of the Caliph's palace complex and both riders were waved into the inner court. The Caliph's guard opened the door, took the reins of the horses and led the men to the Caliph's living room, just off the throne room.

The Caliph was at breakfast as the men strode up. "Your excellency."

"Yes, what have you?"

"It is done. The doctor is at work." Enough said. As the Caliph had planned, Hasdai had been kidnapped under the nose of Ordono and spirited to the camp of Sancho. The Caliph knew the good doctor could not resist the opportunity to cure someone, especially a member of the royalty. He also foresaw that it would be a colossal embarrassment to Ordono that the Caliph's envoy had disappeared from under his very nose. The two Moorish soldiers were directed to make a strong protest while the two Christians were to spread all sorts of rumors. Hasdai's guard had been carefully instructed by the Caliph's generals, but not Hasdai. His reaction must be genuine. And as the riders reported, it had been. Even now, Hasdai was committing Sancho to a course of exercise and diet to win back his people. So far, the Caliph's plan was working.

Later that morning, the Caliph sent a small package of gems to Rachel along with his chief aide. She was told that Hasdai was on a secret mission, that he was safe and would be delayed in his return. She was instructed not to discuss this with anyone or it could cause great harm to Hasdai. Rachel was an intelligent woman and well knew the intricacies of court politics. Silence was always the best course. Meanwhile, a guard was stationed near her out of sight to protect her at all costs. She could never become an Ordono hostage. The Caliph was moving his chess pieces carefully around the board.

That same day, I greeted the very sweaty Sancho as he finished his walk in the warm spring with a tall cool ewer of tea and the female attendants patted him down with cotton towels.

"Whew! That was interesting!"

"Your excellency, when you feel you can do it, you will trot for 200 paces, then walk 200, then trot 200, then walk 200."

"Can I do that?"

"No question. You will be a lean fighting man in no time. Lean as a tiger. You have taken the first step. Just imagine yourself seated in the cool throne room in Leon."

"And Ordono's head on a pike."

"If that helps."

"It does. Now, what's for dinner?"

While the king sat in the shade, I went to the kitchen. There I supervised the preparation of the salad and the cooking of chicken in olive oil and garlic. Fortunately, or unfortunately, what Sancho ate, the rest of his entourage ate.

At dinner, Hasdai explained all this to the senior military commanders eating with Sancho. They cheered at the progress their King was making and vowed to join him on his walks and trots as well. Sancho could not back down now.

Weeks of this were to follow. Fish, chicken, lean pork, egg plant came and went in the diet – all cooked in olive oil and garlic. There were many varieties of fruits and nuts. Plenty of pitchers of wine. Lots of vinegar.

Trout was plentiful, and organ meats – liver, kidneys, hare, frogs legs, and even an occasional lizard.

Sancho's clothes began to sag on him and had to be altered. His walks were becoming trots, and uphill. He was followed at a respectful distance by 20 of his upper echelon commanders all grinning as they pounded up the hilly paths. Soon, the afternoons would be filled with martial training in swords, pikes and javelins. The King's clothes sagged further and now he needed a new set. As the king sat over lunch after the morning's run, his grandmother came in.

"Who is this in the King's place?" she demanded ironically.

The King did not answer, but munched on a chicken leg hungrily, trying to ignore the attention. Indeed, he was just a shadow of his former self. His step was lighter. It was also whispered about that his mistress was happier and lighter in her step.

I had invented a chant to be grunted as the men ran. "The throne, the throne; the throne in Leon." The officers resurrected some of their more bawdy chants imitating the rhythm of the jog up and down the hills.

In the afternoons, the commanders created or resurrected exercises for the abdomen, the back, the shoulders and the arms. It was no longer a chore, but almost a communal dance of men, chanting out verses and numbers.

By summer, the sweat was pouring off the King and his men in rivulets, and they were constantly resupplied with cool water in small gulps. The women of the camp began to line up and cheer the men on as they plummeted down the slope to camp.

At last, I approached Sancho. "Your excellency, I have been with you for almost three months now. I am afraid my wife is worrying and thinks I may be dead. Can I take some time to go see her? I miss her."

"Hasdai, you have been an excellent doctor as I had been told to expect. I will deny you nothing. But you must see that our location, our work, my training, all must be kept in extreme secrecy."

"I very much appreciate that, your excellency."

"Very well then. You have proven your loyalty. I will send you back to Cordoba for some time along with two body guards. But you must remain in disguise the entire time and only let your family know where you are and what you are doing."

"Thank you for your generosity of spirit, your excellency. But may I ask where we are. I have never known."

The King laughed. "Good, very good. Our location is well concealed. In fact, we are in Moorish territory, about twenty miles from Jaen in the fiefdom of Alonso who protects us and keeps intruders from our site. "Jaen? But your excellency, you are practically under the nose of the Caliph. I thought we would be in the north, with Christian vassals you can trust."

"Alas, it is difficult for me to determine who I can trust, and who not. I must tell you that I trust the Caliph and his good will more than my own Christians at this humble time in my life."

"The Caliph? You mean he knows where you are?"

"Quite so. It is with his protection I remain alive and concealed."

"But then he must know where I am and what has happened to me."

"Quite so."

"He sanctioned my kidnapping in Leon?"

"Somewhat. He knew about it."

"Does my wife know?"

"She has been told you are alive and on a secret mission."

"Very interesting. I can see I must observe all efforts at secrecy."

"Quite so. Now you see how deep the plans run."

"Yes. Yes. I see."

"Very well, you may go now, but with the two body guards and in disguise."

"Thank you, your excellency."

HASDAI BACK HOME

Sancho I was quick to grant my wish to go back to Cordoba to visit my wife for a few days. Two strapping Christian soldiers were assigned to protect me along the route which was sometimes dangerous. The King also gave us three thoroughbred Arabian horses to sprint along the old Roman road around the foothills. Of course, I was quizzed on my ability to ride the magnificent Arabian I was given, but I assured them I was up to the task.

Sancho's advisers were a bit squeamish about letting Hasdai return to his home city. What if he should tell the Caliph where they were? Maybe he wouldn't return. Sancho already had enough troubles with Ordono. Did he need to take on the Caliph as well, and in his own territory? Sancho had brushed these questions aside with a knowing smile. He knew something they didn't.

Just before dawn, the horses were saddled and the men took off for Cordoba. The countryside, sometimes threatened by bandits, sometimes bearing nosey travelers, was quiet at this hour. With a few stops for water and to cool off the horses, the trip turned out to be lonely and uneventful. The two Christians pulled off as they neared the outer fringes of Cordoba. I put on my disguise to keep my identify unknown and my mission still a secret. Ironically, I wore a monk's habit with a hood as I rode quietly into the Juderia. As I knocked on the door of my house, Rachel came to the door and started to cry as I pulled back my monk's hood. I slipped inside the door and hugged her as she continued to weep wordlessly and shudder.

"Quiet, my love, quiet. I am only here for a short time and must keep my visit a secret." Between sobs, Rachel blurted, "We heard you were kidnapped and nowhere to be found. The bodyguards came back days ago and we didn't know what to think. Then Eli and Samuel came back and told us of your discussion with Ordono. It seems they had deposed Sancho. What happened?"

"Now you must keep all this a secret. It could mean my life or disaster for the Caliph."

"You may be sure of me, Hasdai. You know that."

"Of course, my love. Well, I was kidnapped by Sancho's people who are hiding in a camp somewhere. They seek peace and help from the Caliph against Ordono. In the meantime, it appears Sancho was deposed because he was too fat."

"Too fat." With tears still streaming on her cheeks, she began to chuckle. "He lost his kingdom because he was too fat!"

"So I am retained as his doctor to cure his obesity."

"Ah, the bottle gourd. I knew it. I could feel your presence. Some woman came to the market day at Jaen when I was there and asked for herbs to cure obesity. When I heard bottle gourd, I thought you must be the only one who could prescribe such an herb. It was you. I knew it."

"Yes. I translated that book of herbal remedies."

"So, how is Sancho doing?"

"Well enough. I have him walking or jogging longer and faster each day. And I have cut out most of his food. His clothes now hang on him. He does military training in secret with his soldiers almost every day. He is making progress, but he complains. I have to remind him of his lost kingdom and the evil Ordono. When he is ready, he wants me to talk to the Caliph about getting his kingdom back."

"Hasdai, you mean the Moorish Caliph would help a Christian king regain his throne?"

"Well, we have to see what the Caliph wants. I don't know yet."

"But you are helping the Christian king."

"I am after all a doctor and he definitely needed one. Besides, I was a captive in a place I didn't know. It was not hard work and he treated me very well."

"You actually look well. More fit."

"I accompany the King on his walks and jogs chanting advice and we are eating very healthy food."

"You even smell good. I thought those Christians were crude barbarians."

"I use the King's bath and his attendants. It is as if I were a rich noble."

"I can't say I am used to you with perfume."

"No, that's part of my bath routine."

"And you smell a bit like a horse."

"We rode about six hours to get here."

"Six hours. Where did you come from?"

"The east mostly."

"So you were near Jaen when you started. And I was in Jaen when the woman came asking about the bottle gourd. She was very secretive about who it was for."

"I too have guessed we are in the forests near Jaen."

"Should the Caliph come to rescue you and defeat Sancho?"

"My guess is no. I will talk to the Caliph and see what he wants. Meanwhile, I am hungry. What have you got?"

"I could warm up the lentil soup. I have nuts and fruit. And I just baked bread last night."

"Perfect." Rachel started to prepare the meal as I pondered my next move: how to meet secretly with the Caliph.

"Rachel."

"Yes."

"Can you get Eli or Samuel over here? I think I will send them to the Caliph."

"Yes. Eli has come back from Leon and is with his parents, just around the corner.

Rachel sent their son, David, over to Eli's house. Although only ten years old, David had been instructed that this was a very important task and that he must be very secretive about asking to see Eli. He did not yet know his father had come home, but seemed to sense something was up by the way his mother spoke to him. He put on his most serious face and walked over to Eli's house. Eli too could sense something was up by the look on David's face. So he came back with David.

As they stood in the small front room, they could hear someone coming down the stairs. As I appeared, David ran up to me crying, "Daddy, Daddy." He had to be quieted and reminded on the secrecy of my mission. He put on his best military face and stood at attention.

Eli too was relieved. "Hasdai, you're back. We were so worried."

"I have to ask how Ordono acted when he was told I had disappeared?"

"Oh, he was angry. You were snatched away right from under his nose. He wasn't done humiliating you or the Caliph. It looked like his city was not safe."

"Did he ever learn where I had gone?"

"Not that I know of. He sent scouts out everywhere."

"So how was your business up there?"

"Oh, great. We sold off a lot of our wares and bought a permanent site at the agora. We hired a local Jewish man to run it when we left. We are assembling new stock this week."

"What kinds of stock?"

"Our knives and daggers went well. But the women's things were best. Goblets, plates, combs, pins, belt buckles, all that kind. They don't have anything like that in Leon."

"Now, Eli, I have something you must do for me."

"Anything Doctor, name it."

"I must meet with the Caliph and tell him what I have seen, but it must be in a secret place."

"I'll go to the palace today."

"Yes, that would be best, the sooner the better."

"How will the Caliph let me in?"

"First, he knows you from before. But give him this letter. It is the one he wrote granting my safe passage and telling the King of Leon I was his representative. Here."

"Very well Doctor. I will go now and be back this afternoon."

"Thank you Eli."

"No, thank you Doctor. Samuel and I owe you much."

ELI AT PALACE

For most residents of Cordoba, a trip to the Caliph's palace was an intimidating event. Eli was no exception. He had hustled on my horse from the Juderia through the narrow streets to the road leading to the palace. Two guards in the bright uniforms of the Caliph's army stood at attention with long spears with curved blades and glared at all passersby. Eli approached, putting the Caliph's letter at arms length for the guard.

"What is it?" grunted the guard.

"I must see the Caliph on a matter of importance," Eli managed to stammer out. "This letter will explain."

The guard looked at the letter cursorily. He was probably illiterate, but he recognized the Caliph's signature and seal. He called for the relief guard sitting in the shade in a booth near the gate. "Escort this boy into the palace." The guard appeared and impatiently waved Eli to accompany him to the palace after checking him for weapons. They walked along the large pond surrounded by cloisters and pushed open the massive doors to the throne room. He was directed to sit in a small antechamber off the throne room. Soon, an elderly clerk came out and asked Eli what this was about.

"Sir, Dr. Shaprut has come back and wants to see the Caliph about a matter of some importance." The clerk nodded and left. In about a half hour, the clerk returned and told Eli, "The Caliph will meet the doctor in the rear of the Christian Cathedral at 6:30 tonight. I have brought a monk's robe for the doctor to wear."

"Thank you sir."

Eli rushed back to my house carrying the monk's robe. "Doctor, Doctor" he whispered at the Shaprut's door. I came down while Eli delivered the message and the robe. The meeting was six hours later, so I went back up to my reading on the second floor.

By 6:00 p.m, I put on the monk's robe and brought the cowl over my head and walked quickly out of the Juderia. It would be bad enough if I were recognized, but a monk in the Juderia would also attract unwanted attention. I went into the cathedral which had mercifully been spared by the Moors and remained an anchor for the cordoban Christian community. I had to admit that the cathedral was indeed a miracle. It had great solemnity inside the thick cool stone walls and magnificent sculpture and carvings throughout. For a brief second, I had to suspend my aversion to what to me and all Jews was a collection of idolatry – statues of Jesus, Mary and a number of saints. Women and men went to the chapels where images of the different saints were depicted in drawings behind a low fence. The parishioners would drop a coin in a box and take a candle, light it from a burning taper and place the candle in a small hole outside the fencing. They then kneeled and mumbled some prayers. "My God," I thought, "They are duplicating the rite of a burnt offering to a lesser god." I quietly recited the second commandment against idolatry. These Christians were a strange lot. Somehow they had taken the words of a Jewish preacher and made it into a religion that was replete with pagan rites. I had to admit that the men and women seemed to walk away from the candles with a serious and calm demeanor. It must be a force for good – at least for them. As a Jew, I shuddered at the notion.

Soon, several men all in monks' robes moved into the bench at the rear of the cathedral on either side of me. Without looking at him, I could recognize the Caliph's voice as he spoke in Greek.

"Hasdai, how good to see you again."

"Yes, your excellency. I received a very rude welcome from the new King Ordono. He appeared totally unresponsive to anything I had to say."

"So I have been told by Eli and the men who traveled with you."

"Yes. There is little to discuss on that score. Then, I was kidnapped and brought to Sancho I's encampment."

"So I heard from Sancho's men."

"Sancho I is quite obese and he wished me to cure him of his obesity. Your excellency, I did so not knowing what his intentions are with regard to you and your caliphate. I must say he spoke highly of you and wished to enter into an alliance. He treated me very well while I supervised his diet and designed some exercises for his weight loss regimen."

"So I have also heard. You did well to cultivate good relations with him."

"You heard?"

"We exchange messengers regularly."

"I see. So you knew I was in his encampment and advising him on his obesity."

"Oh yes. Your good offices are much appreciated."

"I see. So I believe he wants to ally with you to retake his kingdom."

"How do you feel about that?"

"I must say he is an intelligent man, of royal blood, and well educated. He speaks disparagingly of the cost of war to both the winners and losers and is anxious to conclude a treaty and secure prosperity for his people."

"Did you believe him?"

"Although I am a bit suspicious, I would have to say he is quite convincing. Of course, he has nothing now and you are his only hope. A drowning man may clutch at many ropes. Who knows what he will do when he is saved."

"Well said, Doctor. My thoughts as well. I would like to try an alliance and put him back on the throne. This Ordono is an abomination – a crude war-mongering fool."

"Yes, Your Excellency. I described the horrors of war to him. You should see what Salamanca looks like now. A disaster. Unusable for generations, haunted by ghosts of women and children, littered with dead soldiers."

"No. Ordono is not acceptable."

"But Sancho needs an army. I would say there were less than 1000 men in camp. He will need the support of his former vassals and many of your men. I could draw a diagram of Leon. It is protected by thick walls and there is a narrow bridge into the city over the old Roman bridge. Leon could be a problem."

"So I hear. We are investigating other approaches. Would you be willing to look at some of the other towns?"

"Of course, I would always be happy to be of service to you, but I am not a military man. I could not formulate strategy."

"Quite so. Perhaps I should send some of my men to travel with his men to plan an attack."

"If I may speak boldly, your excellency. Your Arab soldiers are your best men, but I think maybe some of your Christians would be best to oversee Sancho's men."

"I see. Yes. I have many I could trust with this. So, will you be returning to Sancho now?"

"I promised him I would. In a few days. My wife is very concerned though."

"I will lend you two Christian riders to accompany you back. I must say, the Arabian you rode in is a magnificent animal."

"Thank you, Your Excellency. What sort of terms will we require of Sancho if we are to have an alliance?"

"Obviously, we must have a permanent truce along the present borders. No weapons or soldiers within three leagues of the borders. Safe passage along all roads between our realms. Free trade between us. The usual."

"So, you do not want any more land or towns?"

"No. Unfortunately, I am beginning to realize that the more territory you have, the more expensive it is to maintain and defend. I am beginning to see that the strength of a country is measured by the strength and education of its people and the wealth of its trade."

"An interesting concept, your excellency. Your Cordoba is certainly a fine example of that."

"Thank you, Hasdai. Well, Godspeed. May Allah protect you and send my regards to Sancho. Tell him I am favorably disposed to an alliance."

HASDAI WITH NICHOLAS

It was now a second day I was free from the Caliph's business. So, once again, I held my medical office open with Yael as my assistant. The line was as long as usual and had people with maladies large and small. Yael collected the fees and I saw the patients. Yael made the notes of treatment and drew up a slip for Rachel to fill as apothecary. It was a bit hectic, but satisfying in a way. There were no moral judgments, only positive help for people in need and very satisfying. It seemed in no time the morning hours had passed away, so I left to have a bite to eat at the Jewish inn. Again, my presence drew a number of men who wished to pose questions. I am not a rabbi, but I am learned in the law and the Torah, so the discussion was lively. Once again, I was not permitted to pay my bill as someone or the inn's owner picked it up. I had to extend my apologies to all when I left to stop by Brother Nicholas' room at the cathedral. I say cathedral, but it was actually divided in two. Part was a mosque and part Catholic church. The Caliph's grandfather, on conquering Cordoba, had wisely let the Christians retain their main place of worship and actually purchased a part of it to make into a mosque. Other conquerors take the first opportunity to tear down or build on top of the previous house of worship, while building a more magnificent house of worship. This disturbs me in more than a few ways. It is like a dog urinating on the spot where another male dog has gone before. It seems sacrilegious to destroy a holy place even if it belongs to another group of worshipers. Often though, Muslims look with favor on the previous prophets of the other religions and consider Abraham, Moses and Jesus to be prophets to be venerated as part of their own religion. Perhaps that is why the Cathedral remains partly under Christian control. And yet, some Muslims would kill those who do not convert as they demand, much as many Christian rulers do now. It is another mystery –

violence in the name of religion that preaches love. But I would now see Nicholas and continue our joint translation effort, rather than attack him with a dagger.

I started in on the pile of translations Nicholas had already made. After a few hours, a woman came in with a tray of pastries and some tea. She put them carefully down on the table and then gave Nicholas a hug and bent to kiss him on the mouth. I knew I should not have been seeing this intimate moment, but I saw Nicholas looking at me and chuckling.

"Hasdai, this is my wife Elfrida." I did not know what to say.

"Oh, Dr. Shaprut, I am pleased to meet you." I was at a loss for words, but held out my hand to shake hers. "Nicholas talks about you all the time. It is a pleasure to meet you."

"But . . . But . . ."

"Yes, Hasdai, you have heard we are celibate. Well, that is only partly true. The doctrine is not altogether clear. The young men are supposed to be celibate, but the church is unsettled on this. I come from a church where that issue is not strict. We only may not have children. This prevents our church being a place where men seek nepotism for their offspring. I subscribe to that doctrine. It prevents the ruinous fights over dynasties most kingdoms experience. But older men and women past childbearing age in some areas may marry."

"But, I thought you believed Jesus was celibate and want to emulate him."

"So some believe. As you know, I am a scholar. The gospels do not say that Jesus was celibate, or not celibate. Some gospels rejected by the Church say that Mary Magdalene was his wife. I don't know the answer; but I have chosen to be married. I come from another area where this is permitted. As you know, my duties here are as a scholar, so I do not mix with the young priests. I do not feel any less holy being married and count it a blessing from God."

"So do we."

"Yes. I know that. And the Muslims can have four wives, but some have more, and some have concubines as well. I do not know the answer."

"The Caliph has four wives and many concubines but I count him among the worthiest of men. He is wise and governs with mercy and tolerance. I am not sure God has a definite policy on marriage. Well, it was nice to meet you Elfrida."

"Yes, Dr. Shaprut, I have begged Nicholas to introduce me for some time. It was a pleasure." She left. Nicholas caught my eye again and resumed chuckling at my amazement.

"A little surprise for your day."

"Yes, Nicholas, it certainly was." We returned to the manuscripts and nibbled on the pastries in the coolness of the cathedral walls. I would leave the rest of my questions unasked.

HASDAI AT HOME

I knew I could not wander the city at leisure. My presence on release from Sancho was still a secret which must be kept. I must go about the city in disguise, so I retired with great pleasure to my library on the second floor. The peace and tranquility of pure research and contemplation was a joy I had missed. That is until Rachel came in and saw a body at rest. There is something about wives that generates a list of chores for husbands in a position of rest. The couch had to be moved, discarded items had to be assembled for charity, help with chopping vegetables for dinner, moving the wine jars – the list was endless. Unfortunately, the tomes of Greek and Arabic references had to be left for another day. My correspondence with Constantine VII of Byzantium to form an alliance with Cordoba had to be put off. My letter to the Jewish state of Khazar in central Asia lingered unfinished on my desk. My review of a Codex of Botany which we were translating with the aid of a learned Greek monk into Arabic lay idle. Rachel's household was a prime concern for now. After few days, I grew restless and sought out some bodyguards for my return trip to Sancho's encampment. Enough peace was enough, back to the fray.

Again at dawn, with two sturdy Christian soldiers at my side, I sped along the route to Jaen and Sancho, who welcomed me warmly. The prescribed diet and exercise were beginning to show great improvements in Sancho, and, if it be known as well, his senior generals who ate with him every meal and accompanied him on his walks which had now lengthened and hastened to jogs of about a league. Sancho's grandmother, Todo of Pamplona, also was happy to see Hasdai and began, almost at once, to question him about an alliance with the Caliph ar-Rahman. For the time being, I was coy and brushed off her advances. I needed proof of Sancho's ability to rule and lead an army as well as his good faith in keeping a treaty with Moors. No, now was not the time to talk or bargain. Let them dangle. Nonetheless, I had brought along with me some of my correspondence and research. In the quiet of my tent, with an occasional fruit drink or cup of tea, I could get things done.

Eventually Todo, pulling Sancho by the hand, burst into my tent. "Just what did ar-Rahman have to say about his support of Sancho?"

"Your highness, he was most pleased with my report of your grandson's continuing improvement of his . . . er . . . health."

"But can he support us against Ordono?"

"I reported on how rudely I was received by Ordono and how, if he were to choose, Sancho would be his overwhelming choice."

"But will he support us?"

"I must evaluate whether King Sancho and his men are ready, not only to fight themselves, but whether his former vassals will support him."

"Quite so. How will you do that?"

"I would like to see some of his vassals in camp pledging loyalty and men for the fight."

"What can we do to persuade you to render a favorable report? We have given you already a serving girl. Are you a rich man?"

"Ah, Queen-Mother Todo, I must only serve my master without outside influences shall we say?"

"What can we do to benefit you? Why does ar-Rahman have a hold on your loyalty?"

"I must say that the civilization ar-Rahman has created is second to none in these dark ages. Moors, Christians and Jews live together in harmony. We advance science, botany, poetry and philosophy together. We are at peace with one another. I would gladly serve a ruler who is able to do this. For the first time in centuries, I and my Jewish compatriots can live together in peace, we can prosper and we can worship as we please. I am afraid the Christian kings in their alliances with the popes are very dangerous to us. I would not sell this peace for my own benefit."

"We can see that. So, you want a pledge of peace for Jews in my kingdom?"

"That is important, but I do not know what the Caliph wants."

"Does he want more territory; does he want an alliance against Castile or Asturias?"

"With respect, your highness, I don't know. In the meantime, I suggest you strengthen Sancho and his army and call in your trusted vassals. That is important."

"Ah, Dr. Shaprut, you are playing with us, like a maiden to her swain."

"What you ask us to surrender is as valuable as what the maiden has to offer."

"Ha! Ha! Very good, Doctor. You are good at this game."

"Your highness is too kind. I am here. The Caliph is interested. He will not support Ordono under any circumstances. That is the best I can say for now."

Queen-Regent Todo looked at Sancho and shrugged her shoulders. Sancho nodded. She turned and left.

Within Sancho's camp, I returned to my work. I had heard of a Jewish kingdom of Khazars in eastern Europe and was anxious to find out who they were. I had many questions and had learned much from previous correspondence. They were not related by blood to the lost tribes scattered from Judea after the Roman conquest in 135 C.E. They were Magyars, a group of Aryans who migrated into eastern Europe from the east. They had set up a kingdom, but were wedged between the Moors and Christian Byzantium. As a political device, they elected to be Jewish rather than Islam or Christian and had brought councilors in from Tiberius to instruct them in the Jewish religion many years ago. In this way, they maintained their neutrality. They were happy to hear from a coreligionist and invited me to visit when I was able. Sadly, reports I had received recently suggested that the Byzantines were courting the Russians to convert to Christianity and offering them an alliance against the Khazars. Since these letters took weeks and months to go back and forth, I was worried about the future of this kingdom.

I then translated some pages from a botanical treatise on the properties of healing herbs.

The captain of the guards came by to ask me to join Sancho and the others on their afternoon run. (Now it was a run, no longer a jog or walk.) Today they would run up the hill and walk down. This exercise left everyone sweaty and groaning. They rinsed off and went in to dinner. A treat at dinner – brook trout sautéed in olive oil and garlic with huge casks of white wine. I heartily approved, ate my fill and staggered off to my tent and fell into a deep sleep.

HASDAI SEEN, RACHEL SOUGHT

Could it be that well laid plans go amiss? Hasdai somehow had been seen during his visit back to Cordoba. Was it some well meaning neighbor who casually mentioned him? Might it have been a betrayal by one of the men Sancho had sent him to or from the camp? Some said it was actually a well laid trap by the Caliph to lure Ordono's men. It could be anyone's guess. But with Hasdai safely back in Sancho's camp, at least no one knew where he was now. His bodyguards as usual had taken a circuitous route back to camp. They were sure none had followed. But word of Hasdai back again laid to rest some rumors. First, Ordono had not murdered him while he had been in Leon. Second, he was alive and probably on some secret mission for the Caliph. And the focus of Ordono had switched to Hasdai – where was he? Did his wife know? She must. At least the Caliph did. Out of some perverse desire to demonstrate his power, Ordono began to believe that kidnapping Hasdai's wife might procure him some bargaining points. What was the Caliph up to, now that Hasdai had been spurned in Leon? A strong possible answer was an alliance with Sancho. Could Hasdai be meeting with Sancho? Hasdai's wife might secure him some answers. So he dispatched five men to take Rachel captive.

The five handpicked men were from Ordono's own elite guard. The success of their mission could demonstrate Ordono's power and embarrass the Caliph. The appearance of power is power. Vassals would be quick to show their allegiance to Ordono, also quick to be wary of the ability of the Caliph to control his realm. In this age, alliances were quick to change, even with Christians joining Arabs. The men rode carefully south, avoiding Merida as they went. At first, they thought it possible to join a caravan going south, but the secrecy of their mission might be compromised. So, after several days en route, the five arrived at the outskirts of Cordoba and donned Arab clothes which more easily concealed their swords and daggers. Surely, this mission would be easy as they strode down to the Jewish quarter. Hasdai's house in the Juderia of Cordoba was not well guarded and an escape with a defenseless woman should prove no difficulty.

So at dusk, as pedestrians of the streets began to go home and leave the path to Hasdai's house unpopulated, the men strode down the street and posted lookouts at each entrance to the narrow winding street. The other three carried a large mace to break down the door. From somewhere a cackling bird call was unobtrusively heard mixed with the din of the city. Suddenly, one of the lookouts was sliced across the back of the neck by a long curved spear of the Moorish military. He fell quietly where he stood with but a low gasp of surprise. The other lookout was run through with a spear through his lower back. On cue, 15 Moorish soldiers hurried into the narrow street and without further command attacked the remaining three of Ordono's men. A windmill blow chopped off the right arm of the first and burrowed into his side. His sword clanged onto the cobblestones. As the second rushed up to the encounter, he was bludgeoned in the head with a massive iron ball mounted on a wooden handle. The ball tore through his helmet drawing blood from his forehead and nose. He fell like a slaughtered ox. The third tried to raise his hands in surrender, but was chopped from forehead to knee by the curved swords of the Moorish soldiers who had crowded into the narrow street. The encounter ended with an eerie quiet at first as the Moors stood panting and wiping their weapons on the clothes of the fallen. By this time, heads of the area residents began to appear out of the second story windows. Aghast at the scene of slaughter and the large collection of Moorish soldiers, they tried to make sense of the scene. Were they under attack by the Moors? No, the slain men were large Christian warriors bleeding in huge gouts of blood. Where were they from? The Christians to the north? What were they doing in the Juderia? They were at Hasdai's door.

Rachel stuck her head out the second story window. She was pale. Her two children also were at her side. What were these men doing at my door? My God, there was blood everywhere. Were they looking for Hasdai? What could they want with me?

The commander of the Moors issued a few curt commands in Arabic. His men began to chop the heads off of the Christians and put them into a large box. Blood flowed in even greater rivulets than before. The other men began to carry the bodies down the street to be thrown on two carts at the intersection. It was not long before the bodies, the heads and the Moorish soldiers left as quietly as they had arrived. A figure on the roof top of one of the houses sent out another cackling bird call and disappeared as well. It took at least 15 minutes before the first brave residents began to come out of their doors and ask questions, for which there were no answers. The Caliph's men seemed to have prevented an attack by Christian soldiers on the house of Hasdai Shaprut. They had been butchered. That is the only fair term for it – butchered by the Moors in defense of the Jews and Hasdai.

By the way, where was Hasdai, Rachel was asked. She shrugged. No answer there. Must be on one of is missions for ar-Rahman. As the reality of what had just occurred sunk in, the women began to see the slowly coagulating blood on the street and among the cobblestones.

They could not let it dry. They could not let the stench of this blood rise up in their block. Without much talk, the women got out their buckets of water and mops and began to wash the blood down the gutters. There was little communication – the Jewish community, for whom cleanliness was a religious obligation, joined in sweeping the blood into the gutter.

Finally, one of them said, "Did you see the way they cut off their heads and let the blood run out?"

Another of the ladies said, "They must have trained as kosher butchers." The joke in the midst of the horror set everyone laughing. Ah, Jewish humor! The women kept mopping, shaking their heads at the scene they had witnessed.

AFTERMATH

There was an uneasy aftermath from the abrupt dispatch of Ordono's men in the Juderia. People would walk by and point at Rachel's door and a few of the remaining blood spatters. David had become a bit of a celebrity at school as he was asked to repeat his version of the fight with a great display of sword strokes and spear thrusts. Eventually, the teacher thought the boys had heard enough of blood and gore and forbade any further discussion.

Soon Samuel returned from Leon with a meager collection of goods from the market up north, but he could describe in vivid detail the reaction of Ordono and his men to the large box tilted on its side in the center of the agora with five bloodied, disembodied heads with Leonese helmets spilling out on the pavement. After a long trip in a combined space, the heads had begun to rot and gave off an atrocious odor. A contingent of servants were sent out to clean up the mess. Ordono had lost at least the first skirmish with ar-Rahman and the reports of the scene in the agora spread quickly through the realm.

A few days after the event, a cart pulled up the narrow street in front of Rachel's house and was unloaded. Several crates were carried inside. They bore some exquisite place settings of plates and soup tureens, serving dishes of finely hammered copper and brass and a true work or art of a Kiddush wine goblet with Hebrew letters hammered around the rim. No card was attached and the donor was not identified. It was easy to deduce that this was a gift intended for a woman and selected by a man with great wealth and fine taste for the woman of the house. Could the Caliph be rewarding Rachel for her role in the confrontation? Had she been a lure for Ordono's men? No one could say one way or the other. The gift was much appreciated and all the women from the Jewish area came to marvel at the fine workmanship.

And Samuel, after he reported whatever he had seen to the Caliph's generals, returned a healthy portion of the loan he and Eli had been given to start their trade with Leon. He at first gave a report of the Jewish Community in Leon which had grown to hate the constant harassment and higher taxes Ordono imposed on them. The King's cruelty and oppression was also sorely felt among the townspeople in general. His soldiers swaggered through the town, harassed the young women and demanded bribes from the merchants. The Caliph had thanked Samuel for his service as he left to take Eli's place at Leon. Samuel was now accorded some praise and status by the men at the gathering outside the Sabbath services that week. He was asked to describe the scene with the heads rolling out onto the main square in Leon, the people who had friends or relatives in Leon, and how his trade had prospered. Such attention was not lost on the young girls of the congregation who stole glances at Samuel through their discretely averted eyelashes in his new found status in the community. He, of course, could sense their looks and resolved to show them up for their disinterest in the past by spending some time with the tall blond Christian beauties in the town. He was still not of marriageable age and could afford a few dalliances before he would have to raise a family.

Slowly, Cordoba returned to its normal affairs and the events of the past few weeks ebbed as a subject for daily conversation.

ZASTRA AND RACHEL AT JAEN

Once again, Rachel and Zastra chose booths next to each other at Jaen's monthly market. Each had brought bottle gourds for the mysterious lady's request for a weight loss remedy. Rachel by now knew who they were to go to, but kept the knowledge to herself. During the day, the women chatted and exchanged herbal remedies for various ailments. Once again, the odious Osric, as they now called him, stopped by in fiery red leggings and a green leather doublet, in the company of his two retainers and, once again, he harrassed Zastra. He was a noble and she a peasant. Her rejection had to be polite and respectful, which to the male ego was often interpreted as encouragement. She had told her Burgomil countrymen of her bewilderment at being unable to discourage this presumptuous popinjay. To the Burgomils, it was no laughing matter. Once a proud independent people living in southern Francia, they had escaped the greedy clutches of the Pope and the Frankish king leaving the rich farmlands and the cultivated vineyards behind. Some said they took much of their gold and treasures with them, a story which they often discouraged, but never completely denied.

They had settled in a high, peaceful mountain valley with a cool climate and rich soil, surrounded by mountain ridges and thick evergreen forests. They had survived several generations, practiced their brand of Christianity and lived an insular life with minimal outside contact. Zastra was one of the few people with regular outside communications. She was usually accompanied by a few of the men on her trips to market who kept a discrete distant but watchful eye on her. They had fully investigated the background of Rachel as Hasdai Shaprut's wife and were pleased with what they found. Osric was a different matter. His father, Alonzo, was a vassal to the Caliph ar-Rahman, not known to be dangerous to them. He seemed to have settled into a working arrangement with the Caliph and enjoyed his independence from the Christians on the other side of the border. While he was a steadfast supporter of the Church of Rome, he had not voiced any desire to rid the world of heretics including Moors, obviously, but also Jews or Burgomils. But he could be dangerous also. As a Christian settled near the border, he would be expected to evaluate his political position carefully and might switch over to the Christians at any time.

Osric was now an irritant. An embarrassing incident might sway his father one way or the other, especially against the Burgomils who resided secretly but close to Alonzo's domain. Now poor Zastra had innocently set in motion this libidinous little prig. The village conferred. Should they approach the Caliph and ask for protection? Should they approach Alonzo and seek amnesty? When Zastra described her friendship with Rachel, it seemed a new path had opened up for Hasdai Shaprut. He had the Caliph's trust, but a well known sense of integrity and discretion. Another faction among the Burgomils elders, of whom about half were women, felt they could never trust anyone again, especially a Moorish Caliph or a Jew. The debate went on for some time, over days. The council decided to trust no one, but elected to send a few of the men to rough up Osric and his men and send them home with their tails between their legs. If Zastra was bothered in any way more than verbal harrassment, Osric and his men would be taught a lesson. Anonymously, but firmly, they would be buffeted about and sent packing.

At the end of the day's market, Osric took a new and bolder course of action. He followed Zastra in the caravan along the trade route east. Somewhere along the way, Zastra and her two bodyguards would have to peel off and ascend along the path leading to the Burgomil village. Osric could never know this path. And so, the course of action was set in motion.

Osric followed the caravan several hundred feet to the rear, laughing and drinking, and much to Zastra's embarrassment, calling her name. It did not take long. Several masked horsemen burst out of the bushes and knocked the riders to the ground. There, they beat them soundly and thoroughly with the sides of their broadswords about their legs, their buttocks and their backs. They did not draw blood; they did not strike the heads, but left many bruises and bumps. For good measure, they took the horses, their purses, and the weapons which had not been drawn, and left Osric and his companions sore and groaning on the ground. The caravan could hear the commotion, but knew better than to look back and become involved. In fact, they sped up to a better pace to distance themselves from this disturbance. The people had paid good money to join this caravan and they were well protected by the men who rode back and forth guarding the front, rear and flanks of the caravan. No one was anxious to participate in any rescue, especially of the drunken young fool who seemed to want to humiliate the nice young girl with the pack mule filled with herbs.

After quite a while, Osric regained consciousness and felt his hammered body parts, as did his men. They were now alone and horseless along the trade route, with no food or weapons. With little other recourse, they began the trek back to Jaen. It would take two days at their slow pace and they slept among the trees. By the next midmorning, they stumbled into Jaen much to the derision of the townsfolk. Using his father's credit, Osric obtained solid meals and a few horses for the ride back home. Now, however, he had acquired a reputation not to be envied in the town of Jaen, where his father was well known and now also an object for some snickering – a reputation no knight would ever court. But an affront to Alonzo he could not ignore.

Alonzo now sat glaring at his son as he stood still in his tattered clothing fresh from the recent fracas.

"Osric, how did this happen?"

"We were riding on the trail behind a caravan when we were set upon by a bunch of thugs."

"Thugs, you say. Were they bandits?"

"They were masked. It was difficult to tell who they were."

"Now, they beat you and robbed you?"

"Yes, father."

"Let me hear from your men, Osric. Step forward you!" One of the retainers, Ethelred, stood forward "Yes, sire."

"What happened here. Now, I want the truth. Out with it." The loyalty to Osric was not as strong as the fear of Alonzo.

"Well, sire, we had gone to the Jaen market day. It seems we had a bit to drink, if the truth be known. Then Osric fancied this shop girl as he had in the past. He urged us to follow her when her caravan left to the east. We were following the caravan. We had our weapons stowed in our saddles when several men came and attacked us. That is all I remember until we started back into Jaen."

"You did not protect Osric?"

"Sire, we were surprised."

"I do not know whether these men were common bandits or possibly an enemy. They did not seem to want to harm you. No. You survived nicely. But you embarrassed us in front of the people of Jaen. Osric, these are difficult times. We cannot allow our enemies to think us weak or ill-prepared. Did the girl have something to do with this?"

"I think not, Father. She is just a shop girl selling herbs and remedies."

"Next market day, we must check into her. Is she Moor or Christian?"

"I believe she is Christian." Well, we will see what happens next market day.

HASDAI – REGULAR VISITS

Once tested, I was now able to return home at frequent intervals. I was always accompanied by Sancho's men up to the outer edge of Cordoba as they journeyed through what might have been treacherous bandits. The Caliph's men were able to convince my townspeople that I had simply been kidnapped by some thugs who had intended to hold me for ransom, but when they could find no takers in Leon who knew me, they simply abandoned the project. This story exonerated Ordono to some degree because, at least Ordono had not mistreated an envoy, but it did show Ordono's inability to govern his capital city. In any case, I was able to go about my usual life as before: regular hours for my medical practice aided by my wife as my apothecary. My daughter also was now learning to be an apothecary and delved into the medical treatises I had collected in Arabic, Latin and Greek. David too, buzzed around the medical office when he was not in school or playing with his friends.

I scheduled my return visits to Sancho when Rachel would be at the Jaen market and David would stay with one of his friends.

Of course, I regularly met with the Caliph to report on the status of Sancho's recovery from obesity and the strength and training of his troops. Generally, the reports were favorable.

Regularly, on my trips to Sancho, I was bombarded by the exiled King and his grandmother about securing an audience with the Caliph to beseech him for aid in reacquiring his kingdom. Each time, I deferred until the Caliph gave me the approval for such a meeting. In the meantime, I continued to bring bottle gourd powder, although Sancho indicated he was getting a supply from elsewhere.

Then one day, Rachel returned from Jaen and, at dinner with me, related an incident in which Lord Alonzo's men had arrived in Jaen on market day and began to question up and down the rows in the agora if anyone knew about the robbery and beating of his son Osric. Although, for the most part, few people were able to give any information, a number of things came out. First, Osric had bragged that a king was in his father's lands and, second, that Osric had been harassing Zastra in the marketplace and was following her caravan home after the market day had ended. He was reportedly drunk and making lewd comments. Apparently, Lord Alonzo was waiting for news of the investigation just outside of town and came quickly into the market to question Zastra. Rachel overheard much of what was said:

"Who are you, my dear?"

"I am Zastra."

"Where do you live?"

"In a mountain village to the east."

"Are you Christian?"

"Yes, Sire."

"What is the name of your village?"

"We just call it 'our place'."

"How many are you in this village"

"Six families, your excellency."

"What was Osric doing to you?"

"He was embarrassing me by his questions and he was always making impertinent comments, Sire. Sire, I am a good and righteous person. I do not wish to be made a fool at the agora." Zastra was treading a very difficult path. Her people could suffer great disaster if Alonzo chose to find out who they were. Zastra could not let this happen and must sacrifice herself for the good of her people. She would never reveal their identity or location. "Your excellency, could you ask your son not to bother me. I am a good woman." She began to cry. A crowd had gathered. Alonzo also knew he must not arouse the crowd against him. These were people whom he did not need to provoke unnecessarily.

"Zastra, do you know the men who robbed and beat my son?"

"No, your excellency. I was in the caravan, but could not see what happened. I only heard a battle taking place."

Alonzo was not satisfied, but left the scene and encouraged the crowd to disperse. It was too much of a coincidence that Osric's beating followed so closely on his harassment of Zastra. He might need to follow Zastra more closely.

Zastra was left heaving great shudders and crying as she turned to Rachel. There was more to this than Rachel could fathom and she sensed a bigger story. She had to tell Hasdai about her friend, who might now be in trouble.

I had listened carefully to the story from Rachel. I stared into space slowly chewing my dinner. Rachel was used to these long pauses and let me consider the possibilities.

"So, this Zastra is your friend. She is a Christian from a small mountain village and she is very wise in the way of herbs and medicines?"

"Yes, Hasdai." Rachel could almost hear the ideas moving about in Hasdai's brain.

"And this Osric has bragged about a king staying on his father's fiefdom."

"Yes, Hasdai."

"Not good, not good. The Caliph must know this and tell Alonzo." More silence. "This Zastra, where is she now?"

"I guess she went home after the market day."

"No, my guess is maybe not. You must find her. She is in trouble if she is whom I think she is. I will speak to the Caliph about this." Rachel felt some relief. Hasdai, like a good hunting dog, seemed to have a scent.

The next day, I went up to see the Caliph.

HASDAI AND RACHEL TO JAEN

The next market day, I joined Rachel and Yael on the trip to Jaen. I felt I needed to investigate this event with Osric. David, seeing the rest of the family depart on an adult adventure insisted on being included. So at dawn in a cart they joined the caravan east. Rachel, as usual, with Yael set up the booth while Hasdai and David toured the agora and went up to the castle on the top of the town which overlooked the surrounding countryside. Since they had eaten only a small breakfast of milk and fruit, David stopped at each booth and wanted to taste what was on display, whether it was kosher or not. Cheeses, almonds, pastries, fruit juice – he seemed to have consumed twice his body weight by the time they came back to Rachel's booth. As they approached, Rachel said, "Hasdai, this is Zastra. Zastra, this is my husband, Hasdai."

"Pleased to meet you, Dr. Shaprut."

"Pleased to meet you, Zastra. I have brought you a translation of an Arab text on herbs and medicines. Rachel says you are very knowledgeable."

"Oh, many thanks, Dr. Shaprut."

And then in a lower voice, I said, "Zastra, we must talk."

"Yes, I know, Doctor. I was expecting you."

"Can I speak to the leader of your village as well?"

"Yes, Doctor. We know of your concern. He is watching us from the corner over there." She motioned slightly with her head to an elderly man appearing to be dozing against the wall. He was dressed in rags and had his hat pulled down over his forehead.

"Can I walk with him someplace private?"

"Yes. Just go over to him and say 'God is good.'"

Hasdai walked over a circuitous route to the corner, and without addressing anyone in particular, said, "God is good." With that the man appeared to shake off his lethargy and slowly painfully got to his feet and ambled with a limp in the same direction as Hasdai. They walked a few streets down from the agora to a small park at the edge of town where they sat. It seemed both had been trained to expect someone to follow them since they turned at intervals to examine some curiosity in the street or in a doorway while looking behind them. Each satisfied that they were alone, addressed each other. Zastra's man took off his hat and smiled. He was a man in his forties with black hair, light blue eyes and a tanned complexion, nothing like the old man in the agora.

"I am Dr. Shaprut. I represent the Caliph. We are concerned about the incident with Osric, Alonzo's son. May we speak?"

"Yes, Doctor. I am Emil. My people came from Byzantium to escape religious persecution. You are a Jew so I believe I can speak to you in a confidential manner. You too know of persecution."

"Yes, Emil, you may speak freely."

"Our religion is Christian, but they consider us heretics among the so-called Catholic Church hierarchy."

"What do you believe that is so dangerous to them?"

"We believe that men and women are equal, so many of our priests are women. We do not believe in the trinity – that system which makes Jesus divine, equal to God the father, and at the same time, part of the father. It is a mystery we do not accept."

"How is that dangerous to Rome and the established order?"

"We do not know. We live a moral life in our community and seek to be perfect. There is a ceremony we have to recognize a member of our community as perfect. We call it Consolamentum. Now, Zastra herself is seeking to be a "perfect" and prepares herself for the ceremony. That is why these approaches by this teenage menace, Osric, are so inappropriate."

"I can see that. They certainly live on different planes."

"Now, we live comfortably in a secluded mountain village – away from the Christians who persecute us and away from the Moors who might be a danger to us."

"Yes, I can see that. So this Osric might expose your community in the mountains."

"Quite so. Can you help us, Dr. Shaprut?"

"I can certainly say that you need not fear the Caliph. He is tolerant of many religions so long as you support his realm and obey his laws."

"How do the Jews fare under the Caliph?"

"We prosper. I am free to pursue my studies, we are never bothered in our worship. We do not serve in the army, but pay a special tax instead. Other than that, we are considered to be citizens in his land."

"Can he protect us from our fellow Christians?"

"I will see."

"Now as to Osric, his father seeks some revenge for the beating we administered to his son. That threatens us greatly."

"Yes, I can understand. I will speak to the Caliph. Lord Alonzo is one of his vassals."

"But he is Christian. Can he rely on his loyalty?"

"We have many Christian vassals, all loyal to the Caliph. You are right to ask that question. We are careful to test their loyalty from time to time. I do not know this Lord Alonzo. We will see what can be done."

"I must also tell you that King Sancho is hiding in exile in Alonzo's fiefdom. We do not understand the alignment of loyalties that may mean. Will Alonzo side with Sancho or the Caliph?"

I now had many secrets to keep. Perhaps the burgeoning alliance between the Caliph and Sancho was a secret, and perhaps the Caliph had arranged for Sancho's sojourn in Alonzo's land. That was not something I knew. But a confrontation which exposed this possible alliance prematurely could be dangerous. Emil had this knowledge, but did not yet know he could exploit it. Certainly, a truce between Emil's people and Lord Alonzo might be necessary. But was it something the Caliph wanted?

"Emil, we have started a worthwhile process. I must consult with the Caliph. How do I reach you?"

"Tell Zastra."

"Is she safe in the agora."

"You cannot see us, but she has several bodyguards who keep watch over her. But I am worried that Alonzo will not wait long to mete out his revenge."

"I understand. I will let the Caliph know."

"Until next time."

"Yes, Godspeed."

HASDAI SEES THE CALIPH ABOUT ZASTRA

As I had many times before, I went up to the Palace and was recognized by the guards who let me pass through to the small antechamber off the throne room. Within a half hour, the Caliph came in.

"Ah, Hasdai. Something must have come up."

"Yes, Your Highness. I am not sure what it all means, but I have a few qualms about recent events I felt I must tell you."

"I always respect your advice. It must be important."

"Thank you, Your Excellency. It may seem to be a minor matter, but it could have farther reaching consequences."

"Please tell me."

"As you know, I have been consulting with King Sancho who has an encampment in exile in the fiefdom of Lord Alonzo, one of your vassals. You are pondering whether to support Sancho in his claims to the throne. Since he already resides in your kingdom, you are exposed to some speculation that you already support him, but since his whereabouts have been kept secret, such speculation is only that. Ordono has taken the throne, but has been cold to any advances we might make to have a treaty. A new but small irritation has arisen. First, Osric, Alonzo's son has been bragging of a king staying in his father's fiefdom. Second, Osric has been harassing a friend of my wife's while the two women share adjacent booths at the Jaen market day. It has been reported that Osric with two retainers had followed this young woman's caravan after market day. They were apparently drunk and made lewd comments. Although several hundred feet behind the caravan, they were attacked by persons unknown. They were robbed, severely beaten and left unconscious on the highway. Osric and his companions made it back to Jaen where they became a bit of a laughing stock to the townspeople. Needless to say, Alonzo could not take such an event without risking a loss of esteem with his villagers and began an investigation. This could lead to the young woman Osric has been harassing. She denied any relation to the attack. I fear this woman may be in some kind of trouble. If she is caught, it may come out that her villagers may try to protect her. I even suspect that her villagers were part of the attack. Alonzo cannot allow the attack to go unanswered."

"I see. Is this not a matter for Alonzo to deal with?"

"Normally, I would agree. Vassals should control their own realms, but I sense that this village the young woman comes from may cause a larger problem. The young woman has supplied a certain remedy for weight loss to Sancho. She may not know who the herb's recipient is, but my wife does and it is Sancho."

"Now, the woman may have been able to connect the two – the herb and King Sancho – since the woman who picks up the ingredient has been very secretive. On the other hand, my wife's friend has also been very secretive about where she lives. Her deep knowledge of medicinal herbs suggests something strange to me. Only a few people know in depth about this curative remedy, the Jews of course, several Moorish experts and, I guess, the Burgomils."

"Ah, the Burgomils. I have heard of them. Christians deemed heretical by the Pope. The French king and the Pope took their lands and slaughtered many of them. A very greedy maneuver, I must say. I have heard of these Burgomils – they have great knowledge of many things and worship Jesus, but as more of a human."

"I too am confused by their beliefs. The Christians have fought for many centuries over theological issues. I simply don't understand."

"So, Burgomils on my land. People with much knowledge on Alonzo's land. Maybe at risk over an adolescent's indiscretion."

"Yes, your excellency. But I feel a confrontation between Alonzo and the Burgomils will uncover the location of Sancho and force your hand in this alliance before you are ready to make a decision."

"Yes, I can see that as a possibility. I have considered this alliance, but am not sure I want to risk a war with this Ordono. It is not a war I can lose. I must feel confident of success. I have already sent my military commanders to explore the possibility of commencing war with Ordono. As you know, they are in Estremadura now. But I have not made up my mind."

"Quite so, your excellency."

"But I have another thought. I would like to speak to this young woman. I have some other ideas in mind. Can your wife find her? I would like to have you bring her to Cordoba."

"I will see what my wife can do. Thank you for letting me bring this to your attention."

"No, thank you. It was quite a valuable alert." I left and explained this conversation to my wife. The next market day would be an adventure.

HASDAI CONSULTS CALIPH ABOUT EMIL

I returned from my meeting with Emil once again by a circuitous route to be sure I was not followed. Once back at Rachel's booth, I nodded to Zastra. She cast a wary smile back. While I thought out the possibilities, I took David on another walk around the agora and the town. David it seemed was determined to eat his way through every variety of food that was not obviously kosher. He also picked out a few trinkets for his mother and sister and a magnificent dagger with mother of pearl inlay and a hilt wrapped in silk cord.

Just after noon, Alonzo's men came through the town once again asking questions about Osric's beating. The people practiced the well exercised tactic of bland ignorance which had preserved peasants for many centuries now. After a few exasperating hours of shrugs and wide- eyed innocence, the men gave up.

At the end of the day, Rachel and Yael packed up, hugged Zastra and joined the caravan west with David and me.

The following day, I made my way up to the palace and was promptly admitted. I was met in the cloistered walkway around the pond by the Caliph. We walked slowly around the water and the surrounding garden. Occasionally, the peacock would scurry across our path. But, we could talk in privacy here.

"Your excellency, I have spoken to this woman's clan leader. It seems they are a community of Christian heretics, they call themselves gnostics, living in an obscure mountain village. They come from near Byzantium and fear they will be persecuted by the orthodox Christians and the Pope for their beliefs. Women are considered equal to men in their religion and this woman seeks to be something they call a "perfect", and is preparing for a kind of ceremony. They seem to lead a monastic life style, but do interbreed. However, Lord Alonzo's son is deeply embarrassing to her."

"Is she attractive?"

"Quite."

"How old is she?"

"I would guess fifteen or sixteen."

"What do they want us to do?"

"Intervene with your vassal Alonzo to convince him to let this insult to his son pass."

"Why should I do this? Alonzo's a Christian vassal. I do not wish to push these people"

"Well, Osric has let slip that Sancho is encamped on Alonzo's lands and this Emil is aware of this and seems to know where he is."

"Has he threatened us with this information?"

"I would have to say no. He mainly wants peace. He wants the location of his community kept secret. I doubt he would take such a risk." "What is your arrangement with Alonzo regarding his providing sanctuary to Sancho?"

"Alonzo asked to accommodate someone he referred to as a friend and I agreed provided his whereabouts were kept secret and I was not implicated."

"So if we confer with Alonzo, he owes you this favor. He also wants to have you support Sancho in his war to regain the throne. I imagine he will be willing to let this incident with Osric pass."

"I would agree. I have no desire to provoke Alonzo, but he must leave these mountain people alone. Go see Alonzo and see what you can work out."

It was mid-morning now. The Caliph had let me have my two bodyguards as we rode to Alonzo's castle in Linares. The trip up the old Roman road from Cordoba was uneventful. Alonzo's castle, if you can call it that, was on the river which runs past the town down to Cordoba. There were some ramshackle huts in the fields outside Linares and as we got closer to the town, there were some mean huts erected in rough concentric circles. The town had an eastern entrance through a series of towers so that only one horse or one man could enter at a time. Guards were posted on the towers to inspect the entrants. I showed them a letter from the Caliph with the royal seal. The guards could not read the letter, but recognized the seal.

"Are you coming from Cordoba?"

"Yes"

"To see Lord Alonzo."

"Yes, just as the letter says."

"Pass on in."

We rode up to the interior wall of the castle and tied up the horses in the post in the interior yard. The castle was constructed mostly of wooden beams with a few stone pillars and walls set at angles. The entire affair was one story with a tall watch tower rising some 40 feet in the air to surveil the surrounding countryside. We walked up to a large wooden door with heavy iron studs. Again we showed a guard the Caliph's letter and again we were admitted. We were escorted to a large room which was set up as an eating hall with wooden tables and benches on the lower level and a higher table on an upper level some four feet off the floor. We were instructed to sit at the bench on the floor level directly in front of the raised seating area.

In a few minutes, a very large man with blond shoulder length hair and a heavy leather tunic came and addressed us.

"Doctor Hasdai, what is this about?"

"Lord Alonzo, it is a delicate matter I would prefer to discuss in private."

"Ah so, it must be important. Very well." He dismissed his retinue of several men also dressed in heavy leather tunics. I excused my men and told them to get the horses fed and watered and stabled for the night. Alonzo beckoned me up to the table where he sat.

I had never met Alonzo before and had little information on his character, his loyalty to the Caliph and his circumspection in dealing with information I might be required to reveal to him. As it stood, I believed Alonzo had no real idea as to why Osric was attacked other than for a robbery. He did not know yet of Zastra and her mountain village. If he were to learn of this connection, it might provoke a feud, dangerous certainly to

Zastra's people, but also to people who were the Caliph's subjects. This, in turn, might disclose the knowledge that Sancho was permitted to hide in exile in Alonzo's fiefdom.

"Lord Alonzo, I must admit I know nothing about you other than that you are a vassal of the Caliph. Does it seem strange to you that a Christian would side with Moors against the Christians in Lyon?"

"Not if you know any history. My father was a knight in the army of the Christians. He supported Ramiro in his battles, but as you know, Ramiro lost out to Ordono's and Sancho's father, and he was forced to flee. The Caliph at the time was good enough to offer our family a fiefdom and protect us against Leon. It has been over 60 years now and the Caliphate has been fair with us, so we are loyal to them."

So, I thought, he is loyal until the political or military tide turns, then he is a Christian again. But his answer was honest and straightforward. Alonzo himself was a large coarse fellow. He spoke bluntly with more than a few grammatical errors.

"Does it bother you that the Caliph has sent a Jew to speak with you on his behalf?"

"Ha, Ha. Jews, Moors, they act the same to me. They are not Christians, but I enjoy peace and prosperity under the Caliph. I pay my taxes and I have assurance of military forces if I am attacked. I do not know any Jews, but I believe they are like the Moors – educated and smart."

"Does it bother you that the church tells you we are heretics?"

"Look, I avoid my contacts with the church. They are always after me for money. It is the same as the Caliph. I was given a Christian education, but I never paid attention and don't get involved with the debates– trinity, no trinity, that sort of thing. The priests drone on in Latin. I don't even know what they are saying. Mainly, they don't pay taxes, they are on my lands. Only my wife listens to them."

"Did you know Jesus was Jewish?"

"No. I was never told that. Why did you kill him?"

"That is a matter of debate. We did not."

"But the priests say you did."

"That is the church speaking."

"OK, I see. Well, it all doesn't matter to me. I collect my taxes, I live well, I hunt, I chase women and I eat and drink well, so I follow the Caliph. I am not complicated. I like what I like and I am happy now."

"Very well, Lord Alonzo. I am going to tell you something about Osric."

"You know who robbed him?"

"Yes, but it is not that simple. I must ask you in advance not to seek revenge against these people because the Caliph wishes to keep the peace."

"OK, I am listening."

"It seems Osric was harassing a peasant girl at the agora, making crude remarks and following her caravan home. She knew he was trifling with her. She is very religious. She told her family and they sent men to protect her. On the day, Osric had been drinking heavily and harassing her both at the agora and in the caravan. Her men folk were just protecting her."

"I will have to talk to Osric about this."

"There is more. Apparently Osric has been bragging that "a king" is hiding in his father's domain. Everyone at the agora has heard him say that."

"Oh, not good. I have heard that you know of Sancho."

"Yes, I have and I must say that I have been helping Sancho."

"Yes, I have heard that also. So I must trust you now."

"Let me make this plain. Sancho seeks the protection of the Caliph who has not decided yet whether to help him regain his throne. You support Sancho. If word got out that the Caliph knew Sancho was on your land, or that you even permitted Sancho to hide on your land, Ordono would send his men after Sancho, you and eventually the Caliph. So we wish to have these things unknown."

Alonzo paused, stared into space and drummed his fingers on the chair arm. "I see . . . hmm . . . Bring in Osric." Alonzo summoned his men from outside the door. As Alonzo passed me on the way to the door, there was an overwhelming odor of garlic, onions and heavy male sweat. I thought I would have to introduce ritual baths or Turkish baths to this town. The Christians did have a water ritual in baptism, but that, for most people, only occurred at birth. Surely, these people knew they emitted strong unpleasant odors. The Arabs and the Jews had raised frequent bathing to a religious level, especially before prayer. As Alonzo returned and passed me once again, the odor returned. It almost watered my eyes.

Osric stood before them with his head down. "Yes, father."

"Osric, the day you were beaten, had you been drinking?"

"Some, Father. But not much."

"Osric, did you harass a young woman at the agora?"

"I don't know what you mean. I sometimes flirt with many girls."

"I mean the one at the herbal medicine booth."

With that, Osric glared at me. "Did this Jew's wife tell you that?"

"Ah, so you did."

"I did say hello to her."

"I understand you followed her caravan at the end of the day. Now, don't lie. This is very important."

"Yes, we did Father."

"Were you making lewd remarks to her?"

"Who is telling you this Father? It is that Jew's wife?" He said looking pointedly at me. "No, she was not in the caravan. Did you or did you not?"

"I don't remember."

"Oh, very nice. OK, send me in his retainers. Who were they this agora day?"

"Ethelred and Theophil"

"Bring them in at once." The room was silent as Osric stood nervously eying his father, and alternately glaring at me. Alonzo stared, fuming up at the ceiling and I stared at my feet.

Some time passed before the two men came in. They knelt and addressed Alonzo, "Yes, my lord."

"The day Osric was beaten, were you armed?"

"Of course, Your Excellency."

"Why didn't you best these attackers?"

"Sir, there were five of them."

"Where were your weapons?" The two men looked at each other. This was not a good time. Which was better, to lie or to admit their negligence. A lie over time would be worse. Yes, the truth.

"Sire, they were in their scabbards in the saddle."

"So, you never drew them?"

"No Sire. Lord Osric was not doing anything, he was just having a lark with this one girl. We thought nothing of it."

"So you did not protect him." A long silence.

"So he was harassing this young girl?"

"Yes, Sire."

"OK, you may go." The men didn't need to be told twice. They were out of the room in a flash.

Alonzo turned to Osric. "So, Osric, it seems you have too much free time that you must go out and embarrass my subjects. Alright. You have become a spoiled young pup. You embarrass me and your mother. Today, you will learn the art of warfare. Every day, except the Sabbath, I will have the soldiers train you until you can no longer walk. I will secure a wife for you and you will beget me heirs. Your days of idleness are over. And . . . and, you will be forbidden to go to Jaen or any agora. You will leave this young girl alone. And you will not harass another woman in my domain. Is that clear?"

"Yes, Father."

"Now, I have also heard that you have bragged that a king is staying in my territory. Is that so?"

"I don't know what you mean."

"Come now. I want the truth or it will be worse for you. When I am privileged enough to grant sanctuary to a king, it is a very important matter. It gives me, and ultimately you, great prestige and favor. Do you understand that?"

"Yes, Father."

"When you try to destroy what arrangements I have made, you are very harmful to me and my domain. Do you understand that?"

"Yes, Father."

"How did you learn this?"

"There is much gossip that King Sancho has a camp near the river. The people in town talk of it."

"Who has said this?"

"I don't know. Just the peasants."

"Do you see that if I have helped Sancho, that Ordono may make us a target and attack us?"

"Yes, I see."

"Why have you opened your mouth and told these secrets in public?"

"I don't know."

"Do you think someone who did something so foolish should ever be allowed to rule a fiefdom?"

A long silence.

"Get out of here, you foolish pup and don't come back until you have grown up."

Osric turned and left. It was possible that he had given way to tears, but Hasdai and Alonzo could not see it for sure.

"Dr. Shaprut, I must apologize profusely. My son has created a difficult situation. What can I do?"

"Most important, you must leave this woman and her people alone. They are the Caliph's subjects and must be left in peace."

"Granted. I will issue the orders today."

"You must move Sancho to a different location."

"I can see all that. But I must ask, when will the Caliph support Sancho?"

"That is difficult to say. Sancho, himself must prove that he is no longer obese and will be ready to fight. His men must, of course, be ready. And, most important, his former vassals must be willing to support him. We must be assured he will have sufficient men to defeat Ordono."

"Do you have any influence with him?"

"Me. No. I am not a military man. These are military questions."

"How can I help?"

"Prepare your men for the fight and contact those former vassals of his with whom you have some influence, of course."

"I see. Well, Dr. Shaprut, you have been most helpful. Give my regards to the Caliph and let him know that I am his loyal vassal as always."

"Thank you, Lord Alonzo. You have been most helpful."

"Is there anything I can do for you?"

"I work for ar-Rahman only and do not expect anything for my services from those I speak to on his behalf."

"Then please stay the night, enjoy dinner here and I will send something with you for the Caliph."

"Thank you for your kindness."

HASDAI AT REST

The rest of my stay at Linares was pleasant, but I was eager to return home. We rode at night to avoid detection.

I awoke at dawn and went into our garden with some tea, some of Rachel's charoset and some yogurt. Behind my plain house on the narrow street sat my garden, an oasis of calm in the midst of the city. This day, like my garden, was a respite in the midst of my travails. The garden had a small pool in the center surrounded by plants and flowers from an exotic collection – a profusion of oranges and blues, pinks and purples, reds and greens. We had attracted a few wrens who chirped happily flitting from the branches of the trees and bushes which lined our walls. In the midst of our pond was our mikveh, a private ritual bath where we could sit up to our eyes in the cooling waters and soak away the cares of the day as we contemplated God and our lives. The mikveh would have to wait until this evening before sunset as we began our preparations for the Sabbath. But this Friday would be a day of work and peace.

Today, I could resume my prior scholarly efforts in which I took such joy. First, I would go to the abbey where the Christian monk, Brother Nicholas, and I would resume our translations of ancient Greek medical texts. He had been diligently translating from Greek to Latin and I from Latin to Arabic the work of Pedonius Dioscorides which would tell the world we knew of many cures and remedies, many operations and procedures to heal all of God's people. It had been a gift from the Christian ruler of Constantinople, Constantine VII, to cement relations with the Caliph's father.

Brother Nicholas would have many pages for my review since I had been away so long and I would have many to add to our volumes. As

I walked to the northern part of the city, the magnificent Cathedral of St. Vincent and its surrounding buildings sprawled across the public gardens and walkways. The Moors had permitted the Catholics to retain their cathedral, but purchased half of it for use as a mosque. And now, I, a Jew, was walking peacefully through the gardens to meet a monk to enrich the world's knowledge. Brother Nicholas greeted me warmly and expressed his delight at my safe return from captivity. He said he had prayed for me. And together, we returned to our joyous labors. There is something about the written word that always brings me joy and I can feel the same resonate in my brother here, the Irish monk. I avoided holding open my office for medical cures. Before me lay cures for asthma, foot fungus, bronchitis, cancer, constipation, diabetic ulcers, earache, gingivitis, menopause, irregular heartbeat, headaches, shingles and yeast infection. Brother Nicholas had arranged neat stacks, in alphabetic order in Latin as I sharpened my quill and took out a sheet to write on. The dictionary close at hand, Nicholas and I would work side by side in the cool room against the Cathedral wall. I could hear Nicholas humming softly some Christian hymn as he scratched out his pages from the ancient Greek codex rescued from Alexandria and brought to our shores a few centuries ago. In the process of rooting out heretical gnostic beliefs from the libraries and burning them, a few courageous monks had rescued this volume as well as much of the Greek wisdom of centuries past. Except for a few moments of respite to stretch and bend, to refresh our cups of tea, the morning went past in a trice and pages of new translations lay stacked in neat piles. Space had been left here and there for Nicholas' brothers to make illustrations of a few plants, as well as whatever struck his fancy from the Bible. It was well past noon when Nicholas excused himself for the prayer bell and I returned along the streets to the south.

My next stop was a long postponed visit to the school we had formed with Moses ben Hannoch. Alas, ben Hannoch had been dropped off at the port of Cadiz, poor and friendless. He had been a renowned scholar in Byzantium, but no one knew that. When he went to the local synagogue to ask for help and explained that he was a scholar, somehow I learned he was in al-Andalus and brought him to Cordoba. It immediately dawned on me that he should start a school to equal that of the one in Syria. I knew the Caliph should be told. He too saw the wisdom of having a school of the Mishnah and the Talmud in Cordoba and immediately endowed it. We bought a building near the synagogue with an apartment for Moses on the top floor. Moses' eminence drew scholars from all over – Morocco, Sicily, Byzantium and even Syria. Soon their commentary rivaled that of Damascus. But from this school poured poetry, Hebrew poetry in the melodious, extravagant style of the Moors, mathematics and geometry, and all manner of science. It became a bouquet in the Caliph's garden, amply aided by the Caliph's own library of 400,000 volumes in all manner of subjects. I dropped into various rooms as the scholars discussed and debated, some heatedly, some in a refined disciplined manner. Feeling that the school was in good hands, I left for home not far off and the mikveh bath, a reward for a fruitful day. But as I paced the inlaid lanes of the Juderia, one of the Caliph's men appeared.

"Dr. Shaprut, I bring news from the Caliph. Sancho has left the lands of Alonzo. I cannot say more but you must see the Caliph. He knows it is the Sabbath and must see you first thing Sunday."

"I see. Tell the Caliph I will be there at first light. Thank you." And so to the mikveh bath. What was now afoot? My peace had been all too short lived.

HASDAI TO CALIPH (AFTER SABBATH)

I made my now familiar way up to Madina al Zahra, the Caliph's magnificent complex to the north of the city and was immediately granted entrance through the gates and escorted to a small antechamber off to the side. Already the Caliph was there dressed only in a plain white shirt. It was to be a meeting known only between the two of us.

"Hasdai, please sit." There was already tea and pastries on the polished inlaid table of many differing woods. I sat.

"King Sancho has moved to Navarre." He said without ceremony. "It seems that Alonzo's son has blurted out Sancho's presence in his father's land. I now deem it unsafe for Sancho to remain in my Caliphate. Alonzo agrees. I have decided to support Sancho's quest for his return to power. My men tell me he is ready and his troops are ready. More importantly, he has many former vassals who will support him against Ordono, who has pleased no one it seems." I nodded. It was only a matter of time.

"Sancho does not know that I will support him. My presence must be kept a secret in this. The Christians may desert him if they know a Muslim supports his return. I need you to persuade Sancho to come here and pledge secret loyalty to me and guarantee the peace if he is successful. His appearance must be a secret." I nodded. The Caliph was calculating accurately.

"But I will send him some of my Christian troops in disguise. They will be happy to no longer have conflicted loyalty. They will serve the new Christian king while remaining loyal to me."

"Yes, your highness. It is complicated, but I see the wisdom of it."

"Go now to Sancho. You have earned his trust. Persuade him in this plan and bring him here in disguise. I will send you two bodyguards for the trip and an excellent horse. Your family will be protected and provided for as always."

"I knew somehow this would happen and have been ready for it." I will leave this morning."

"As always, I am grateful for this service." We shook hands and I left the small antechamber. Immediately outside the door on the cobblestone way were two large men mounted on fine Arabian horses holding a third already saddled for the trip. We would stop briefly at my house so I could assemble a few things. We trotted quietly down the street to my residence. I went in, kissed my wife who was still warm and drowsy in bed and left. As we reached the old Roman road, we broke into a gallop until Cordoba was far behind us.

Sancho had probably chosen a better place to hide. His grandmother was Toda of Pamplona and was his principal adviser. She was a Basque through and through. For many years, her people had been fiercely independent of the Leonese or the Castilians. But now, Sancho was in the open, his presence known and an easy mark for Ordono.

Matters had to be decided quickly. And quickly, I and my Christian bodyguards rode through the hills and into the flat dry land of the north. Camping briefly and eating on the run from the dried foods the bodyguards stowed in their saddlebags for the trip. After many days in the saddle, I was able to see the city of Navarre in the foothills of the Pyrenees to our north. We were now in dangerous territory. Ar-Rahman III had had numerous battles with the Christian rulers as had his predecessors. Sometimes this territory would be conquered and securely under the Caliph's control. When this happened, the people were not disturbed in their Catholic faith, but were required to pay the vizya, a tribute tax to Cordoba. At other times, they were able to throw off the Arab yoke. For now, it was hostile territory to the Caliph's men. While I carried a letter in three languages from the Caliph which designated me an envoy, the Christian soldiers often could not read any of the three languages and might just as well bring our heads to their king. It was more useful to let my Christian bodyguards do the talking, although they were mostly visigothic, while the Navarrese were mostly Basque. As I said, we were in perilous territory. We hoped that King Sancho had persuaded Toda to let us through unharmed, but such messages might be easily misunderstood, lost or simply ignored. My two bodyguards, however, were sturdy fellows well trained in combat if it should come to that.

The first encounter occurred as we attempted to ford a stream in the land of one of the nobles. Several men rode up to collect tribute. This unkind welcome was met with considerable negotiation. The noble's men were anxious to acquire a not insubstantial portion of the tribute. As our recalcitrance to pay grew more obvious, the five men started to circle us menacingly. At a sort of battle grunt from one of my bodyguards, they drew their broadswords in one swift motion and unhorsed two of the men with massive gouges in their chests. Their horses bucked and whinnied with wide eyes rose and galloped away. The remaining three men seemed a bit more reasonable and backed off a few paces. They would suffer much abuse from their noble at losing two good men and not securing their tolls; but they were not about to sacrifice their own lives in the face of such formidable bodyguards. My horse mercifully rose up only slightly and I was able to remain mounted, but I did manage to draw my short sword from its scabbard on the saddle. We took the weapons of the three men and had them lead us until we were out of the territory. I was able to see that the three men were no larger than I, while my bodyguards were both large men. These must have been Basques we encountered. They had very white complexions and black curly hair. My men were massive Visigoths, at least several stone heavier and many hands taller. I thanked the Caliph for his foresight and took out a piece of dried beef to munch on to keep my teeth from chattering as the waves of excitement and fear swept over me. Being an envoy was not at all like the life of a doctor, but somehow I was still drawn to it.

We trotted peacefully behind our would-be toll takers for a few miles and then left their horses tethered and tied them up. This would provide us with several hours of respite as we galloped out of the greedy noble's land on to Navarre.

We descended into the Ebro Valley and started our climb up the foothills of the Pyrenees. As we came into a view of the city, we saw ramshackle huts with children and dogs wandering through the dirt streets. At the bottom of the basin lay the center of the town. We had been forewarned that there were bandits in the area and little else of profitable economic activity.

Occasionally, a few horsemen on mangy animals trotted by, took a cursory look at my imposing bodyguards who now rode with their swords in hand as we cantered past. There was no resistance at all as we came up to what passed for a castle or a fort of some kind. There were liveried guards at the entrance to this building. It seemed a few of what looked like old Roman walls were still standing at odd intervals, some stones had been rolled in between with splotches of plaster holding them together. At other points, wooden partitions blocked the entrance and completed the perimeter. This was a poor excuse for a fortification. Clearly, it had been attacked and destroyed many times and not fared well.

About 200 years ago, the Moors had pushed this far north, but in the meantime, the area had been overrun by the Franks and the Vikings from the north and was occasionally under some self rule by the Basques. The inhabitants wandered about in rags and the children cried. Mangy dogs and feral cats stalked the streets. It was worse than Salamanca and bore the evidence of many destructive wars by many parties over the years, motivated for little other than pride or greed over the very meager assets of the populace. As we rode in, we drew some stares, but mostly dull glances.

I presented our letter from the Caliph to the guard and he disappeared inside for several minutes. Without much delay, both Sancho and a man he identified as his uncle and the "King" of Navarre came into the courtyard to greet us. We dismounted and several stable boys came to take our horses for feed and water. Other servants came to take our saddle bags.

I must say, Sancho looked in good health. He was much leaner and tanned. The other man, Enecco Crista, was somewhat plump and looked dissipated and unkempt. He had survived advances from the Franks to the east, but had not dealt with Moors for some time. Sancho greeted me warmly, but it was obvious that Enecco regarded us with suspicion. While he shook hands, he said little other than a mumble of some of the local dialect. He was short and stocky, had rough hands and was very pale with curly black hair which hung down his back. I was told that these people were Basques, an independent and unruly group. To myself, I noted that this land of Navarre was of little value and could not understand why anyone would want to conquer it or rule it. It certainly would yield little in tribute and cost much in military supervision. Nonetheless, Enecco seemed puffed up with his position as king and had his servants executing their duties with great ceremony in a language I could not understand.

Sancho bade me join him and Enecco for some wine at the table in the courtyard near the fountain and pond. As we sat, Toda, Sancho's grandmother and chief adviser, came to the table. While women were not often given much say in business matters, it was apparent that Toda bossed both men around and was given great deference.

"So, Hasdai, what does the Caliph say these days?" Toda was characteristically blunt.

Not many niceties.

"Your Highness," I said turning to Sancho, "I have given him my report that you are fit and trim as are your men. I see they have thrived on the diet I prescribed. I must congratulate you on your efforts."

Before Sancho could speak, Toda blurted, "Yes, Doctor, you have done well and we thank you. Now, what does the Caliph say?"

"Yes, Queen Regent, he wants to know what support you have from your former vassals."

Enecco now had to be heard. "Sir, may I ask who you are to question the King? You are a Jew, are you not?"

"Yes, Your Highness, I am a Jew. But I am the Caliph's envoy as you can see by the letter I have brought, sealed by his ring."

"Why would the Moor send a Jew?"

"Would you rather have a Moor or a Christian?"

"That is the question. Can we believe what the Caliph says, or does he seek to reconquer the north lands again?"

"Sir, he seeks an ally and peace."

"I do not like this alliance of Jews and Moors with us."

"I see. Well, then I will so advise the Caliph and you and Sancho may pursue your fortunes without him" I moved his chair as if to leave. We had already traveled a good distance and would not brook this insolence from parties seeking our Caliph's aide.

"Wait, wait," said Sancho. "Enecco, you have been most kind to afford me asylum, but Dr. Shaprut here has been most helpful and the Caliph's aid would be most helpful." I could sense the split growing in these men. Whom to rely on, Toda, Sancho or this Enecco? Could we lend our aid to Sancho and be betrayed later? Sancho and Enecco were two different men. Sancho, was educated but spoiled and self indulgent. Enecco, while unschooled, was perhaps crafty and mean spirited. He had narrow shoulders, a long pointed nose and small dark eyes. I thought of a plump raccoon. Toda was grateful to me but was able to vouch for Enecco, a relative of hers, and also guarantee Sancho's good faith.

"Sir," I said, directing my words to Enecco, "You must know that it was I who gave King Sancho the word of Alonzo's son which betrayed his location on Alonzo's land. King Sancho and Lord Alonzo determined it was no longer safe for Sancho there, so he sought refuge with you."

"That is true, King Enecco." Said Sancho. I could barely suppress a smirk at the notion of this man being referred to as a king – this unkempt ruffian.

"May I ask what troops, you sir, will contribute to King Sancho's campaign?" I directed my question to Enecco. He was not happy to be questioned by a Jew representing a Moor and he grimaced.

"None of your business."

"I am afraid, sire, it is the Caliph's business and thus, mine because he must evaluate the chances of success before expending his men in support of King Sancho."

Toda intervened, "Enecco, we must rely on our allies and we will need all we can get." Enecco shook his head in frustration. Here he would have to answer to a Jew, and a Moor and maintain a proper attitude to gain their support and appear to like it. I noted that this man would one day be an enemy and knowledge of his military assets would be useful.

"King Enecco," My words almost stuck in my throat, "What types of warriors do you have? Horse or foot? Do you have archers?"

"Why, do you think to attack us?"

"To what end, King Enecco? I see little of value in your region." I said it and immediately regretted it. It was said in spite and I had been provoked, but this man would prove to be a nuisance. We might not need him at all.

"We, sir, are on the pilgrimage route to St. James de Campostelo and host many wealthy travelers en route. They bring us much information of Ordono and much to pay for food and lodging on the way." Enecco was bragging of his meager economic assets.

"Ah, I see. And do you know Ordono well?" It struck me that he could easily become a traitor.

"I have known him for years." A vital piece of information. Who would this man choose to aid, Ordono or Sancho. More questions for the Caliph. What were the family connections and how strong? It would take much consideration before the Moors would intervene in a battle for a Christian throne and not receive anything in return other than a pledge of peace.

"Who will the Vikings back?" The Vikings were a constant threat to the north shore of Hispania. They were huge and wild charging out of their odd looking crafts and swinging axes. They roused themselves into some kind of frenzy and would be a dangerous foe.

Sancho said, "Yes, these Norsemen are a constant threat, but they will side with no one. They do not seem to be interested in ruling, only plunder and rape. No, they will ally with no one."

"Well, we have discussed enough for today. Let me consider what you have said and we will meet tomorrow."

Toda spoke. "Yes, Hasdai. You have much to consider. We will see you at dinner." And so, I retired to the wing of the soldiers' barracks where we were directed and took a late siesta. When I awoke, my bodyguards had returned as well.

"Dr. Shaprut, how did we do?" I was happy to hear 'we' because I was the only Jew and there probably were no Moors. It was comforting that my Christian bodyguards considered me to be their charge.

"Well and not well. This so called King Enecco is not friendly. Did you speak with his men?"

"Yes. They do not like him. He is very poor and pays them little. It seems the entire region is poor and lacks food. These men are mostly Basque and have some anger towards the Christians who were Visigoths or Franks. They are a strange breed. It seems that Enecco now runs the inns where the pilgrims stay on their way to Campostelo."

"Interesting. We will go to dinner soon. Be sure to explain how rich the Caliph is and how fair he is to the Christians and the Jews. I do not relish the idea of this Enecco sending my head back to the Caliph. Nor should I wish him in our rear if we attack Ordono."

Dinner was a solemn affair. A large bowl of some kind of stew was served from large pots into dinner bowls. Some bitter wine was poured liberally. I knew better than to ask if this meat was kosher, or the Arabic form, bilal. It had been a long day and a hard ride. God would forgive me for the indiscretions occasioned by necessity. It was very salty and fatty. I assured

God in my prayers later that I took little pleasure in it. I was punished later however by painful heartburn as I tried to sleep on the meager straw pallet Enecco had given us. Apparently, our Lord also punished my bodyguards in a similar fashion. They were most grateful I had brought along ginger and peppermint, which we made into a tea. For this respite, which must have cured their painful condition equal to my own, my bodyguards swore eternal loyalty. Tomorrow, we would have a bland breakfast of eggs and bread with more peppermint tea. And so we went to sleep.

Sometime after midnight I could feel a beautiful young maiden stroking my arm as I rose through the layers of darkness to wakefulness. Had Enecco sent me some comfort or had Sancho? Maybe even Toda. I grew more and more conscious only to see an elderly woman tapping me and saying, "Dr. Shaprut wake up!" Her accent made her request unclear, but she was at pains to get my attention.

I shrugged myself awake as my head spun through layers of reality and unreality. As I sat up on my straw pallet, the woman in some strange accent said, "King Sancho must see you now." I threw a robe on over my night shirt and slipped into my sandals and followed the woman to the stables not far off. There, Sancho and Toda sat and beckoned me to a vacant chair.

If this was a ploy to catch me unawares, it had succeeded. I was still quite groggy. It must be past midnight. The moon was descending, but shown brightly still. What were these people saying?

"Dr. Shaprut, you must help us. Will the Caliph lend us men? Will he fight for us?"

"I must tell you that I was of a mind to go home because of this Enecco. He would be poison to us."

"Yes. We know that, but we had no choice. After leaving Lord Alonzo, there were few who would grant us asylum. He is a relative and means no harm."

"So, you wish to start a campaign soon and must ask the Caliph for help."

"Yes, yes, Doctor."

"You must understand that he is Muslim. If you wish his protection, you must come to his court and prostrate yourself before him. If you do that, by his law, the Quran, he must protect you at all costs. Do you understand how deep his commitment will be?"

"So I have heard."

"If you betray him after he has granted you protection, his revenge will be terrible and he will never forget."

"We must have his help."

"You must swear an oath of loyalty."

"Yes. We will do whatever."

"Does Enecco know of this?"

"No. That is why we must meet in secret."

"What will you grant Enecco if you are successful?"

"He has not made his requests known, but I think he wishes to control the whole north of Hispania."

"If you ask me, I would insist that he take no part in this and receive no recompense later."

"I see. Will the Caliph say this?"

"I believe he will follow my recommendation."

"Now, who are the lords that will support you in this?"

"We will bring a list. But we think there will be 15,000 men."

"What types – horse, archer, foot soldiers?"

"We will include this in the list for the Caliph."

"You should keep in mind that the Caliph is a very devout Muslim, but also a man of great learning. We are fortunate that he interprets his Quran to respect both the Christians and Jews as worthy but inadequate predecessors and respects both the Jewish prophets and Jesus, whom he does not consider to be divine. In fact, he and the other Muslims do not believe Jesus died on the cross. He speaks Greek fluently and reads Latin as well as Hebrew. If you wish him to support you, you should demonstrate your own learning as well as your tolerance of Arabs and Jews. One word from Enecco will destroy your chances."

"I see. I have no issue with these things."

"I would bring him a gift of some example of your knowledge and education. Gifts of material value alone will mean little to him."

"May I ask what he expects in return? Tribute? Hostages?"

"That is his to determine. I do not believe he wishes to extend his realm to the north into Estremadura, and he certainly has no designs on Navarre."

"Dr. Shaprut, I thank you for all your advice and counsel. I have gained much respect for your Jews and I believe, you are entitled to much tolerance. My family and heirs will always grant deference to your people. They will never again have fear in Hispania."

"I thank you for that, King Sancho."

"You must come in disguise to the Cathedral of St. Vincent in Cordoba in ten days time. You, King Sancho and also Toda. You must be prepared to prostrate yourself in front of the Caliph. He will review your list first and then summon you to court if he will take up your cause."

"You must exclude Enecco from all of this."

"I understand. We will see you in ten days time at St. Vincent."

"Ask for Father Nicholas and he will tell you where to go."

"Doctor Shaprut, how can we ever thank you?"

"I serve the Caliph. Show your gratitude to him."

HASDAI RETURNS TO CALIPH

I felt I could travel at leisure, protected as I was by my two Christian bodyguards. As we were leaving Navarre for the long ride back, Sancho made sure to provision us with many delicacies including cured meats, dried fruit and ample skins of wine. It had obviously not occurred to Sancho at the time that none of these items were kosher. Relying on the rule of necessity, I helped myself to many of these delicacies on the way home, but promised many prayers of repentance and periods of fasting. Even the squirrels and pigeons the bodyguards hunted and turned on a spit by the evening fire had a nice flavor in view of the feeling of success I enjoyed as I envisioned the advances I expected as Sancho returned to his throne.

As we trotted, or just ambled along the way, I permitted my mind to drift into the many things I should consider when back in Cordoba. First, of course, was my wife and family, but then it drifted onto the Khazars, to Byzantium and the east.

The Khazars were a large pagan nation living in the Caucusus Mountains who, for reasons never very clear had converted to Judaism en masse and now wished to be instructed further in its learning. The Khazar king probably felt pressure both from the Byzantine Christians and the Syrian Arabs and so chose neutrality symbolized by a faith in Judaism.

The world was in flux just now; the rise of Islam just three centuries ago and its rapid expansion, the overthrow of old Rome and the many disparate so-called barbarians in the west who now espoused Christianity spread fear and confusion on the earth. Could the Jews survive? Who knew? They had outlived the Roman empire which had destroyed their homeland. The decline of paganism had left religious vacuums. But mainly poverty, sickness, famine and war after war by brutal men seeking power, plunder, slaves and recognition embroiled the known world. Would mankind ever find a way out of this chaos? The Caliph of Cordoba was a shining beacon in the world of tolerance and knowledge, of science and the arts, and prosperity. I could feel a glow of satisfaction as I hoped to bring peace to al-Andalus and Hispania by restoring the educated Sancho to power and pacifying the peninsula by a treaty of his creation. It certainly was God's work and I said a prayer as my horse jostled me along the path. Soon they came upon what was left of the old Roman road and were joined by many travelers to and fro.

I must also write to the Queen of Byzantium, Helena, and make a connection between her Byzantine Empire and that of ar-Rahman. I knew enough from sailors and other travelers from the east that Byzantium was hard pressed. It was an excellent time for the Caliph to pursue a connection with this ancient but respected empire against its enemies. Letters of greeting and negotiation passed between the Caliph and Constantine VII to shore up mutual exchanges of art. I, of course, knew that Queen Helena was the power to direct his correspondence to. So, while the letters were between the Caliph and Constantine, they were read by Helena and Hasdai.

Constantine VII was an ugly and shy man who had been designated an heir to the Byzantine throne since the age of two. He had been the first born but bastard son of the previous king. His regents nonetheless deemed him the "prophyrogenitus" – to the purple born, meaning of royal descent, since his mother made sure to give birth to him in the royal throne room to legitimize his right to succession. As regents came and went, Constantine grew up, but remained a life-long scholar willing to leave politics, war and governance to his regents who squabbled, assassinated one another, and defended the realm on his behalf.

The Caliph felt a kinship with this scholarly emperor and made contact with him, although his wife and most powerful regent controlled this as well as other liaisons.

In my head, I prepared long letters to the king of the Khazars and Constantine VII. I foresaw a world of peace stretching across the northern Mediterranean with commerce, science and the arts flowing back and forth among cultures led by enlightened rulers of different faiths.

Yes, this I dreamed as I trotted along the old Roman road, which had survived where Rome itself was a looted and unpopulated cow pasture. It was the middle of the tenth century and the world seemed full of possibilities.

GENERALS REPORT TO CALIPH

I was again summoned up to Medina Zahra, the Caliph's huge complex north of the center. The guards waved me through and I was directed to a large hall with a polished oak table running almost the entire length. Large shields and crossed ornate spears were hanging in between hanging arrases of silk or wood in a variety of geometric designs. Several of the Caliph's Moorish advisers were seated at one end of the table drinking tea and helping themselves to trays of fruit and pastries. At the end, two Moorish generals in full formal attire stood with what looked like large scrolls at their sides. I greeted everyone. Two Christian counselors of the Caliph, Rodrigo and Alphonso came in shortly thereafter. They were large fellows in heavy leather tunics with designs of eagles hammered in gold on the chest. I made myself a cup of tea and took a macaroon and waited for ar-Rahman with the others. Suddenly, the two double doors at the end of the hall were thrown open and the Caliph with several attendants strode down the hall. He took his place at the head of the table. With a nod from the Caliph, the two generals came forward and spread two scrolls out on the table placing weights at the corners to hold them flat. The scrolls were each maps of north al-Andalus showing the entire region from Navarre, going west to the edge of the kingdom of Leon and the ocean. Notations had been added at certain points of each map. With another nod from the Caliph, one of the Moorish generals began to speak. He was a large, broad shouldered man in the dress uniform djellaba of the military. He had a number of ribbons around his neck, each holding a medal, some in hammered gold or silver, some in cloisonné, awards from various campaigns he had been on in service of the Caliph and his father before.

As he spoke, I understood that he had fully debriefed Sancho as to who the nobles were in the north and which of them would back Sancho and which might side with Ordono in a war. Sancho's people had their regions outlined in red with inked notations as to how many fighting men we might expect to support Sancho. Below the total numbers were listed the numbers of each military specialty – archers, horsemen, engineers and foot soldiers. Sancho's number exceeded Ordono's by a substantial amount – 13,000 to 8,000. However, we were cautioned to take this information with a grain of salt, since Sancho needed our support and might well be exaggerating. Sancho claimed he was assured of victory.

It did not take long to dawn on me that the Caliph had succeeded in getting the entire military assets of the northern Christians to be used in the event of future war with them. The

Caliph, of course, had from his various spies, assembled similar numbers, but this was perhaps more accurate and reliable. It came from a Christian monarch himself.

This intelligence would be stored away for future use in the event of perhaps another march northward or a defense of his own territories later. Most of all, it described the troops and defined how later battles might be fought. Archers could fire from a great distance and flood the battlefield indiscriminately with missiles, sometimes flaming, on the infantry and mounted forces. The number and skill of the engineers told the Caliph about the use of catapults, arbalettes and other machines necessary for sieges. The ability to erect large towers for placing men on and over the parapets of a walled city was a vital factor. For the most part, the general was optimistic that the northern Christians lacked planning and sophistication as well as funds. Their favorite form of attack was for these large foot soldiers and mounted knights was to charge downhill screaming with lances, axes, broadswords or maces. The fury of their battle cries and the size of the average soldier would intimidate many enemies. The battle would result in a large area covered with bleeding bodies which would stink mightily for weeks depending on the weather, and swarms of mosquitos and maggots.

The Arabs had learned battle tactics from the Greeks and Romans, which usually involved luring the main force into a trap while encircling their flanks and attacking them from the rear. The use of terrain – swamps, rivers, and the protection of forests – were by now second nature to these generals.

Next in the general's speech was the choice of terrain for the Caliph's men. The Moors were far better horsemen and could use speed to their advantage. Their weapons were of finer steel and sharper. But most of all, their engineers were the most capable. They could break different battle machines down into component parts and reassemble them on the battlefield to great advantage. Siege towers and catapults could rain down burning oil, stones and pieces of jagged iron on the foe. Arbalettes were large cross-bows which were mounted on a large device with a handle which propelled arrows or darts by using gears to increase the strength of the force necessary to pull back the bow string and accelerate the dart down a guided path. The darts could fly with tremendous speed and pierce armor. The Moors had used the same principle to impel large spears for long distances into the ranks of advancing forces.

The use of speed in attacking and flanking the line of the enemy was further aided by the use of chain mail, much lighter than plated armor. It could still deflect most arrows and glancing sword strokes, but permitted the mounted horsemen and foot soldiers much greater maneuverability.

With this in mind, the general then considered a direct attack on Leon itself, going directly at Ordono's men. The surrounding village and the number of innocent inhabitants would have made such an attack slow and difficult.

The best chance of success would be to lure Ordono into an open field for combat. Hopefully, they would be in a valley where they could be susceptible to being surrounded or outflanked. Terrains of different sorts were considered and suggested. After his lengthy discourse, the general and his colleague were directed to sit at the table while alternatives were discussed.

One of the Moorish advisers, al Hakim, an elderly man and on the previous Caliph's counsel stated, "Gentlemen, I believe it will be difficult to coordinate the battle plan if we mix Moors and Christians together. It might be best if we assign specific responsibilities to each. This will avoid miscommunication and even possible infighting. We should encircle the edges of Ordono's advance while the Christians supporting Sancho hold the center. Our archers and arbalettes could fire at signals from a distance."

"Yes, al Hakim. A worthy suggestion."

Al Hamsur rose. "I think we could expand on that point. We could be hiding in a protected location and once the battle is joined we could descend on the enemy from a more strategic angle and surprise them at their weak point."

Finally, the Caliph arose and spoke. "Gentlemen, I am lucky to have such wise counsel. We will incorporate your ideas. But we must allow Sancho to plan the attack with our aid and guidance so that he will not be suspicious of our motives. It might be too easy for us to turn on his men and defeat both sides and regain the north. That is not my goal. I do not consider the north a valuable asset. Salamanaca, Navarre and Pamplona are poor and have been devastated by prior wars as have many of the areas in the north. I do not wish to expand the area I must police and defend, and take into my populace unruly elements which oppose me. We will fight solely for the limited purpose of restoring Sancho, who then will sign a peace treaty and enable al Andalus to be a peaceful and prosperous oasis in the midst of the strife and confusion to our south. Do we all agree to support Sancho in his effort to regain the throne?"

The consensus was strong in this regard.

"Very well, I will send my generals to negotiate a battle plan with Sancho's men. I believe they have been well counseled on how to proceed." The Caliph rose, turned and left. The war counsel now also rose, nodded to each other and were escorted out different gates of the Medina Zahara.

As I reached the outer gate with the others, one of the guards motioned me over to him and told me to go to a small office just off the large promenade to my left. I went as instructed and saw a servant standing by one of the doors along the way. "Ah, Dr. Shaprut, please come in and sit. The Caliph will be with you shortly." I went in and sat. Soon the Caliph came in without ceremony and joined me at the table.

"Hasdai, I would like to discuss some of these events with you alone. Needless to say, what we discuss does not leave this room."

"Yes, your excellency. I fully understand."

"First, is Sancho ready for war?"

"From what I hear, yes. As we heard, his men outnumber Ordono's and his compatriots are more loyal. He is better liked and few people trust Ordono. In general, I would have to say yes."

"Does he need us?"

"I would guess no. He is sufficiently prepared without us."

"Then why should I cooperate with him?"

"Two reasons. First, if he wins, we may have a grateful ruler to our north and future peace. I believe you are correct when you say you do not wish to expand the area you rule. Better to consolidate what you have and have a secure border to your north while the Berbers attack you from the south. You do not need to have battles on two fronts. Second, it is always good to be on the winning side. If it does not cost much, it is better than not participating at all."

"How do I limit the cost?"

"First, I would never agree to be under the command of one of Sancho's generals. I would keep my forces entirely separate as you said. We should be in reserve, not at the front lines. We should use our archers and arbalettes rather than our foot soldiers. But, mostly I would avoid an open battle altogether. Perhaps a siege. We surround them, starve them out until they surrender."

"Hasdai, I must say you confirm my thoughts. But first, we must have Sancho beg our cooperation. That is the key. He must feel he needs us and will be loyal to our treaty afterward."

"Agreed. But Excellency, I have another idea as well. I do not think we should attack Leon itself. In a siege, the people of Leon may grow to hate us. I suggest we go after a small town first and lure Ordono into a battle there."

"What do you have in mind?"

"Zamora. It is to the west of Leon. It is well fortified, but does not have many sources of supply around it and will not withstand a siege for long."

"I can see that."

"Plus, we can reach it by water. It is on the Douro River. We could load our forces on at Cadiz, then travel quietly up the coast and go east on the Douro and land our forces there. We could cut off any enemy forces coming from the west or south. It would prevent a long difficult trek over land from here north and conceal our presence until the last possible time."

"Interesting. A water passage versus a march overland. I will have to consult my generals. And Zamora. I have been there. It is extremely well fortified and will be difficult to use a direct attack. It has very good stone fortifications, but it sits on a flat terrain. The Romans used it as an outpost years ago. So, Zamora versus Leon. Another question. Of course, we must see what Sancho wishes to do before we suggest it to him."

"Yes, of course, excellency. Just my humble thoughts."

"Always valued, Hasdai."

"How are your merchant boys doing in Leon?"

"Quite well. They are quite profitable and, I understand, have already repaid a large portion of your loan."

"Yes. They have. But have they been threatened?"

"They say no. They seem to have fitted very nicely into the small Jewish population there and no one has come asking about them."

"Good. We will need more reports as we prepare for war. I will double my messengers to them. I must say, I believe I will help Sancho, but on my terms. I will summon you when he and Queen Toda come to court."

"Very well, your excellency." The two parted with a warm hand shake.

CALIPH'S GIFT TO YAEL

On the way back from the meeting with the Caliph, I stopped first to see Brother Nicholas and spent a few hours translating pages for their new Arabic encyclopedia of herbal medicine. This was a relaxing and refreshing time to spend after the tension of the meeting. The quiet solemn presence of Nicholas always served to soften the pace of my life. Somehow, the solid walls of the cathedral also were a calming influence, permitting me to think and turn things over in my mind. By midday, I was hungry and left for a meal at one of the taverns back at the school near the synagogue. This tavern was kosher and run by one of the local families. A stew of chicken in lemon and olive oil with a few bits of pita bread was just what I wanted. Sitting outside at a long table, my presence always attracted a few men who stopped to pass the time and engage me in a few troubling questions of Jewish law, medical problems and the politics of the Caliph. I always enjoyed the company and the deference these men paid to my answers. Often they wanted to pay for my meal, but I politely refused, even when the innkeeper refused to let me pay. After all, my presence had attracted more than a few customers.

The school was next. I was presently surprised to meet a few of the new scholars arrived recently from Byzantium and Morocco. They wished to learn some of the specialties of the school so they could return to their homes and broach these new subjects to their own followers. Again, I was bombarded with novel questions by the students who wanted my response to some of the knottier problems they had been discussing. Again a pleasant time in debate and response – the exercise so familiar to Jewish men over the centuries. No part of the Torah or haftorah would ever grow too old or too familiar not to provoke debate.

And so, relaxed and refreshed but longing for a bit of solitude, I came home. It was late afternoon and I could hear the shrieks of my daughter, Yael as I came in the door. Torn to pieces on the table was a package, apparently just opened by Yael. Rachel stood to one side with her hand over her mouth.

"Hasdai, what is this?" Since I had just come in the door, I had no answer. My daughter was prancing around holding a beautiful new djellaba up in front of her and emitting nothing but teenage girl squeals.

"When did this come?"

Rachel, the only other coherent one in the room said, "A servant of the Caliph just delivered it, addressed to Yael."

"It must be a gift in recompense for my work."

"Oh, father, I love it." At last, from Yael.

It was indeed a beautiful garment of cotton and silk in colors of red, orange and yellow, with gold thread glistening here and there.

"Yael, you must not wear this except for special occasions. It will make the other girls jealous."

"Oh mother, can't I just wear it one day to our school. I want some of the girls to die of envy."

"That is what I was afraid of."

"But to have it and not to wear it is such a crime. And some of those girls from the rich families are such snobs."

"Your strength is in your brain and your character, not in material possessions. We have talked about this."

"But just once! I want them to gasp in jealous rage."

"That is not our way. Remember Joseph. No good came to him over his coat of many colors."

"I know, but just once?"

"Alright, once, then it goes into the trunk for special occasions."

"Could I also wear some kohl on my eyes?"

"No, out of the question!"

"Aw,"

I could only look on in amazement at my women. The Caliph had given my daughter a blessing – the perfect gift and it fit perfectly. How had he known? He was indeed a smart man. Yael continued to prance with the djellaba as her mother crossed her arms and looked skyward.

HASDAI SPEAKS TO THE MERCHANTS

As I left the meeting, I rushed to speak to the merchants who sailed the coasts of Portugal up to Britannia and back. I took a short ferry ride down to the port of Cadiz. There, I stopped in at the local Jewish quarter and began to ask for the merchants. They were not hard to find. Jews had dispersed from Palestine and outward for several hundred years and established small outposts in the seaports and river cities throughout Europe. Even in biblical times, nearly 40% of the Jewish population lived outside of Palestine. The merchants of Cadiz maintained their own chandlery – a shop for provisioning vessels of all sorts with dried food, salt fish and meats, grain, water, rope, sails – in fact, everything a ship might need except cargo and even some of that. A small café with tables sat outside the chandlery. It was a cool breezy day as the winds blew off the Atlantic. The chandlery was surrounded by all sorts of industry of a port city. The smell of fresh caught fish was a perpetual presence, of course, but men labored continually rolling carts back and forth between large warehouses and the ships across the wooden planks of the dock area.

I was directed to the café and told to ask for David Rabeeya, one of the Jewish merchants. As foretold, he was seated with several other merchants, smoking a pipe and sipping from a glass of tea.

"Senor Rabeeya."

"Yes, that is me."

"May I speak to you about a matter of some importance?"

"By all means, please sit with us."

I sat and ordered a glass of tea and was introduced to the other men.

"I am Hasdai Shaprut. I have been asked by the Caliph to provide some information about navigation routes."

"Wait, I know of a Dr. Shaprut, a famous doctor from Cordoba. He pays the passage for scholars to come to Cordoba from Morocco."

"Yes, I have done that."

"Then you are most welcome. So a Jew on a mission for the Caliph."

"Again. This is what I am doing here."

"So, you are among friends. Many of we Jews have warehouses in the port. How can we help you?"

"The Caliph would like to explore the possibility of opening trade with the north of Portugal, to the port of Porto and along the Douro River. He has been told it is possible. But I wanted to check with those possibly more knowledgeable."

"So the port of Porto and the river Douro, eh? Yes, we can do that." He looked at the other men at the table. They nodded.

One of them, looking weather beaten and grey-bearded said, "The winds are strong, blowing east as you go up the coast and you can make good time going north. When will you sail?"

"September."

"A good time. Just before the cold winds blow down from the north. The town of Porto has a large harbor and my cousin Avram works out of there. There is much timber and excellent sweet wine."

"How about the river Douro, is it safe to travel? How is the current?" "As you probably know, the current flows from the mountains toward the west into the sea, but in October it will be lower. The snow will long have melted. March to June are not good months. The current is too strong. You may need to row the whole way. In September, you may use some sail and the river will be calm."

"How about the people who live along the river, are they dangerous?"

"There are a few farming settlements here and there. Some river traffic, mostly small boats. The south of the river is controlled by the Moors. The Peres family rule the north."

"Who governs that land?"

"No one really knows. For a while the Christian Visigoths, but they were somewhat disorganized. Then the Arabs came in, but did not seem to take much interest. The area is mountainous and rocky. There are some old Visigoth towns, but I think maybe it belongs to the Arabs. Sometimes the Vikings attack the town of Porto, rob the settlements, rape a few women, but they leave and go back north."

"What will the Caliph do up there?"

"I'm not sure. Maybe a colony. Maybe a port. His navy tells him it is safe, but they have never been there on a regular basis. I guess you each have."

"I buy some timber up there. There are also some old gold mines, but that is too dangerous. They have a sweet wine I buy sometimes. And, of course, olive oil."

"Have you ever been up the river?"

"Many times. It is wide enough. In the summer, it is a decent cruise."

"So, Dr. Shaprut. You are from the Jewish area in Cordoba. Do you know my cousin, Solomon ben Hannoch?"

"Why of course, he is a merchant on the river there."

Soon requests for other names flowed. Some I knew, some I didn't. I was not a merchant, but it was a small town for Jews and I knew most of the community and had treated the families.

"Please Hasdai, (now it was Hasdai), please share a plate of sardines with us." The sardines were large and grilled in a buttery garlic baste. I could not resist this seaside treat. The men sat for several hours, eating, exchanging gossip on those they knew in each city. As the sun passed midday and started to sink, I had to leave to catch the ferry back to Cordoba. I left, but added a list of names for the Caliph to contact in Cadiz. A list of reliable commercial contacts and loyal subjects.

MEETING WITH CALIPH'S ADVISORS

Today was the regular meeting of the Caliph's advisors, two Christian nobles, two Arab nobles and Hasdai. As usual, the men were escorted into the large conference room at Madina al Zahra, the Caliph's magnificent complex of official buildings, mosques, ponds, cloisters, and gardens filled with exotic flowers and shrubs as well as colorful birds. Peacocks strutted slowly around the gardens and doves cooed under the eaves.

Servants bustled in and out of the conference room bearing trays of fruit, pastries and ornate ewers of tea. I marveled at the way the Caliph had welded together alliances with the Christians his predecessors had conquered. Conquered is too strong a word for what happened as the Moors came north. The Visigothic kings, warlords, nobles and knights were not liked. They were brutal, disorganized and basically knew only the art of battle, drinking and hunting. Many towns welcomed the urbane Moorish rulers and secretly aided their short sieges of the towns. But then, the Caliph's grandfather and father developed an allegiance with the Christian nobles. Intermarriage, of course. Although the Christians' young daughters very much feared being one of four wives and living in a gilded cage their whole lives, but word got back that they were well treated, lived in luxury and could raise their children in peace. This life was different from that where their brutal husbands might come home drunk, beat them and then run off to their concubines. Perhaps it was the alcohol, perhaps it was the Christian disdain for women – even those made to preserve strategic alliances. St. Paul had made that clear. The castles, such as they were, were cold and damp. The marriages between the Moors and the Christians proved not to be difficult for the Christian women. But the Christian men could often appreciate the alliances as well. Often, long standing blood feuds had chased some knights and nobles out of the northern Christian alliances. Occasionally, a history of treachery was repeated among the nobles and warlords. But the Moors were tolerant. Even in their holy book, the Quran, they respected the Christian religion, worshipped their prophets and allowed them to retain their cathedrals and churches. No, life under the Moors was not bad. And so, their leaders sat on the Caliph's council as trusted advisors.

Soon the Caliph swept into the room. He was dressed in all white with some gold thread at the borders. He was handsome and well groomed.

"Gentlemen, I've much to discuss. Mostly, the new alliance with Sancho I. You have reviewed our war plans and I now seek your advice." It was a subject all had anticipated.

The first to speak was one of the Christians. He was tall, a head taller than the Caliph and Hasdai. His blond hair hung long and lank from his head. He wore his leather breast plate.

"Excellency, I have reviewed the list of Sancho's so-called allies in this battle. I do not like or trust them. I feel Sancho will be surprised when they desert or may even switch sides. It has happened before with some of them."

"Could you give my scribe a list and some of the history of these nobles? They should be isolated from Sancho's main force so as not to corrupt it. We should also be in a position to advise Sancho of any bad faith they show. When he forms his government, he must not reward them with lands or positions of power. These men are corruptible and would make poor allies for us to cultivate."

"Yes, Excellency."

The men reviewed the map of the area around Zamora, at length describing the elevated areas, the forested areas, the watercourses and swamps. They discussed the positions of the archers and the arbalettes and catapults. The battle plan began to take shape.

I now rose. "Excellency and esteemed members of the council, my sources tell me that we may expect some difficulty as we enter the mouth of the Douro River. The land is controlled by the Peres family who have been in power for over a century, since Urmara Peres ousted the Moors. They are more situated in the area north of the Douro. As we proceed east, we may expect a fight or an ambush. The river Douro is quite wide and we could not be reached by arrows from the shore I am told, but we may be attacked by small boats. I am sure there will be men on the shore prepared to ambush any land-based troops. We will need to make some provision for this. We will have a large and vulnerable flotilla."

The men nodded.

One of the generals looked at the Caliph who nodded. "Dr. Shaprut, the Caliph has been aware of this problem since our route was planned down the Douro River. Yes. The Christians do control the area north of the Duoro and yes, we think, if our plans are discovered, there will be some opposition. We don't think moving 5,000 men and supplies will not go unnoticed. We also believe Ordono may have spies who have told him of our plans. We are prepared for this trouble, but do not think the Peres family who rule the area or Ordono can afford to focus too much attention on us when he will face Sancho and his allies coming west on the route to Campostello. It may in fact be to our advantage for him to split his forces."

"I see. Well thought out, General." The general nodded sternly.

"Oh and Dr. Shaprut, we may have a surprise for the Peres family if they want to aid Ordono by harassing us on the Douro. The General looked to the Caliph and the Caliph nodded in approval. The consensus at the meeting was that this was a subject best left alone."

The conferees moved on to other topics and as the noon approached, they rose to leave. As they were being escorted out, the Caliph had one of his men detain me discretely and ask me to stay.

When the room was empty, the Caliph beckoned me to a seat near him at the table.

"Doctor, we have been receiving very good reports from your men in Leon. Your "Samuel" and "Eli" have been able to provide our daily messengers with much information – who visits Ordono, the troop buildup, the expense of acquiring material, all very helpful. I can see I made a wise investment in those two. By the way, it is not yet a year and they have paid off much of my loan. I must ask though, are they in danger?"

"As you know, your Excellency, Jews are always in danger of some kind. The men are now well established in the Jewish community there. They are receiving many approaches from marriage brokers. At the least, they can hide in the small Jewish community there. Ordono would have to do something dreadful to the entire community. But they all pay their vizya–

the tax that supposedly frees them from military service, but is actually a rather hefty tax on the Jews. Ordono needs the money now. He is a bad governor and is careless with his finances usually, but now with the war buildup he is even shorter than usual. He needs his Jews. We are like a sponge. We sop up money because of our superior commerce and the ruler squeezes us when he needs funds."

"Will you let me know if they need to be removed from Leon?"

"Of course, excellency. May I ask you a question?"

"What is on your mind?"

"The Berbers in the south who threaten you. Who are they and should we worry about them?"

"As usual, a good question. Yes, it is always bad to be fighting wars on two fronts. That is why I support Sancho in the north, to gain a cease fire and a no man's land in Estremadura. The investment of 5,000 men, horses, boats and material is small, and risks little. We will see little of the fighting and lose few men while the Christians will exhaust themselves, between Ordono and Sancho and their allies. A peace up north will let us concentrate on the south."

"These Berbers are an uncouth lot. They follow a different hadith of the Quran. You see, we Muslims are not all one. Although we believe in Mohammed and the Quran, we have many political factions which arise. Some are based on the rich versus the poor, but mainly they are tribal. Rather than seek accommodation with one another, the tribes prefer to fight. It is the old desert warfare from before the Quran. Many people do not understand this and see us as one people. Because the Quran makes many different statements on the same subjects, it is possible to adopt one and exclude the others."

"Yes, I have tried to read the Quran and have often become confused."

"And so with our people. These Berbers chose to follow a hadith – a teaching or interpretation which permits them to be brutal, warlike and greedy. We Sunnis believe in education, good government and peace. I fear that these Berbers threaten our occupation of al-Andalus and will bring down the golden age we have allowed to grow. You see, we are like the Jews. We believe in the rule of law, we adopt your prophets and even your Torah. We see the Allah who wants peace and justice. Others see only war and conversion by any means."

"How goes your war against them?"

"So far, they are a nuisance, but an expensive nuisance. They weaken us against the Christians from up north who have already begun to recapture territory. They call it the reconquista."

"Is there anything I can do to help?"

"No, I am afraid this is a matter we Arabs must decide among ourselves."

HASDAI AND THE TOWER OF BABEL

While the Caliph and his generals set about preparing for the assault on Zamora, I had some time to myself. As I had done sporadically over the past few months, I declared my medical office open for business in the morning hours. Patients of all sorts turned up outside the office. My daughter, Yael, served as my receptionist and wrote down each patient's name carefully and the complaint. She then went into the Doctor's treating room and took notes as I examined and treated the ailment. Yael wrote down the prescribed treatment and gave a list of herbs or medicines to the patient to be filled by Rachel, her mother. The hours moved by briskly and the office cash box filled rapidly with coins of all sorts. As the sun reached its height at noon, I had to rest and told the line of patients I would be back the next day, but had to retire for now. Some mumbles and groans arose from the crowd.

Because all the family had worked so diligently, I took the two women to the Jewish restaurant and ordered a stew of chicken in lemon sauce with rice and a large pitcher of tamarind juice. Yael, even at 14 was quick to pick up the regimen her father prescribed in various cases and kept notes of them. She would soon exhaust all the levels of teaching at the local synagogue school and would go on to the university. Although Arab women never attended, some Christian women, especially nuns, were among the few females. Among the Jews, there were also a few women attending. She had visited the university several times and loved the atmosphere of debate and argument in the cafes near the university where professors regularly lectured. The Caliph's massive library was open to all students and in its cool sheltered halls, students quietly absorbed the wisdom of the ages – the Greeks, the Arabs, the Jews – all sorts of books, scrolls and codexes were stacked or shelved around the walls. There was a musty smell in the place which the students and scholars from all over grew to love. It was an oasis of peace. Soon, Yael would attend and join the rarified, if musty, air of wisdom. While Hasdai and Rachel had received very pointed overtures from the richer Jewish families to broker a marriage for their daughter, both held firm that she would also become a physician. Although she could never treat Arab men, and Christian men would disdain advise from a woman, she would be able to treat women of all sorts and could study their particular ailments and concerns.

After the midday meal, we sat in the coolness of the garden in the rear of our house and said nothing, just resting among the potted shrubs and flowers around the small pond. Soon it would be time for me to drop by the school I had founded and see Moses ben Hannoch , the scholar imported to run it. After a brief nap under the shade of the palmetto tree, I rose and walked over to the school rooms. My appearance there drew not only the school boys and melameds, but also a number of men of different callings to hear what wisdom I might impart. The class today would take place in the small ampitheatre. As I walked in, a smattering of polite applause greeted me.

"Ah, gentlemen, always a pleasure to address you. I learn as much from you as I hope you do from me. Today, I have a prepared message, but I would like to do something different. I would like you to pose some questions and I will respond, or you may also respond if so inclined. So please, raise your questions that we might enlighten each other." While the men were used to a healthy debate and discussion every Sabbath, this formula for a school was something new. I had been perhaps reading Socrates and Plato and was trying to adopt their form of learning by dialogue. The Greek was once again influencing the Hebraic.

After a few moments hesitation, one of the boys just recently called to the pulpit to read his Torah portion for his bar mitzvah, ventured to stand.

"Doctor, I have wondered about this for some time. God has been part of many religions and religions from what I hear preach love, respect for our neighbors, and a respect for the law, but yet almost every religion fights with the other religions and tries to force others to convert. I don't see how you can force a man to believe what he does not want to. But why, if God made the world, does he permit men to fight each other in the name of religion?"

"Excellent . . . excellent, . . ."

"Joshua, sir."

"Excellent Joshua. The great question. Let me think." He paused a few moments, staring up to the sky. Was he in prayer or just organizing his thoughts? "Alright." At last. "The ways of God are unknowable and beyond our comprehension, but sometimes we see a glimmer of light. I have thought of the Tower of Babel. As we know, often the Lord created the flood and destroyed much of the wickedness in the world, he saved Noah and his family. Somehow, these descendants decided to build a tower to each god in the heavens. When our God saw this, he confused everyone by having them all speak a different language. And so, the vast building scheme went for naught as the people of Babel scattered about the face of the earth. We all know this story."

"As I see it, man's greatest skill is the use of language. With it, he can communicate with others, make laws, create art and poetry. To take that away from him is truly a severe punishment. But just as God seems to have punished Adam by giving him the knowledge of good and evil, the separation of man into different languages may be viewed as a punishment or a gift. Perhaps a test."

"The separation of man into different religions may also be like the Tower of Babel. It may be a punishment, a gift or a test. A gift, you ask? How so? Perhaps we are meant to strive to manage a world with our knowledge of good and evil until we achieve the kingdom of God, by our own will, by our own free will, and not merely by a gift from God."

"Many rulers use religion to encourage men to go to war, when it is really to enrich themselves and gain new land. This would be a false doctrine. Just as God separates us by language, he separates us by religion. It is a test. We must learn to live together and learn each other's language, accommodate each others' religion and reach a level of peace and tolerance by ourselves."

"We are in such a world now. Here in al-Andalus, we live in peace, we tolerate each other, and we exchange the knowledge our separate languages have denied us so far. Could this be what God intends for us?"

A stunned silence ensued. Joshua, who was still standing, sat. Then a few mumbles among the men sitting together, then some louder voices. At last Simeon, one of the older men from the back, rose and spoke. "Brilliant, Doctor, brilliant. And what are we the Jews supposed to do?"

"Is that Simeon? Yes, that is you Simeon. I don't know, Simeon. The Jews are still a mystery to me. God keeps us around for some reason. Maybe, we are a test; a test, a punishment and a gift – all in one. We suffer, we learn and we endure, and a remnant remains. Enjoy these times in al-Andalus, we are at peace, we prosper and we survive."

I had sparked a lively debate. The popular issues – What does God think?, who are we and what are we doing here. The discussion went on all afternoon, some citing the Torah, some even the Greeks and Moslems. I sat back and listened with interest. I had done my job. They were educating themselves, the secret mission of a teacher. In the late afternoon, I walked home through the narrow streets deep in thought. Yes, it was a good day. On the way I saw David coming home from school and bought each of us an orange drink from the street vendor. We sat in the shade as David told me what he was doing in school. When we got home, Rachel was roasting a few fish on the grill. There was a salad of fruit and a mixture of peas, endive and a cactus pear or two. I mused how the Caliph had dinner. Did he chose a wife and her children? Did he dine with his close associates? Did he enjoy family life? It was not something I could ask the Caliph. Ah well, another mystery to ponder – monogamy and family, or many wives and total dominance.

FERRY BACK FROM CADIZ

I was glad to have my plan confirmed by local merchants who were in the sea lanes and river lanes every day. Somehow, although I had no distrust of people in the Caliph's pay in this regard, but I would look to those who gambled their own money on the success of their sailing knowledge, and especially Jews talking to another Jew. And then the idea struck as it often does when I am thinking about something totally different. If the troops from Pamplona began to march so as to arrive at or before October 1, the word of their advance would surely reach Leon. It was, of course, as we had planned it. The feint at Leon, the maneuver south to Zamora. The residents of Leon would panic and begin to hoard food and supplies. As always in war, the price would go up rapidly. And who should profit? Not the favorites of Ordono who got the advance knowledge, but my boys Eli and Samuel, already well entrenched part-time residents of Leon. But this would be an even more clever maneuver. They could buy up hoarded items well in advance, and then, before the feint south, dump them on Ordono's speculators before Sancho's men headed south to Zamora. A double profit, on the way up and on the way down. I could trust Eli and Samuel with this knowledge and expect their discretion in this.

As they had arranged, either Eli or Samuel would be in Leon while the other was in Cordoba. Every few weeks, they would exchange places and carry a load of items for sale. They would meet at the halfway point at Merida to exchange information, settle upon their profits and then continue on their way. I could also get the latest of information about Ordono and Leon.

After dinner that night, I headed over to their parents' street. As it happened, Samuel was at home but about to leave for the trip north in two days. We went out for a long walk in the narrow streets of the Juderia while I described my plan. These temporary dislocations in the markets were the times fortunes could be made. Samuel understood this well and was overjoyed by this warning. He was also relieved that Leon itself would not be attacked. He had become so entrenched in business and the Jewish community that he was already being bombarded with marriage proposals from the town's marriage broker. He was getting to be the proper age to marry and every day he could feel the mothers and fathers sizing him up as a prospect. The girls themselves were much too shy or proper to do it themselves, but he could catch a very fleeting glance even from them as well. Now, with a killing in the market, he would have enough for the bride price and to pay back the Caliph.

I am not a merchant, but tried to help Samuel plan his foray into this venture. By now, Samuel indulged me in my advice, but kept his own counsel. He also planned how he might speculate on Zamora as well. A more important element however, was safety. If his buying and selling were discovered, Ordono might well suspect he had advance knowledge and was in league with the Arabs. If Ordono should, by some chance win, Samuel and Eli's business would be dead, as well as they themselves might. True discretion was important. Samuel went home from our walk with ideas spinning in his head.

I went home tired but relieved that my water route could be successful and Samuel and Eli could profit.

HASDAI AT HOME

Once again peace had returned to the Shaprut household. I wandered between a desk in the garden at the rear of the house and my small den on the second floor to write letters. On some days, I would go up to the cathedral to catch up on my translation of pages in Latin and Greek into Arabic on my encyclopedia of medicine and herbs. My chats with Brother Nicholas were always refreshing as we discussed the nuances of certain words. Intermingled with the sheer technology were lengthy discussions on the meaning of God, the Christian revelations and Jewish law. I could not help but feel refreshed from these endeavors.

At other times, I would visit the school of Jewish study which Moses ben Hannoch was leading. Every day rabbis and scholars from all over came to learn, debate, read and reflect in the rooms and the library of the school. I was asked to give a number of guest lectures on a number of his favorite topics. I loved most the lilt and nuance of the psalms and verses of the torah. As I read aloud the verses, I could parse out the many double meanings and ambiguities the ancient writers had embedded in their texts. Some possibly from Moses, some from David, some from Solomon, or others writing in their names. Maybe even a few Babylonians writing in the midst of painful exile. All were in the same tradition of the desert, the same as the Muslim poetry, the same as the Jewish poetry of late. But the mind was always free to create and fly like a bird. Long discussions always followed my presentations and the teachers of the school, the melameds, applauded the erudition of my exegesis. These times of peace and learning were a gift from God, as I waited the appearance of Sancho and Toda.

The Caliph was ready for Sancho's visit and had planned with his scouts and generals an alliance with Sancho – a major coup for al-Andalus.

I had briefed him on his many meetings and discussions and sat in on the plans for an attack. The terrain, the weaponry and configuration of the possible battles had been researched and coordinated at length. But the Caliph wished to keep Sancho on edge, in doubt as to his intentions. Eli and Samuel had both returned from their business in Leon and had tested the temper for Ordono's allies. They described in detail the meetings with Ordono's vassals as they rode into town. A few well placed inquiries, attendance at late night sessions in the taverns as the visitors bragged on their plans, and a few well placed bribes to Ordono's generals could easily define an entire system of defense. The Caliph had left little to chance and with proper counsel, would formulate a formidable attack on Ordono. But Sancho could not know this yet. The Caliph needed assurance of his good faith, as well as his military backing.

After a few days, a young novitiate knocked timidly on the door of my residence. David came to the door and then ran to the garden in the rear to get me. I brought the novitiate quickly back to my garden. I knew what the young man had come to say, but his presence in the Juderia would draw attention and certainly speculation. Yes. Sancho had arrived and was staying at the monastery attached to St. Vincent. I hastily scribbled a note to the Caliph, sealed it with wax and dispatched Moses to give it to the guard. The note read: "The beggar seeks his alms. Brother Nicholas will officiate." The Caliph was now to send his two generals to interview Sancho to evaluate the strength of men, catalog the knights, horsemen, archers, arbalettes and foot soldiers. They would also review the plan of attack. When all was in place, then and only then would the Caliph entertain Sancho.

SANCHO TO MADINAT AL ZAHRA

Some days passed while the Caliph kept Sancho and Toda waiting impatiently at the Cathedral. They were, of course, sent feasts and even wines in the Muslim country and were nightly given concerts and dances of Arabic origin. Eventually, the day of Sancho's audience before the Caliph was announced. I was summoned for the mid-morning event at the new throne room at Madinat al Zahra to the north of the city. It was to be the first ceremonial event in the new complex.

I passed through the gate and into the hall. I was directed to a seat of honor to the right of the throne. Lining the walls of the hall were shields bearing the coat of arms of the Arabic houses represented in the Caliphate and in between were hung silk hangings in traditional designs from many of the Arabic clans. Below these shields in full battle array were soldiers in colorful mail with painted helmets and bearing a long spear with the curved blade gleaming. Various of the Muslim nobles assembled and took their places alongside the long promenade from the massive double doors and leading up to the throne.

The Caliph, a handsome figure dressed in white with a purple trim in his robe, was seated first. Since he was short, he did not wish to be seen next to the tall soldiers or his courtiers, he entered from the rear of the throne and sat. After surveying the hall and approving the assemblage, he clapped twice and the double doors were opened. Through there, Sancho and Queen Toda entered first, followed by several of their noblemen who gaped awkwardly at the scene of wealth and power they encountered. As they reached a certain mark on the floor, the Caliph's minister of protocol bade them stop and kneel. All obeyed calmly.

To my dismay, I was able to see Enecco in the row behind Sancho. Why was he here? I had warned the Caliph of his impression of deviousness and bad faith. Yet here he was, still in Sancho's company. Of course, he was related to Queen Toda and had offered refuge to Sancho when he had been forced to leave his encampment in Alonzo's territory. We would have to see how this played out.

As expected, Sancho recited a long introduction of praise for ar-Rahman and beseeched him for aid in pursuing the return of his throne in Leon. To appease the Caliph and to show his worldliness and sophistication, the entire speech was in Greek, instead of his native form of Leonese Latin. Since the Caliph was known for his learning, it was meant to be a major compliment to his wisdom. It also concealed from many of his supporters and many of the Caliph's people, the true message of submission and the high praise and pleading tone of his address. Certainly, a churl such as Enecco would never grasp the import.

When he was done, one of the Caliph's ministers, at a nod from the Caliph, told Sancho that the Caliph would consider favorably this request. At that signal, Sancho, Toda and the rest of his entourage knelt and in Islamic fashion bent fully to the floor of the hall, touching their heads to the polished stones and swore allegiance to the Caliph if he would grant their request, even Enecco. The Minister then told Sancho they might retreat and come to one of the offices for a more complete discussion of the terms of the new treaty to be negotiated. As Sancho and the others rose, ar-Rahman left to the rear of his throne and the Leonese and their contingent turned and left. It had been brief, but impressive. The Caliph would review the terms of their entreaty which had already been discussed in detail with the generals.

As I left the hall to go to the meeting in one of the offices, a servant of Sancho's came up to me and handed me a soft bag of goatskin. I could feel the precious stones inside, but would wait for later to see what this gift was. The office was not far off. I took my place at the right side of the seat reserved for the Caliph at the head of the table.

Sancho's men and Toda were already arrayed at the other end. The Caliph had not yet arrived and would be sure to keep everyone waiting to demonstrate his superiority. Although the path from the throne room to the office was a bare five minute walk, the Caliph did not arrive for 20 minutes while Sancho and the others fidgeted.

The room was decorated with maps executed in fine inks of many colors on parchment of the many parts of the known world: Byzantium, Khazaria, even India and Britannia as if to demonstrate the reach of the Caliph's influence to these crude bumpkins from the north. The table which ran the entire length of the room was highly polished and inlaid with various woods, some even exotic including ebony, rosewood and bamboo. The Leonese should be cowed into admiration of the Caliph's sweep and power.

The Caliph entered briskly as was his style and promptly asked Sancho how he intended to conduct his campaign and what role he expected of the Caliph.

The generals and nobles assembled at Sancho's end of the table looked at each other as if surprised by the question stated so bluntly and so directly. At last, Sancho stood. He spoke some Arabic, but occasionally lapsed back into the Hispanic form of Latin of his region. A translator then spoke in Arabic.

"Gentlemen, we intend at the appropriate time, to begin to march west from Pamplona and be joined at intervals by my allies who have agreed to participate on our behalf. We will also obtain provisions from them as our tribute. I have made a number or promises as to what they will receive if we are successful, so they know of the venture. I have promises in return from them of men, horses and equipment. When we reach Leon, we will attack from the east in full force."

"Thank you King Sancho." (He was clear to use his past and hopefully future title.) "How will you array your troops for battle?"

"In the usual manner. We will set up a long line of armed foot soldiers at the ready. We will use our archers to rain down on Leon a mighty hail of flaming arrows. Then our mounted men will approach their line followed by waves of foot soldiers."

"On which terrain will you fight?"

"Why . . . just outside of Leon to the east."

"Have you made provisions against an ambush?"

"What do you mean?"

"You have told us that you will march west from Pamplona. Your line will stretch several miles with your supply train at the rear. If you are not prepared, they may attack at the middle of your line and outnumber you, while killing off many of your men. They may choose a hilly or heavily forested terrain and conceal themselves until the attack. Your approach will be well known since it will take at least a week to cover the distance."

"I see, General Gamba. What preparations have we made for such an eventuality?"

"We will devise a plan. Mostly, we will send out advance scouts on horse to reconnoiter."

"King Sancho, may I speak plainly." One of the Caliph's elderly generals stood. "Please do."

"We believe Ordono has long awaited such an attack and may not come out of Leon to confront you directly. Instead he may have laid in provisions to withstand a siege of months or even years. He will use his allies to harrass you on the flat terrain to the east of Leon in a series of skirmishes designed to weaken you and have you expend your provisions while he prevents you from gaining new provisions from the countryside."

"What do you suggest?"

"We make a feint at Leon and attack Zamora to the south."

"What will that do?"

"Ordono will keep maybe all or the vast majority of his troops at Leon. When he hears we have attacked Zamora, he will reluctantly be forced to send a contingent of his troops southward. In this way, he must divide his forces. His troops will also be on a hasty unplanned march out of Leon and be vulnerable to attack by our forces. We will vastly outnumber him then and can easily defeat him in open battle. At the same time, we will lay siege to Zamora, which will not expect our attack. They will not have expected us and will not long withstand a siege."

"What will the Caliph's forces do?"

"We will be assembled to the west of Zamora. We will bring siege towers, arbalettes and men sufficient for a long siege. We will also have access to provisions from the Muslims of northern Portugal."

"So, you will not march with us?"

"No. We will appear unexpectedly to the west of Zamora."

"How will we coordinate an attack?"

"We will send messengers back and forth over the days. When you have passed Leon to the south, we will appear to Zamora's west. From there, we will use trumpets and tubas to send messages to your troops."

"How will we know you will be there?"

"You will send a full contingent of riders to stay with us, before you leave Pamplona. They will be your riders so you may trust their messages."

"So we will never fight side by side."

"No."

"But we had a place for your excellent horsemen. In the front of our assault."

"I see. Well, we will discuss this more, after we have agreed on the ultimate battle plan."

With this, Enecco, who had listened quietly now slammed a fist on the table. "This plan is yours, not ours. How do we know there will not be some treachery."

With this I rose. "Lord Enecco, my Caliph will be committing 5,000 men, as well as horses, equipment and other necessaries. He will expend large sums of money in this endeavor. You may have your men stay with us to observe our preparations and report back to you. Your forces only number about 10,000 and they come from different sources. They have not trained together. You will have many different generals. We will be a united fighting force and will assume full responsibility for the western half of Zamora. When Ordono may appear to your west after you have marched past Leon, we will bring our mounted squadrons to the fight on the river Esta. We, as you know, have excellent horses and can cover great distances swiftly." I well knew Enecco wished to put the Caliph's forces in the most vulnerable location in the battle where they would suffer the greatest casualties. If Sancho attacked from the north, the people of Zamora would try to flee to the west. Their flight would be cut off by the Caliph's men. The heaviest fighting would occur to the north or east of Zamora, as Ordono came down from Leon. In this way, only Sancho's Christian allies would be in the battle, with the Caliph's in reserve, if needed. But no one could object since the Caliph had committed 5,000 men – equal to the total of Sancho's own men. The total of 20,000 would much outnumber Ordono's army, estimated to be about 10,000. The Caliph's word must hold sway.

"I also must say," I said, "Ordono has no great love for Zamora. When his father, King Ferdinand I, on his death divided the kingdom of Leon, he put Sancho on the throne of Leon, and put Sancho's sister, Dona Urraca and her husband on the throne of Zamora. While Ordono has a treaty with Dona Urraca, after all she was never friendly with her step-bother Sancho, she is also very wary of Ordono. She looks more towards Portugal for comfort. I suspect that Ordono will be of a mind not to aid Zamora, but will aid her nonetheless because it is so close to Leon. We may take advantage of this lukewarm aid from Ordono, take Zamora and have a secure base of operations from which to attack Leon both east and west with Ordono in a weakened condition after his loss at Zamora."

The Christian lords who sided with Sancho sat back in awe. How did this Jew know so much of the politics of their own northern alliances in their Hispania? Of course, it was a masterstroke to drive a wedge between the tenuous relationship between Zamora and Leon and gain a foothold against Leon. It could now be seen as obvious, but why hadn't they thought of that? Only Enecco objected. He wanted a direct confrontation with Ordono and he wanted the Moors at the center of the line. He was waved down and chided for his insistence on what had become a bad idea and an obvious play to have the Caliph bear the brunt of the fighting.

Yes. The answer was to attack Zamora. Feint at Leon, but bypass it and go for Zamora. Only one question remained, or rather two. When would we meet at Zamora? Fall was a good time – not too hot and an easy trip from Pamplona. So October 1 it was. The second question, how would the Caliph get his men in place to meet them on that date.

"That is our problem. You may be sure we will be encamped on the west of Zamora and send our messengers out on our fine Arabian horses to make contact with your troops coming west. Leave that to the Caliph." I said. He certainly did not want these Christian allies of Sancho knowing their plans to travel up the Douro River. There might be spies for Ordono here.

A few more details were discussed. A small midday meal was served and Sancho and his men left for their quarters at the cathedral. When they were alone, the Caliph's men drew together at one end of the table and, while nibbling at the remainder of pastries on the tray, asked me.

"How do you suggest we get to Zamora?"

"I have discussed this with the Caliph. It will be easier and less costly than you think. The Caliph has already begun building cargo ships in an isolated area west of Cordoba. We will load the ships with our men, horses and material in the secrecy of our own port, sail to Cadiz, then travel northward up the coast of Portugal, enter the mouth of the Douro River and sail up to about ten miles from Zamora, just over the Portugese border and unload at the small town of Toro. We will complete the journey with no difficult overland travel. We will not alert any of Ordono's people along the way and will arrive fresh and intact. Only, the horses will need to be exercised. The men will be well rested."

"Do we need help or permission from the warlords of northern Portugal?"

"I will see to that." I knew that the Arabs still held the area south of the Douro and would protect their flank as they sailed east up the river. Christians held the area north of the river.

MOORISH ARMY MASSING

The Caliph's generals had acquired a large field on the Quadilivir River south and west of Cordoba to begin to assemble the many components of the army to attack Zamora to the north. The plan was to float down the river to Cadiz and then sail north on the Atlantic to the mouth of the Douro River, there to offload and camp until all the troops had joined them. Once assembled, the entire fleet would row up the Douro and offload just west of Zamora at Toro. The field below Cordoba now was beginning to fill up with tents as the horses and mounted troops, the foot soldiers, the archers, the engineers and the supply line began to drift in. Every day the men trained and every day a fleet of ships would leave the newly constructed piers and carry the army to Cadiz. There, the ships would raise their sails and take a reach out into the Atlantic, and then tack back in on the trade winds just south of the mouth of the Douro where another encampment awaited them. This massive movement of a 5,000 man army had to be carefully planned and coordinated by the generals and their subordinates on down the line. The horses and livestock were the most difficult since they did not at all like sea travel. The ships themselves were immense floating barges with a low draft and unwieldy in the choppy waters of the north Atlantic. For several weeks, ship after ship left Cordoba, rounded Cadiz and tacked north. Soon a large encampment was assembled on a plain south of Porto.

More than most military men, the Caliph understood the value of good logistics and had insisted on personally overseeing each phase of the generals' operation. He was also mindful of the threat from the Christian held lands to the north of the Douro. He had made a few discrete overtures to the Peres family that held the land to aid him or at least to remain neutral in the impending battle. The response was neither for nor against.

This probably meant that they owed some loyalty to Ordono and were afraid to defy him, but this was never confirmed. Sancho had also sent envoys to Peres, but got no clear response. The family probably would await the outcome before choosing a side and remain on the good side of whoever the winner might be rather than risk creating an enemy.

In the meantime, the Caliph had dispatched 500 guerilla warriors to the north of the Douro to spy and where appropriate, harass and attack Peres family soldiers possibly massing for an attack on the Caliph's ships as they cruised up the Douro. Scouting reports and spies had provided regular reports of the activity north of the Douro. The Peres family ruled a relatively calm, but poor area. The land was mostly forested with a few farms here and there growing olives and grapes. There was no army assembling and few standing army soldiers training near the Peres castles. They had probably elected to remain neutral, but would send some token offering of troops to Ordono. There were no attack boats docked on the north of the Douro. While these reports were favorable, the Caliph still would have fully armed war galleys floating up and down the Douro as they passed the Peres lands. Archers would be placed on the side of each ship to rain a hail of arrows on any threatening vessels from the shore.

I made several trips with the convoy ships down to Cadiz and up the coast to Porto. There, I would chat with the Porto merchants over a glass or two of their sweet wine at the docks. I also took in reports from them and passed them on to the generals.

After a few months, the Toro encampment was full. Men trained regularly. It would only take a word from the mounted scouts for the army to march the few leagues up to Zamora. Meanwhile, a tension hung in the air.

The Christian and the Moorish divisions trained separately. Their weapons and battle tactics were vastly different, as was their language and battlefield commands. That is not to say they were hostile to each other. They simply had separate encampments and commanders. They both spoke the Iberian dialect which was a combination of old Latin, Visigoth and some Frankish words, as well as Arabic. The Christians did not chafe under Arabic command, quite the opposite. They had faith in the Arab generals who were well organized and precise in their commands. It is extremely frustrating to the common soldier not to receive logical orders based on sound strategic planning. Soldiers without that confidence in leadership can become desultory and even rebellious. And there was often no love lost between the Christians fighting for the Arabs and the Christians of the north. Often, family feuds had divided loyalties between clans, especially the well remembered brutality of some of the Visigothic rulers just 200 years past. And they were prosperous. They were often well paid, had nice farmland and could pursue their religion in peace. The so-called mesarabic Christians were content to support the Caliph when called upon.

Besides men, especially Christians, enjoyed war. They trained frequently, often hunted and could become bored with mundane family and farm chores. The opportunity to rape and plunder, to travel bonding with other males, training during the day and drinking at night was a welcome respite. Few men lived past 40 and to die a noble death on the battlefield in your 20's or 30's wasn't so bad. Only debilitating or disfiguring injuries were truly painful.

Reports were now coming in every day from spies in the cities of the north that vassals of Ordono were assembling to march toward Leon, most often along the pilgrim trail which ran across the north from the Pyrenees to Santiago de Compostela, forcing the pilgrims to the side of the road.

Eli had returned from his shift in Leon. Yes. The vassals of Ordono were assembling in a large field to the north of Leon. The Jews were being assessed a large vizya, a tax paid in lieu of military service. The Jews grumbled and begrudgingly paid their assessments while profiting handsomely and secretly from the economic shortages engendered by the run up to war. Otherwise, the Jewish section was quiet. Every day, troops from the west were coming into town and buying up foodstuffs, clothing, weapons and horses while consuming vast quantities of wine and brandy. To travel the streets at night was foolhardy, as drunks sang and swayed past brandishing their weapons. Some of the Jews thought to travel south to avoid the side effects of war, but decided it was better to stay and defend their homes from burglaries and confiscation in their absence.

Rachel made her regular trip to the fair in Jaen. There too, men, horses, wagons and arms were headed off to fight for the Caliph. She had made up large packets of medicines and herbs for the many diseases and injuries of war: aloe for burns, echinacea astragalus and garlic for infections, willow bark for pain and ginger for nausea. Women bought things for their men, but shook their heads at the stupidity of war while Rachel commiserated. Zastra still had the stall next to Rachel's and also spoke ill of war which had harmed her people so badly in the past. Osric no longer came to the fair since he was now a soldier training for the battle. In fact, the men had now largely deserted the city leaving only young boys and old men along with the women. It was quiet with an ominous tension. Which of the men would return? Who would be a widow without protection or income? Would the city recover from the vast economic losses by the disruption of war, or the loss of its manhood? Who knew? Nonetheless, women bought up the stores of small daggers and hid them under their skirts. Teenage boys were sent out to family farms to avoid being enlisted in the fight. The war would affect all parts of the peninsula.

But Cordoba was quiet. Since the Caliph's army assembled well to the west of the city and the new loading docks for the army were well down the river, the city felt little of the actual fever of war. There were shortages of some items and the smelters and ion workers were busy turning out weapons and armor. But there was little other disruption.

Soon, all awaited the signal from Sancho's army to commence the sail up the Douro to Zamora.

THE WAR FOR ZAMORA

Word came in from riders from Pamplona, from Leon, from the roman road to Campostella and other places that Sancho was ready to march and the Caliph sent his riders out that he too was ready. Slowly the vast assemblage of military forces groaned into movement. With much fanfare, Sancho's forces sounded war-time tubas and huge drums beat cadences as the battle line began to wind down the pilgrim road. The partially Roman road which stretched from the Pyrenees west to Santiago de Campostela and was the route a horde of pilgrims trod daily to the shrine in the west. The city of Leon was on the route. Ordono had been waiting in Leon for months to hear about the advance of Sancho to retake his throne and had been calling in his vassals for his defense. Sancho too had been contacting allies along the north to join him. Usually, vassals promised help to each side in differing degrees of enthusiasm, but the promises, of course, might or might not be fulfilled at the time of confrontation. Sancho hoped to create as much noise and display as much military might as he could to persuade the northern lords to support him. Some held grudges, remembered slights, and judged the probability of success. If they chose the wrong side, their comfortable fiefdoms would be confiscated and divided among those faithful to the winner. It was a precarious choice, but one that had to be made. As Sancho's army marched, he was conveyed in a hugh red and gold carriage with wood carvings of shields and emblems on the side. Tubas blared along the road and Sancho sat in the open air bench behind the drivers who clucked to the six white horses pulling the regal conveyance. As vassals rode up to join the entourage, their leaders, the lords of the fiefdoms along the way, rode up and bowed in their saddles, doffing their caps and announcing the name of their family and vowing allegiance to Sancho. Sancho rose from his seat at the top of the carriage and welcomed them in effusive terms. He asserted the victory was certain and the lords' loyalty in this venture would not be forgotten. The lords then would ride back to their assembled troops and fall in line with the other troops while they greeted their compatriot lords as they went down the line. These lords would each fight as separate units – only coordinated by Sancho's generals shortly before the battle. It was not yet known that Sancho's battle line would appear, approach Leon, then veer south to Zamora. This stratagem had been a closely guarded secret since it had been decided upon at a meeting in Cordoba. Riders came back every half hour to report that Ordono's troops were assembling on high ground to the east of Leon. Of course, the riders had been instructed to note by the flags and standards of the assembled troops who had joined Ordono and how many men were assembled. How many archers, horsemen, foot soldiers and how arrayed across the battle line were all relayed to the generals' wagons as they sorted through all the information. The line now stretched for almost a mile and was vulnerable to attack at somewhere in its midsection. Our riders galloped in lines parallel to the line of march and kept careful watch for any ambushes, especially where the road narrowed and strung the troops further out.

The march from Pamplona was not long and Sancho stood waving to the troops in a magnificent robe of red and gold while brandishing a gleaming sword from the top seat of his carriage. As they approached the Rio Esta to the east of Leon, he abruptly descended into the carriage and changed into the suit of mail and tunic of the foot soldiers from his once royal house. One of the soldiers donned Sancho's royal robe and put on the regal helmet and ascended the blocks up to the top carriage seat to impersonate Sancho. He bade the line halt. A small contingent drew up around the royal carriage. It was possible to see the dust from Leonese troops of Ordono as they assembled in the distance on the other side of the Rio Esta, where Ordono hoped to cut down Sancho's men as they crossed the small river.

As was now relayed down the ranks by the general's riders, the main body of the line turned smartly south along the eastern river road which followed the Rio Esta south to Zamora, less than a day away. While Sancho's regal carriage sat amid choruses of martial tuba and heavy drum beats, Ordono's riders came up to view the oncoming enemy and could see a vast array of forces on either side of Sancho's large red and yellow carriage.

In less than eight hours, the main body of Sancho's forces that had gone south were assembled to the east and north of Zamora and began to lay out lines of archers and catapults to rain stones, fire and arrows down inside the walls of the city. Sancho watched as the generals and their adjutants rode up and down the line of 8000 men barking instructions. Tubas sounded both to frighten Zamora and to tell the Caliph's troops of their location. The town walls were undefended as yet and no one ventured out to meet them. Since the castle and walls were along the Douro River to the south and west of the city, Sancho's army were arrayed to the north and east where most of the residents lived outside the walls. It became apparent that the small force protecting the city had retreated back inside the castle, leaving the major part of the city open to attack. The archers and catapults advanced to the edge of town where the castle grounds would be in range. Frightened residents came out with their hands up and a few belongings. They were herded into a field outside town.

Meanwhile, Ordono had by now discovered the southward march of Sancho's troops and ordered a hasty march to the south on the western side of the Rio Esta. This march was not orderly and not strategically planned so his vassals followed in clumps of men behind Ordono's own troops. As had been previously arranged, some of Sancho's troops had peeled off to cross the Rio Esta and set up an ambush along the western road. As Ordono and his allies hurried helter skelter down the road, they were first met by a hail of arrows from the archers hidden behind trees or behind ridges. Panic ensued as men fell left and right. At that time, the 500 horsemen sent by the Caliph to the north of the Douro to guard against any attack by the Peres people, having met with no resistance, were now directed to join the ambush of Ordono's army going south on the Esta river road.

A troop of Sancho's horsemen rode up as some of Ordono's men tried to retreat back to Leon and were cut down as they fled. When they again retreated south, they ran into the men retreating northward. Confusion reigned. Some of Ordono's own troops maintained discipline and fought their way through the ambush toward Zamora. Over 2000 men lay dead or dying with few losses of Sancho's men who now pursued Ordono's men to the south, most were Ordono's vassals.

CALIPH TO ZAMORA

Earlier, most of our troops had encamped along the Douro below Zamora in Toro, a small town upriver from Porto. The Caliph, his generals and I had boarded a barge below Cordoba on the Guadalivir River and drifted down to Cadiz, rounded the point and on out to the trade winds in the Atlantic, and caught the reach back to Porto. There, our men rowed us up to the encampment where the Caliph's men, 5,000 strong camped, awaiting our arrival. We received word that Sancho had turned south from Leon and was on his way to Zamora. We quickly marched to join Sancho at Zamora and could hear the tubas of Sancho's forces. Riders came in every once in a while. They told of the slaughter of Ordono's men coming south. We awaited the arrival of what was left.

As I sat on a horse by the Caliph's side, we were undistinguishable from the rest of the forces. We wore only standard soldiers uniforms and carried ordinary weapons. Around the Caliph was his usual cadre of bodyguards. The rest of the men were archers scanning the shores for evidence of the enemy ready to attack us.

The march up from the Douro otherwise was quiet. Resistance from the Peres family to the north never came and the shore was quiet except for the usual freight vessels coming in and out of the docks. We had formed up several miles below Zamora at a town known simply as Toro. The Arab generals carefully guided each contingent to their assigned place in the march. After a brief meal at noon, the line formed up for the short march to Zamora.

Our responsibility was the south and west of the city. The Douro flowed immediately south and we marched up the western road of the Esta. Eventually, Zamora came into view. There was a decent sized castle perched on a hill overlooking the river. An old Roman bridge ten meters wide came from the south, and the road connected to a drawbridge over the moat which surrounded part of the town. A wall about three meters high surrounded the castle and part of the town. We could see riders scurrying off to the castle, to announce our arrival. They were unnecessary. We came in full force with tubas blaring, heavy drums beating and an enormous dust cloud. The men wore cloths across their faces to screen out the dust. We were here and we wanted them to know. Boats off loaded south of the river. Immediately, catapults were erected and archers took up positions in range of the castle. Boiling kettles of flaming oil were set up and arrows dipped into the bubbling concoction. Soon arrows were flying over the castle walls into the interior. Catapults launched cascades of rocks at the walls and over. Occasionally, a few stragglers would come out with their hands up or pulling donkeys with household possessions. These people were herded into a rear section and kept under guard. Zamora was now under siege and would be as long as the people might want to hold out.

A rider came down from the north around the outside of the city. We were told that Ordono's men had been ambushed on the way south and a smaller contingent was coming south. Sancho's men were already aligned in a siege to the east of the city and were prepared for a small assault from Ordono's men coming south from the ambush. Without hesitation, at the sound of Sancho's tubas, the Caliph ordered his horsemen to follow the rider back to join Sancho in the combat with their battle standards aloft. He wanted full credit for the victory and wanted his men in at the end. About 300 horsemen and some 1500 foot soldiers left following the rider. In the meantime, Zamora was under a hell storm of fire. Hail after hail of flaming arrows and heavy clumps of boulders hit the walls and beyond. We neither heard nor saw anything from inside.

As the Caliph's horsemen rode up to the battle scene, it was clear that Sancho's overwhelming forces were fully engaged with Ordono's remaining troops. The general in charge of the Caliph's horsemen directed a charge at the western flank and rear of Ordono's position. With little opposition, men were now cut down and the entire western flank was being rounded by the Caliph's men, surrounding and entrapping Ordono's. Soon a few weary stragglers raised their hands and dropped their weapons. It was over.

Within an hour, a leader of some sort and few others emerged from the gates of Zamora with hands raised. It was clear they had now surrendered. They asked to whom they had surrendered, Arab or Christian, Sancho or the Caliph. They were brought back to Sancho's tent where the Caliph's representatives including me, explained that we were a joint force of Arab and King Sancho. We would leave the town in peace if they would become vassals to Sancho, and sign a treaty not to attack lands of the Caliph. They were a bit confused at first. But peace was peace. They would remain Christian and pay taxes to Sancho when he accepted the surrender of Leon. Of course, they had little choice but to agree.

AFTERMATH OF ZAMORA

As the furious hand-to-hand combat and the thundering charges of the horsemen subsided, the pants of the exhausted warriors who stood bowing at the waist, hands on knees could be heard. Groans and shrieks of the wounded pierced the air. Slowly, a heavy calm descended on the battlefield. Sancho's men and the Caliph's wearily walked off to the side and stood looking out over the plain which was now filled with death and bloody bodies.

As if on cue, the peasants from inside Zamora and from the surrounding huts crept onto the field and began to scavenge among the fallen. A ring here, an amulet hanging on a necklace there, a helmet, a sword, a dagger were picked from the dead and handed to the family member following them. Soon carts bearing barrels of salt wheeled in among the dead and began to butcher the fallen horses before the meat started to rot and cover it with salt to preserve the flesh for later. Fights and squabbles sprung out as the human vultures began to fight over the valuables, such as they were. The generals directed the engineers and foot soldiers to pick out their own dead and wounded and bring them to carts to be buried or tended to as their conditions were assessed.

The Christian and Arab generals began the grim body count of the dead. With much lower resistance from Ordono's men who had survived the earlier ambush, it was apparent that Ordono had not fared well. The death count was reaching several thousand and growing rapidly. The Caliph's men numbered 35 dead and 60 wounded, some slightly, some heavily. Sancho's men numbered 120 dead and 400 wounded. Ordono's men had few wounded since many were summarily stabbed where they lay groaning. There would be no time wasted on the wounded for the losing side. After several hours, the field bore nearly 3000 Christian dead, left to be eaten by dogs and birds or rot in the sun.

A long tent was hastily assembled on a far part of the battlefield. The generals, both Christian and Arab, from the Caliph's and Sancho's armies sat on heavy wooden benches to decide the next step. The two sides had been opposing each other in battle for over 100 years and had little affection for each other. Yet today, the Christians had to keep their thoughts to themselves. Clearly, the strategy to veer from Leon south along the Rio Esta to Zamora had proven brilliant and was acknowledged to come from the Arab counselors. This move had set up the ambush as Ordono's troops rushed south in pursuit and left his numbers decimated and disorganized. The battle for Zamora had become an easy victory. Yet the Christian generals felt some contempt. After all, their glory was in rushing headlong into the enemy forces and, by superior size and strength thrashing weaker men. It was the fury that engulfed their minds that brought them elation - a surge in spirit that made them feel like gods as they rushed into battle. With this infusion, they could fight for hours with otherwise devastating wounds. To win by evasion and strategy was beneath them. But a victory was a victory. Besides, hacking the limbs and heads of an opponent was a joy that could not be matched. Of course, Christians had been slaughtering Christians with Arabs by their side to help. This thought dimmed some of the glow of victory. Yet victory was victory, and blood lust was blood lust.

The Arab generals knew their place. They were in enemy territory now and had aided a Christian ally against other Christians. In itself, this was not unusual. Frequently, along the shifting border between Arab and Christian territories, one side or the other sought out allies from the other religion. After all, the stakes were high. Gaining a new fiefdom for a lord, whether Christian or Arab, could mean a major elevation in annual taxes and prestige. The use of a perceived enemy was soon forgotten if the objective had been obtained.

Now the forces were joined. The next battle would be for Leon – a weakened Leon. The entire kingdom was at stake for Sancho. At stake for his Christian allies would be large new fiefdoms, towns and farms paying taxes into the lordly coffers, as well as many new serfs, forests for hunting and an unending supply of crops, wines, silver and trade goods. A complete victory in which a lord's participation in the victory was acknowledged by King Sancho would elevate any soldier to new levels of wealth and status. With the Caliph's participation of 5,000 men – foot soldiers, horsemen, archers and engineers, as well as a well-stocked supply train, victory was assured. So all enmity between the sides now allied was forgotten. The generals for each side agreed easily on a swift march the next day northward in an orderly fashion up the Rio Esta to Leon. There, they could expect little opposition. Maybe a siege, maybe an easy surrender, but little risk, few if any casualties. Tonight their troops would feast, drink and be assembled and ready for the short march up the river.

The Caliph had attended the meeting dressed as a general's aide. He was already a short man and presented an insignificant presence. I too was a general's aide. We both listened calmly to the summary report on the battle and the decision to march the following day. We both silently nodded approval to each other. Clearly, the winner of the day was Sancho. But the Caliph had gained much as well. His Christian opponents to the north had lost, between the ambush and the battle of Zamora, over 4,000 men. He also now knew who would side with Sancho and who now would suffer defeat as a follower of Ordono and all the losses that went with it. And he hoped he had gained what he most sought – peace in the north. Sancho had pledged to be an ally and declare the area south of Zamora to the Arab border area to be a non- combat zone to be preserved by both sides. Some under the jurisdiction of one, some under the other. As this area of Estremadura was poor, the actual taxes and control of the area was of minor interest. The peace was paramount. For 50 years now, the Caliphs had to worry about the berbers to the south and the Christians to the north. Now, he could concentrate on the berbers and consolidate his kingdom.

As planned, the two combined armies, now consisting of over 15,000 would march north and rendezvous on a plain outside Leon to the south. There, they would meet and plan a siege - distributing out responsibilities based on reports they had from their spies and observers. But the rendezvous was first, then the planning.

The men returned to their respective encampments and joined the feast and merriment already in progress among the troops.

MARCH TO LEON

Undoubtedly, the news of the total victory over Ordono's troops at Zamora had reached Leon. Ordono had suffered huge losses and now faced the prospect of defending his capital city. He would not have the resources for an open battle. To withstand a siege was the only option. The question was whether he had laid aside enough food and water.

So there was no hurry in the march of the Caliph's and Sancho's men along the Rio Esta river road. There would be no tubas, no drums, no grunted marching cadence and no haste. The army under the Caliph was under the command of the generals and closely coordinated. Sancho's army consisted of separate groups each under the command of a different lord. The Caliph's men maintained discipline, and marched at the same pace. Sancho's assortment were an array of differing styles; some marched, some walked at an easy pace, weapons askew, uniformed or not. However, the march was short and the units as they approached the field to the south and west of Leon were directed to their respective encampment areas. The last stragglers came in about late afternoon and were followed by the supply wagons.

Sancho's magnificent red and gold carriage once again pulled up, this time with Sancho on the top bench waving at the troops. The royal tent and supporting structures were laid out in the center of the camp. Sancho dismounted from the carriage and took up residence in the royal tent. The retainers, courtiers and even his grandmother, Toda, were accorded brightly colored tents. This was not a preparation for battle. Soon Sancho would be presiding over a ceremonial retaking of his throne. He called for an assembly of his generals, his loyal vassals, and the Caliph and his entourage. There, a late afternoon repast was served of chicken, fresh fruit, wine and pastries. As the invited dignitaries trickled in, they were seated in rows before a dais. At the appointed time, Sancho, Toda, and his major allies strode onto the dais. Sancho remained standing and raised a goblet of wine while he waited for silence.

"Friends, and my many loyal allies, I wish to thank you all for supporting my return to the Leonese throne. I am grateful for your assistance and I will not forget you. Even now, my clerks are tabulating the territories and towns the allies of Ordono held and will be divided among you for your service."

This was greeted with loud applause and shouts.

"I recognize also the help the Caliph from Cordoba gave us in our struggle. While I was in exile, he provided us with many things. Most of all, I wish to recognize Dr. Hasdai Shaprut for the medical assistance and comfort he gave me. I should note that he also devised a brilliant battle plan. I pledge now two things: For the Caliph's help, I will maintain a peace with his country to the south. A non-combat area will be defined along our borders. The Caliph has graciously declined to receive any further lands or tribute from us and has sought only peace. Also with the peace will come free and open commerce."

A smattering of applause followed.

"For Dr. Shaprut, I pledge that his Jews in my realm will be treated fairly and permitted to pursue their religion without interference. His people may live in peace among us throughout Hispania."

A trickle of applause.

"But the war is not yet over. We must assemble tomorrow and confront the inhabitants of Leon. Their fate is in their hands. We will be ready for whatever they may choose, but I assure you this, we will retake Leon."

Loud chants and cheers. As the noise died down, the men returned to their heaping plates and enjoyed themselves.

SIEGE OF LEON

The following morning, the troops of both Sancho's allies and the Caliph were in full battle formations around the city of Leon. At dawn, the tubas began to blast and the drums beat. They knew we were here and they had to decide: surrender and save the inhabitants or hold out for a siege and starve to death. They had known we were coming for some time and they must have hoarded provisions, but would they be enough? They would have water. They were near two rivers and must have ample wells. Could they feed their people or might they begin to starve and die? Might they revolt? Sancho held off firing flaming arrows and catapulting boulders into the city. He had ruled it once, knew its people and wished to be welcomed back by the residents, rather than hated for the devastation and death he might cause. So he stood in his magnificent red and gold carriage at the center of the formation and blasted the town with horns and drumbeats. No barrage of arrows, no hail of fiery stones had been unleashed; only the martial sounds of the drums and tubas.

Every few minutes, a few people, or a small wagon would emerge from the gates to the south and ask for safe passage. They knew well what a siege might mean. Or worse, they knew that would happen if the walls were breeched and hordes of armed invaders rampaged through their streets. Those crossing the battle line were herded into a circle and watched.

As I expected, Samuel came out eventually with a small cart and a donkey. I recognized him instantly and rode up to greet him. Sancho and one of the Caliph's generals were interrogating all those who had left, so I followed Samuel over to the tent where these interrogations occurred.

"Samuel, good to see you are safe."

"Thank you, Hasdai. How did it go in the battle?" I explained how Sancho had veered south to Zamora, leaving Ordono no one to fight outside Leon. Then the ambush on the road south. Then the skirmish outside Zamora.

"Amazing, Hasdai, amazing. Well done. So now what?"

"Either there will be a siege or a surrender. How are things inside?"

"Until Ordono was left with no one to fight, every soldier was swaggering around town, boasting that Sancho would be crushed. Then we heard nothing. There was no battle. The soldiers did not return and it was quiet. Then a few bloody and wounded men began to straggle in. We heard about the ambush first, then the loss at Zamora. Some of Ordono's men returned and now man the walls and the gates."

"How many do you think?"

"I would say less than 1,000."

"They can't defend the city with that."

"No. We all guessed that. People are now afraid you will come into the city and loot everything. There is much hysteria."

"Where is Ordono?"

"We don't know. He went south to Zamora, but we have not seen him since."

"So what happened to you?"

"When we saw your troops and knew of the defeat at Zamora, I sold off everything I had and packed up."

"How did you get out?"

"Once they heard I was Jewish they let me through."

"Did you manage to keep your profits?"

"Don't you worry about that, Doctor, I have prepared well in advance of this day and am well fixed."

"Good, good." By this time, the line into the interrogation tent had shortened, so I left Samuel and sought out the Caliph.

HASDAI AND THE CALIPH OUTSIDE LEON

I found the Caliph still in the disguise of a junior officer in the tent of the generals. He was making notes of the reports from the various posts as horsemen came up to the tent.

"Ah, Hasdai. How goes it?" I told him about Samuel and then I went into my suspicions about Enecco.

"Yes, yes. Quite so. I have my doubts about this peace. In every change of monarch, there is confusion. Some follow, some do not. Some never follow. I know we will continue to have trouble, but now I have an important document – an agreement of peace. If we are attacked by a vassal, Sancho cannot defend him. We will severely punish anyone breaking the truce."

"Good. I knew you would anticipate this."

"Yes. People never understand that trade and prosperity is always better than war and poverty. Now, Hasdai, I do not expect the city to hold out very long. Soon I will go back on the barge to Cordoba. I want you to come with me as far as Porto. You made very good contacts there. I want you to meet with those people again. I want two things – a good trading relationship and regular reports on what they hear from their area. The Peres in the north, the Leonese people – whatever they hear."

"Of course, excellency."

"You also sent me two good men in Eli and Samuel for Leon. I would like the same in Porto."

"It would be my pleasure."

"Let me know if Eli and Samuel can continue to remain safely in Leon. If not, move them to Porto. If they can remain, find me two new men. I will again lend them the funds for a trading stock."

"You were most generous last time."

"Hasdai, I was repaid within a year. You need not thank me. Thank them for me."

"Yes, Excellency."

LEON'S SURRENDER

Without much ado, the gates of Leon opened. The massive wooden doors in which six horsemen could enter or exit abreast, swung open. An elderly man dressed only in a white robe and sandals, accompanied by two young pages came out of the massive entrance. He held his hands up as a sign of peace and walked slowly and, it appeared, painfully almost 50 meters to the center of the battle formation, up nearly to Sancho's carriage. Three of Sancho's senior men rode out to the man. The scene of the elderly man and two young boys facing three men on battle chargers fully armored and draped in the colors of their respective houses was almost laughable. The horsemen were in full chain mail, helmed in painted, plumed iron devices which covered their necks; they carried lances in their left hands and had, at the ready, broadswords dangling in halters on their backs. The horses, always ready for battle or a fast gallop, chafed, reared and turned as they approached the elderly man.

"I am Lord Thudon of Tiburon. I seek peace and surrender."

"We accept. Have your men come out of the walls and drop their weapons behind you." The old man turned and waived to the walls. Slowly, in clumps of two and three, the men came straggling out through the huge gate and assembled behind the old man. Soon a massive pile of bows and arrows, pikes, spears, swords and shields mounted in the dust. The men numbered 1,240. They stood in loose groups, a few attempted some formation, but gradually gave up the effort.

"Where is Ordono? Where are his generals?"

"Fled."

"Which way?"

"We do not know. They left yesterday out the west gate as you were coming north."

"Who were they?"

"Ordono and his retainers."

"They are all gone?"

"Yes, sir."

"Who are you leaders now?"

"Lord Hugo and Lord Carlos."

"Where are they?" The old man turned and motioned two men from the ranks. They walked slowly up to the three mounted horsemen.

The two lords were asked where Ordono was.

"We don't know sirs. He and the generals left yesterday."

The three horsemen motioned for a rider. Soon, a young man rode swiftly out to the group in the center of the battlefield. He was told Ordono and the generals had left and Hugo and Carlos were the new leaders. They asked for guidance from Sancho. While the three horses continued to rear and circle, the rider returned and whispered to one of the horsemen.

"Sir, we are told to accept your surrender and let you return inside without weapons. Each of you must pledge never to take up arms against Sancho again. You may return now."

The old man relayed the instructions to the dispirited men behind him and they turned in a slow desultory walk back inside the gates. Soon, Sancho's troops were marched into the city and began to take up posts along the walls and in the streets.

As Ordono's soldiers came back inside, they were greeted by their wives and children who wept and clung to them. They all would survive. Their prayers were answered.

Soon, Sancho mounted on a massive white horse draped in red and gold trappings marched at the head of a column of mounted men all draped in the colors of red and gold, all fully helmed, all wearing chainmail and carrying lances. Next the foot soldiers also draped in red and gold with swords hanging from belts at their waists and shields and their backs. Then the archers in gold tights with red doublets with bows and quivers of arrows strung over their shoulders.

At intervals, musicians with horns and tubas and large base drums played pleasant tunes with a heavy marching beat.

The procession took nearly an hour. But there was to be no mistake. King Sancho was back in his rightful place on the throne of Leon. Soon, his men would begin to interrogate the villagers to see who supported Ordono, who might be a spy and who would be left in peace. As was to be expected, most of the villagers had little interest in the politics of the court and would support whoever was now on the throne.

I visited the Jewish section. My presence, which hopefully augured a new era of peace, was greeted warmly. As it happened, the day was Friday. So Samuel and I took a long peaceful dip in the local mikveh built in preparation for Sabbath services.

As we sat in the mikveh up to our eyes in cool water in the heat of the day, we each became lost in our thoughts. For me, the tension of the war and the battle began to fade and a calmness took over my senses in this ancient ritual. I was preparing for the God-given Sabbath and cleansing my mind and body – a new beginning. The ritual in this brief moment had taken over my soul. I praised God silently.

We joined the locals in the small circular synagogue with the pulpit in the middle. I was given the honor of being in the minion, the ten men surrounding the pulpit, as the torah was brought out and read. I and the congregation bobbed and chanted the 18 benedictions in ancient Hebrew. People wept as we said the prayer for peace. As the service drew to a close, the congregants, in addition to shaking the rabbi's hand, came up to greet me, thanking me again and again for ridding them of Ordono. I recited Sancho's pledge of peace and tolerance to the Jews. Some wept, some cheered. Could Leon become like the Cordoba they had heard about?

Not to be forgotten was Samuel's unmarried state, an unworthy state not to be ignored by the women of Leon. As Samuel's supposed father-surrogate, I was inundated with invitations to engage in matchmaking for Samuel. He might now be expected to remain in Leon. And Jews, never slow to count the contents of another's purse, had watched Samuel's business acumen and the shrewd dealings he had concluded as Leon prepared for a siege that never came.

RESULTS OF THE BATTLE

The street near Sancho's new palace was filled with women and children. Every few minutes new visitors came to listen in the square. Over 3,000 men from Leon and his allied regions had died in the battle and 1,500 were captives awaiting their fate as Sancho judged those men who had betrayed him before. The women knew full well that the loss of their men would destroy their lives. Some nobles would be cast out of their rural castles and become serfs, their surviving widows abandoning their finery and servants to work in the fields or the kitchens of their new lords. Some of the women and children might starve. As each name of a dead soldier or knight was read out, cries of anguish rose and signaled a life of poverty and danger and virtual slavery. Their men's bodies lay rotting in some distant field without a decent burial. Wars caused massive upheavals in the lives of the peasants and nobles alike. And whole towns losing perhaps 500 to 1,000 able bodied men would suffer a generation of misery before they could again become productive. The women, with the vastly depleted male population, could only look forward to lives of drudgery or prostitution. Without men to work the land, it would be at least a generation before the fields would yield enough to feed the population.

ENECCO AT THE FEAST

As the now presumed King of Leon was magnanimously including all his allies and supporters in the success of the taking of Leon, I had a lingering sense of dread. Maybe it was my biblical training that in every good event is evil, and in every evil is good. Yes, there it was. A small coterie of men hung at one end of the raised table around Enecco. At times during Sancho's speech, they did not look his way, but muttered among themselves. When Sancho recognized the Moors' part in the victory, I could feel a cold glower in our direction. It would mean a small fissure in what was supposed to be a treaty of peace, a détente and an era of peace. It is always difficult for me to understand man's desire for war. Of course, there was always the relief from the grindingly dull life of daily labor, to be replaced by a chance to loot, to rape and to seek glory on the battlefield. Somewhere in the makeup of men was this urge for violence, for savagery. Every few years, a chance would arise and men would desert their residences and take up arms to join in fraternal bonds to kill. And yet, the life of Cordoba was so much more refined - there was beauty, prosperity and peace. The emotion was more delicate, something that had to be learned to be appreciated, perhaps. Men like Enecco would never understand this. Perhaps it was because Jews had so long been denied access to this brotherhood of warriors. Perhaps, it was because they had learned to appreciate peace and learning. God must have denied Jews access to military service and put them in servitude or occasional danger from the ruling overlords, but gave them something instead, to be enjoyed and savored in their synagogues, in their schools and in their studies. Was that it? God worked in mysterious ways. Or was it just an accident? I could feel the blood lust of a victory, the warmth of combat camaraderie, and it was an elation. Yet, I also could see the field of dead and mortally wounded as the peasants pulled off their rings and made off with their boots, their coats of mail, their weapons, as the birds and dogs picked at their remains. Was this what God intended for man? And the devastation and poverty that followed. Burned houses, bereft widows and children, populations with no able bodied men to work the fields and bring in the harvest. Zamora was spared much of this since they surrendered, but still the stench of death would be in their atmosphere for weeks and poverty would reign for a generation.

What was Enecco thinking? Would he breach the truce and create more war between the Christians and the Moors? As I thought about how deftly the Caliph had handled the war, I saw the depth of his intelligence. He had lost few men, he had full credit for his support of Sancho, and he had gained valuable knowledge about the lords who supported Sancho. If the peace were not to last, he would be ready for battle. He knew their battle tactics, their allegiances among themselves, and the strength of their attachment to Sancho.

But certainly, I would have to discuss with the Caliph the possible danger of Enecco, although I knew the Caliph would always be on guard. He would not trust this peace.

RETURN TO CORDOBA

With Sancho now safely on the throne, and a treaty in hand, the Caliph and his army slowly began to board the barges and drift down the Douro. As planned, I got off at Porto and went to the docks to seek out my acquaintances from before. The small Jewish community welcomed me. When the time came to talk business, I asked for a list of things that Porto could supply and a list of things they needed. Olive oil, of course, the Iberian peninsula was always awash in olive oil. Sweet wine, called Porto or Port, was available in large casks. A few sips told me it would be a favorite in the south. And fire water. The trade in fire water was a little known fact. The Arabs coined the word alcohol even if their religion forbade it and they were prominent in the trade. For centuries a trade in fire water had gone on along a route from Leon to Merida and south. Casks regularly come to the Porto docks. This brew was so strong that men could drink but a small cup before losing their senses. And yet the trade was small but regular.

A swift inspection of the markets revealed many items had been denied the residents of Porto. Fine silver and copperware, knives, daggers and cutlery of all sorts, silk and fine cotton and medicines of all sorts were needed. The opening of this trade with Cordoba bode well for all involved.

The Caliph needed to know what was going on in this part of the peninsula. Currently, the Norsemen were raiding up and down the coasts. They would beach their ships and dash headlong unannounced into the seaside areas. Bashing heads with heavy hammers or maces, slicing limbs and skulls with huge swords, the men would simply run into the towns, stealing, smashing and grabbing as they went, occasionally raping or simply destroying. Their great size and fierce cries shocked the residents into immediate paralysis. This was the most feared element lately. The Peres family had ruled quietly for at least 100 years, but they had little and wanted little. Mostly, they kept to themselves. Of greatest interest was the passage of boats and ships through the port. Who were they? Where were they going and what were they carrying? The Porto merchants readily agreed to include coded letters on their soon to be regular shipments to Cadiz and Cordoba. Of substantial interest was the extensive trade with Britannia. This Porto connection would open new possibilities for this traffic. I also had to ask the merchants to accept another merchant house of two young Jewish men into their group – backed of course by my credit. I would not reveal that I was backed by the Caliph. My word as a scholar and doctor was good enough.

HASDAI IN PORTO FISH MARKET

I prepared to sail south to Cadiz. When I arose just after dawn, the merchants of Porto were already busy at work on the docks. Their offices lined the area between the wooden walkways and the paved street where horse drawn wagons were loaded from the docks and consigned for overland routes in all directions. The sea air, that fishy smell and, fortunately a cool Atlantic breeze greeted me as I strolled down the narrow street from my inn. I knew where to find them. The Jewish merchants by midday were seated around a wooden table as platters of grilled sardines and fresh greens were deposited in front of them. They were busy in conversation discussing the recent battle at Zamora and speculating on the outcome.

"Gentlemen, may I join you? I can enlighten you on the battle. I was there." Several of the men drew back giving me suspicious looks. Others beckoned me in. "So who are you and how do you know this?"

I showed them my letter from the Caliph. As they passed the letter around, some beckoned me to taste the fish, another poured me a cup of the sweet wine. I launched into as accurate a version of the Christian forces and Arab forces coordinating the attack, and the bloody victory over Ordono. Instant information on the outcome of wars, or the shifting alliances was very important in this world, especially among merchants. It directly affected the safety of their shipping and the supply of certain goods for their markets. They hung on my words as I gave them the list of Ordono's allies defeated and Sancho's regions rewarded. Each took careful review of the goods and products flowing to and from each area. Each recalled their contacts in each city and made mental notes to verify my account. A single miscalculation, a misdirected shipment could cost them a fortune, a hasty analysis of the new market opportunity could mean a huge profit.

The fish was indeed tasty. Sardines with some garlic, oil and lemon. The wine was that sweet wine of the region – watered down for the midday meal. I ate my fill as the men debated what prospects had come to light from Sancho's victory.

It was now my time to negotiate trade arrangements with these men between Cadiz and Cordoba. They too were much involved in trade with Britannia. I assembled lists of goods available at all of these new ports for the Caliph and, of course, Eli and Samuel to exploit.

HASDAI FROM PORTO TO HOME

I t had been a productive trip so far. Ordono has been crushed with the Caliph's help and I had made new trade contacts in Porto. My merchant friends got me a ride on a freighter bound for Cadiz in the morning. I was up early and sat on the docks as my freighter was loaded until it was low in the water. The captain, a grizzled heavy-set old Visigoth came up and slapped me on the back.

"Shaprut, is it, are you ready to go?" He was a jolly sort. I picked up my pack of clothes and things. They loaded on the vessel my crate of different trade items I was bringing as samples as well as quite a few bottles of the local fortified sweet wine.

"Yes, Captain, thank you very much."

"No trouble at all. Just sit on deck as we drift south." By now, the winds off the Atlantic had gotten stronger. It was very cool as I stepped aboard. I found a comfortable spot on deck on a pile of cow hides – or at least they smelled like that. My clothes would need a good airing on my return. I lay back and peered out into the gray waters which were quite turbulent now. We shoved off from the dock and the sails were hoisted and caught some heavy gusts. Soon we were breasting the waves on a speedy run south. We covered the distance in very good time. I got a nice inn at the docks of Cadiz that night and would get another lift the next day up the Quadilivir to Cordoba. Cadiz was a very rough town with many nationalities swaggering along the narrow streets. It had been a port town for ages, but was now under Moorish rule. Trade was brisk and the harbor was jammed with barges and ships waiting to pick up or drop off cargo. The men were anxious to get moving, but wasted little opportunity to spend their wages on strong drink, even in this Muslim town. Nor did it lack for loose women ready to avail themselves of the loose money from the well oiled sailors. It was a loud and raucous scene and one best left to others. I sought the solitude of an inn in the Jewish quarter and a kosher meal – maybe roast chicken. Yes, that would do nicely. The Jews freely referred to this city as Tarshish and recognize it as a port Solomon traded with.

I walked along the lengthy sea wall which connected the island of Cadiz to the mainland. Once on land, the scene changed as if I was in a different world. The streets were wider and the houses taller and wider. I was directed to the synagogue by a local and not far came upon a neat square surrounded by white-washed houses with flower pots along the walls. I stopped at the local market and asked for a room for the night. A man addressed me in ladino – the slang Jews often spoke among themselves. I answered him cheerfully. As we talked, passersby stopped to join in the conversation. They all wanted to know about the war at Zamora and the defeat of Ordono whom they roundly hated. After catching everyone up on the latest news, and a description of the wondrous city of Cordoba, I was sent to the house of a widow who took in boarders. I was told she fed everyone and was an excellent cook. So, on to Esther's. One of the teenage boys took me there and introduced me. Esther, it turns out, loves to talk. She named every resident of Cordoba she knew, asked if I knew them and began an endless series of anecdotes about each as I stood there with my pack in my hand. Finally, one of the boarders came in.

"Esther, give the guy a rest. He's been on a long voyage. You can talk later."

Properly chastened, Esther showed me my room, took my money and gave me the rules. Dinner at 6:00 and don't be late. I did not need to be told twice. I set my pack down and descended on a narrow pallet on the floor for a welcome nap.

By dinner time, I splashed some water on my face and went in for dinner. Several men sat around the table. At the head was the apparently self-appointed master of ceremonies, a Baruch ben Jusuf, an elderly fellow. He started to quiz me about who I was and where I came from. I certainly didn't want to reveal too much about my mission for the Caliph, so I just told him I was back from the battle at Zamora. At once my tablemates wanted a complete narrative. I obliged. I mean it is always nice to have an appreciative audience. Then they wanted to know all about Cordoba.

When I bragged about the beauty of the city, the peace and culture among the Jews, Muslims and Christians, they were happy to hear. Most of the outlying cities of the Moorish realm feared a return of the Visigoths whom they had heard about mostly by legend and hearsay from generations back.

Then Baruch, not to be outdone, told the story of Cadiz. He claimed it was the biblical Tarshish founded by the Phoenicians in King Solomon's time and was the "end of the world." With this, a debate sprung up among the other men. They claimed there were islands west of Cadiz and that sailors came back telling of a different race of people. This debate went on for a while. Meantime, the dinner, a chicken stew, was wonderful. Esther, like a mother hen clucking over her chicks kept ladling more on the plates and scolding those who didn't eat fast enough. "Eat, eat. You do God a disservice to waste my food." Soon groaning with way too much, we sat back. I broke out a bottle of my wine from Porto and poured a short glass for everyone. Esther was not slow to take her share. Everyone agreed it was wonderful and the bottle died a happy death. By now, the sun had sunk in the west and we trundled off to our rooms with happy thoughts. Tomorrow, I would get my crate on a ferry up to Cordoba and home. It would be Friday and the Sabbath with the family.

CONFERENCE AT MADINAT

It was difficult not to feel the dread after my days of peace from the Sabbath. The calm days of scholarship, of healing, of warm family life had made me feel as if God had descended on this land and blessed it. Harmony, peace and calm. But the summons to the Madinat at Zahra the Caliph's immense palace and grounds, could only mean one thing – danger. As directed, the next morning on Sunday, I went to the livery by the Alcazar and had my horse saddled. He looked sleek and gleaming in the morning sun as he pranced from the stable. I could tell he was eager for the journey as he trotted spritely up to the road to the palace some leagues away. As usual a group had assembled at the way station waiting for the armed guardians to guard the small caravan. I was saluted with great ceremony by the guards who recognized me from the past as the other members of the caravan whispered to themselves, "Who is this little man on the fancy horse? He looks Jewish. Why the salute?" It made me chuckle. I had not chosen this prestige. I was a humble doctor and scholar.

I fell in with the ranks as we slowly stretched out in a line on the road, my horse just bouncing as he wished to race ahead. I got a few appreciative nods from the rest of the group. They were all sorts. A few minor noblemen seeking favors from the Caliph through his chamberlain, a few servants returning from a visit to their relatives in Cordoba, a few soldiers back from leave, merchants carrying foodstuffs, provisions, produce, crockery, flatware and all things necessary to the Caliph's household. Some sang old songs, some chatted as we went through the countryside of dried grass and a few acacia bushes. As we approached the palace grounds, the road split in several directions. The servants and food merchants took the lowest, the soldiers went to the military gate, the noblemen went to the government seat where they would await an audience with the chamberlain. I alone trotted on the road up to the Caliph's residence at the top of the hill. I could feel the stares and hear the murmurings of my fellow travelers. Who is this fellow on the fancy horse? How does he get to see the Caliph? The guards saluted me at the gate and waved me in. A groom took my horse and I walked through the path amid the ponds and trees. I went to the small room off the large throne room. Several generals were already seated at the polished table of inlaid wood marking out a map of al-Andalus in oaks, cherry woods, ash and ebony. Large trays of fruit and pastries were being passed around and servant girls poured tea into porcelain cups with the seal of the Caliph on each. Around the walls were shields and battle flags of the Caliph's forces. Around the ceiling were moldings of dark wood carved into grapevines and flowers. Several men holding large fans slowly pushed breezes around the room. I knew some of the generals from our recent campaign to Zamora and Leon. They greeted me warmly and I them. They wore military tunics in the colors of their regiments with decorations and medals they had earned over their years of service. Soon the chamberlain came in along with a few aides and scribes. After the long hot ride in from Cordoba, it was pleasant to sit and have a few pieces of fruit and sip the tea. But there was an air of foreboding in the room. While people greeted each other, they reverted to frowns and sat with great seriousness at the places around the table.

After all summoned were assembled, the Caliph, all in gleaming white, and several aides swept into the room from the double doors to the throne room. As all rose to greet and salute him, he motioned for us to sit.

"Gentlemen, we have much to discuss. I have brought together my best advisers and seek your counsel. Please, bring in the first!" He signaled to the door at the rear and one of the nobles from the north came in. "Lord Acklind, please tell us what you have heard and seen."

A large plump man, in Christian attire of leather jerkin with a crest tooled into the right chest, came in and crossed his arms. "All hail, your excellency. I come from the north of Linares where I have been the Caliph's vassal for several generations. My grandfather aided ar-Rahman I take Seville and I was awarded our fiefdom 60 years ago. I am a loyal bondsman to the Caliph and sent 600 men in aid of Sancho to regain his throne on your orders."

"Now I am under attack from the north. I believed our treaty with Sancho would mean a safe border. This is not so. Some men from, I believe,

Pamplona have broken the peace and raid my towns. I seek your help and protection." He was nervous and had obviously memorized his speech. It came out stiff and halting.

One of the generals spoke in a deep rumbling voice. "Near Linares, you say. Maybe Pamplona. Why do you say that?"

"Some had old tunics from Pamplona. And I've been told they had an accent from there."

"What did they do?"

"Mostly theft. They rode around and stole. They burned crops. A few women were raped. Several men killed."

"Christian women?"

"Yes. We are almost all Christian."

"Did you recognize anyone?"

"None so far. I'm told the leader was dark, black hair, stocky." The general turned to the Caliph. "We don't know if these were Sancho's men or Ordono's."

The Caliph spoke. "Send some men up there to find out. These men may just be losers from Ordono's party. Losers in the fight for control of a kingdom often turn to banditry."

Eli came in next from Leon. "Your excellency." He bowed. Few knew Eli had been aided by the Caliph to set up shop in Leon and keep his eyes and ears open. I did of course. Most could tell Eli was Jewish by his clothing. "There is much activity in Leon. After your armies and Sancho's won, Ordono escaped with a small party. Sancho's men rounded up the rest and hung quite a few. Some are still being questioned. The city is full of men claiming to have aided Sancho in his victory and seeking favors or land. His generals are busy trying to verify their stories of providing men. There is much spending of money, much drinking and many people have armor and horses to sell from the dead on the battlefield. The city has at least three times as many people. Many come to pledge support to Sancho, but many who were loyal to Ordono now claim they aided Sancho. When people come to testify against those who were loyal to Ordono, there are fights."

"Are the people behind Sancho?"

"It is difficult to tell. Some pledge loyalty. Some are waiting to see what he will give them first. I would say, there is total confusion. Sancho is trying to sort out the men who are loyal to him."

The Caliph turned to one of the generals to his left and had a whispered conversation. This went on for several minutes. He then thanked Eli and dismissed him. The next one in was Alonzo, the noble whose territory included Jaen. The Caliph remembered the incident involving Alonzo's son Osric. Apparently, Osric was still missing from the battle at Leon but had not been found among the dead.

"Ah, Alonzo, nice to see you again." I greeted Alonzo. He seemed worried about Osric, but was hoping for the best.

"Good morning, your Excellency."

"Well sir, what can you tell us?"

"Well, your Excellency, I too have had some of my holdings attacked here and there along the border."

"Any idea who might have done this?"

"We are pretty sure they came from Pamplona. Some people recognized a few of their men."

"Any names?"

"I will give you that. My son Alaric has a list. He has come down with me."

"I see. How did he do in the battle for Zamora?"

"It was his first real action, so he stayed with me and the commanders. He does not have the training yet to be on the battlefield. I am also sorry to say that Osric has not returned from the north. We are very worried."

The Caliph nodded to one of his generals who stood to leave and get Alaric's list. "How goes it otherwise, Alonzo?"

"Your Excellency, we were very pleased with our victory. Otherwise, a brilliantly conceived plan. But I hear of intermittent attacks, not only in my fiefdom but along the border. Would it be possible to lay an ambush for some of these bandits and bring them in for questioning?"

"Excellent idea, Lord Alonzo. I will have my generals draw up a plan immediately. I cannot permit this breach of our treaty to be taken lightly. Sancho must assert better control over his subjects."

"Thank you, your excellency."

More reports of border incursions came in and followed the same pattern. Small bands of men marauding small northern towns. It became obvious that this breach be laid at the feet of Sancho and relief demanded forthwith.

The Caliph at last signaled he had heard enough. He excused the men and asked only the generals and Hasdai to remain. The room slowly emptied leaving four, the Caliph, two generals and Hasdai.

"Gentlemen, what do you suggest?"

The large swarthy general with the deep rumbling voice spoke, "As Lord Alonzo said, we must lay an ambush and capture some of these bandits. Are they sent by Sancho, or are they independents who do not respect our treaty?"

"Quite so. See to it. I suspect this may be occurring in the area south of Pamplona. Let us try that area first."

"At once, your Excellency." He and the other general left. "Ah, Hasdai. You have been quiet. What say you?"

"Reluctantly, I must suggest that I go to Leon as your envoy to inquire with Sancho what he intends. We have some spies in his court now, and we also know who is most loyal to him. I will meet these men as well to see if this can be attributed to Sancho, or to men who seek to advance their own influence."

"Then, Godspeed, Hasdai. When can you get back to me?"

"Now that I know the route by water, I can be in Leon in less than a week and back in let's say, three weeks."

"Excellent, Doctor. We must evaluate this threat."

"Quite so, your Excellency."

HASDAI TO LEON

After the conference at Madinat, I pushed my horse over the road back to Cordoba and went swiftly to all the merchants to assemble a crate of merchandise for Leon. Since Leon was relatively poor and had little trade, it was not difficult to assemble an inventory of things for sale: knives and copperware, dried fruit, nuts, women's clothing. I also sewed into my clothes several handfuls of gemstones, rings and brooches. I arranged for passage on the next barge to Cadiz that afternoon.

When I went home to begin packing, Rachel walked in for her midday meal with Yael. "Oh, Hasdai, not again."

"Yes, dear, it must be. The treaty to the north is not being kept and I must confront King Sancho."

"Will it be dangerous?"

"I think not. The Caliph has given me a letter with his seal identifying me as an envoy."

"Why is Sancho doing this?"

"We don't know. We don't know if Sancho is even behind it."

"Suppose he says he is not, but in truth is?"

"I must judge by observing Sancho."

"How do you do that?"

"That is the art of negotiation. We shall see."

"When will you be back?"

"Maybe three weeks."

"Then I shall go to the markets in Jaen and Linares."

"I must say, my dear, that some of the trouble is in that area. Perhaps the Caliph will give you bodyguards. I will send a messenger to ask him."

"That would be a comfort." I continued packing and took a carriage down to the docks to meet the barge. The barge itself was a dirty old scow which must have been carrying livestock. The stench was overwhelming so I perched on the bow and let the eastern winds waft past me for some relief.

The trip to Cadiz was by now routine. I now had to hire someone to take me up to Porto. An obliging young man, an Italian named Columbo, with a two-master was willing to take me to Douro and even beyond so I hired him. As with the army before, we sailed well out into the Atlantic and caught some strong tradewinds on the westward reach to arrive at Porto. Since we had few in crew, I sat with Columbo and asked him about the ocean. He told me of some islands he had heard of from some Norsemen who were raiding the northern cost. They claimed that someone from their country had sailed far to the west and found land. He said he was curious about it and was studying the wind currents further out to sea. All too soon, I arrived at Porto and stopped by for a midday meal with the merchant friends I had made before. We traded a few of my goods. As before, I ordered the excellent sardines grilled and basted with olive oil and garlic. It was delicious, especially in the cool air of the sea winds off the dock. I negotiated a load of that special sweet wine I had had before and said that I would be back in about a week. Columbo had joined me for lunch. Surprisingly, he spoke some of our Jewish Ladino. He told me he would be back in a week to take me back to Cadiz, which was now his home port. It was an excellent connection. He also liked the Caliph's money in which I paid my fare and a deposit for my return.

With the war over and Sancho firmly in charge of Zamora and Leon, it was not difficult to get passage up to Zamora where docks were being built to facilitate trade with the Moors. Again, I lightened my inventory by trading almost all that was left, and hired a carriage and guard to convey me up to Leon. This was a short ride now with no opposition. As we passed Zamora and the battlefield to the north, it had an overwhelming smell of death and heavy smoke. The locals were burning the corpses of men dead for a few weeks. Piles of uniforms, tunics, mail and weapons were assembled here and there as Sancho's men kept watch on the gruesome work.

I went to the house Samuel and Eli shared in the Jewish quarter and took Samuel out for a fine dinner at one of the better taverns pilgrims frequented on the way to Santiago de Campostella. I went over what Eli had told the Caliph and for the most part he agreed. New faces had joined the royal court, and the King's allies in the war plead their cases in search of new lands and titles. It had been very festive since the victory and the women were anxious to acquire new finery as might befit their new station which their husbands had expected. Eli and Samuel had amassed a quiet fortune buying up essentials before the war, and the anticipated siege and now were displaying all manner of women's and men's hunting gear. They had sent their last payment to the Caliph and were doing well. The town of Leon itself was doing fine. I had sent my letter from the Caliph to King Sancho and requested an audience. That evening, there was a message that the King would see me in his private study at noon tomorrow.

So far, so good. A meeting in a private place. No posturing in front of followers. A frank discussion. Sancho owed it to me and the Caliph. We were certainly the impetus to put him back on the throne. He owed us. So I slept soundly that night and in the morning went for a walking tour of the city. As Samuel had said, the place was lively and bustling. Shops were open, the open air market was full of buyers. Soldiers in various colored tunics swaggered up the street, accosting young girls. Even the elderly and the juveniles were not safe from their affronts.

Leon had never been happy under Ordono and most of the citizens felt they had been liberated. There was no sign of discontent under Sancho and many of the men toasted the King at the open air taverns. I could never be sure if these toasts were in earnest or simply to curry favor with the new government. But hearty and drunken they were, even under the midday sun. A noon invitation usually meant a sumptuous midday meal. And Sancho, a trencherman of great repute, would not be stingy in the offerings of his table. I could feel my stomach rumble in anticipation. I presented my letter of introduction and was escorted by two guards, no less, to the small room where Sancho wanted to meet. As expected, the table groaned under the delicacies on offer. A young piglet, roast whole, some sea bass, flagons of many different kind of wine, trays of fresh fruit arranged artfully. Alas, most of it not kosher. I had often confronted these obstacles and selected a tame looking chicken pie and a heap of fresh salad. The wine, though not kosher, was a bit too sweet for my taste, but very rich and fruity. As I nibbled away waiting for the King, an entire assemblage, including the King, his grandmother, Toda, various generals and numerous toadies who had already been able to ingratiate themselves to the king, came into the room. I was surrounded by about 20 people in what was called the "small antechamber." The place soon began to reek of garlic, body odor, hair oil and what have you. Although dressed in rich fabrics of many colors, with crests of their respective houses, this assemblage of nobility was to a man unkempt. Hair and beards were riddled with bits of straw, dirt and dust particles. This was the new ruling class of Leon.

"Ah, Hasdai, a pleasure to see you again." Toda, my confidante at Sancho's encampment in exile and co-conspirator in the weight loss regimen, greeted me warmly.

"Yes, Hasdai. You are always welcome." beamed the King. He introduced those around the table at great length including their full names, lineage and the tales of repute of both the men and their ancestors – all noble. "What can we discuss?"

I felt it best to relive our days of cooperation in exile and the marvelous victory which the Caliph had aided. The fighting men were happy to join in recounting the war plan – the feint at Leon, the march to Zamora, the ambush of Ordono's men and the taking of Zamora. Sancho broke in. "Hasdai, as I recall, you had no small part in that war plan. So I have heard."

"Your excellency is too kind. I am but one of the Caliph's advisers."

"No, no, no, I heard you were in it down to the details."

"I was of some help." Sancho seemed anxious to endear me to the new government and to soften me up for our discussions. As a seasoned envoy, I was well aware it was all a ploy, but enjoyed it nonetheless. His generals knew well my part in the plan. The careful dance of exchanging niceties was a diplomatic ploy, a stalling tactic to have one side or the other reveal how anxious they might be about the subject of the talks. I was an experienced envoy and could play this game for hours and had reserved at least a week to dangle my mission before Sancho and his advisers. Meanwhile I could size up the emotions on the other side. I knew well to becloud my emotions while observing those of the many men Sancho had assembled.

Perhaps they knew of these raids on the Arab lands, perhaps not. Had Sancho directed it? Or were these uncontrollable allies who would not keep the peace? If it was Sancho all along, should we retaliate. If not, would

Sancho retaliate if we sent a force to quell these attacks. The delicate dance of diplomacy continued. I got a full report on the health of all of Sancho's family, but could observe the alacrity with which the King attacked the meal before him. Once back on the throne, Sancho had abandoned his diet and exercise routine. His self discipline had earned him the respect of the nobles and the military before, but he would soon lose it with his present excesses. As they spoke, I took careful note of the generals and nobles. They had greeted me warmly as a fellow of the recent campaign at Zamora and Leon, but were these smiles valid? Were they fading with the length of these talks? Did they view me as the voice of the Arab enemy to the south or a long term peaceful neighbor?

I would test these attitudes subtly. I asked about the allies who were not at the table. I was most curious about Enecco, the noble from Pamplona who had never been entirely fond of the Caliph, the Arabs or the Jews. A few smiles faded. Were they in league with Enecco? Perhaps he was the least capable of honoring the treaty. Sancho, not entirely deftly, avoided answering this query. More names of the vassals who supported Sancho before were not present. Had they returned home or might they still be at court trying to urge Sancho to reward them with the lands of the defeated? The dance continued. It became apparent that the nobles backing Sancho were but a loose confederacy, not joined by any idealogical or hereditary ties, but merely assembled to scavenge over the last lands of Ordono. There was little loyalty here, merely a pursuit of self interest.

Ordono himself had fled. No one seemed to know where. Could he be behind these raids? An army with little to do might often resort to theft by violence.

At last, Sancho tired of the game. "So, Hasdai, we are both aware you come to inquire as to the breaches of our treaty. Is that not so?"

"You observe correctly, your excellency." I had won. Sancho could not deny it, nor feign a lack of responsibility. "What do you intend?"

"Good Dr. Shaprut, I must say that I do not condone any such incursions."

"Can you aid us in preventing them?"

"In all honesty, I do not know who they are. I have been busy re-assembling my government and have not directed our attentions to this matter." Essentially, this was a no. He could not risk having his Christians fight the rebel Christians on our behalf.

"As you must concede, these are troubling to us and our vassals. We must pursue a remedy. If we engage these bandits, will you intercede for them? We wish to avoid a conflict with you."

"Quite so." Sancho must be seen at least to keep the treaty and certainly did not wish to engage in a large conflict so soon after the battles at Zamora and Leon. He certainly must deny complicity in the attacks, he must avoid a large conflict with us. These positions were known. Would he call on his vassals to engage Christian troops in support of Moorish one against Christians not keeping the peace treaty? Too much to ask. Certainly. Now he must be backed into a corner where he would not retaliate if the Caliph engaged in punitive campaigns against Sancho's possible allies not keeping the peace. Sancho was left with little choice. He must disavow his own allies or risk open war with the Caliph, especially after the loss in forces he had incurred in the battles at Zamora and Leon.

"I see, Dr. Shaprut. We do not support those who breach the treaty. They are outlaws and may be attacked by the Caliph at will."

"Thank you, King Sancho. My wish is that we remain at peace." But it was not the wish of many of those at the table. Many were bound to the dissident vassals by blood and by marriage. They had only recently fought side by side and been victorious. Now, Sancho was permitting this pipsqueak of a Jewish envoy to trap him in a promise not to intercede if the Caliph attacked their good friends, neighbors and allies – all Christians. It was the barely concealed wish of all at the table to rid Hispania of all Arabs. Now, Sancho had crumbled to the implicit threat of warfare against the Moors. To these men, warfare was an honorable pursuit, and warfare in pursuit in furtherance of the church, but really to enhance their land holdings. I carefully noted the most hardened faces and resolved to lay this before the Caliph. I did my best to appear at ease as I finished my meal, took my fill of sweet wine and pastries. As we finished and men got up to leave, I bowed to all and passed out some exquisitely wrought daggers of Toledo steel, with cloissone handles with a design of the seal of Zamora, our mutual victory. A few men came up and clapped me on the back, a few skulked out of the room, avoiding the sight of me. So be it. I had a full report for the Caliph. I let out a healthy burp from the excellent meal and made my way back to Samuel and Eli's house for a quiet nap in the heat of the afternoon.

The Caliph sometimes wanted me to travel incognito, unknown, unseen, as his personal envoy. This time we agreed I should be seen. I represented the treaty between Sancho and ar-Rahman, and memorialized the aid the Caliph had given Sancho in re-acquiring his throne. So I had Samuel announce I would be holding office hours the next day. Word apparently spread quickly and I was greeted with a variety of ailments the next day. By now, Samuel and Eli had an assistant, Ahab. So Ahab was sent to help me with the patients and to collect the fees. He was a pleasant lad and seemed to enjoy great prestige to be working with me. I asked him if he knew who he was named after, but he did not know. I told him to beware of Jezebel and was rewarded with a puzzled glance. Maybe I had awakened in him a quest for knowledge. Nonetheless, he was somewhat competent at keeping the patients in order and collecting my fees. After a few days of these office hours, I gave Ahab a handsome bonus, pocketed my fees and left for Zamora hoping to find Columbo waiting. I took a wagon down to the Douro docks so I could make notes on the audience I had had with Sancho and my impressions on each of his vassals. I had to count my visit a success because Sancho had reiterated his desire to keep the treaty, but I had to note his reluctance to discipline those vassals who did not. He certainly would not risk his status by making enemies of his own allies who attacked us. He simply had not consolidated his power as yet, not did I think he ever would. He seemed to have returned to his old habits and was well on his way to regaining the weight he had lost.

Columbo was glad to see me and had already put a number of crates on the vessel of his own. I had also used my medical fees to buy some goods. We cruised down the Douro with the current at an easy pace. I stopped by Porto to pick up my purchase of inventory of their excellent sweet wine, had dinner with my new-found merchant friends and joined Columbo for the occasionally perilous sail out into the Atlantic down to Cadiz and thence home to Cordoba. We arrived after a two day sail late in the afternoon. I consigned my inventory to a warehouse and went home. It was Friday and some daylight remained so I slipped into our own ritual mikveh bath to prepare for Sabbath services. Rachel came home and started the preparations for the Friday dinner and the Saturday servings. The tensions of the previous days eased as I sat up to my eyes in the cool water in the heat of the afternoon. I got up and dressed for the Sabbath and walked with my family to the synagogue. As the ritual prayers and chanting swept over me, I could feel a sense of peace. Always lingering in my thoughts however, was the presentation I must make to the Caliph on Sunday. For now, I was at peace.

REPORT ON SANCHO AT MADINAT

Sunday came all too quickly. I went early to the livery at the Alcazar to get my horse and rode up to the road out to Madinat. A few early stragglers were on the road, but otherwise it was empty. My horse would not be held back and cantered happily along occasionally breaking into a full gallop. It must be a wonderful time for him to be so free. I barely had time to nibble at the fruits and goat's milk in my saddle bags before the magnificent Madinat al Zahra rose against the hill in the distance. I must have signaled my excitement to my horse as he gaily galloped up to the highest gate, lurching to a stop with dust flying everywhere. The guards saluted, took my horse's bridle and ushered me into the gardens and pools in front of the Caliph's palace. The chamberlain had been waiting for me apparently and waved me in the door to the Caliph's study. I came in and sat at the polished ebony table as servants bustled in with trays of fruit and cakes. Each bowed their way out of my presence. Soon the Caliph, all in white, and two generals joined the chamberlain and me.

"Hasdai, what do you have for us?"

I explained the curious atmosphere in my talks with Sancho. Some were happy to see me, others not. Sancho, of course, claimed shock and dismay at the attacks on our northern territories, and agreed to speak to those involved. Since he claimed not to know who they were, that, of course, would be an empty promise. Nonetheless, he reiterated our peace treaty and agreed to aid us in enforcing our borders. It was my impression that he had little control over his allies in these early days after his conquest and would be reluctant to take any real action. I presented a list and general location of the allies who did not seem happy to see me. A vague piece of information at best. I should note that these possible dissident allies of

Sancho were mainly situated in the eastern part of his realm – the furthest from Leon and directly south of Pamplona. At the very least, Sancho clearly agreed not to oppose us if we policed our borders. Small comfort.

The Arab generals immediately understood that they must launch some punitive expeditions to confront and capture some of these marauders. They began to discuss with the Caliph the type of forces and the number of men. Certainly a few ambushes would be set up along the routes south to our northern settlements and towns. This would require archers and horsemen. A series of districts were delineated on the map and responsibilities divided among various cohorts. Scouts and spies would be dispatched along the border. Our northern allies would be reinforced. The concept was to capture as many men as possible, interrogate them into confessions as to who had instigated the attacks, and mount major offensives against them. Names of possible commanders were discussed, locations of towns and outposts were put forth and supplies were calculated. I sat quietly with all this planning and allocation of resources. It was decided to divide up the responsibilities and mark out the territories each contingent would patrol. Once a few prisoners were taken and interrogated, a larger force would descend on the land from which the men came. I could add little to this careful planning and sat back to enjoy the pastries. The Caliph did set a fine table; no sense letting it go to waste. I could tell the Caliph was very disappointed that Sancho had so quickly ignored the treaty. I certainly was. This meant more war and conflagration in Andalus, a prospect which foreshadowed evil for all inhabitants. As the meeting broke up, I saluted the Caliph and got my horse for the long ride back to Cordoba.

PEACE AT CORDOBA

While returning from my conference with the Caliph and the generals, their plans began to turn over in my head as my horse trotted smartly along. We would be covering a frontier of 250 miles with 5,000 men in cohorts of 500 each. It might happen that a superior force might come on the men and overwhelm 500. This could send a disastrous signal to whomever was making this happen. There had to be some way to summon the neighboring 500 men to and in the battle. Then I remembered how the ancient Hebrews signaled the beginning and end of our holy week from Rosh Hashanah to Yom Kippur. They used a shofar – a hollowed out ram's horn to call from mountain top to hill top the nightfall of the New Year and the conclusion of the day of atonement. Yes, I would send a message to the Caliph immediately. Trumpets or maybe tubas – which might carry further? As I entered the city gates of Cordoba, the synagogue was just ahead. I grabbed a short scroll and wrote my message and rationale for the Caliph. I dashed to the city gates where a small caravan was assembling for the trip to Madinat and handed it to the ranking soldier with strict instructions to hand it only to the general in charge.

I knew the results of our campaign against these Christian raiders would take some time to bear fruit, so I resumed what I always enjoyed as my weekly routine. First in the morning, Doctor's hours with Yael placing the patients in order of the severity of their maladies and collecting my fees. I would then choose my afternoon depending on how I felt. If it was a time for peace and quiet, I would join Brother Nicholas at Saint Vincent in translating the marvelous compendium of medical treatments the Greeks had compiled. Jews have always been fascinated by the human body and its treatments. For that reason, men who practiced these arts were deemed holy. Jesus certainly was one of these men. Often they traveled circuits throughout Judea, the Galilee and Asia Minor in their healing missions. I felt I was now in a long line of Jewish healers and was fulfilling my destiny as I puttered about my small room in the Juderia treating my patients. When I could make a difference in someone's life, I felt it was a gift from God.

On other days, I would go to the school we had founded. I must admit when I appeared, I was introduced to the classes as if I was a celebrity. I was nothing more than a traditional Talmudic scholar in my own mind, but the students were expected to accord me great deference. Of course, being traditional Jewish students, they saw this as an opportunity to attack what I said more vigorously and often savagely than ever. Ah! It was a fine old Jewish tradition to belabor the teacher. It was, in fact, an honor to be belabored. So I began to explore newer ideas than the traditional themes of exploring and closely reading the Torah episodes looking for some insight into the mind of the divine.

I began by discounting the literal language of the Torah and seeing it as metaphor and myth. This change in direction had been foreshadowed for many years by our learned scholars but to examine it at the yeshiva level was new. I must say some of the more conservative members were repulsed, but the younger men seemed to hunger for new ways to prise out the languages and meaning of the stories. It was fascinating to hear some of the theories. A teacher often learns more from the time teaching than from solitary study.

I introduced the study of my good friend from several centuries past— Aristotle, in the study of nature and the development of the law. I tried to reconcile God and nature and the Torah which was met with much vociferous debate. I could feel the fervor of mental development and growth in these scholarly debates, usually followed by tea and cookies. I could walk home from the school exhausted but fulfilled. I walked in the footsteps of scholars at least 1500 years in the past and felt a warm kinship. But I had to calm down. I would sit under the fruit trees in the rear of my house and stare at the pond, thinking nothing, thinking everything. Soon Rachel or Yael would call me in to dinner. It had been a full day – a true gift from God.

PRISONERS FROM LINARES

The ambushes set by the Caliph's generals did not take long to bear fruit. Soon a few prisoners were carted into town. Apparently, some local farmer had been seeing horsemen riding across his fields near Toledo and sent his son to the garrison nearby to warn of the possible raid. The local farmer was feeling much in debt to the Caliph who had provided money and expertise to the locals to revive the old Roman aqueducts and irrigation systems. There was visible evidence of the green and lush fields of the Caliph's serfs and those beholden to the Leonese and their allies. So the son rode up to the nearest garrison with warnings of a massing of horsemen. The next day the sounds of tubas echoed through the hills around Toledo. Scouts combed the hills for signs of horsemen. Toledo had been the center of much warfare over the past 100 years the Leonese kings, the Berbers, the Caliph's family, the Ummayads, had ruled, then been deposed in wave after wave of combat for generations now. At present, the lord of Toledo had been placed in control of the city by ar-Rahman III's father, but his position was always precarious. Toledo was an excellent place to start a recapture of the south by the Christians. The massing of horsemen was no surprise. As the tubas announced the massing, the Caliph's and the local lords' troops began to converge on a plain to the north of Toledo. Reports from scouts now had located the horsemen on a river trail coming west to Toledo. The Caliph's general immediately dispatched troops in several directions to head off and ambush these raiders. Soon the Caliph's men were told the band numbered perhaps 100 to 200 with some 50 archers. They were climbing up the foothills in a mountainous area along an old Roman road which ran parallel to the Tagus River. The generals staked out a pass which ran between two large hills and assembled archers above the pass.

For several hours, the Arabs waited in silence until they could see the first of the horsemen trotting along the roadway. At the moment the general gave his command, a few tubas blasted bass notes into the air. A wave of arrows began to plummet from the sky into the ranks of the horsemen. From their rear, about 500 Arab horsemen mounted on faster Arabian horses charged up the mountain pass at the rear of the formation where usually the supply wagon and archers rode. From the front, a cohort of more Arab horsemen charged at the column. For no more than a half hour, the air was filled with cries – horses dying, men screaming and the clash of weapons. As the Arab cohorts met in the middle, the band of still unknown horsemen had been decimated and lay wounded and dying in the road. A few horses trotted idly confused and dazed.

The Arabs swiftly picked through the fallen men to take into custody those that were wounded the least and could speak. The supply wagons were emptied and about 20 of the most coherent men were loaded on. They were all carefully bound and had black hoods placed over their heads. The rest of the men gathered in the stray horses and the salvageable weapons. The remaining enemy were left to die and rot in the sun. Of course, a few of the arab soldiers still picked through the dying ones to take possible jewelry, change purses or serviceable riding boots. The entire operation had taken but a few hours. The loaded supply wagons now sought out the trail to Linares where the Caliph's chief commanders had assembled to interrogate the prisoners. It was early evening as the wagons rumbled into Linares after two days travel in the hot sun. The prisoners lay on their backs, bound and hooded, without food the entire trip. Often their cries or shouts filled the air. At last, the column drew up to a farm outside the city and the prisoners were unceremoniously dumped inside a small barn. Guards were assembled and some meager bowls of stew and barrels of water were brought in as the prisoners were unbound.

Meanwhile, a tent had been set up just outside the barn. A few posts had been sunk in the ground with large hooks screwed into the tops and bottoms.

At a table in the tent sat several generals and their aides to question the prisoners. The last man to enter was a diminutive man in the uniform of a general. The senior military officials recognized him as the Caliph, but were given hand signals to keep his identity a secret. He sat quietly to one side.

The first of the prisoners was lead in. He had a severe shoulder wound and his left arm hung loosely by his side. His wrists were wrapped in leather bonds and he was then suspended by hooks at the top of the post with his back to the generals at the table.

"You, who are you?"

"Felix"

"Not so lucky, were you?" The interrogator was making a joke on the word felix which meant happy. "Are you happy now?"

"No, sir."

"Where are you from?"

"Pamplona."

"Who is the commander?" No answer.

"Who is the commander?" Again, no answer.

"Who asked you to join this raiding party?" Again, no answer.

The men had been told not to reveal the names of their leaders. "What is your occupation?"

"I am a squire to a knight."

"Who is this knight?" Again no answer.

"Do you realize you will be tortured if you do not answer?"

"Yes."

"With that, his shirt was torn down the back and he was whipped with a leather thong several times."

"Did you feel that?"

"Yes, sir."

"Will you speak now?"

"No, sir."

"Have they said they would harm your family if you spoke?"

"Yes, sir."

"Then you have a choice. Tell us in private or be tortured and possibly killed. If you tell us, no one will know. Will you tell us now?"

"No." More strokes of the whip. He was then stripped of his pants and bent over with his wrists attached to the lower end of the posts. Now his buttocks and privates were exposed. He was then thoroughly whipped, but still refused to talk.

The torture process went on for two days. Men were brought in, beaten, stripped, beaten again. It became apparent that they had been severely threatened. Probably their families were at risk. The solution was to go one of two ways: more painful torture, or a bribe – the stick and the carrot. After briefly discussing it with the generals, the Caliph decided to split the prisoners into two groups. The prisoners selected for torture would listen to the screams of the men as their fingers were cut off, hot pokers were put on their most sensitive areas. Those to be bribed were offered a chance to resettle their families in remote areas with a grant of land and farm animals. Soon, a few answers began to trickle off the prisoners' lips.

It seems they were all from Pamplona, their leader was none other than Enecco and they had been encouraged by Sancho's grandmother, Toda. The Caliph was particularly angry that Toda had not honored the treaty that she and Sancho had come to his court to ask for aid in regaining Sancho's throne. The Caliph had only asked for peace – a peace with the north that might last for generations. Yet she now sent men to break the treaty and bother the Caliph with this nuisance. And Enecco – Hasdai had warned the Caliph about Enecco before. Now all the Caliph's careful planning was a nullity. He still had war and two traitors on his hands. They must pay dearly for this. Sancho was not to be trusted.

As the questioning went on, it was revealed that Enecco was one of the prisoners. His presence was the reason the men were so reluctant to talk. Any weakness on their part must be met with even greater pain if Enecco could report that they had spoken to the enemy.

With this information, the Caliph called a temporary moratorium on the questioning. He sat in his tent and stared off into space. The servants brought in some tea and a plate of fruit. After a few hours, the Caliph called in his men. He had written a few lines and was referring to them as the men came in. Once they were assembled, he began:

"I have a few ideas as to how to deal with these prisoners. I invite any suggestions you might have."

"First, we will load up a few crates with the heads of the men from the battlefield and mix in a few heads with the prisoners who refused to talk. If we can find out, I would like some of the heads to be of noblemen. Some of the crates will be delivered to Pamplona, some to Leon. The crates will be delivered by ordinary tradesmen. The heads will be covered in tea and rose leaves to keep down the smell. The crates will be left in the middle of the central square, unopened. This will draw the curiosity of the townsfolk until they are opened in view of everyone."

"A few of the men who refused to cooperate will be fed, clothed and set free to return north. They will be bathed and their wounds dressed. They will return home. Obviously, they will be considered to have cooperated with us, and so they will be dealt with harshly by Toda and her band of treaty-breakers." "I want to know the names of all noblemen among our prisoners and the names of all those who died on the battlefield. We will demand a ransom for each – dead or alive. Of course, we will not disclose those who are dead."

"The rest will be fed, cleaned up and sold as slaves. I want them on a ship to the slave markets of Africa. We will bring the surviving nobles back to Cordoba for display in a march through the city and further questioning. I will devise further plans to deal with Sancho and Toda."

There was a silence when the Caliph finished. It was an awed silence. The Caliph had plotted his retaliation carefully. The march of the captured noblemen would rouse Cordoba to a patriotic fervor, but the later interrogation of Sancho's allies, Sancho the betrayer, would yield valuable information – which of his allies were now our enemies and which not.

The generals rose and directed their men to various tasks. The crates of heads were delivered to the common draymen in Toledo. The nobles bound and hooded to be lain on the wagons to bump along the way to Cordoba. Others cast adrift to wander back to Pamplona. By next dawn, the men were ready. Some of the generals departed to reconnoiter with the cohorts and scouts still in the countryside. Other troops of enemy horsemen would be dealt with similarly. And so, the battlefield lay abandoned to the wild dogs and birds to scavenge the bodies.

PRISONERS FROM CORDOBA

As the prisoners were slowly and triumphantly paraded past the Alcazar, past the Mosque and thence around the city, I knew I would be summoned to the Madinat for further interrogation and planning. By late morning, Eli knocked on my door and with great excitement announced that we both were to confer with the Caliph on the following morning. As I stood in my doorway, Eli showed me a magnificent Arabian stallion which strutted and pranced as Eli drew him around by the bridle. "A gift from the Caliph," he whispered. Eli and Samuel had been the Caliph's eyes and ears in Leon for some time now and must have been relaying valuable insights from the court around the once and present King Sancho. I took great pride in now having the boys taken into the Caliph's confidence. The boys had done well since they opened up their trade route, but they no longer took the arduous journey overland through Merida and Salamonca. Once learning of the water route from Cordoba to Cadiz, through Porto up to Zamora, they had shipped their goods by barge. They also had used my contacts in Porto to open my trade in dried fish and that marvelous sweet wine people were now calling Porto. Even the Catholic church had begun to order through them. With the boys no longer away from Cordoba for lengthy periods, their marriage prospects began to blossom. The same merchants' daughters that had scorned them before now batted their kohl-lined eyes at them in the streets and at the market. Marriage brokers descended on them at their homes. I must say I was very proud.

So the following morning, Eli and I got our horses from the livery near Alcazar and trotted the route to the Madinat and our meeting with ar-Rahman III. The guards saluted us at the gate and carefully inspected Eli's letter with the Caliph's seal. As a new invitee, he was carefully searched as we entered the highest gate admitting to the residential gardens and ponds. Eli could not help but gape at the rare birds flitting among the fruit trees and flowering bushes which surrounded serene ponds reflecting the sky. We were shown to the large conference room where the generals and the Chamberlain were beginning to assemble. As always, a sumptuous spread of fruit and pastries greeted us while servants whisked in and out pouring tea. After a while, double doors opened and in swept the Caliph and a full entourage. No longer dressed as a minor general, the Caliph glowed in blue and yellow flowing silks and a gleaming white bejeweled turban. When he was seated, one of the generals rolled out a large map with colored splotches all in the northern Christian regions of Hispania.

"Gentlemen," the Caliph stood and pointed with a slender walking stick, "these are the domains of Sancho's territories. The same Sancho who seems to have betrayed our friendship after we helped him regain his throne. I must exact revenge on such perfidy. As you can see, I have outined the territories of those vassals of Sancho who accepted our military help, signed a treaty and now attack my allies and vassals. Some other of these territories are the former allies and vassals of Ordono, whom we defeated. We do not know who has acceded to these fiefs. It is my intention here today to determine a strategy to conquer and possibly recapture some of these territories and punish Sancho and his vassals. I will designate certain of my forces to attack certain of these areas. Responsibility will be divided. We know from our previous alliances with Sancho which of his vassals are superior foes and which are not. We will pray on the weaker forces and the most connected to Sancho. We will secure overwhelming victories and intimidate the others. We will mass our forces and destroy the longer forces in strategic places of our choosing. Am I clear on this?" After a brief pause, the generals nodded, some rose to review the map.

"Sire," One ventured. "Are we not to pursue the richest?"

"No, Rafiq. My goal is not riches, or the expansion of my realm. It is to punish those who would sign a treaty, use our help and then betray us at the first opportunity. We wish to demonstrate our power and create chaos among the north."

"Ah, I see."

"Now, General Rahm will describe those places we will first attack and then I will assign you to different sections of the map. You will devise a strategy for that territory and present it to me for review. Am I clear on this?"

"Sire," ventured General Mafouz, "Some of us are better at certain terrains than others. Might we have a say in who is assigned where?"

"Good point, Mafouz. First, then, let us pick the vulnerable areas I wish to attack first. Then each of you will describe to the best of your knowledge how such area may be attacked. I will leave you for several minutes to review the map and make your suggestions. Meanwhile, I will withdraw for further discussions with my advisers." With that, he swept out of the room. One of the men from his entourage beckoned Eli and me to follow. We were directed into a small room down the hallway.

"Hasdai, good to see you again. I am glad you have brought your protégé with you. Good day, Eli."

"Your excellency, it is a great honor to be called to be of service. I thank you for the most excellent steed you have given me."

"Your service is valued Eli. Now, what can you tell us about things in Leon?"

Eli looked warily around the table to see how he should proceed. He had an irrepressible personality, cheerful and occasionally irreverent – a fine aspect for a salesman and negotiator, perhaps not so well suited for an audience with the Caliph. Nonetheless, he plunged in.

"Much to the dismay of my head and stomach, I have been frequenting the taverns of Leon. I am not used to drinking so much, but I bought many rounds to lubricate the tongues of my fellow imbibers. As they spoke, I hoped to have remembered who they were and what they said. I would put them in several categories. Obviously, there are those who all along were close to Sancho and had been or expected to be richly rewarded for their service in helping him to regain his throne. There were other supporters who felt they had not been rewarded enough for risking life and limb, as well as defying Ordono. There were a few who doubted Sancho would be much of a king – he had been cast out by the nobles before and might be again. Those thought him too educated and aloof from his people. I have listed them each in their category with the name, the residence, and their attitude. Sometimes in taverns which catered to low company, I even heard from some who still supported Ordono. I have some information on where he may be in hiding. It was generally agreed that he was a bad king who relied on ignorant thugs for his support and was cruel and abusive to the lords. Now he is very unpopular, but still has a small loyal following."

"For the most part, Sancho's closest and warmest supporters come from the area around and south of Pamplona. Those closest to Leon and in the north are not entirely happy to see Sancho on the throne, but consider him to be the lesser of evils. I have included their names in the notes I have prepared for your excellency."

I could tell the Caliph was well pleased with the report and he carefully perused Eli's notations at length with many "hmms" and a few "ah ha's." He passed the notes to the generals. "Well done, Eli." The Caliph said, "Perhaps you could stay while we interrogate the prisoners a bit further." Eli looked at me for assurance and I nodded. Watching this kind of interrogation was a frightful experience. The methods were brutal and shocking, particularly where the prisoners were deeply antagonistic towards the Arabs. The Caliph already had much of the information he needed and suspected these men were mostly from the Pamplona area and closely allied with Sancho, but we had to know whether Sancho encouraged or condoned these raids on Arab territory. Already, the Caliph was planning massive counter attacks if Sancho had indeed breached the treaty. Arabs are not a merciful lot when betrayed, and these prisoners and their allies to the north would regret their actions.

Elli and I walked over to a café near the large mosque and had a bit of lunch. We would return to observe the torture antecedent to the interrogations at the Alcazar prison.

ALCAZAR INTERROGATIONS

It was an eerie feeling to sit next to Eli at a table of interrogators at the Alcazar. As enlightened and educated as the Caliph was, we were now about to witness the horrifying prospect of barbaric torture methods from the desert from which these Muslims had come. Alongside us were several generals and the Caliph himself all hooded and concealed from the prisoners as they were brought in.

For the past two days, the prisoners had been isolated from each other in cells which were only four feet high and were chained to the wall. The cells were damp since they were at the lowest end of the city near the Quadilivir River, so bugs and vermin of all sorts oozed from the walls. They were fed a bowl of watery gruel and scraps of whatever was left over from the soldiers' mess. Before they entered the interrogation chamber, they would be lead past several torture devises where men practiced in these arts prepared to receive recalcitrant prisoners. There was, of course, the rack where they might be stretched until their arms and hips popped from their sockets. In another corner, there were pokers on the brazier heated to a white hot glow to touch a man's most sensitive areas. Other odd looking pieces of metal or wood fixtures lay strewn on the floor for future use. The prisoners were then lead out and chained to a chair to face their inquisitors. Each was a bedraggled, dispirited lump of humanity. The question was, "had they given up the will to resist interrogation?" In most cases, they had. While they were soldiers who had volunteered for these raids on Arab-held settlements, they were used to picking on the weak. In battle, of course, where their life was on the line, they could and did fight with intensity. Now, hungry, tired and alone, they were not so brave.

The initial questions were directed to find out who their leaders were, where they lived, and why they had joined this band to conduct the raids. Evaluations would be made as to whether they had any value to be held for ransom or be sold as slaves. Most of the men were lowly peasants who believed they could have an easy time of it stealing from the smaller Arab towns and raping the occasional woman. It was a holiday from the drudgery of farm work in the barren hills of northern Hispania. It seems the men were recruited mostly by the nobles near Pamplona, and their families were given some advance pay as their men marched off for war. There was no particular loyalty to Sancho. Like most peasants, they eyed each leader warily and sought only their own self interest and self-preservation. These men would be cleaned up, fattened up and put on barges to be sold as slaves in north Africa, where large grain farms could easily use another able body.

A few of the men were minor nobility or knights who might be ransomed back for a hefty price. These men were instructed to write home and beg to be set free by their relatives.

Then two startling revelations came out. Several of the men spoke of the capture of Osric, son of Alonzo, during the battle for Zamora. Apparently, Osric had either fled the scene of battle or faked an injury and was found by Leonese soldiers also fleeing the battle scene. Osric, in his colorful battle garb as the son of Alonzo, was easily recognizable. His value was immediately apparent and his ransom substantial. Efforts to learn where he was being held bore no fruit, but some ransom demand would undoubtedly be forthcoming.

Next, as men were questioned, it slowly came out that Enecco was one of the prisoners and had been leading the raids. He had been the most adverse to my efforts to aid king Sancho and reviled on every occasion both the Arabs and the Jews. Ah! Revenge might be sweet. Before Enecco was brought out for a second round of questioning, the Caliph called me aside for a conference.

"Hasdai, we need to decide whether to ransom him or not. He may be valuable, however, in telling us whether Sancho is encouraging these raids. He was close to Sancho before and knows his royal family well."

"Your Excellency, as you have clearly seen, his position with Sancho is extremely important. If at all possible, we must find out whether he is doing this on his own, or with Sancho's blessing."

"Quite right. Let us squeeze him for more information."

Enecco claimed not to have had any discussions with Sancho about his raids on the Arab south. After several trips to the instruments of torture, it was decided that his value as ransom would diminish. Before he left, I had to ask a few questions.

"Sir Enecco, why is it not possible to live in peace with the Arabs?"

"Sir, they are not Christian. We must convert these heathens to our faith."

"Does not Jesus encourage love of one's neighbor? Yet you raid our villages, steal our goods and rape our women. Surely Jesus would not condone that?"

"Sir, war is war."

"But do you think this will cause people to convert to Christianity?"

"If not, let them go back to where they came from."

"What about the Jews?"

"They must convert or die."

"Didn't Sancho say he was grateful to the Jewish doctor and would permit the Jews to remain and worship as they pleased?"

"He said that. I disagreed."

"Why not leave the Jews in peace?"

"They do not follow the ways of Jesus."

"But Jesus was a Jew."

"No, I have heard that said, but he was not."

"Was Jesus the same as God?"

"So some monks say. I do not understand this business about the trinity, it makes no sense. I believe what our priests tell us, and they say he was a god, but not the God."

"So you are an Arian?"

"I don't know what that is. The priests say we must reconquer Hispania and that it is a holy mission. It must be all Christian."

"Even with war, with stealing, with rape?"

"That is part of war. They read us that from the Bible."

The Caliph motioned with his head to me and shrugged his shoulders. I left the room to speak with him.

"This man is dangerous as an enemy. Should we ransom him back or sell him off?"

"Your excellency, I fear that many people will follow him if he remains up north. He is dangerous and must be sent to Africa."

"Good, I agree. First, we will castrate him. We want no sons seeking revenge. He can still work in the fields, but must never fight in battle again."

"I think that is best, Your Excellency."

Two days later, the men having been well fed and scrubbed clean, and would be loaded onto a barge and chained to the gunwales. They would float down the Quadilivir River, round Gibraltar and head for a slave auction in the Barbary Coast, Tunis to be exact. These robust fighting men of white skin would fetch a fine price. The Chamberlain was quick to total up the cost of the expedition against the proceeds from the sale of slaves. Although a slight loss, the venture encouraged the Caliph to launch further expeditions.

GENERAL FROM CALIPH ABOUT OSRIC

It was a quiet, pleasant night as my family sat down to dinner in the garden behind our house. Rachel, with Yael's help, had prepared a chicken stew over noodles. The fountain in the pond tinkled peacefully. The city noise had muted, as soon the stress of the day would melt. I had a full morning of patients and an afternoon at the school ben Hannock now ran with my oversight. Scholars and poets were coming to Cordoba almost daily to sample the intellectual fervor of our school and the entire Cordoban community. And then, a rap on our front door.

I opened it to find General Rodrigo in common Arab attire nervously pacing. "Ah, Hasdai. We must talk. Can we find a private place?"

"Certainly, General, come into my study." Rachel called from the back, "Hasdai, who is it?"

"Just a moment dear, some business matter."

Rodrigo followed me into the study and I closed the door. "Dr. Shaprut, Osric has been taken, we just heard."

"Osric, you mean Alonzo's boy? The one who was harassing the girl?"

"That's the one. It seems he was aiding his father in the attack at Zamora and disappeared. We didn't know of this until much later. Alonzo feared he was dead and sent out search parties through the battlefield to no avail. Osric had been sent with a message to another general on the battlefield and he seems to have vanished."

"So how did we learn this?"

"He is being held for ransom. Someone must have discovered his value after he was taken prisoner."

"Who is holding him and what do they want?"

"It must be someone connected to Enecco because they want to exchange him for Enecco."

"Is Enecco still here? I thought he was to be sold as a slave."

"True, but he had not been sent out to Tunis yet."

"So we could make the trade if we wanted?"

"If we wanted."

"This is not a good trade. A skilled and ruthless enemy for an immature boy who is a troublemaker."

"True, but he is Alonzo's son and Alonzo is a valuable vassal on our border. He wants his son back."

"I can see that. What does the Caliph think?"

"He wants you to go up to Toledo and negotiate a trade."

"I see. He is willing to let Enecco go, just like that?"

"There is more to the story, but I cannot discuss it."

"I see. So he wants me to go. When?"

"As soon as possible. Two of my men will ride with you as bodyguards."

"Should I leave tomorrow morning?"

"That would be best."

"Tell the Caliph I will go then, but I want to hear more about this deal."

"We will send one of the Caliph's advisers who will give you more information. You will also meet Alonzo and his party in Toledo."

"Very well, have my guards join me at dawn in the Alcazar livery ready to leave."

"The Caliph and I thank you. Good evening."

TO TOLEDO FOR RANSOM

The next morning, I went to the livery where my horse Tariq was readied by Aziz, the stable boy. "He knows he's going somewhere in a hurry, Dr. Shaprut. He can't wait."

The two bodyguards were standing by their mounts and awaited my orders. They were the same who had gone to Leon with me. They were armed and looked happy to see me again. "Dr. Shaprut. Always a pleasure. We remember. No dead game. Bring them in alive so we can bleed them like bilal butchers."

"Ah, you remembered. And I remember. Prayer stops along the way."

We traveled nearly 40 miles every day from dawn to dusk with stops for the Muslim prayers. There was precious little game around so we bought grain and fruits as we went, often eating in the saddle. Soon the foothills of Toledo came into view after four days. We showed the guards on the main road north our letters from the Caliph and were greeted warmly by the mayor of the town. The party representing Enecco had not arrived yet, so we settled our horses with the military horses and were escorted to rooms in the castle. I took a lengthy nap. These long rides were wearing on a man of my age, but I awoke for dinner. The mayor had been instructed that my mission was to remain clandestine, and that we were not to be entertained. My guards stopped by as the sun was setting and we went for a walk to discover an appropriate inn for dinner. My guards followed the Muslim faith quite carefully and did not partake of alcohol. It was no imposition on me to refrain as well, so we sought out a Muslim cafe. Toledo was a prosperous town so there was no shortage of pleasant cafes. The facades of the cafes were handsomely decorated in colored tiles in hues of blue, gold and orange. As we sat at the "Persian Songbird" we were immediately brought pots of a sweet mint tea as the waiter recited the menu. Apparently, this restaurant had a Persian cook and so the entrees were of that style. At the urging of the waiter, I often am suspicious of such urging because it usually means the restaurant was unable to dispose of the item for several days, nonetheless, we ordered the pomegranate walnut stew. It turned out to be a mixture of tart pomegranate with chunks of chicken, ground walnuts and onions and we ate heartily, wiping our dishes with pita bread to sop up the sauce. Eating with Muslims, I had few concerns about observing Kosher practice. Mohammad must have been very close to the Jews in Mecca and Medina as he was formulating his revelations and adopted most Hebraic food rituals. After dinner, we walked around the city which still had many Roman temples, agoras and a very fine ampitheatre still in use. There was a substantial Christian population who mingled freely with the Arabs. I was reluctant to ask my guards to go to the Jewish section. That would wait until tomorrow.

Toledo was not under the control of Cordoba or its Caliph. Nearly every two or three years, Muslim commanders sought to declare themselves rulers or kings of Toledo, only to have internal rebellions break out or outsiders assail the city walls. Some were successful and some were not, causing the city to remain in a constant state of flux. As the northernmost area of Moorish al-Andalus and its least stable, Toledo was not a place to engage in political talk. So, I and my guards assiduously avoided any contact with the locals – Arab or Christian, which might reveal our mission. Only the mayor and a few of his trusted advisers knew. So we walked the city and went to bed early.

The next day, I went to visit the Jewish area. For centuries, it had been the subject of harsh treatment by the ruling Visigoths. Now, unfortunately, was no exception. The ruling Muslims were not as enlightened as my Caliph and the occasional successor to the previous ruler did little to enhance the intellectual life, the arts and sciences, much less a tolerance for the Jewish community. My walk to what I was told was the Jewish community was a sad one. I found people living in poverty, frequently under attack or harassed. They were forced to wear yellow emblems designating their Jewish status, and were barred from most trades or professions. They were heavily taxed, but managed to eke out an existence in and among the various trades. Things did not bode well for the future of this community. Yet still it remained. There was still a small market place, a pen for the ritual slaughter of animals and a synagogue. I returned for a midday meal in a depressed mood.

My guards met me in our rooms. As we walked out to a nearby food stand, we met Alonzo, Osric's father. We were informed that the other contingent would arrive by 4:00 p.m. and we could use the mayor's dining room for a conference. As we walked out to the row of stands, I had to prepare Alonzo.

"Lord Alonzo, since we are here to secure the release of your son Osric, I must advise you on my plans for negotiation. We use the same principles as those to purchase a plump capon at the market."

"Dr. Shaprut, your wisdom comes highly praised. I await your good counsel in all of this. I know of your many experiences."

"First, you must not appear to be Osric's father. I will also suggest the possibility that he is only a step-son to Lord Alonzo."

"Why so?"

"We must cheapen the value of what they offer. If they are aware that you are his father and have a strong influence on the Caliph, enough to have the Caliph bargain on your behalf, the price will go up. They will play on your sympathies and cause you to put greater pressure on the Caliph's man – namely me. You must appear rigid and uncommunicative. Can you do that?"

"Good Doctor, if it will help you, I will do as you ask."

"If I suggest that Osric has little value, you must not flinch."

"I see your purpose."

"Next, it seems that Enecco's negotiators are late. They try to gain the upper hand by implying that we are more anxious for the trade than they by making us wait. I have arranged for men to tell us when they arrive and we shall have left the building. They are very intent on regaining their leader Enecco and cannot fail in this mission. So, we will appear to have left to return home, they will use great efforts to bring us back here. So we will leave now and wait at the livery stable. Do not fear, they will come pursuing us rather than us waiting nervously for them."

"I see."

"I will also insist that they produce proof that Osric is alive and well in their custody. They may try to make him appear to be pitiful and increase our urgency to make a deal. Do not be moved by this. We must make our mission purely a passionless business transaction, nothing more. You must steel your resolve."

"You may count on me, Dr. Shaprut." All men filed out to the livery to await the contingent to bargain for Enecco's release. It was not long before one of the mayor's men came bursting into the stable. "Dr. Shaprut, they are here. Where are you going?"

"Home. We thought they no longer wished to bargain."

"No! No! They are here and await you. They are quite dismayed."

"Oh, I see. Well then, we will return. You may go and tell them." The man left in a hurry. I turned to Alonzo and my guards. "Now we make them wait. Take a moment, and then we will stroll leisurely back to the castle." Alonzo could not suppress a grin as he shook his head. "Dr. Shaprut, you are an experienced negotiator. You would have the butcher chasing you down the aisle to sell you his best plump chicken at half price."

"Thank you, Lord Alonzo." The guards smirked as well as we strolled up to the castle.

As we entered the dining hall, it was nearly 5:00 p.m. Dinner was to begin at 6:30 so we had just an hour and a half to talk today. Time is always a factor in negotiating and I meant to use it to my advantage.

Across the table from us sat three large men dressed in heavy leather tunics. They were rough and unkempt and already the room was heavy with the smell of body odor and horses.

"But, Dr. Shaprut, you say Osric is a stepson to Lord Alonzo. Is this so?"

"From what we hear, his wife had a son from a previous marriage. He is no blood relation, nor an heir." The price was going down.

"We have heard he was his very own son."

"We cannot confirm either way, but are told he is a stepson."

"So we must ask, how is Enecco?"

"We were about to sell him into slavery and were feeding him well so he would fetch a decent price in Tunis. So, I would say he is in fine shape."

"Was he tortured?"

"I would guess not." That was an obvious lie to all. If Enecco was a leader of this raid, he undoubtedly would have been tortured for any information.

"So what is your offer?" A naïve play in negotiation. It is always best to have the other side make the opening offer and then you negotiate downward from there. "Well that depends. You have a stepson to offer. One who has shall we say not distinguished himself in battle, one who is not an heir, and for what? You wish to receive back an experienced military commander, who upon his return to your group, would lead further raids on the Caliphate's north border. Have I stated out respective positions correctly?"

The men looked at each other. Someone or some group wanted Enecco back and as soon as possible. Osric by himself was doing them no good. As I stated the basis of the transaction, it certainly sounded unbalanced. Their deficiency in language kept them from articulating it in a way more favorable to them. Surely, they could depict a mother and father fearful for the well being of their son, coward though he be, and they were under pressure to secure Enecco back in a timely manner. Yet they were already delayed.

"Before we can make any arrangement, we must see to this boy's condition. Can I send a man to observe him?" It was agreed to send a man to their camp blindfolded.

"Hearing nothing more for now, I suggest we return tomorrow morning at 9:00 a.m. promptly to start again. Please formulate your position by then."

The three men turned to one another and shrugged. OK, tomorrow it would be. They rose and left. I and Lord Alonzo followed.

As they were safely in the street outside the castle, Alonzo turned to me, "Do you think they meant to capture Osric all along?"

"I can't say. Would Osric have run from the battle?"

"It is hard to say. He has had some military training. On that day, he was only a messenger bringing orders from the command to the field. It is hard to say."

"Whatever, it diminishes his value."

"What do you seek?"

"I don't know yet. At best, peace, but we know such pledges are worthless. Money or ransom, always a possibility, but I don't believe they have much to offer. They certainly are not aligned with Sancho and do not have access to his territory. I suspect they are from Pamplona which is not a wealthy area. But we shall see, we shall see." We walked and talked further until a friendly Muslim inn beckoned.

GENERAL'S TAIL TO FARM

An entourage of armed men from Pamplona surrounded the hooded figure, one of my bodyguards, and began to mount horses in the courtyard in Toledo. A rather plump old peasant in a straw hat and poncho sat by the roadside. A muddy plow horse kicked at the dirt by his side and was munching on the apple he had been fed. When most of the armed men were mounted and the hooded man righted in his saddle, the peasant too mounted up. He peered around as if lost and scratched his belly. As the troup of mounted men left on the road north out of town, the peasant followed at a discrete distance. The road was a wide old Roman road with much traffic in each direction until the further outskirts of the city and then there were but a few travelers – some in carts, some on horseback. The armed troup walked and trotted at a leisurely pace. The dust they rose could easily be seen from at least a half league back. At that distance, the peasant's horse plodded forward. After several miles, the troup turned left and followed a dirt track between farm fields. The peasant followed. After an hour of uneventful walking, they turned onto a farm and began to drift behind a storage barn. From the roadway, the peasant could see a number of tents and a ring of horses. Without entering the roadway into the farm, the peasant could see the troup dismount and shift the hooded man from his horse. The peasant was careful to note the family name at the entrance way, "Espero per Cielo", hope for the heavens, the name of an old Visigoth prayer. Yet, the farm was still in Moorish territory, a bare ten miles from the castle in Toledo. The peasant slowly turned his horse and headed back to the Roman road where he noted the stone mile marker by the roadside. His horse ambled back to Toledo.

9.4 miles to the castle, look for "Espero per Cielo." The peasant munched on some pumpkin seeds in his saddle pouch and hummed softly to himself. He must ask the mayor who owned the Espero.

On the way into town, two riders on beautiful Arabian stallions pulled up to the peasant.

The one rider asked, "General Rodrigo, where is he?"

"Look for marker number 9.4 and go to the left. The "Espero per Cielo" farm is on the right. They are about 100 yards in a field encampment. I would guess about 30 men in all." The riders lurched their horses to the rear and galloped south. General Rodrigo and his horse were in no hurry and would see Hasdai at his room in a few hours with a full report.

SECOND DAY OF OSRIC NEGOTIATIONS

We got up early this morning and had a leisurely tea and yogurt at one of the Muslim inns as the people passed by on their everyday pursuits. As the church bell struck the ninth hour, Lord Alonzo rose, "Hasdai, it is time." Our bodyguard reported he has seen Osric in the farm outside town and he was indeed, alive and well.

"Relax, Lord Alonzo, they were late yesterday. Today they won't be. It shows we have the upper hand. They have been contemplating the values of our deal: A cowardly stepson for an experienced military leader. Not an equal bargain, yet they are under great pressure to get one of their elite back. It will appear that Lord Alonzo is only seeking to calm his wife, about whom my Caliph cares little. That is our line. Relax, have another cup of tea. It will allow us to stall these negotiations further when you ask to relieve yourself."

"Hasdai, your wisdom prevails," he said pouring more tea and reaching for another apricot. The sun rose over the buildings on the town square. I rose and Alonzo and our guard followed. To be very late would be an insult provoking anger, somewhat late must be excused as a personal eccentricity.

We walked into the conference room. Two of yesterday's men were seated and looked anxiously at a third man who had been pacing along the opposite wall. One of the men from yesterday spoke, "Dr. Shaprut, we have been joined by Wamba. He will conduct further dealings." Even better, we had now drawn the apparent new leader who had dismissed one of the former men.

"Pleased to meet you Sir." I chirped happily.

He ignored my pleasantry and proceeded. "You Sir have been stalling," with a burst of hostility. "We have a noble son of one of your vassals we would exchange for one of our countrymen. What is the problem?"

"First, Sir, we must understand who you are. We had believed that we were aiding Sancho in his quest to be reseated as King of Leon and that we were allies. Lord Alonzo and his men fought alongside you and King Sancho. Now you kidnap his son and ask for ransom."

"Sir, I will not play your Jew games as if I were at the market haggling over a chicken. You have taken Enecco prisoner. He is ours."

"But he and, I would guess, you have broken the very truce we agreed upon with King Sancho. All we asked in return for our aid was a peaceful north. Now, you and Enecco seem to have ignored the truce but enjoyed the benefits of our considerable military assistance both at Zamora and Leon. Do you represent King Sancho? Is there no truce."

"We were not part of that agreement."

"Ah, but Enecco was. He came with King Sancho and his grandmother, Toda, and asked in Cordoba for our assistance. And Enecco was there and agreed. So I ask you, can you be trusted to engage in a deal to exchange prisoners? I might add, you acquired your prisoner as he was fighting on the same side as you and Enecco when you kidnapped him." I could see this Wamba clenching and unclenching his fists. He had to recognize the truth of what I said. But he was a large fellow used to fighting in battle. He had long hanks of dirty blond hair hanging straight to his shoulders. He wore a military leather tunic embossed with a shield of some sort at his belly.

"Sir, this is all irrelevant. You have Enecco and we have Osric. Let us exchange and be done. No more of these games."

"You mean we should release a leader of perfidious men who would disavow treaties and who will be a nuisance at our northern border. For what? A coward who hides from battle."

"What do you want?"

"We want peace at our northern borders. Can you give us what we have already bargained for and earned? Should we trust Enecco again only to have him ignore our deal just days after we supported him in battle."

"We may execute Osric then."

"So you might, and we Enecco. What then? Who has lost the most?"

"Bring Lord Alonzo here. See what he says."

"Lord Alonzo does not have Enecco and cannot deliver him to you. If you wished to bargain with Alonzo, you should have asked him directly. Now you ask the Caliph and he has been betrayed before. Why should he bargain with you now? Where is your proof of good faith?"

"A Jew asks for good faith!" He bellowed. He pounded the table. "What do you want? You entangle me in webs. Shall we fight in the ampitheatre, you puny purse snatcher?"

"So, it has come to that. Threats. Good Lord Wamba. Perhaps we should retire for the day so you can regain your composure."

"No." he shouted. "No, no, no! We wish to exchange, yet you ask for what we cannot give."

"What? Peace. A guarantee of peace. You would ask for us to accept your word of a guarantee of peace from someone who has defrauded us before?" I know I was pushing beyond a comfortable point. "Sir, we will leave now and return after a midday meal. Perhaps you will have mustered a more amicable perspective." I rose, Lord Alonzo followed my lead and we left. Wamba and the other two sat agape, open-mouthed, but silent.

As we walked out of the castle to the large open square, a plump elderly peasant in a straw hat and a ragged poncho came up begging for alms. He said, "All is in readiness. They are at a farm two hours from here. Is there any reason to delay?" Lord Alonzo looked at me, puzzled. I turned to him. "Lord Alonzo, we will surround and capture the men holding Osric if you think it acceptable."

"Dr. Shaprut, your wisdom has prevailed so far. Do what you can."

"General Rodrigo, you may proceed." I said handing him a few small coins. He bowed and nodded and scurried off.

AT ESPERO PER CIELO

A few men crept slowly through the underbrush on several sides of the farm. They peered at a small group of men loitering about a few tents which were pitched haphazardly behind a storage barn. Soon, the air was filled with a few whistles and cackling sounds similar to the local birds. On three sides, armed men came to the edge of the farm. At the sound of a trumpet, horses were spurred to action and leaped over the brush and raced towards the tent area. The men around the tents screamed and ran about. They were not able to get to their horses in time, nor reach their weapons. When the mounted men came to twenty yards away, shouts of "fall to the ground," "hands up" rose over the noises of the horses rearing to a stop. Soon, without a single confrontation, the horses surrounded the men who were standing with their hands up. A senior officer dismounted and asked, "Who's in charge here?" The men pointed to a tent and several other men dismounted and ran to the tent brandishing long pointed spears with a curved knife blade at the end. "Come out, come out" was shouted at the tent. Slowly, a flap was pulled back and a large man came out. He was agape as he stared at a circle of mounted men surrounding his encampment and his troup standing with their arms raised.

"Who are you?"

"I am Ludovic. Who are you? What do you want?"

"We are soldiers of the Caliph. We want your prisoner. Where is Osric?" Of course, he knew who they were and of course he knew they wanted Osric. He hesitated, looked around, saw his men with their weapons on the ground and their hands raised in surrender. He also saw 120 men mounted on horses and carrying long pointed spears with curved blades. It took some time to occur to him, but he began to see that his entire troup was surrounded and taken, quietly and without a fight. A massive disgrace sure to be spread. He motioned for one of his men to bring Osric out. As Osric came out, he blinked his eyes in the bright sunlight and shaded his brow. He was still in the military garb he had worn at the battle for Zamora, but now it was dirty and tattered. Two men dismounted and brought Osric away from his captors.

"I am Akheem. I am a captain of the Caliph's army. You are my prisoners now. Kneel where you stand while we collect your weapons." Several more men dismounted and started to collect a large assortment of swords, maces, daggers and bows. Some were in good condition, some in disrepair and barely usable.

From a distance, there was a rumble as two large wagons drawn by large horses came bumping down the farm road and across the field to the encampment. As the wagons rolled to a stop, more men dismounted and began to throw the weapons into the wagons and take the prisoners' horses to be tied to the back of the wagons. When all was assembled, Akheem said, "You, Sir Ludovic, form a line with your men. The first ten will be tied and will walk tethered to the wagons. The next ten will sit in the wagon. And the last ten will be mounted across the backs of your horses. Every ten miles we will rotate the men so the ones walking will not slow our pace. Now, move quickly." The men moved slowly but obeyed the orders of Akheem's men. A defeat and capture without a fight was an embarrassment and they hung their heads. They knew several fates awaited them: first a long and grueling march to Cordoba; next, interrogation and torture, and last, either death or a life of slavery. In their zeal to follow Enecco, the men were always aware that this was a possibility, but overlooked the thought of capture or death for the prospect of looting, rape and a life of excitement, free from the toil of a farm.

As the train of wagons, prisoners and men were finally assembled, they returned to the farm road. The train went south for a while and veered east to go through the back roads in order to avoid going near Toledo. This journey would take several days, slowed by the march of prisoners and the pace of the wagons.

Before veering off the old Roman road south to Toledo, two riders continued on to Toledo. As they entered the town and the main square, they sought out a drowsy plump peasant leaning against a wall. "It is done," they said, nothing more. They remounted and continued south.

The old peasant nodded. He rose painfully and limped to the castle. As he approached the guards at the gateway, he was addressed.

"Halt, you have no business here. Go away."

"Sir, I have a letter." He handed up a document with the seal of the Caliph. At once, the guards drew to attention and saluted. "General Rodrigo, please pass." Once inside the gateway, the old peasant straightened up and resumed with square shoulders and a brisk military stride into the castle, escorted by one of the guards to the dining area where Dr. Shaprut and Wamba were meeting. The guard knocked on the heavy oaken door with his spear. Dr. Shaprut's guard opened it and rose to attention on recognizing General Rodrigo.

"Hasdai, I would speak with you." I came to the door and into the corridor. "We have retaken Osric and we have taken 30 captives, all of whom are on their way to Cordoba. Their leader is Ludovic."

"I see. Do we have any intentions of taking the men in here as prisoners for the crime of betrayal."

"If they admit participating in Osric's capture, they are criminals. Then yes. They are not emissaries."

"Very well. Have your men stand by to arrest." I returned to the dining table. "So Wamba, I must know when you were aware of Osric's taking."

"What difference does that make?"

"I would know if he was a deserter or simply a prisoner of war. It matters to my Caliph as to his value."

"I see. I observed it with my own eyes. We rode up on him. He was wearing the military garb of his father, Lord Alonzo. His horse was standing nearby and he was sitting on a fallen tree."

"Did he make any resistance when you rode up?"

"No. There were about ten of us. Resistance would have been futile."

"I see. So you knew he was a soldier in the service of Lord Alonzo at the time of his arrest, or should I say kidnapping? What did you intend to do with him."

"We would hold him until Enecco decided what his value was."

"So you did not intend to return him to Alonzo?"

"No. He was to be used for ransom."

"I see. So, even though you were fighting on the same side as Alonzo you were holding hostages against him and the Caliph?"

"Dr. Shaprut, we have been at war with the Arabs for centuries. Alonzo was aligned with the Arabs, we with the Christians. Alonzo was an enemy."
"So, you are now an enemy. In that case, you have breached our treaty with Sancho. You have taken a hostage."

"Whatever you call it."

"Sir, I am sorry then. I must ask the Caliph for further instructions. I will send a messenger today with full details."

"So when will we exchange for Enecco?"

"Perhaps you should ask Ludovic when you see him in Cordoba."

"What does that mean? How do you know Ludovic? In Cordoba? What do you mean?"

"You may also ask Enecco."

"Will we see Enecco?"

"Yes, in Cordoba."

"What do you mean?"

"That remains to be seen. Good day Sir." I rose and Lord Alonzo and the guard followed. I spoke no word until we were safely outside.

"Lord Alonzo, we have recaptured Osric. He is safe and will see you shortly. We have also taken all of Wamba's men as prisoners. They are on a long trek to Cordoba by back roads."

"Oh, Dr. Shaprut. That is incredible. I owe much to you and the Caliph."

"Sir, you are a faithful vassal and deserve our full support."

"What can I give you? I owe you much."

"Sir, I am in the employ of the Caliph. I ask only that you treat the Jews in your community with respect."

"Of course Dr. Shaprut. I will establish one of those schools of yours. Would that be acceptable?"

"Most acceptable. Thank you kindly."

"So what will happen to Wamba and the others?"

"I think you will see Wamba taken prisoner if you look just at the gateway to the castle."

As I spoke, we turned to see ten armed men surround Wamba and the two aides just at the gateway. There was some shouting. Some use of swear words I should have noted for my dictionary of the new Iberian tongue evolving out of Latin, Frankish and Visigothic. Mostly, I think they were referring to dumb farm animals and the chastity of our parental lineage. Alonzo and I strode with our guard to a nice Muslim inn to sip some mint tea. I gave a quick salute to a plump peasant dozing in the shade by the wall.

BACK IN CORDOBA

My two guards and I were elated by the results of our trip to Toledo. Our horses must have sensed it too, so they were happy to gallop and prance along the well worn road south. While the horses glistened with sweat in the sun, we wiped them down and the guards were off for their regular prayers. We remounted and covered great distances in between prayer stops. Of course, we reached Cordoba way ahead of the train of wagons dragging prisoners behind them. My guards split off at the outskirts of town and went on to Madinat al-Zahra and the Caliph. He would want all the details. I dropped my horse off at the livery at the Alcazar and walked home to the Juderia nearby. David was just back from school and sat in the garden staring off into space while eating from a fruit plate.

"So, Father, how did it go?" I described my trip, Toledo, the "negotiations" and of course the capture and arrest. I was careful to explain how to negotiate and why I took some of the positions I had. I'm sure he didn't absorb it all, but the more exposure to skills in life the better. Soon Rachel and Yael came home and began to prepare supper.

I went about my daily affairs for a few days – translations with Brother Nicholas, mornings with medical patients, visits to ben Hannoch's school. On the third day, a train of soldiers guarding the wagons and a trail of ragged prisoners traveling on ropes came through the city. The Caliph and a large entourage was assembled to greet General Rodrigo and his men. There were trumpets and tubas and men leading cheers while jeering the prisoners. It was not unlike a Roman triumphal march. At the west of the city, the soldiers were relieved and the prisoners hauled off to the prison cells in the Alcazar. Determination as to their respective fates would be made after they were interrogated. Most of the healthy ones would be sold as slaves after a brief voyage over to Algiers. As expected, the interrogations yielded little.

Apparently, Enecco was an independent adventurer who was leading a gang of thugs on raids of Arab settlements along what was now the northern border area. Although Enecco claimed some legitimacy by urging his men to recapture Christian lands from the Arabs, it was as usual the opportunity to attack lightly defended farming communities to loot and rape.

When questioned as to how their Christian faith was somehow urging them to overwhelm weaker and innocent farm people, they could only shrug. They seemed to know they were destined to become slaves in North Africa where their living conditions would be brutal. They did not seem to blame Enecco to whom they continued to express loyalty.

When asked about the whereabouts of Ordono, some believed he had fled to what they called "Finisterre" or "lands end" in their language. This generally meant the area in the northwest of the Iberian peninsula near Santiago de Compostella. They claimed no loyalty to him, but seemed to look toward Pamplona where Enecco came from.

Soon the prisoners were to be cleaned up, fed well and exercised in the prison yard so they would fetch a better price at the slave market. Their particular skills were catalogued, but the men for the most part had very few valuable skills, could not read or do arithmetic and seemed to know only farming and fighting. Most were descendants of the Visigoths, intermarried with the Romans and all held unsophisticated Christian faiths. It was not a very valuable assembly of slave material, but this many men would at least pay for the expedition to arrest them.

Their horses were a different story. For the most part, their horses were sturdy, deep chested and large. Not like the delicate Arabian thorobreds, but more fit for plow horses and as patient, plodding animals capable of bearing riders and their baggage long distances. They had been well cared for, as in most cases, they were the prize possession of the prisoner and his family. They would also make excellent war horses because of their strength and stamina.

The question of slavery has always had me perplexed. The Torah permits the ownership of slaves, but requires that we treat them humanely. But when we were slaves in Egypt, I believe we were taught a lesson, as the Torah does so frequently. I can feel the pain of a slave, so I do not own any myself, but other Jews do. They, of course, are not permitted to own Christian slaves. I content myself as do many Jews by redeeming those of us under slavery's rule. Many of my teachers at the school were learned men whom we redeemed. Jews, however, rarely are permitted to own land, and so rarely employ slaves at the most difficult tasks of agriculture. But it remains a difficult question for those of us whose ancestors made bricks for the Pharaoh. But these prisoners belonged to the Caliph. It was his determination to sell them into the markets of North Africa and often to the cruelest masters. Such was the fate of men who made war and lost; as was known and accepted as one of their fates.

It was not long before barges were loaded to float down the Quadalivir to Cadiz and back through Gibraltar. In little time, the men would be tilling the vast grain fields of the Arabs all along the southern coast of the Mediterranean. If they were lucky, some might become soldiers again, but most would end their days in back-breaking toil in the grain fields.

The Caliph, as he often did, rewarded my efforts with a large bonus of gold. It was my son's turn to receive a special gift. Waiting for him after school were two horse soldiers who escorted him to the military stables where a beautiful young bay colt, freshly bathed was waiting with a new bridle and saddle. David would be trained with the sons of the soldiers and the nobility in horsemanship. It would not be long before David would parade his thorobred before his school mates. I, of course, gave him the paternal lecture on the danger of lusting after material possessions and the joy of searching for the treasures of the mind. I was not sure if he fully absorbed this wisdom as he was stroking the animal's mane at the time and nodding in partial awareness of my talk. Ah, the education of our children is one of the burdens the creator has put upon us. Only sometimes are we successful.

REPORT ON SANCHO'S BANQUET

I was summoned once again to Madinat-al-Zahra to a meeting. I already knew the subject of the meeting was to be Eli's report on the banquet held in Leon by Sancho I. Eli had rushed by the now frequently used water route down the Douro River to Porto, along the Atlantic coast to Cadiz and then by barge up the Quadalivir to Cordoba. My protégé had become a merchant in Leon backed by a loan from the Caliph to keep an eye on the politics in Leon. I had my horse readied at the livery and rode the distance west from Cordoba to the Caliph's new palace complex. Dismounting at the upper tier and going directly to the large throne room, I was met by the usual assemblage of the Caliph's advisers – the chamberlain, the generals and others whose official duties were never clearly specified to me. Eli was already there and happy to see me. He was nervous and fearful of addressing this august group, but I calmed him down, reminded him he was named after a Hebrew sage and told him to organize his thoughts, but expect to be interrupted and questioned from time to time. He took a gulp of tea and nodded.

Soon the Caliph swept in through the heavy oaken double doors at the end of the room. He and his entourage of aides sat at one end of the long table. The Caliph was quite a handsome man, but short. He sat at a raised throne-like chair and waved Eli to the lectern at the center of the northern wall. The men assembled scarcely had time to rise and salute the Caliph before he sat. It was obvious that this was to be an important and urgent meeting.

Eli moved to the lectern and stood in front of the large mosaic map of Iberia which adorned the wall.

"Your Excellency, assembled gentlemen, as you know, I have been a merchant in Leon for many months now and endeavored to report on the political events in that kingdom in the service of the Caliph. I have frequented the taverns and fostered relationships with those in power. As a result, I was invited to one of the regular large banquets the recently installed King Sancho I had ordered. These are held frequently now in a large field outside the city. Large gallery pits are set up, masses of soldiers surround the field and wagonloads of produce, vegetables and fruit sit by the side. Kitchen workers of all sorts scurry back and forth from the castle to the field, and in and among the tables. The guests enter through a series of banners and pennants and a large archway while their horses remain tethered or tied on the outside. Each banquet is a regal display. The king himself has once again grown in girth to immense proportions. He weighs over 30 stone and must be guided up the stairs by several aides to his place on the dais with his wife and grandmother and other notables by his side.

Politics in Leon have not been kind to the King. He has had to quell numerous disputes among those vassals who helped him in the battle for Zamora and Leon. Ordono seems to continue to plague him from wherever he is in exile. Sancho issues orders, summons vassals to his castle, sends troops against recalcitrant subjects, to no avail. In general, he does not enjoy the respect of his vassals. He is too fat again to ride a horse. Because he is well educated and speaks with lofty ideas, his nobles feel unable to understand or connect with him. He has attempted to foster the arts and sciences, but they feel he has neglected military training. Disputes still arise over his division of the land from Ordono's nobles and no one is happy with his treaty with you. The nobles enjoy these raids on our northern territories, but claim they are obligated to bring Iberia back under Christian rule. I must also say that the nobles are for the most part an uncouth lot who seem to enjoy fighting, hunting and drinking the most and have little regard for learning or the arts."

At this, a few of the Christian generals and nobles under the Caliph's power began to shift uncomfortably in their chairs. A low hubbub arose. The Caliph broke in.

"Gentlemen, you can see that we are blessed with a diverse mixture of religions and blood. It supports the civilization we enjoy. It is easy to see that Leon is having trouble now, as did the Visigoths before them. Lack of stability, constant armed conflict, and many different leaders harms everyone. We, of course, welcome you all into our Caliphate and we do enjoy peace and prosperity. But, please, Eli continue."

"Thank you, Your Excellency. These banquets had become regular events, but often, the men fortified with the ample stores of wine, had become more unruly, sometimes happily, sometimes fighting among themselves. "I have been careful to notate those nobles who seem to fight with each other most commonly. But I must say that those near Pamplona and the east are the most unruly and fight the most."

One of the generals, Theodis, barked, "Enough of this flowery description. What in the name of hell happened that brings us here?" Theodis was known for his fiery temper. A descendant of the Visigoths, he resented this Moorish control of his old lands, but still was a staunch and reliable supporter of the Caliph under whom he had enjoyed much success and enrichment.

Eli looked panicked at this outburst and blurted out, "Sancho was poisoned." The room gasped. The Caliph had already heard this as had I, but it was the first for most in the room. Eli went on. "I could see the king grab at his throat, fall forward onto the table knocking it over and fall off the front of the dais." The room fell silent.

"Who did this? Are we sure it was poison? How did the poison get into his food?" A flood of questions filled the air. When this subsided, the Caliph spoke.

"Eli, tell us about the investigation."

"Yes, Your Excellency. The king's doctors of course ran to the king and could smell the bitter almond of cyanide. The King had vomited up a bright red blood and defecated profusely. The cyanide was often found in the death of cattle and the doctors were familiar with it."

"Who might have done this?"

"The king's usual diet each day consisted of seven meals with 17 different meat dishes. All of these were featured at the banquet and served by different servants, usually slaves. The remaining foods on his table were tested, but no conclusion could be reached."

"Who could have done this?"

"Some say Ordono, some say the nobles of Galicia and Castile to the east. The leader last to oppose him was Fernan Gonzalez of Castile, but he was executed when Sancho returned."

"So, no answer."

"Nothing definite, your excellecy."

"Who succeeded him?"

"His son Ramiro." The room was silent. The Caliph stared up at the ceiling with his fingers forming a bridge.

At last he spoke, "Well, gentlemen, what do we do next?"

Another long silence. General Rodrigo at last cleared his throat.

"Your Excellency, I am sure we can expect more raids from the Galician and Castilian nobles. They will be difficult to predict. At least we must establish scouting posts all over the northeast." Heads nodded. The old general was well respected and had recently captured Osric's kidnappers. He was still a hero.

General Aziz spoke up. "We must retaliate in force. Maybe capture and sack a few Christian towns where it will hurt most."

The Caliph sighed. "Ah, more warfare. It is costly and leads to more warfare." He stared at his fingers. "I had hoped for peace in the north, but it is not to be. We cannot allow these raids to go unanswered. Very well, Rodrigo, assemble your generals and select the best targets for attack. Come back to me with suggestions." The assemblage rose and left the conference already beginning discussions on where to make war.

I had hoped I could have achieved peace to our north, but it was not to be. I knew the only resolution for now would be a continuous series of raids back and forth. It was inevitable that war benefits no one. Men are killed, farm lands are burned, cattle and horses are destroyed, women live in poverty and culture, the most perishable of all commodities, vanishes.

I went home with Eli and a dark cloud of depression hung over us. I prayed silently asking God for answers. There was no reason to harm this beautiful civilization we had built in Cordoba.

I sat in our garden at the table and began to compose my notes into a diary of the events since I had first gone to Leon. The day was hot even under the shade of the trees around the pond in the middle of the yard. I had written a few pages, but was beginning to feel drowsy. I had been feeling successful with all the events after my capture by King Sancho. It had resulted in a successful treaty between my Caliph and Sancho. The king was able to lose weight and be restored to the throne after our successful campaign at Zamora and later Leon. But Sancho had been unable to control his allies – especially Enecco and now he was dead. His young son Ramiro II was now the nominal king, but controlled by regents. Now, our former allies in the war against Ordono were breaking our treaty and leading raids on our northern towns. We had sent a clear message that this meant war if they persisted and then they persisted by holding Osric for ransom. We could only accept so much confrontation. Now war was inevitable. Brutal, bloody war with many slaughtered men, lost husbands and fathers. All trade would cease. Maybe some of our Christians would change sides, maybe some would remain as spies. I could only remember the utter devastation of Salamanca – burned houses and fields, dazed women, hungry, crying children. We almost had a wonderful, lasting peace. But now I was irrelevant. I was not a soldier. My skills were of no use. I went to lie down on a bench in the shade. I fell into a light fitful sleep.

In my dream, I could see Jews weeping, boarding ships and borne off in all directions – some to safety, some merely to be marooned in unfriendly foreign lands where they would starve and die or be sold as slaves. My efforts to build schools of learning were destroyed; Christians took over and desecrated our synagogues, rampaged through our neighborhoods. Vicious rumors would arouse the peasants to acts of violence. The Caliph's noble dream of an educated enlightened society would be lost. Maybe never to be revived as brutal monks in fierce vows to follow the teachings of Jesus would force thousands into false conversions or be burned at the stake in front of cheering mobs.

Then, in the midst of the crowds, I heard my wife calling, "Hasdai, Hasdai." I slowly drew out of sleep. I was bathed in sweat, a deep nervous sweat. My clothing stuck to me. I opened my eyes and could see Rachel standing over me with a worried look on her face. "Are you alright?" I rose slowly to a sitting position and rubbed my eyes.

"Yes, Rachel, yes. I had a bad dream." I stared off into the perfect sky above. "I think I saw the future. Bad things. This new war with the north cannot be good. I saw devastation and death and the destruction of the Caliphate, and the exile or forced conversion of the Jews. I have heard of such things in other countries, but not here. I saw the end of the Caliphate's rule – a wonderful time of peace and the advancement of learning. Not since early Roman times has the world experienced such wisdom and such a golden age. And now it is to end."

"When, Hasdai, when?"

"Not soon, but in the future. These wars will cause it."

"Why?"

"I do not know God's plan. Perhaps we had a small taste of the Kingdom of Heaven. Perhaps we have sinned and did not deserve it. But I cannot believe that. It is all so wonderful. The Muslims have permitted Jews and Christians to thrive together. When can that happen again? What does God intend? Rachel, let us pray."

We knelt and recited prayers with Rachel next to me. Was God listening? The children looked out into the garden at their parents. They turned and stared in puzzlement at each other and then went to start supper.

Yes, supper. The family came together and recited the evening prayers. Tomorrow was another day.

EPILOGUE

The tenets of Islam are difficult to decipher. As per the orthodox belief, Mohammed as a wealthy middle-aged merchant began to go to a cave to meditate. There, he received from the Angel Gabriel revelations directly from Allah. From a pagan worshipping several deities, he began to worship Allah – the sole diety. The teachings Mohammed received from Gabriel are in the form of Suras – or a sort of sermon. Unlike the Torah, which often relies on a narrative of human activity, or a series of legalistic compilations, these suras are a sort of free form, often disconnected, series of thoughts which contain in places here and there laws or directives for his followers. It makes for very difficult reading to derive a common central philosophy from these suras, which have a dream-like asymmetric quality. However, read aloud they are an excellent, melodic form of prayer or meditation.

They ardently adopt much of Judaism, the Jewish laws, and especially Abraham and the prominent Hebraic figures of the Hebrew Bible as well as Jesus and the prophets. While they also recognize and purport to accept Christianity, they make little specific reference to it. It is quite obvious that the development of Islam relied heavily on Judaism and has incorporated within Islam much of Judaism. It has no central authority like a pope, it has similar dietary laws, it practices circumcision, and its scholars have, like the Jewish Talmud, codified and interpreted the Quran into specific laws and practices. While the Quran is deemed to be the word of Allah alone, the Hadith is the commentary on it of Mohammed and other Islamic scholars. It is as if the Quran served as an amorphous spiritual inspiration, which its sages have codified into more closely defined laws.

In view of the fact that the Quran is believed to be the direct word of Allah, as related by the Angel Gabriel directly to Mohammed in his cave meditation, any change or deviation, or any criticism of the suras is considered to be heresy. That being said, Mohammed during his lifetime was believed to be illiterate until he was commanded by Allah, "Read!" and from then on, he could read and write. Nonetheless, the Quran is not believed to have been in written form for at least fifty to a hundred years after Mohammad's death. Early versions of the Quran which have actually been found, date only after that. So, in terms of human intervention alone, the Quran may have been improperly transcribed by humans subsequent to the revelation to Mohammed. It is also believed that there are missing suras which were never canonized into the Quran. So, like the Bible, the Torah, the Gospels, etc., some human error in transcription, translation, copying and editing may exist, although it is considered heretical to assert this.

There are also changes in the attitudes from one sura to another. As we know, Mohammed initially lived in Mecca and the suras of that time speak very positively of the Jews and Jewish practices. Mohammed left Mecca and went to Medina. The suras after the Mecca period are less favorable and often antagonistic towards the Jews. In the Mecca period, the Jews were helpful to him and supported his monotheistic mission. Once in Medina, politics shifted and some Jews opposed him. The suras reflect that change.

Nonetheless, over the centuries, the Muslims have usually had a friendly relationship with the Jews. The Muslims, however, consider themselves to be more advanced than the Jews. Especially in Spain between 800 and 1300 C.E., the culture created by the interchange of knowledge and friendship created a golden age even the midst of the so called Dark Ages. Only when the Christians reconquered Spain did the Jews start to suffer from the intolerance of the Dominican monks which culminated in the Inquisition in the late fifteenth century.

Unlike Judaism, however, Islam is a fatalistic religion very similar to Calvinistic pre- destination. Everything is planned according to the will of Allah. An oft repeated saying is "Insh Allah" – God willing. At the same time, Islam demands submission or acceptance of the discipline of the Quran and the proper way or path (Sharia). To deviate from the path means suffering and rejection from heaven (Gemna) and an eternity in hell (Gehenom). Between the belief in pre-destination and acceptance of the discipline of Sharia, there is little choice offered to Muslim believers.

Jews believe in the choice between good and evil and, therefore, the freedom of will. The Christians have a variety of different interpretations of the same concepts. However, as a result of the strong Muslim compulsion to accept the will of God and to have their acts pre-determined, they rely heavily on the law as propounded over the centuries by a number of legal scholars who interpret the Quran. However, since there is no central authority figure, as the Pope, Muslims, like Jews, have different authorities to interpret proper behavior. One significant split is between the Sunnis, whose authority comes from scholars in Egypt, and the Shiites, whose authority comes from Qum, i.e. Khomeini, in Iran. There are many variations of the doctrines of these authorities in between. Often, the deviations reflect ethnic, political or economic differences. While all Muslims look to the text of the Quran, there are many variations among the beliefs and practices that arise from it. To lump all Muslims together then as one would be a mistake. To determine with the initial tenets of Islam, the motivations of a particular group, it is important to understand the diverse ethnic, tribal and religious forces at work. Often, these do not fall along national lines, but other diverse alliances.

It had just been less than two centuries since the Moors had pushed the Visigothic Christians out of South Hispania and named it Al-Andalus. While nominally Christian, the Visigothic rule had been brutish, cruel and hated by Jews and Christians alike, and yet blessed with the many roads, castles, bridges, ports and other amenities the Romans had built. The early Jewish settlers had fared nicely under Roman rule and were permitted to govern themselves and worship as they pleased unabated. With the advent of both Christianity and the many attacks by the barbarian Visigoths, Jews were herded into ghettos and taxed heavily.

The Visigoths were undisciplined and made war frequently among themselves. They never established dynastic order for the succession of rulers and rarely coalesced under a single leader. They did adopt the Christian church, but remained confused over church doctrine – many refusing to accept the trinity concept and relying on a belief deemed elsewhere to be heretical called Arianism which rejected the trinity, and on occasion, the divinity of Jesus. Over 130 years or so of Visigothic rule, there were over 18 so-called kings from 15 different families. Regime change was accomplished by war, assassination, poison and murder.

As disputes raged over the succession to the Visigothic throne, the heirs of one King Witiza opened the gates to a small Arab expeditionary force from Morocco. With almost no resistance, the Moors bloodlessly swept through South Hispania with little objection from masses weary of Visigothic misrule and instability. The Moors were not vindictive to the Christians who were permitted to retain their churches and their practices. And so, much of southern Spain became Al-Andalus under enlightened Arabic rulers. Just as the Christians were permitted a degree of tolerance, so were the Jews for whom the Arabs held a kinship even expressed in their holy book, the Quran. And a golden age of tolerance, intermingling of cultures, education and in general healthy cross fertilization occurred. It was in this time that Hasdai pursued his path to meet with the Caliph ar-Rahman III in his magnificent palace complex named Madinat al-Zahra.

ABOUT THE AUTHOR

Richard Malmed, now retired after fifty years of practicing law, is able to pursue his first love since he was an Honors English Major at Yale. His work have a won a few awards. He lives in Philadelphia with his wife and spends his spare time thinking creatively while working out at the gym. He holds world record in the bench press for his age and weight group (320 pounds at age of 78 and weight 173). He writes historical fiction and lawyer's adventure novels.